Star of Gypsies

BY **Robert Silverberg**

Star of Gypsies

DIF

DONALD I. FINE, INC.
New York

FOR KAREN

O Star of wonder, Star of night,
Star with royal beauty bright,
Westward leading, still proceeding,
Guide us to thy perfect light.

ONE

In a Snowy Season

These are the Three Laws:
    What is holy is what is efficient.
    Those who live by common sense are righteous in the
    eyes of God.
    The One Word is: Survive!
This is the One Word:
    Survive!

1.

WHAT HAD LED ME TO ABDICATE IN THE FIRST PLACE WAS
the realization that the time had come to drop everything and run for
it. One of my favorite tactics, with which I have often had great success,
is attacking by means of retreating. Passive aggression, you might call
it.

And so in a snowy season I left Galgala behind, my throne and my
house of power and everything, and went off to the world called
Mulano, which means the World of Ghosts. What I was looking for on
Mulano was nothing more than a quiet place to live—me, who always
thrived on noise and bustle and excitement—and that was what I found
there, in the middle of all the snow-white brightness. I was a hundred
and seventy-two years young and so far as I was concerned I had never
been King of the Gypsies in my life and I was damned if anybody was
going to talk me into being King of the Gypsies ever again.

I didn't miss the throne. I didn't miss living in my house of power.
I didn't miss Galgala. Except for the gold, I guess. Yes: I did miss the
gold of Galgala. For its sheen. For its beauty. (Certainly not for its
value. *What* value?)

On Galgala everything is golden. The cats and the dogs, or what you
might have called cats and dogs in the old days on Earth, have liquid
gold running in their veins. There's gold in the leaves of the trees, there
are grains of gold in the sands of the deserts, there are specks of gold
in the paving-blocks of the streets. That's right. On Galgala the streets
are literally paved with gold. You can imagine what the discovery of
a planet like that would have done to the galactic economy if we had
still been on the gold standard when they found Galgala. But of course
that quaint though sensible ancient idea had been obsolete for centuries
by the time the first exploration team landed there.

Gold is pretty much worthless everywhere in the galaxy now, thanks
to Galgala. Even so, the stuff still has its fascination for us foolish
mortals, despite the hatchet job that the discovery of Galgala performed
on its value in commerce. Especially does it fascinate the species of
foolish mortals that other folks call Gypsies. My people. Your people

too, most likely: for I hope and believe that most of you who read this will be of my own kind. (By which I mean those who call themselves the Rom. Who have called themselves by that name since before Earth was.)

We Rom have always loved gold. In the old days our women used to festoon themselves with gaudy masses of gold coins, threading them on golden chains and letting them dangle down over their lovely jiggling bosoms like so much braided garlic. You practically needed a hacksaw to get through the gold to their breasts, dancing around under those masses of yellow metal. And we men—oh, what tricks we played with *our* gold, back there in Hungary and Rumania and all those other forgotten places of old lost Earth! The roll of gold napoleons wrapped up in a handkerchief and stuffed into your pants to make a bulge, so you'd look like you were hung like an elephant! Imagine the Gypsy lass' surprise when the trousers came off.

(But of course you can't really surprise a Gypsy lass, because she's seen everything already. And it isn't size that your clear-thinking woman looks for, anyway: it's craft and cunning, and some vigor.)

Well, I had given up Galgala and all its golden glitter forever and ever. My power and my glory were behind me now. And Mulano was my home.

Mulano was a good peaceful sort of world. It was chilly but it wasn't really inhospitable. There was a silence about it that I loved. I had plenty of ghosts and snow-serpents and even a doppelganger or two to keep me company. And then too there was the bird called Mulesko Chiriklo, the bird of the dead. I think I never was happier in all my years. I had told them all to go to hell, all those who had never understood what I was driving at and what was driving me. You want a king? Good: go find yourself a king. I want to be by myself for once. That was what I told them. And even though I was by myself I was still as full of joy and mischief as ever: joy has always overflowed in me. And mischief. On Mulano I felt as sweet as a lamb that is sleeping in a carload of newly harvested garlic and wild onions. Chapite! Which means, in our old Romany tongue, It is true!

The day on Mulano is fourteen hours long and the night is fourteen hours long and also there is a time between day and night that is seven hours long, when both suns are in the sky at once, the yellow one and the blood-orange one. That time of day I called Double Day. I would stand outside my ice-bubble for hours, watching the warring shafts of light collide and crash and struggle until one had enfolded and transformed the other.

And there was always a time at the end of Double Day when the two suns dropped below the horizon in a single instant, so that the sky turned green and then gray and then black between one breath and the next. The stars would come out in that moment. And that was the moment of Romany Star. I would see very suddenly, blazing in the forehead of the sky like the torch of the gods, the great gleaming red ball of hot light that long ago gave my people birth. And I would drop to my knees wherever I might happen to be at that moment, and scoop up snow and rub it on my cheeks to keep myself from crying. (I don't mind crying for joy but it sickens me to cry out of sadness and longing.) And then I would say the words of the prayer of Romany Star. If there was a ghost with me—Thivt, say, or Polarca, or Valerian—I would make him say the words too.

And when we had spoken the words I would say, "You see it up there, do you, you Polarca?"

"I see it, yes, Yakoub."

"How far is it from here, do you think?"

And he would say, shrugging, "Six hundred leagues and then a mile or two."

And then I would say, "The journey of ten thousand years ends with but a single step. Is that not so, you Polarca?"

And he would say, "That is so, Yakoub."

And we would stand there in the cold red glow of distant Romany Star until we could feel the cold snow beginning to melt under our star's hot embrace; and then we would go inside and sing the old sad songs until the night was done. And that was how it was for me on Mulano, among the ghosts and the snow-serpents, in that snowy season, in that time when I had never had been King of the Gypsies and was never going to let them make me King of the Gypsies again.

2.

BEING THE KING, WELL, THAT WAS MY DESTINY. I WAS marked for it. I was caught up in the kingship from my childhood on, the way a swimmer can be caught in rough surf and tumble over and over and over, altogether unable to fight his way free. What the swimmer learns is, you will never escape the turmoil of the waves unless you go slack and easy, and let the waves have their way with you, and wait for the moment when you can regain control. The same with being king: if you are marked for it, no sense struggling against it. Go slack and easy, and let your unchangeable fate come up over you and take you where you are meant to go. That is what destiny is all about.

I knew I was supposed to be king because the ghost of an old woman came to me and told me so, when I was just a little Gypsy boy. I didn't know she was a ghost; I didn't know whose ghost she was; I didn't know what she was trying to tell me. But I knew she was there. I thought she was a dream that had somehow detached itself from my sleeping mind and was walking around, free and clear, in the light of common day. This was in the city of Vietorion on the planet Vietoris, my native world, one of the worlds of the great Imperium of the stars. I was— who knows?—three years old, four, maybe. A long time ago.

She was horribly ancient and withered, the oldest woman who ever was. I knew at once that there had to be something magical about her, seeing those signs of great age in her face, because even in those days it was an easy thing to get a remake and there was hardly anyone who looked old. Here I am today, with practically two centuries behind me, and my hair is black as ever, my teeth are sound, my skin is firm. You would have to look into my eyes, and beyond them into my soul, to discover how long my journey has been and how far it has taken me.

But she looked old, my childhood ghost. Her face was seamed and wrinkled and I think there were gaps in her teeth and her nose was sharp as a blade. Out of her lean and parched Gypsy face blazed her eyes, two dark stars lit by fiery mysterious furnaces. She was something out of fairy-tales, the witch-woman, the magical crone, the old Gypsy fortune-teller. Hobbling into my little room, putting her claw of a hand on my little wrist. Muttering magical names to me:

"You are Chavula," she whispered. "You are Ilika. You are Terkari."

The names of kings. Great names, names that went booming and roaring down the corridors of time.

I was never afraid of her. She was the old wise woman, the mother of mothers, the seeress. What we call in our Romany language the phuri dai. How could I fear the phuri dai? And I was too young to fear anything, after all.

"You are the chosen one," she sang to me. "You will be the great one."

What could I say? What did I understand? Nothing. Nothing.

"You were born at the midnight of noon," she said. "That is the hour of kings. You are Terkari. You are Ilika. You are Chavula. And they are you. Yakoub Nirano Rom, Yakoub the king! You have the sorcery in you. You have the power."

She was chanting prophesy at me, and I thought it was a game. She was laying my life's destiny upon me, weaving the inescapable web of my future around me, and I laughed in wonder and delight, comprehending nothing of the burdens she was giving me. There was a glow around her, a magical shimmer of electricity. Her feet never touched the floor. That was the best of it for me, the way she floated. But of course I was very young. I had never seen a ghost before. I understood nothing of the principles. All magic explains itself, if only you live long enough to let the answers come to you, and later I understood everything. Later I knew that in truth she was prophesying nothing, but only telling me the things that she had already seen come to pass. That is what it means to go ghosting: to carry the future, the absolutely delimited and altogether unchangeable future, backward into the past. I would meet the old woman again much later. When I became king she would be my wise adviser, my phuri dai indeed. But for now I was only a child struggling with the perplexities of my knives and forks, and she was the magical floating woman who came to me by day or by night in a shining aura of sparkling light and touched her hand to mine and whispered, "You will be the one who brings us home."

3.

WHEN I WENT TO MULANO I WASN'T TRYING TO ESCAPE
from my destiny, however it may seem to you. Believe that or not, as
you choose. I know what I was doing. How can you escape your
destiny? That's like saying, I was trying to escape my skin, I was trying
to escape my breath, I was trying to escape my thoughts. On Mulano
I wasn't trying to escape anything: I was trying to fulfill that great
design of destiny which I had known all my life I was meant to fulfill.
Sometimes it's necessary to run very hard in what seems like the wrong
direction if you hope ever to get where you need to go.

Of course the whole universe sent emissaries to bother me when I was
on Mulano. Nobody can stay hidden for long in a galaxy as little as this.

The first one who came was Rom, naturally. I would have been
surprised and probably sore as blazes if he had been Gaje. Rom are
always quicker than anyone when it comes to picking up the signs of
a trail. You know that already, if you are Rom; or at least you *should*
know that, and I pray to whatever god is closest at hand that you do.
And if you are not Rom—if you are of the other kind, if you are Gaje
—read and learn. Read and learn!

Four or five years earlier, however many it was, when I decided to
put the worlds of the civilized Empire behind me and headed out to lose
myself in the snowy wastes of Mulano, I took good care to leave a trail.
It was only common sense. Even when you've gone off by yourself to
think, or to heal your wounds, or simply to hide for a while, you want
to leave the patrin behind you, the trail-signs. If you don't, how will
your family find you? And if your family can never find you, who are
you?

In the old days on lost Earth the patrin-signs spoke of simple things,
and they were posted in simple ways. We were a lot simpler people then.
A few marks scratched in the ground, or some charcoal strokes on a
wall: that was sufficient. When your path took you far from the wagons

of your kumpania, you left the signs behind you to show where you had gone and also to guide your kin as they traveled the same path. There was the sign like this— ⊙ —that meant, "There are very generous people here who are friendly to Gypsies," and there was the one like this— + —that meant, "Here they don't give you a thing," and the one like this— /// —that meant, "We have already robbed this place." And then there were signs that said that water was available for the horses, or that there were pigs and chickens for the taking, or that in this town lived many stupid people who wanted their fortunes told. And also you could leave clues to be used in the fortune-telling by those who followed you: "This woman wants a son," or "They are very greedy for gold here," or "The old man will die soon."

All this I know not only because it is the tradition but because I have walked the trails of old Earth myself, the Earth that existed a thousand or two years ago, when I used to go ghosting around to see what was to be seen.

Do you doubt me? But why would you doubt me?

Believe me. I know whereof I speak. How could it be otherwise? When I tell you something it's because I know it to be true. I'm too old to lie, at least to lie to myself; and what I say here I have to say to myself before I can say it to you. I would lie to you in a flash if I saw anything to gain by it. But not here. Here I can only gain what I want to gain by telling the absolute truth.

(Maybe a *little* lie once in a while. I'm only human. But no big ones. Believe me.)

When I went to live on Mulano I left my own patrin behind me in fifty places. Of course my patrin wasn't just a matter of charcoal marks scrawled on walls. These are the days of the Empire, after all, when everyone has magic at his fingertips. So I marked my trail in signs of fire in the sunset sky over Galgala, and I wrote it in gleaming blue and gold on the shells of a tribe of wind-scarabs on Iriarte, and I buried it in the nasty dreams of a smelly little thief on Xamur. And I posted it in other ways in other places here and there about the Imperium as well. I had no doubts that I would be found. Only let them not find me too soon, is what I prayed.

The first one who found me, as I say, was Rom. That was gratifying, that a Rom would be the first. You want your own kind to confirm your prejudices about them. He was young and very tall and he was wearing his skin midnight-dark, with glittering white eyes and teeth and a mane of shining black hair tumbling about his shoulders. Because he was so long and slender there was a kind of beauty and fragility about him that made him look almost like a woman, but I could tell he was strong enough to crush rocks in his hands.

He came up to me while I was spice-fishing on the western lip of the Gombo glacier. It was so long since I'd seen another real living human being, not a ghost, not a doppelganger, that for a moment I was really taken aback. I almost wanted to run. I could feel powerful waves of life-vibration emanating from him, clanging off my soul with the impact of a thousand gongs.

But I held my ground and pulled myself together. Whatever he wanted, he wasn't going to get it from me, and if push came to shove I was going to do both the pushing and the shoving. Kings are like that. You don't have to be a son of a bitch to be a king, but you don't usually get to be king by being a patsy, either.

He gave me the Rom sign and the old Rom greeting:

"Sarishan, Yakoub."

Then, still speaking Romany, he wished me long life and many sons and the continued favor of the gods and angels, and a few more medieval flourishes of the same sort.

"I speak Imperial, boy," I told him when he seemed to be done. A little gratuitous snottiness is useful, sometimes: it keeps them off balance while you're trying to figure out what they're up to. Although this one looked too innocent to be up to much.

He bit his lip. He had expected me to answer in a patriotic gush of Romany. The Great Tongue and all that.

Staring at me in puzzlement, he said, "You *are* Yakoub, aren't you?"

"What do you think?"

I imagined I could hear the gears going round in his head, clank, gnash, clank. Yes, yes, he might be telling himself, this is Mulano and that is the place where Yakoub has gone, and this man looks like Yakoub and there's nobody else living on this planet, so this must actually *be* Yakoub. But maybe he wasn't thinking that at all. He was so young and pretty that I tended to underestimate him, I now suspect.

Finally he said, "There were two rumors circulating everywhere, one that you were dead, the other you had gone to some world outside the Empire."

"Which one do you want to believe?"

"There was never any question. Yakoub will live forever."

Oh, Lord! Hero-worship, a bright purple case of it! He was trying hard not to tremble. Quickly he made three of the signs of respect, one after another without pause, including one I hadn't seen for at least forty years. I began to wonder whether he was really all that young, or simply a good remake. But then I saw that he had to be young. There's a look of rapturous awe that comes into a young man's eye in the presence of true masculine power and authority that simply can't be faked and absolutely can't be built back into anyone past the age of thirty by some remake artist. This boy had that look. He knew that he was standing before a king; and that knowledge was melting his bones.

He told me that his name was Chorian and that he came from the world known as Fenix in the Haj Qaldun system and that he was a Rom of the Kalderash stock. That is my branch of the tribe as well. He told me also that he had been trying to find me for three years.

None of that was particularly interesting to me. The first impact of his presence was dying down now. It took a moment or two, but I was calm again. I turned away from him and went on with my fishing.

In this part of the glacier the ice was perfectly clear and you could see the long tubular forms of spice-fish, both the red kind and the superior turquoise variety, gliding serenely through the depths of the frozen river fifty meters down. I had a vibration-net down there, fluttering in the molecular breeze.

He said, "The Lord Sunteil instructed me to find you."

Now *that* was interesting. Sunteil floated into view in my mind: the emperor's right-hand lordling, the favored successor, smooth and slippery and perhaps a little sinister. I glanced back over my shoulder and gave Chorian a long slow cool look.

"You're in the service of the Empire, are you?"

"No," he said, "I'm in the pay of Lord Sunteil." There was a wink in his voice. "That's not the same thing."

Yes, I definitely *had* underestimated him. That was a fine distinction, very nicely put: he had allowed himself to be bought, but he hadn't sold them anything. I wanted to hug him for that. The Rom blood may be running thin, I sometimes think, but it hadn't yet turned entirely to water if this boy was any evidence. And of course Fenixi in general have a well-earned reputation for slyness and slipperiness. I had let Chorian's air of seeming naivete mislead me.

I didn't give him so much as a glint of approbation, though. I didn't want him to get too smug too soon. That's a peril to any Rom; you start bamboozling the poor Gaje before you've cut your first teeth, and you find out how easy it is, and it can make you smug, which is just one province away from being careless. We have never been able to afford to be careless. So instead of praising his nice little distinction I simply shrugged. In any case I had my fishing to attend to just then.

My net was nearly in position. The moment was critical and called for all my concentration. It's a ticklish business, lowering a vibration-net through solid ice. I ran my fingers over the keyboard as if I was coaxing a tune from my zither, and the net dipped and bobbed and billowed.

Down in the ice a turquoise spice-fish picked up the song of the net and swung around to stare at the net's gaping shimmering mouth. Come on, you lovely bastard, wriggle right in! But the fish wasn't about to do that. He looked up through the ice at me and I saw his huge golden-green eyes, wise and solemn, glowing like twin suns. That is one smart fish, I thought. That fish has Romany blood in him. I could hear him laughing at me through fifty meters of ice. That fish is my cousin, I thought.

"You ever do any vibration-fishing?" I asked.

"There's no winter on Fenix. I've never seen ice before."

"Ah. I should have remembered that."

"I went a lot of places while I was searching for you. I was on Marajo, I was on Duud Shabeel, I was on Xamur. I never saw any ice in those places either."

I tickled the keys and swung the mouth of the net away from the turquoise spice-fish. I wasn't eager to catch him any longer, not after the way he had looked at me.

Chorian said, "Xamur is where I finally was able to find out where you had gone."

"God gave you a nose. It's only right that you should use it for smelling things out. Why did Sunteil send you?"

"The Lord Sunteil is afraid that you're planning to return to the Empire," the boy said. "He thinks this abdication of yours is some sort of ruse, that you're just biding your time until you're ready to come back. And when you come back you'll be more powerful than ever before."

That went right to my gut, those words. In amazement I realized that Sunteil was actually on to me. Even though none of my own people, apparently, had managed so far to figure out my game, somehow Sunteil had.

Which meant not only that Sunteil was smart, which I had known for a long time, but that he might be smarter than I had allowed for. That could cause trouble for us when the old emperor finally died and

Sunteil, as most people expected, succeeded him. For I had no doubt at all that I was going to have to deal face to face with Lord Sunteil, I or my immediate successor, concerning matters of the highest importance to the future of the Rom people, when Sunteil became emperor.

But if he had fathomed my strategy, what was the point of his sending Chorian all the way out here to tell me so? There had to be a trick somewhere.

"I don't get it," I said. "The Lord Sunteil sends a young Rom to find out whether the old Rom king means to make trouble? What sense does that make? Does he really think you'll spy on me for him? That's too simple."

"The Lord Sunteil is a subtle man. And devious."

"So I have heard, yes."

"Perhaps he thinks you'll tell me things that you'd never tell a Gajo. And maybe he actually does hope that I would tell them to him."

"And would you?"

Chorian looked at me in horror.

"I have strong loyalty to Lord Sunteil, and he knows it. But I would never carry the secrets of the King of the Rom to him, not for anything. Never. Never."

"Even if I wanted you to?"

"What?"

"Look," I said, "Sunteil's all wrong about what he thinks I'm up to out here, and it isn't in any way useful to anybody for him to go on believing any of that stuff. I want you to tell him the truth about my abdication. That can't be construed as betraying me. You took Empire money for this job, didn't you? Well, give the Empire what it's paying for. Go and let the Lord Sunteil know that he doesn't need to fret about my coming back to cause trouble. I have completely lost interest in power. Completely."

God, could I ever lay it on! But just then I believed every word I was saying. That's the first rule of successful lying: believe your own bullshit, or no one else will. Right at that moment I knew as clearly as I knew I had two balls between my legs that I was done with being king. I hadn't felt that way five minutes ago and I probably wouldn't feel that way five minutes later, but what I was saying was what I believed with all my heart, right at that moment.

Chorian stood there listening in that rapt adoring open-mouthed way of his, as though he bought every syllable of the nonsense I was spewing.

Grandly I went on, "I've had a bellyful of it, boy, and I'm finished with it. The whole power thing has burned out, for me. The time has come for me to step aside for good. Mulano is where I mean to live. If the Lord Sunteil knew how good the fishing is here, he'd understand."

A nice flourish to finish with, I thought.

But Chorian was more complicated than I had been giving him credit for.

"I'll tell the Lord Sunteil that, yes," the boy said sweetly, when I was done. "And should I tell your cousin Damiano that also?" All innocence, just a good-looking young messenger-lad running errands for his betters. "That you have no plan to return to the Empire? Even though there is great trouble among the Rom, because there has been no king? Even though you are the one who is best able to bring the crisis to an end?"

4.

I WASN'T EVEN REMOTELY EXPECTING THAT. IN MY amazement I hit the keys so hard that the net turned mouth-downward just as an elegant red spice-fish was becoming curious about it. I should have realized that this was all going to be much less simple than it had seemed at first. Who was this kid really working for, anyway?

"Damiano?" I yelped. "What does he have to do with this? Where did you talk with my cousin Damiano?"

"On Marajo, at the City of Seven Pyramids. I told him that the Lord Sunteil had sent me after you, and he said, Yes, go, find the king and tell him that his throne is waiting for him."

My heart started to pound in a nasty way.

Calmly, calmly. How I hate it, when alarm bells start ringing like that inside my old bones! But between one eyeblink and the next I went into myself and turned down the adrenal flow. Sometimes wisdom is nothing more than proper control of your ductless glands.

"I never had a throne," I said. "I never was king of anything."

Chorian wasn't having any more of that line now, though.

"You were Rom baro," the boy said. "The big Gypsy. The top man."

"Never. Absolutely not. Get that whole idea out of your head." My hands were trembling a little. I didn't want Chorian to see that. To distract him I pointed and waved my arms and cried, "Look, there, do you see that fish nosing around the net?"

It was another turquoise one, not as wise-looking as the first. I gave him my full attention. It was a convenient way of changing the subject until I had had a chance to work things out a little in my head.

I could taste the spice-fish's sweet flesh already on my tongue: rosemary, turmeric, cumin, golden pepper. I made the net dance for him. I let it flutter toward him, I pulled it back, I made him beg to be caught. His long nose twitched as he zigged and zagged about. With marvelous agility he swam the crystalline depths, parting the ice as though it were not there.

Come, pretty bastard! Come glide right in!

"What's this crisis you were talking about?" I said carefully.

"That there is no king. That ships of exploration are going forth and there is no plan. That disputes are arising and there is no one to settle them."

I stared down at my fish, as though I could snare him by the power of my mind alone.

"There are ways of managing these things even without a king," I said.

"They have. For five years. But things are getting difficult and tense. Damiano says to tell you that now the high ones of the Rom want to elect a new king. They won't wait for you any longer, even the ones who never believed you were serious about abdicating. If you're definitely not going to come back, they're about ready to elect someone in your place."

So that was it!

That had been meant to hook me but good, that quiet statement just now. Push was coming to shove; Sunteil was not the only one who had figured out what I was really up to; and now my cousins of the Rom Kingdom were matching my bluff with one of their own. That was the real message Chorian had come here to deliver. He might be in Sunteil's pay but the one he actually served was Damiano. Which is to say that he served the Rom; which is as it should have been. Sunteil wanted information, yes. But Damiano wanted to make me come back. And this was his way of getting me to do it.

Even now I wasn't going to let myself go for the bait. I couldn't, not now, not yet.

"They need a king? Let them find a king, then."

"But *you* are king!"

"You didn't hear me the first time? How can they elect someone in my place when I never had a place?"

"But that isn't so! How can you say you weren't king when you *were* king? You *are* king!"

He was bewildered. He should have been. I had been working hard at bewildering him. I laughed. I left him to puzzle it out and went back to my fishing again. Swiftly, smoothly, I closed the net's mouth and swept it toward the surface of the glacier. The turquoise spice-fish leaped and sprang and writhed. I had him. I pulled the net up until it breached the glacier's skin, and I kept on lifting until it rose twenty meters into the air. The orange sun was high in the east and a streak of scarlet fire ran over the frozen land like a river of molten gold. In that brilliant light my fish changed colors a thousand times, screaming at me from every corner of the spectrum as I held him aloft. Then I sent a quick shaft of force through the rim of the net and the fish was still.

"There," I said. Pride flooded through me. Even an idiot can be a king, and I can list plenty who have, but fishing with a vibration-net is a different story. It takes a quick eye and a pretty wrist. I was years in learning the skill and I doubt that there's anybody better at it. "You see that?" I crowed. "The timing, the coordination? There's real art in what I just did." The boy was gaping, mind still lost in the tangles of interstellar politics. I turned to him. "Boy, you are invited to join me for dinner tonight," I told him expansively. "At least once in your life you should know the taste of spice-fish."

"Your cousin Damiano—"

I glared. "Bugger my cousin Damiano with an ivory tusk! Let *him* be king, if he wants."

"The kingship belongs by rights to you, Yakoub."

"Where do you get all these idiotic ideas?" I said, sighing. "I never wanted to be king. I tell you ten thousand times: I never *was* king. I was king in their heads, maybe. All that is behind me. If they need a king, let them find someone else to be their king. Here is where I live. Here is where I'll die."

I said it with real ringing conviction. I would have taken an oath that

I was sincere, too. I can remember times when I swore eternal fidelity to Esmeralda with the same throbbing sincerity. And meant it, too.

"Yes," I said again, grandiosely. "I have made my farewell to the Imperium. Here is where I'll die!"

"No, Yakoub!"

His eyes were glassy with shock. It went beyond mere love and reverence for me. I had messed up his head completely with my contradictory speeches and with this talk of living out my life on Mulano. Handicapped by his youth, he wasn't able to keep up with my swings and swerves. And when I spoke of dying, it was as if he saw in the mere possibility of my death his own unthinkable extinction sweeping inexorably toward him. If I could die, so could he. He grasped my arm and cried out with the wild silly romantic fervor of the truly young, "You mustn't speak that way. You will never die. Never!"

I shrugged. "Be that as it may. If ever I was king, I'm king no more. Clear?"

"And the succession—"

"Bugger the succession. The succession doesn't interest me. I don't care an ox's foreskin about the succession. That's why I'm here instead of somewhere else. That's why I mean to—"

Chorian gasped. His eyes went very wide. He made a little strangled gargling sound.

It didn't strike me as likely that the web of confusions I had spun around him could have shaken him so profoundly. And I was right. Chorian gasped and gaped and gargled some more, and finally he managed to point past my shoulder, and I looked backward and saw what was really bothering him.

Three snow-serpents had arrived on the scene.

Death's lovely handmaidens, beautiful chilly ribbons of emerald green streaked with ruby and sapphire and speckles of gold leaf. They must have looked horrific to him, even though these were only small ones, no more than eight or ten meters long, each one melting a wide glistening track for itself as it slithered in easy curving glides toward the place where we stood.

They had their eyes on my spice-fish. They were zeroing in on it from three different directions.

"Oh, no, no, cousins," I murmured.

Suddenly there was an imploder in Chorian's hand and he was fiddling with the focus. A vein stood out thick as a finger on his forehead. The grand gesture, again. I sighed. You have to be very patient with young men.

"Don't," I told him, reaching up and pushing the weapon back into his pocket. "They're only scavengers. They won't harm us and it's a crime against God to harm them. But I'm not going to let them have my fish." I walked out to meet them. They wriggled down against the ice and became very still, like whipped dogs. The heat and throb of life bothers them. I could have killed them with a touch: I have a lot of heat in me. "Sorry, cousins," I said gently. "This is a matter of me or you, and you ought to know how that has to come out. He's my fish, not yours. I worked damned hard for him."

They wriggled a little. They looked sad and disconsolate. My heart went out to them.

"I tell you what. Tonight let the king enjoyed his royal feast, cousins. Whatever's left will be yours in the morning. Is that all right?"

Plainly it wasn't. But there wasn't much they could do about it. They looked to the fish, to me, to the fish again. They made little mournful sounds. My soul wept for them. This was a hard season. But I held my ground and after a moment they turned tail and went slithering away.

Chorian was staring at me with that look of awe again.

"They aren't dangerous," I said. "Big, yes, but sweet as pussycats and not half as ferocious. They're strictly carrion-eaters. You know that carrion-eaters are sacred, don't you? For they restore life to the worlds."

But he had forgotten about the snow-serpents already. Something I had said was agitating him now.

"You've been telling me over and over that you never were king. But just now you spoke of yourself as the king. The king will enjoy his royal feast tonight, is what you said. I don't understand you. Are you king or aren't you?"

"I am not the king," I said. "But I am kingly."

He looked at me, baffled.

"You spoke of yourself as the king. I heard you."

"A figure of speech."

"What?" He was lost.

"I have kingliness about me, and so I can speak of myself as the king, if it pleases me. And I can say I have been king, or I can say I have never been king, as it pleases me. Because the kingliness remains forever. The kingship may go, but not the kingliness, not ever, boy, not ever. Once you've taken on that burden and learned how to stand up

underneath it, that strength never leaves you, even if the burden does."
I slung the spice-fish over my shoulder. It must have weighed fifty kilos,
but I wasn't going to let that trouble me. "So tonight you dine with the
king, boy, and what you'll eat will be royal fare. And in a day or two
you go back to wherever you came, is that understood? And you tell
them that Yakoub meant it when he said he was tired of being king.
Yakoub has abdicated. Permanently. Absolutely. Retroactively. You
tell that to Sunteil. You tell that to Damiano. You can tell it to the
emperor himself. It would be a mistake to doubt me."

I heard laughter in the distance. I knew, without looking around, that
it was the laughter of ghosts. Mulano is a place of many ghosts. There
are the native ghosts and then there are the visiting ghosts, and the two
are not at all the same sort of thing. The native ghosts are life-forms
that happen not to be flesh-life; there are billions of them and they are
everywhere, glowing at you in mid-air like little lanterns, a friendly
presence but not much for conversation. Those are the ghosts that gave
this world its name. Mulo, ghost, a fine Romany word. Mulano, place
of ghosts. It was a Rom who named this world, for all the ghosts that
live there. But since I came to Mulano a good many ghosts of the more
familiar kind had taken to visiting it, my cousins, drifting across the
void of space and the gulfs of time to this icy place to keep me company:
Polarca, Valerian, sometimes Thivt, who is also my cousin even if he
is not Rom, and various others now and then. You don't need to know
who they are, just yet. Old friends, coming to visit: that's enough for
now. A dozen times a day I felt the electric crackling of their auras on
the air and the lilting of their laughter drifted towards me, and I knew
that someone close and dear to me was hovering nearby. I could feel
their presence now. They were laughing now. These were cousin-
ghosts. The other kind don't laugh.

I knew why they were laughing.

"Don't any of *you* doubt me either," I told them.

5.

I HUNG MY FISH UP TO STEW IN A GRAVITY-GLOBE, WHERE
the juices would circle round and round and baste all sides equally.
Some Mulano ghosts attracted by the electromagnetic stresses of the
cooking process came nosing around to see if there was anything for
them to eat. They weren't after my fish, only the fish-flavored infrared
waves that were emanating from it. It's possible to impart flavor to
energy anywhere along the spectrum, you know, simply by cooking
something interesting in it. Maybe *you* aren't able to detect it, but just
ask any Mulano ghost.

While the fish was cooking the yellow sun began to crawl into the
western sky and Double Day began. The usual auroras of Double
Daybreak started to jump around behind the mountains, and the ghosts
immediately lost interest in my fish: there were much better things for
them to eat outside. Chorian stared at the amazing lighting effects in
disbelief.

"What's going on?" he asked.

"Happens every day about this time. Go and watch."

"Can't I help you do anything in here?"

"Go and watch," I said. "You don't see stuff like this on Empire
worlds."

He went out. I love cooking but I hate having an audience. For other
things, yes, but not when I'm trying to put a meal together. Cooking,
like lovemaking, needs to be done in private. I went on bustling around
inside the ice-bubble, calling up items for dinner, a flask of chilled
Marajo wine and a bunch of gleaming black Iriarte grapes and a platter
of Galgala oysterines, out of the various dimensional pockets where I
stored such things. When everything was organized I stuck my head out
of the bubble to call the boy. Gaudy winding-sheets of sinuous color
were flapping like tremendous electric banners overhead and the broad
ice-fields were ablaze with a million subtle shifting shades of aquama-

rine and emerald and jade, ruby and burgundy and scarlet, citron, cobalt, amethyst, magenta, gold.

The lights hit me all at once and I felt a torrent of ghost-force come rushing toward me out of the past, tumbling over me like an avalanche.

I hadn't done any ghosting around since I had come to Mulano. It wasn't that I was too old or had lost interest; it was simply that it seemed more important for me to remain rooted in present time here than it did to cut myself loose and go floating through other epochs. But that didn't mean that other epochs wouldn't go floating through me. There's no escaping the past. Either you ghost it or it ghosts you; and that night in the sudden dazzle of the aurora the walls of time swung back and a million yesterdays engulfed me in a wild crimson surge.

"Are you all right, Yakoub?" I heard the boy saying, far away. "Yakoub? Yakoub?"

The blue pearl of old Earth hung suddenly in the midst of a deafening hush of pure silence between one sun and the other. It was the only quiet thing in that noisy sky but once it appeared I wasn't able to look at anything else. Even when it existed Earth must have been far from the most beautiful planet in the universe, but seeing it appearing now out of nowhere in all its ancient cool blueness was so wonderful that the sight of it held me in an unbreakable grip.

"What do you see, Yakoub? What's there?"

It wasn't really Earth, of course. It was just Earth's ghost. You think it's only the ghosts of people that go wandering around the continuum? Planets have ghosts too. The difference is that people-ghosts can go only one way in time, from front to back, but planet-ghosts can move either way. Earth lay a thousand years away, but here it was reaching out for me across half the galaxy. It was like a special gift. For me, only for me.

"Hey," I said. "Hey, Earth! Earth, look here! It's me, Yakoub! Here I am! I'm who you came here to visit, you Earth!"

This was magic. I forgot all about Chorian. I laughed and waved to that dazzling blue planet up there, and put my arms high overhead and shook my fists into the blazing sky, and burst out onto the ice-field and began to dance and caper. And sang Rom songs of love to the Earth at the top of my lungs with my head thrown back and my shoulders high.

Maybe that seems strange to you. Why should I give even half a damn for Earth? I wasn't born there and I had never lived there and in fact I had never even really seen the place. How could I have? It perished long before my time. I had ghosted it often enough but there was no way I could have visited it in the flesh.

Yet I loved it, in a peculiar way.

Consider that Earth was our second mother, and don't ever forget that: a harsh mother but one who shaped us well. Romany Star may have given us birth but it was Earth that was our shaping-place, the forge in which we were tempered. For us Earth was a miserable place of exile, and maybe we should have hated it for that; but how could we hate the place that had made us strong? On Earth we were made fit for the life we now lead as we voyage among the stars. So I sang to it and danced to it and cried out my love to it, to that ghostly blue world, separated from me by centuries, hanging there in silence between those two alien suns. "Here I am," I yelled. "Me, Yakoub. You remember me?"

"You can see *Earth*?" Chorian whispered. I could barely see him, he seemed so far away. But I saw his eyes. They were shining. "Where is it? Show it to me, Yakoub!"

I saw Earth and I saw much more. It was all flooding upon me at once. I was a boy-slave again, swimming for my life through the warm living mud of Megalo Kastro and feeling an entire planet pulse and throb against my bare legs and belly. And then I was at the controls of my starship, feeling the energy of the cosmos shuddering through me and taking it and focusing it and hurling it back, and sending the great shining vessel leaping across the light-years. And then I was standing at the kinging-session of the great kris on Galgala, the high hall of judgment where destinies are decreed, looking down at the nine solemn krisatora of the Rom, the judges who hold the reins of the universe in their hands. They were offering me the kingship, for Cesaro o Nano who had been king had died; and I was refusing it. And then one by one they made the sign of kingship at me again until I was bowed down under the ninefold weight of their force, which was the collective will of all my people since the beginning of time, and I nodded and knelt to them, and then they knelt to me, and I was king. As the old woman had said I would be, the withered and wrinkled phuri dai who had come to me with magical words when I was hardly out of my cradle.

And now, still caught in visions, I was at my estate by the shore of the gentlest of the oceans of Xamur, which I think is the most beautiful of the nine kingly planets. But this must have been earlier, before I was king, because my son Shandor stood before me, the first of my sons and the one I loved best, and he was only a little child. There was defiance in Shandor's eyes. He had done something forbidden, and I had spoken with him, and now they had brought him to me and they said that he had done it again. I hit him and the mark of my hand sprang up on his cheek and still he defied me, and I hit him again. He looked to be eight, nine, maybe ten years old. I loved him terribly then, God only knows why. I raised my hand to him a third time. "Stop," someone said, and I said, "No, not yet." And they said, "He's only a child, Yakoub," and I said, hitting him again, "I have two things to teach him. One is to respect the Law, and the other is to feel no fear. So I hit him to prevent him from being lawless, and I hit him to keep him from becoming a coward." And I saw anger and love in Shandor's eyes, which was what I felt for him. So I hit him again and this time blood ran from his lip.

And the blood was the color of the hot sea that bathes the shores of Nabomba Zom. The palace of Loiza la Vakako was there, who was more than a father to me, though he never once lifted his hand against me. We stood side by side in the red surf under the stupefying thunder of the great blue sun of Nabomba Zom and Loiza la Vakako said to me, "You know, Yakoub, that every Rom is given two lives, one in which you live as you please and make as many mistakes as you care to make, and then a second in which it is your task to atone for the errors of your first life." And I laughed and said, "I'll try to remember that, father, when I enter my second life." But the sly face of Loiza la Vakako turned solemn and dark and he said to me, "This is your second life, Yakoub." That was just before I was taken by force from Nabomba Zom and sold into slavery the second time, to suffer like a miserable frog in the terrible tunnels of Alta Hannalanna. It was on Alta Hannalanna that I first felt the sting of the sensory-whip lash my forebrain, which nearly ended me before I had fairly begun. I saw the overmaster again raise the whip now, and swirls of yellow force blared in the heavens, and I rushed toward him and took the whip from him, saying, "Now the blood of your soul will flow." For there are many kinds of blood and I have seen them all.

There was no end to it. All my wives marched in a vision before me, the ones that I loved and the ones I did not, Esmeralda and Mimi and Isabella and Micaela and also some others that I have pretty well forgotten, and some women that were never my wives but through no fault of my own. I embraced my lost Malilini again, my first true sweet love. And Mona Elena, my forbidden Gaje woman. And golden faithless Syluise. Friends came and I threw my arms around them, Polarca, Valerian, Biznaga. A hundred alien landscapes danced in my brain. Worlds with rings in the sky, worlds with many suns, worlds with none. My God, what a vision it was! I had a hundred seventy-two years of ghosts in me and they were all on a rampage at once. Like a good Rom I have been everywhere and seen everything and it all lives in me, and it all is happening at the same instant, for such words as "past" and "present" and "future" are mere Gaje foolishness, really. All there is is now. Now I stare at the auroras sizzling in the sky over Mulano and now I walk the flowered meadows of Romany Star and now I stand in the Plaza of the Thousand Columns in Atlantis and now I advance toward the throne of the Fifteenth Emperor, and now I sharpen the blades of the Frankish swordsmen who will take Jerusalem from the Saracens in the morning, and now I sit in the royal council of the Rom on golden Galgala with old Bibi Savina the phuri dai beside me, and now I am with my father in the city of Vietorion as he points toward a red star in the sky. Sometimes my lady Syluise is by my side, and sometimes it is someone else, and sometimes I am alone. I see crystal temples and bridges that span the skies. The visions will not end. A thousand thousand souls crowd in on me, Rom souls, Gaje souls, the souls of creatures that are not at all human; and they are all my own. There is an infinity of worlds and I am everywhere. I writhe in the mud and I soar between the stars. And wondrous laughter rings out, filling the heavens so that there is scarcely room for anything else. The laughter is mine.

I was a hundred meters from the ice-bubble and hordes of Mulano ghosts were swarming all around me, orbiting me like furious insects. I must have been putting out enough energy to feed their entire nation for a month.

Chorian, brushing them warily aside, put his face close to mine. "Yakoub? Can you hear me, Yakoub?"

"What do you think? Of course I can, boy."

"I didn't know what was happening to you. I thought you might have been ghosting."

I shook my head. "No, boy, I was being ghosted. It's not the same thing."

"I don't underst—"

"You don't have to. Dinner's ready. Let's go inside and have ourselves that royal feast."

6.

THE BOY STAYED WITH ME FOR ANOTHER FOUR DAYS OR so, and I had to put up with his awe and reverence the whole time. That look of utter adoration, the hushed deferential tone of his voice, the unwillingness to let me do even the simplest task without jumping up to offer to help—it got so I wanted to kick him to bring him to his senses. My very belches were ecstasy for him. Nobody had ever behaved like that toward me when I really *was* king. The way this boy was carrying on, you'd think I was some frail and pampered lord of the Empire, some pallid decadent Gaje prince, and not true Rom at all.

Well, he was very young. And, Rom though he was, I gathered that he had spent more of his short life in high Imperial circles than he had among his own people. So perhaps he felt that that was how he ought to behave in the presence of the King of the Gypsies. Or maybe—God blight the thought!—maybe that is how deeply the Empire has corrupted and perverted the young Rom these days, so that everybody goes around bowing and scraping and kowtowing to anyone of superior rank and power.

King of the Gypsies! The whole idea was nothing but Gaje nonsense in the first place!

There never was such a thing as a King of All Gypsies in the old days on Earth. That was only a myth, a fable that the Rom folk invented for the sake of befuddling the Gaje, or perhaps the Gaje invented it to befuddle themselves, since that is often their way. We had kings, all right, plenty of them, one for every tribe, every kumpania, every roaming band. There had to be a chief of some sort, after all, someone with intelligence, strength, a sense of what is just, in order to maintain authority within the tribe and hold it together against all challenges as it traveled about through hostile lands with strange laws. But a *king*? A single mighty King of the Gypsies to rule over millions of wandering

Rom scattered across the six continents of Earth? There never was such a thing.

We were poor people then. Scum of the Earth, that was us, dirty shabby wanderers that no one trusted. Because they feared and mistrusted us so much the Gaje were always prying, bothering us, asking us a host of foolish petty questions. It was their way of trying to make us fit into their foolish petty way of life. When we came into a new place we had to apply for residence permits, for citizenship documents, for passports, for all manner of absurd papers. We had no respect for those requests, for why should we have been bound by Gaje law when we had perfectly good laws of our own? Still, Earth was Gaje territory and they were many and we were few, they were rich and we were poor, they had power and we had nothing, and so we played their game, we answered their questions. We told them what they wanted to hear, because that was the simplest and most efficient way of dealing with their idiocies.

And one of the things they most wanted to hear when one of our caravans came to their town was that we had a leader, a man of high authority who could maintain some sort of control over us and keep us from spreading chaos in the town. If they found out who our leader was, they would have someone to deal with, and in that way they could control us. Or so they imagined.

Who is in charge here, they would ask us. Why, our king, we would say. (Or our duke, or our count, or our marquis, whatever title seemed to please them best.) He is that man right over there.

And the king or duke or count or marquis would step forward and tell them, speaking in their own language, everything they wanted to hear. Usually he wasn't the true chief of the tribe. The real chief tended to keep himself in the background, so that the Gaje couldn't take him hostage or otherwise interfere with him, if that was what they were minded to do, and sometimes they were. Instead we would send forth someone who *looked* like a king, some tall broad-shouldered Rom with bright eyes and long flowing mustaches, who might have been a nobody in the tribe but who enjoyed strutting about and speaking in a loud voice and playing the part of a great man. He would tell the Gaje everything they wanted to hear. Yes, he would say, we are good law-abiding Christians and we mean no trouble for you. We will just stay here a little while, mending your pots and sharpening your knives, and then we will move along.

So the word got around that the way to deal with a tribe of Gypsies that came to your town was to find the king of the tribe— because every tribe had a king—and deal with him; otherwise it was like trying to deal with the wind, the waves, the sands of the beach. And sooner or later they would think to ask, Is there a king of kings, a king over all your tribes? And we would tell them, Yes, yes, we have a great king. Why not? It pleased them to hear that. They had a powerful need to believe that: that we were a nation scattered among other nations, that we had a king just as they had a king, and his word was law throughout all our tribes in every land. It was exciting and frightening to them to believe that. We were strange, mysterious, we were alien. We had our own customs and we had our own language and we came and went in the night, and we told fortunes and picked pockets and stole chickens and given the chance we would run off with pretty children and turn them into Gypsies. And we had a king who ruled over us and directed us in the secret war that we were waging against all of civilized mankind. So they liked to believe; so they *needed* to believe.

Give a Gajo a foolish fantasy and he will embrace it and embellish it until it becomes truer than the truth. Whenever five of our tribes came together in the same place for a festival the Gaje would imagine that we were convening to elect a new king. Is that what you are doing, electing a new king? And we would say, pulling long faces, Yes, yes, our old king has died, now we are choosing the wisest and strongest and best among us to rule over us. Sometimes we actually did hold an election of sorts, if we saw something to gain by it. We came forth and told the Gaje, Here is our new king, King Karbaro, King Mijloli, King Porado, whatever his name. Those are all filthy words in the Romany tongue, but what did the Gaje know? The filthier the name we invented the better the joke. And we would find some strong handsome fellow of the tribe with more vanity than brains and we would jump him up to be King of the Gypsies and he would stride around waving and nodding and smiling, and the Gaje would be tremendously impressed. They paid good money to watch the coronation feast, and paid money again to take pictures of us dancing and singing in our quaint tribal costumes, and while all that was going on we moved among them and picked their pockets besides, not because we were criminals at heart but simply to punish them for their silliness. And the Gaje went away feeling pleased with themselves because they had seen the coronation of the new Gypsy king. And then we also went on our way and nobody among us gave another thought to King Karbaro again. But the Gaje continued to believe that we were the subjects of a supreme ruler whose powers were absolute and whose commands traveled mysteriously across the world by secret couriers.

Eventually came a time when they stopped believing it. This was in the twentieth or perhaps the twenty-first century, when all knowledge became available at the push of a button and every jackass began to think that he knew everything.

This is the modern world, all the jackasses told each other solemnly. And they all felt very proud of themselves for living in the modern world. Nobody was ignorant any more, nobody was superstitious, nobody could be fooled by glib mumbo-jumbo. Among the things that everybody knew now was that there never had been such a thing as a Gypsy king, that the whole notion was nothing but a hoax, one of the innumerable frauds that those wandering rogues the Gypsies had dreamed up to confuse and delude the poor credulous yokels on whom they preyed.

Not only did those well-informed people who lived in the modern world stop believing in the King of the Gypsies, I think they stopped believing in Gypsies altogether. There was no room in that shiny modern world of theirs for Gypsies. Gypsies were ragged and unkempt and untamable; Gypsies were unpredictable; Gypsies were simply an untidy concept.

So they began to think we were extinct. That we were mere antiquarian folklore, the raggle-taggle Gypsies, O! Oh, yes, there had been Gypsies once upon a time, yes, the way there had been smallpox and public hangings and bitter wars over religion; but all that was done with now. This was the modern world, after all. The Gypsies, they said, have all settled down in ordinary houses and married ordinary people and live ordinary lives. They vote and pay taxes and go to church and speak nothing but the language of the land. The Gypsies of old are all gone, swallowed up in modern civilization, they said. What a pity, they said, that the quaint old picturesque Gypsies are no more.

And right about that time, when we had become all but invisible to the whole Gaje society because we had come to seem to belong to it, when we had vanished clear out of sight—that was the time when we understood that we needed to organize ourselves properly and come forth as a true nation. That was when we really did begin to form our Gypsy government—no fantasy, this time, but the genuine item—and elect our first real Gypsy kings.

We had to. Invisibility has its advantages, but sometimes it can be a drawback. The world was changing very fast. Those were the years when the Gaje first were starting to leave their little Earth and go off to nearby planets. Before long, we knew, they would be voyaging to the stars. If we stayed invisible we would be left behind. So we had to emerge from our Gaje camouflage. In that lay our only hope of getting home again. Earth was not our home, though we had never dared tell the Gaje that; our true home was far away, and the one thing we longed for was to return to it and give up our wandering life at last.

So it came to pass that we began to have kings. That was a thousand years ago, on Earth, in the earliest days of star travel, before anyone knew that we would be the ones to lead mankind upward from Earth into the heavens. Chavula was the first king, and after him Ilika, and then Terkari, and then—well, everyone knows the names of the kings. They were the men who took us to the stars and made us what we are today, masters of many worlds, lords of the roads of night.

And eventually in the fullness of time they came to me and said, "The king is dead, Yakoub. Will you be our king?"

What could I say? What could I do? No one in his right mind wants to be a king; and whatever else I am, I have always been in my right mind. Trust me on that score. But I am also a man of my people, and, powerful as we now may be, we are nevertheless a people in exile. That imposes certain responsibilities on you. I was born in exile and so was my father and so were my father's fathers for fifty generations back. If I was the man who could bring that long exile to an end, how could I dare refuse? In any case I had lived all my life under the lash of the knowledge of my fate; and it was my fate to be the king.

When I was a small boy my father took me to the lookout point near the steep summit of Mount Salvat on Vietoris, which is the world where I was born, and he said, "Where is your home, boy?" And I told him that my home was on such-and-such a street in the city of Vietorion on the world Vietoris. Then he showed me the bright red eye of Romany Star blazing in the black forehead of the sky and he said, "You think this place here is home? No, boy. *That* place is home. And some day our king will lead us there again." And he looked at me and the look in his eyes told me, more clearly than any words could have done, that he hoped I would be that king. I had never told him of the visions I had had when I was very small, the ghost of the old woman coming to me and planting the seed of the future in my soul; and I found myself unable to tell him now, so I had no way of saying, Yes, father, yes, I will be that king, I will be the one to lead us home, there can be no doubt of it: the ghost of an old woman told me so, bringing the word to me out of the future. I wish now that I had had a chance to tell him that. But I never told him or anyone else. I suppose that is every Rom father's hope, that his son would be the one. He was a slave then and so was I, and not long afterward I was sold away from him in the marketplace of Vietorion and I never saw him again. But I have seen Romany Star every night of my life from whatever world I found myself on, and I feel the warmth of its light on my cheeks no matter how cold the night; for it is the light of the star of home. And when they came to me and said, "Will you be our king, Yakoub," how could I say no, when I might be that very king who would lead us home again? So I let the kingship come upon me, which in time also I relinquished, and which I know will come again, as it must, for there are great fulfillments that have to be worked out and I know that I am the vehicle of their doing.

7.

WHILE THE BOY CHORIAN WAS STILL STAYING WITH ME, Polarca's ghost came around to visit. Chorian was out on the ice at the time hunting cloud-eels with my loop and trident: he was young and agile and energetic, and sending him off to hunt was one good way of getting him out of my hair when I grew weary of all that endless adulation.

There was a hum and a buzz and a crackle in the air and Polarca said, out of the mantle of green radiance that he liked to affect when he went ghosting around, "Is he bothering you? I'll scare him away."

"He'll leave soon enough on his own."

"A pretty boy. What did he come here for?"

"To tell me to get myself back to Galgala and be king again, I think."

Polarca considered that. He and I have known each other better than a hundred years, since we were galley slaves together in Nikos Hasgard's synapse pit on Mentiroso. Polarca is Rom of the Lowara stock and he claims to come from a long line of emperors, popes, and horsetraders on Earth. I believe only the part about horsetraders but I would never voice suspicion about the rest. He does more ghosting than anyone I know; he is a very restless man.

"You aren't going to go," Polarca said finally.

"Are you asking me or telling me?"

"Both, Yakoub."

"I'm not going to go," I said. "That's right."

"Even though Damiano says that a new king will be elected if you don't."

"You overheard that, did you?"

Polarca smiled. When a ghost smiles, it's more like a tiny flash of lightning. "I was standing right next to you. You didn't see me?"

"If they need a new king, let them have a new king," I said. "I'm going to stay here."

"Absolutely, Yakoub. Beyond any doubt that's the wisest thing."

The trouble with Polarca's ghost is that he doesn't speak with punctuation, so that half the time I can't tell a question from a statement, and he doesn't speak with inflection, so I can't tell sarcasm from sincerity. That isn't a characteristic of all ghosts; it's just Polarca's. Polarca is a smartass and so is his ghost.

"You think it's wise, do you?" I said.

"Of course it is. Just like it was wise for Achilles to go sulk in his tent."

I still couldn't tell if I was being needled or supported. There aren't many people who can keep me off balance the way Polarca does.

"Don't give me Achilles," I said. "He isn't relevant and you goddamned well know it." Then I said, "I actually saw him once. He was nothing at all."

"Achilles? You saw him?"

"A hoodlum. Little mean eyes and thick lips like chunks of meat. A natural-born sulker. Big and strong but there wasn't an ounce of nobility in him."

"Maybe you saw somebody else," Polarca suggested.

"They said Achilles."

"Ghosting that far back, how can you be sure? There's mist all over everything."

"I saw his shield," I said. "It was the right shield, a real masterpiece of art. But he was nothing but a hoodlum. What I'm doing, it isn't the same thing that Achilles was doing in his tent." I was silent a moment, wondering if I might be fooling myself about that. After a time I said, "Sunteil is mixed into this also. Did you know that?"

"The boy is in the service of Sunteil, yes."

"No," I said. "He's in the *pay* of Sunteil. There's a difference. Didn't you hear him say that? You've been skulking around here all week."

"I went away for a time. I was in Babylon when he said that. I was listening to Hammurabi proclaim the code of laws."

"I bet you were. Sunteil sent him because he thinks my abdication is phony and that I'm probably up to something suspicious by hiding out here on Mulano."

"Aren't you?"

"And so he sent the boy around to spy on me. That's what the boy says, anyway."

Polarca's mantle crackled and hummed and leaped up-spectrum a few notches. "Send a Rom to spy on the Rom king? Sunteil's not that silly, Yakoub."

"I know that. Then what is Sunteil doing?"

"He misses you, Yakoub. This is his way of asking you to come back."

"Sunteil misses me?"

"The balance of the Empire is askew. The Gaje emperor needs a Rom king as a counterpoise to keep things steady, and right now there isn't any king."

"Do you know this or are you just saying it, Polarca?"

"What's your guess?"

"Don't play guessing games with me, you bastard. That's *my* trick. You've got me at an unfair advantage already because you're a ghost. How far in the future do you come from, anyway?"

"You think I'm going to tell you that?"

"You pig, Polarca!"

"Do *you* tell, when you go ghosting around?"

"That's different. I'm the king. I'm not required to tell anybody anything. And if I request information from one of my subjects—"

"One of your subjects? I'm not anybody's subject. I'm a ghost, Yakoub."

"You're the ghost of a subject, then."

"Regardless," he said. "What you're trying to get from me is privileged information."

"And I make a privileged request. I'm the king."

"Bullshit, Yakoub. You abdicated five years ago."

"Polarca—" I sputtered. I was getting exasperated.

"Besides, no ethical ghost ever reveals the point in time from which he's ghosting from. Not even to his king."

"Even when the welfare of the Rom nation is at stake?"

"What makes you think it is?"

"You're trying to drive me crazy," I said.

He laughed. "I'm trying to keep you on your toes, Yakoub. Look, just be patient and everything will make sense to you, all right? Trust me. I see wonderful things ahead for you. Here—let me show you. The truth lies plainly visible in your palm, if only you have eyes to see. For a small fee, no more than a couple of little coins, the wise old Gypsy will pull back the mysterious veils of the future, he will reveal to you—"

"Get the hell out of here," I told him.

And he did, in the twinkling of an eye. I sat there blinking at the place where he had been. A dozen or so native Mulano ghosts, attracted by the little zone of negative energy that Polarca had left behind, came roaming in to feed. They hung in the cold air in front of me like a cloud of shining gnats. And then Polarca came back, sending the Mulano ghosts frantically scrambling out of his interpolation zone.

"Where'd you go?" I asked.

"None of your business."

"Is that the way you talk to your king?"

"You abdicated," he reminded me again.

"I think you're enjoying this."

"I went to Atlantis," he said. "For six weeks. They had just dedicated the Temple of the Dolphins and there were golden flower-petals strewn half a meter deep all along the Concourse of the Sky. I thought I saw your lady Syluise there, riding in the chariot of one of the great princes. I would have given her your regards, but you know how misty everything gets when you go ghosting that far back."

"You saw Syluise in Atlantis? Are you serious?"

"I am if you want me to be."

I love Polarca, but I hate dealing with his ghost. You expect your fellow Rom to tickle and poke you a little once in a while, especially if he's known you a hundred years or so and thus is an expert on the right places to tickle and poke. And he expects you to tickle and poke back at him. But Polarca, when he's ghosting, holds all the cards. A ghost knows not only past and present, but a good chunk of the future too. I've told Polarca many times that he takes unfair advantage. A lot he cares. He boxes me in on six different sides at once. He makes me feel like a simpleton, sometimes, and I'm not accustomed to that. He makes me feel like a Gajo trying to deal with a Rom. And yet I know he loves me. Even when he plagues me like this, he says he does it out of love.

8.

*AGAIN POLARCA DISAPPEARED. I WAS LEFT WITH A RESI-*due of uneasiness and irritation. He had seen Syluise, he said. In Atlantis, no less. It was a long time since I had even thought about Syluise. I wished Polarca hadn't taken the trouble to bring her to my mind now.

I could just see her, riding around in chariots back there in Atlantis. Driving the ancient lords of that great city berserk, and probably the ladies too. What would they have made of her there, with her golden hair and all? They would never have seen anyone with golden hair before, those swarthy dark-haired Atlanteans: she would have glittered among them like a goddess. Like a Venus, a bright shimmering Venus.

Atlantis was a Rom city, you know. Whatever other fables you may have heard, the real truth is that we founded it, we created its wondrous grandeur, we were the ones who suffered when it sank beneath the sea. It was our first settlement on Earth, long ago, when we came there after the destruction of Romany Star. Later on the Greeks tried to claim it as their own, but you know what Greeks are like: a shady bunch, half ignorance and half lies. Atlantis was ours. Not for five thousand years after it was destroyed did the Gaje of Earth build anything that even remotely approached it in architectural splendor. It was Earth's first city. And I don't just mean magnificent buildings and marble colonnades. We had sewers and flush toilets while the rest of the population of Earth was still dressing in animal hides and hunting with throwing-sticks.

A great city, yes. Too good to last. Anyway it was never our fate to be a settled people. Maybe it was presumptuous of us to build anything as wonderful as Atlantis. It *had* to be taken away from us. The volcano roared, the Earth heaved, the sea ate Atlantis, and we went forth in ships, poor battered survivors, to follow our luck on the highways of the world. (That's where the notorious Gypsy aversion to travel by sea came from, you know: the horrendous sufferings we experienced during the escape from Atlantis.) But it was wondrous while it lasted, and those of us who know the secret of ghosting go back there often to stare in awe. Getting there takes some work: Atlantis, we found out long ago, lies just about at the limit of our ghosting range. And it's hard for us to see things in much detail there, because as you've heard the farther back you ghost, the more deeply everything gets shrouded in mist. But we go all the same.

And Syluise—golden hair flying in the wind as she rides in the chariot of some Atlantean lord—

No woman in my life has held such power over me as Syluise. For better, for worse. I can never escape her spell. That infuriates me, that power of hers over me, and yet if I could change the past and remove all trace of her from my life, God knows I would not do it.

Estrilidis is where I met her. Fifty years ago? Something like that. Cesaro o Nano was still king and I was a diplomatic envoy. A hot humid world, Estrilidis, dense unspoiled forests, all kinds of strange creatures. The cats have two tails there, that I remember. And the insects—ah, the insects, what amazing things they are! Like rubies on legs, like emeralds, like blue diamonds. I was watching them one night marching up the walls of my lodging-place, an astounding procession of great gaudy bugs, when suddenly I saw something even more astounding: a golden woman, bare as the dawn, floating past my window. Perfect pink breasts, swelling hips, long supple legs. Shining like wildfire, shimmering like a ghost, she was. But how could she be a ghost? She was plainly no Rom, not with that glistening yellow hair, not with those startling blue eyes. And only Rom can ghost. Of course she *was* Rom, for vanity's sake totally transformed to that lustrous Gaje form. I found that out afterward. But even so, not a ghost. This was the real Syluise that I saw, magically holding herself aloft. She beckoned. I followed her into the night. She floating like the will-o'-the-wisp, I running behind her. She smiling, I staring. Gaping. Awed.

In the depths of the forest she halted and turned to me, and when she rushed into my arms I felt that I had captured a flame. We sank down together on the warm moist soil. She laughed; she raked my bare back with her fingernails; she arched her neck like a cat.

"Do you want me to make you a king?" she asked.

Rain was falling, but the heat of our bodies was such that it burned the water away before it could strike us. It was like a fever.

She laughed again. My hands to her breasts: nipples hot and hard, throbbing against my palms. I stroked her silken thighs and they parted for me. And then she clasped me. Oh, the sweetness of that embrace! I closed my eyes and saw the light of a thousand stars of a thousand colors. And felt the heat of those thousand suns searing me. You might have thought she was my first woman, it was so shattering a moment for me. And me a hundred twenty years old then, more or less. But in that thunderclap of a moment all those who had preceded her in that long life of mine were eradicated from my memory. There was only this one. Who was she? Did it matter? Did I care? I was lost in her.

As we moved she began to speak, a soft low chanting; and after a moment I realized that she was speaking in Romany, that from those perfect lips was coming an astonishing flow of the vilest words in our tongue. How could she have known those words, this Gaje woman? Well, of course, of course, she was as Rom as I, beneath her assumed facade. As she crooned and murmured that startling filth to me I looked at her in wonder; and then I began to laugh, and so did she. And then she swept me away with her.

"I am Syluise," she said afterward.

That was the beginning. When I returned to Galgala she came with me. When I became king a short while later, I thought of making her my wife; but when I went to her to speak of such high matters with her, she had disappeared, and it was a year before I saw her again. That was when I began to understand what Syluise was like. But by then it was too late.

9.

BECAUSE MULANO IS NOT AN EMPIRE WORLD, THERE'S NO regular starship service. The only way in or out is by relay sweep, which is a little like trying to travel by tossing yourself into the sea with a hook fastened to your collar and hoping that some giant bird will scoop you up and carry you where you want to go. Chorian, having delivered Damiano's message and having had my answer, was ready to leave, but he needed the better part of a week to set up his sweep for departure. So he was my guest all that time. Not that I begrudged it. I had come to take great delight in my solitude, and I wanted it back as fast as I could have it; but a guest is a guest. Maybe the Gaje will turn kinsmen from their door, but a Rom, never.

It wasn't so bad having him around, really. Aside from overdoing the worship more than slightly—and he couldn't really help that; I was five times as old as he was, and a king besides, or at least a former king, and legendary on fifty or sixty worlds—he was pleasant enough company. He wasn't nearly as naive as he seemed on first encounter; what I had taken for naivete was mostly just his style of wide-eyed innocence, which was probably nothing more than an artifact of his tender years. And it wasn't fair to blame him for being young. That wasn't his fault, and it would wear off soon enough anyway. There was happiness within him, and strength, and a good Rom heart. Besides, he knew all the court gossip. I was surprised how keenly I yearned to be brought up to date on all the petty trivial intrigues of the Capital's inner circle; and he seemed to know everything, the names of the old emperor's current mistresses, the current relative standings of the Lords Sunteil, Naria, and Periandros in the emperor's favor, the latest non-ecclesiastical escapade of the Archimandrite Germanos, and all the rest.

I asked him how he had come to be in the employ of the Empire in the first place.

"I was sold into it," he said. "Our kumpania broke up in the years of the great drought on Fenix and I was put out on offer for slavery. I was seven. The Lord Sunteil's phalangarius Dilvimon spotted me and bought me for fifty cerces. I was Sunteil's slave until I was seventeen, and when he gave me my writ he asked me to stay on in the civil service, and I did. He trusts me and he treats me well. And I think it's good for our people for there to be a Rom at the Lord Sunteil's right hand."

He sounded altogether casual about having been a slave. As well he might; to be sold into slavery is no big disgrace, and, as my own revered mentor Loiza la Vakako put it when I myself was going off to be sold for the second time, it can be a highly educational experience for a young Rom. It is in the water, after all, that you learn how to swim. But I know there are some that don't think as highly of the institution as I do.

I said, "So you're Empire on the outside but you're still Rom within?"

Chorian grinned broadly. "What else? True Rom, blood and bones," he said. "The only thing that the Lord Sunteil can buy from me is my time. My soul has never been for sale." We had been speaking in Imperial, but for that last he switched to Romany. Of course. When it's necessary to speak the absolute truth, a Rom speaks it in the language of his own people.

True Rom he might be, even to knowing the Great Tongue. But Chorian had grown up among the Gaje and there were sad gaps in his education. No one had ever taught him the old songs and the old dances; he knew nothing of conjuring and spells; he had no idea how to ghost. Worse, he hadn't had any opportunity since he was a boy to steep himself in the Swatura, the chronicles of our race, and the course of our history was beginning to grow jumbled in his mind.

Naturally he was familiar with the events of the past thousand years, how the Kingdom had come into being and the way it had arranged itself in its strange relationship with the Empire. If nothing else, Chorian's responsibilities at the imperial court would have required him to make himself aware of that part of the story. But of the rest of it he knew only the merest hazy outlines, bits and fragments here and there: something of our early days on Romany Star, our going forth into the Great Dark, our wanderings in space and our arrival on Earth. He had some knowledge of the greatness of Romany Atlantis and of the catastrophe that destroyed it. He knew a little about the terrible years of our life as outcasts among the Gaje of Earth. But none of it had any solid meaning for him. It was all cloudy, vague, abstract, mere *history*, a murky tangle of practically meaningless old migrations and persecutions, long ago and far away. Somebody else's history, at that. He had no sense that any of it had happened to *him*. But it had; of course it had. Everything that has happened to any Rom has happened to all Rom. If you aren't one with your history, you have no history; and if you don't have any history you aren't anybody at all.

In the few days he stayed with me I tried to help him. Just before the moment when Double Day was ending, I took him out on the glittering ice-fields and showed him where to find Romany Star. "There," I said. "The great red one. O Tchalai, the Star of Wonder. O Netchaphoro, the Luminous Crown, the Carrier of Light, the Halo of God. You see it up there? Do you see it, you Chorian?"

"How could I not see it, Yakoub?"

And he went to his knees before it on the ice.

"There are sixteen streams of light radiating from it," I told him. "One for each of the sixteen original tribes. You can see that on the banner of the Kingdom, the star of sixteen points. That star has one world, Chorian, and it is the most beautiful world in all the billion galaxies."

"Have you been there, Yakoub?"

"In my dreams, yes."

"But you've never seen it with your own eyes?"

"How could I? It's holy ground. It's absolutely forbidden for any of us to go there—the worst kind of sacrilege. No Rom has set foot on that world in ten thousand years."

He had trouble understanding that: why we didn't simply jump into our ships and go zooming off to reclaim our ancient home world. It would be so easy. Who could stop us? We can go wherever we like, can't we? The young are so impetuous. And they have no real comprehension of the nature of the invisible world, of the unseen ties that bind and constrict us. I explained to him that it was a matter of the fulfilling of our long-range destiny, of a plan that was beyond our ability to grasp. I told him that we could not go back to Romany Star until we had received a sign, a call, that the time had come.

And then I said, "But I mean to get there before I die, boy. Why do you think I've lived so long? I've taken an oath. No death for me, boy, until I've touched the soil of Romany Star with both my heels."

He gave me a peculiar look. "Even though it would be sacrilege?"

I rounded on him angrily. "What are you saying? I can't go until the call comes, don't you see? But the call will be coming soon. I know that,

Chorian. I have absolutely certain knowledge of that. And when it does
—the moment it does—"

"You'll be the first one there."

"The first, yes. Showing the way for the rest of us. Now do you
understand?"

He nodded. He stared at the black bowl of the sky. Mulano's air is
cold and clear and there are no city lights to blur the skyward vision.
I have never known another world from which Romany Star can be
viewed as readily.

"If it's so beautiful there, Yakoub, why did we ever leave?"

"We had to," I said. "A wise mother casts her children forth to make
their own way in the universe; and Romany Star was a wise mother to
us."

Was that so? Suddenly, for a moment there, I wondered. To drive
us forth from our home with a flaming sword and force us into thousands of years of dismal wandering—this is wisdom? This is mother-
hood?

I listened to what I was saying, that glib line about the wise mother
who had cast us forth, and for one weird instant my whole sense of the
architecture of our destiny wavered and wobbled and shook. Sometimes
all this mouthing off of proverbs is just one way of sweeping anguish
and pain and even resentment under the rug. But what you sweep under
the rug has a way of crawling out again to bite you, and that isn't just
a proverb. It's an observation.

Cast forth by our wise mother. Well, yes. Or our father. Romany Star
was our mother and God was our father, and God had noticed us, smug
and happy on Romany Star, and He had said to Himself, These fat and
sassy Rom are getting complacent. They're getting arrogant. They're
starting to forget that this universe is really a vale of tears, a chancy
risky place where it's only by great good luck that you get through any
given day without some monstrous catastrophe. They've had it good for
too long, those Rom. All right. I'll throw them out on their asses. Let
them learn what life is really like. And so had He done. And we have
been suffering for our ancient good fortune ever since.

There was a Gaje people on Earth once called the Jews, who thought
they were God's special people. He tossed *them* out on their asses too,
just to teach them that He doesn't have any favorites, or, that if He
does, He can give His favorites an even rougher time than He does His
enemies. It's a very similar story, in its way: suffering, persecution,
poverty, exile. But He wasn't as hard on them as He was on us. *Them*

He made into lawyers, doctors, professors. *We* had to be knife-sharpeners and fortune-tellers. What kind of a lesson was He trying to teach us, anyway? At least He relented a little later on, and gave us some classier occupations. There are still some Jews around but I don't think many of them pilot starships. I'm pretty sure that none of them are kings, either.

Well, maybe it *had* all been worthwhile, I told myself. The casting forth into exile, the wandering, the suffering. So I answered my own question with a resounding Yes. Of course it had. Who was I to complain? There was Chorian, looking at me with rapture, me the wise man, me the old king, the embodiment of our race, and he was saying with his eyes, Tell me, Tell me, Tell me, Yakoub. Tell me all our great and wonderful story. How it all happened, how it began. I felt ashamed that I had wavered even for an instant, that I had begun to resent, to question.

And as we stood there in the darkness and the cold, I told him the old tale, the oldest of all our tales, the Tale of the Swelling Sun, just as my father had told it to me while we were standing together on that steep slope of Mount Salvat one night on Vietoris long ago, and just as I had told it to my many sons over many years on many different worlds.

10.

*I SPOKE OF OUR ANCIENT DAYS OF GREATNESS, THE WON-*drous cities of Romany Star, the shining palaces and splendid towers, the vast concourses and broad highways, the gleaming columns and plazas. I told him how the sky over Romany Star was forever ablaze with the light of all the heavens. I told him of the eleven moons that were strung like brilliant jewels from horizon to horizon. I told him of rivers that sparkled like new wine, of mountains that challenged the stars, of golden meadows and dazzling lakes. Of the handsome, happy people.

Then I told him of how we came to learn that the splendor would all be snatched from us. First Mulesko Chiriklo, the bird of the dead, making her nest on the highest battlement of the Great Temple. Then the woman's voice crying the mourning-song in the night, which we heard in every city at once; and then the wind that blew from the south, where the dead souls go to live, and would not stop for fourteen months. And other omens after that: a year when there was no summer, and a day when the sun did not rise, and a night when no stars could be seen anywhere in the world.

We had no way of understanding these omens, for we had known nothing but happiness on Romany Star. There had never been a drought, nor an earthquake, nor a flood, nor a plague. The seasons came round in their time and the earth was fertile. There was no sickness among us, and when death came to us it was sudden and clean, in great old age. So when the omens began the call went forth for wise ones who could interpret them for us; and from every part of the world the wise ones came, gathering in the great plaza of the capital city. For ninety-nine months they conferred and studied and asked the gods for guidance. Then in the hundredth month the king locked them all in the Long Chamber of the Great Temple, and let them know that they would have neither food nor drink until they told us what was about to befall us and how we should deal with it; and there was no word from them for ninety-nine hours, but in the hundredth hour they signalled that they had been granted a revelation, and then they were allowed to come forth.

Our sweet Romany Star, they declared, has resolved to cast us forth into the universe to make our own way, and there is no use weeping or wailing or praying, for the time is short and swift action must be taken.

A change, they said, will soon come upon the sun who is our mother. She will swell and grow huge, and in place of her warm life-giving red glow there will come a savage blaze of blue light bearing terrible heat that no living thing can withstand. In one monstrous murderous noontime, the wise ones told us, deadly fire will march across the fields and meadows, the mountains and valleys, the cities and the plains. The world will turn black and the seas will boil and all life will end on Romany Star. And then the sun will subside as swiftly as she had erupted, and her gentle red light will return, but now it will fall on the charred and shattered ruin of our dear world.

At once there was weeping and there was wailing and there was praying, and the people cried out to the king to save them; and the king said, "This is something that is fated to come upon us, and we can do nothing to prevent it. But there is one way to save ourselves." And the king proposed that we build as many spacegoing ships as we could, and fill them with people and animals and plants and all the treasures of our world, and go forth into the Great Dark with them and wait out there until the cataclysm had run its course; and then we could return to Romany Star and rebuild our life there. So the weeping ceased, and the wailing and the praying; and the building of the ships commenced. But very soon it became clear that we could not possibly build enough of them. For the time of the cataclysm was almost upon us, and we had hardly enough ships to bear one person in a thousand into space. And then came news that was even worse: that there would be not one swelling of the sun but three, during the course of the next ten thousand years, so there was no point in trying to return to Romany Star; whatever we might rebuild would only be destroyed once more in the next swelling, and again in the one after that.

So we knew that most of us would die and the rest of us were to be driven forth from our home to dwell a long time in exile. We could not understand why God had chosen to do this to us, but we knew that it was not our place to find reasons for the doings of God.

"But only one in a thousand could go?" Chorian asked, horrified.

"Not even as many as that," I said. "One in five thousand, perhaps. One in ten thousand. We had only sixteen ships. There was a lottery, and names were chosen, and the sixteen ships went off into the Great Dark. And one day they looked behind them and saw a new star in the sky that was blazing a brilliant blue-white, and Romany Star's red glow was nowhere to be seen; and that day they wept and they wailed and prayed, and afterward they turned their faces forward, for they knew there was nothing behind them that they would want to see."

"And these were the Rom who settled on Earth?"

"Yes," I said. "Though we went to a few other places first; but Earth was most like Romany Star, and that was where we chose to live."

"Even though the Gaje were already there?"

"*Because* the Gaje were already there. The Gaje were shaped very much like the Rom, you see, so much so that one race could even interbreed with the other; and that was the proof that the Rom would be able to live and thrive on Earth. So there we settled, on a large uninhabited island of our own where the Gaje would not be able to trouble us; for the Gaje were a crude and stupid and backward people and we knew that they would harass us and bother us and make war on us if we tried to dwell in their midst. We took that island—they were helpless to stop us—and in time we built a great city on it and came to live almost as splendidly as we had on Romany Star; but when night fell we would look toward the heavens and we could see the red light of Romany Star shining there, and we dreamed of all that had once been ours, and we told ourselves that some day we would go back to our own world and make it what had been in the time before we had been cast forth."

"Romany Star had turned red again?" Chorian asked.

"Yes. Exactly as the wise men had predicted, so did it come to pass: it had turned brighter, all of a sudden, and had flailed out with a quick lethal flare, and then it had subsided and all was as it had been before."

"But we didn't go back, even so."

"That had been only the first swelling of the sun. We knew there would be two more."

"And have there been?"

"One," I said. "Almost six thousand years after we left. We saw it in the sky, a great blue-white blaze. That was at the time when Jesu Cretchuno was born, the Christ-child who some say is the son of God; and perhaps you know the tale of the three kings who came to worship him in his cradle. One of those kings was Rom; and he knew that the star that had announced the child's birth was the star that had given us birth also, and that it was blazing up for the second time, just as our wise ones had foretold."

Chorian stared at the sky for a long while. Then he said, "And the third swelling?"

"Soon," I said. "Another thousand years. Or five hundred, or maybe tomorrow. That's the sign we're all waiting for, the call, that third swelling. And then at last it will be safe for the Rom to return to their true home. If your precious emperor will let us have it, of course. Which is our chief task in the universe, to work toward regaining possession of our star; and I tell you, boy, I'll be there to see that day."

A sudden shadow darkened the darkness, cutting a black swath across the stars. For an instant Romany Star vanished from sight; and I heard the deep hooting voice of the bird of the dead, who had just passed overhead and was roosting now in a nearby tree. Her enormous black wings enfolded her like a shroud, and her sapphire eyes glinted in the night.

"Mulesko Chiriklo," I said. "A bird of good omen. She follows the Rom from world to world."

I waved to her, making a Rom salute; and Mulesko Chiriklo hooted her greeting to me in turn. I knew what she was saying. It was what she always said to me. She was offering the King of the Gypsies the blessing of the night, and the hope of a swift return to the ancient motherland. I looked at Chorian. He seemed terrified. His teeth were chattering and he was standing in a peculiar hunched way not at all proper to one so young and strong.

I slapped him on the shoulder.

"Come, boy. Let's go inside and see if there's some decent wine left."

As we headed for my ice-bubble I heard the laughter of Rom ghosts on the night wind.

11.

BY THE FOURTH DAY CHORIAN HAD HIS SWEEP ANTENNA tuned to its farthest vector and it was time for him to go. He packed the few belongings he had brought with him into the smallest possible space, and unfurled his journey-helmet, that soft webwork of coppery mesh, no larger than a handkerchief when it is folded for storage, that would protect him during his lonely flight through the interstellar spaces.

Just before he put his helmet on he turned to me and I saw him struggling to say something, but the words wouldn't come for him. That troubled me. One Rom should never be afraid of saying the true things of the heart to another.

I went close to him and put my hands on his shoulders. I had to reach far up, though I am not small.

"What is it, cousin? What do you want to tell me?"

"That—that I'm going to leave now—"

"I know that, cousin," I said, very gently.

"And I wanted to say—just to say—"

He faltered. I let my hands continue to rest on his shoulders and I waited.

"I was trouble for you, wasn't I, Yakoub?"

"Trouble?"

"I came here where you had come to live by yourself, and I bothered you when you had no wish to be bothered. And you put up with me because it is Rom law that guests must not be turned away, but you were angry within that I was here."

"Dinosaur dung," I said, and I said it with vigor, and I said it in Romany, which was not easy, for although there are many words for "dung" in Romany there is not precisely one that means "dinosaur." Nevertheless I said it and he understood what I had said.

"You've been very kind, Yakoub."

"Enough preamble, boy. We are Rom. Tell me what's in your heart."

He looked down and scuffed the tip of his boot against the fresh snow. He was very young and getting younger every minute. Watching him, I tried to understand what it was like to be so young, tried to remember how it had been. My God, it was so long ago! To exist in the moment, not yet wound in layer upon opaque layer of experience. To be transparent, bones visible through the skin, every motivation lying in clear view just below the surface. I hadn't felt that way for a hundred fifty years. Perhaps not ever.

"These past few days—" he began, and faltered again.

"Yes?"

"I never knew my father, Yakoub. I was sold away from my kumpania when I was seven."

"I know, boy. And I know what that's like. I was sold at seven myself, the first time."

"The Lord Sunteil's been something like a father to me, in his way. He's not evil, you know. He's a Gajo and he's the emperor's right hand but he's not evil, and as close as anyone's been a father to me, it's been Lord Sunteil. But it isn't the same. He isn't of the blood."

"I know what you're saying."

"And these past few days—these past few days, Yakoub—"

He turned away and stared off to his left, far across the snow-field, as though thinking that he had to hide from me the tears that were threatening to break through and burst past his eyelids. He pretended to be searching for the sweep aura, but I knew what he was really doing, and I felt sad for him for thinking that he had to conceal his soul from me. This is what comes of growing up among the Gaje, I thought.

"Listening to you as you told me the stories from the Swatura— hearing from your own lips about Romany Star, the Tale of the Swelling Sun—" He took a deep breath and swung around, looking down at me, and, yes, his eyes were moist, and sell me again into slavery if mine weren't getting the same way, just a bit. Then he said, all in a rush, "For a little while these last few days I understood what it must be like to have had a real father, Yakoub."

So he had managed to get it out at last.

There was nothing I needed to say in return. I smiled at him and embraced him and kissed him on the mouth in the old Rom fashion, and gave his shoulders one good hard final squeeze and lifted my hands from him, and we stood there together in silence. Double Day was dawning now. The orange sun was coming into the sky opposite the yellow one and the ice was ablaze with warring colors.

After a time he said, "I fear that I'll never see you again."

"Because you think our paths will never cross, or that you think my time is nearly over?"

"Oh, Yakoub—"

"The first day you were here you told me that I'd live forever. I don't think that's true and I don't think I want it to be true. But I have to last long enough to set foot on Romany Star. You know that. And you know that I will."

"Yes. You will, Yakoub."

"And we'll meet again long before that day. I don't know how or where or why it will be, but we will. Somewhere. Somewhen. And meanwhile there are tasks waiting for you, boy, which you ought to be off and doing. Go now. Take care. May you remain with God."

"May you remain with God, Yakoub."

He grinned at me. I think he was relieved to have all this weepy business of farewell behind him, and I have to confess that I was too.

The sweep aura now was rising. A surging fountain of brilliant green light came from the antenna that he had mounted out on the ice-field a few hundred meters away.

"You'd better go out there," I said.

He slipped the journey-helmet over his head and the flimsy folds of coppery mesh tumbled down about him almost to the ground.

Just before he touched the switch at his shoulder that would make any communication between us impossible, he looked down into my eyes and said, "You are still king, Yakoub. You will always be king."

Then he touched the switch and the frail web lit up and bellied out like a balloon, sealing him in a protective sphere of chilly Mulano air that no force could breach. So long as the helmet's field remained activated he would be shielded in that sphere against anything. Even the awful darkness and cold of the void that lies between one space and another.

For a long time I watched him from my doorway as he stood out there on the ice, bathed in the green glow of the sweep aura and the blended orange and yellow of the double suns. He was waiting for some roving scanning-strand of a relay sweep to find him and carry him away, back to the worlds of the Imperium.

I felt sorry for him. Relay-sweep travel is not at all jolly nor is it exhilarating. In fact, it's a great pain in the buliasa. Believe me. I have had plenty of opportunity to find that out at first hand over the years. You stand and wait; you stand and wait. At a thousand different nexuses around the inner universe the sweep-stations sit like giant spiders, stroking the nether regions of space with their far-ranging arms. Sooner or later one will find you, if you are patient enough and have set up the right coordinates on your beacon. And then it will seize you and lift you and carry you away, and shunt you through this auxiliary space and that, not following any route that particularly serves your needs, but simply one that suits the pattern of openings in the space-time lattice that it happens to find. And sooner or later, but usually later, it will deposit you—no more ceremoniously than it would a bundle of laundry—at a relay drop on one of the Empire worlds. It's a slow and cumbersome and basically humiliating process, in which you surrender all control of your destiny to an inanimate force that is not only unresponsive to any of your wishes but also completely beyond your comprehension. For hours, days, months, sometimes years, you drift like a child's toy lost in an infinite sea, floating along inside your protective sphere with no way of amusing yourself and no company but your own remorselessly ticking thoughts; for although your metabolic processes are suspended while you are held outside the ordinary space-time continuum, your mind goes right on working, business as usual. A tiresome way to travel. Not that I mean to whine. There are too many worlds, not enough starships, for the Empire to be able to run standard tourist service to places like Mulano. I had come here by relay-sweep myself; and when the time came for me to leave here, that was how I would go.

Chorian stood straight and tall like a good soldier in the light of the two suns for what seemed to me like an eternity and a half without moving. After a time I began to think that perhaps by watching him I was somehow hindering the coming of his sweep-strand, for things sometimes work that way. So I went inside and I conjured up the bahtalo drom for him, the spell of safe voyage. I wasn't sure that it would have any effect, since Chorian was enclosed in his protective sphere where possibly even the spell of safe voyage couldn't reach. But it was worth trying. The spell of safe voyage is one of the true spells, one of the ones that reliably does the job. It isn't simply witch-nonsense, something that some old drabarni of the Middle Ages might have put together out of bathwater and scythe-blades and the wombs of frogs; it is grounded in the great lines of force that run across the curving axes of the universe from shore to shore.

At any rate I wove the spell for him; and then I think I must have fallen into a light sleep; and when I went outside again to look for him, he was gone.

The suns were setting. I said a little prayer and waited for the moment of Romany Star.

TWO:

The One Word

I was with Loiza la Vakako when a messenger came to him and told him that a certain wild Rom of his family, while drunk, had challenged five Gaje to follow him across a mountain pass that was not much wider than the blade of a sword. All six of them had fallen to their deaths, but the Rom had been the last to fall, and those who had watched this event had praised him extravagantly for his courage.

Loiza la Vakako laughed. "Sometimes courage about dying is cowardice about living," he said. And he never mentioned the man again.

1.

A DAY OR TWO AFTER CHORIAN LEFT, I DECIDED TO PICK
myself up and move to some other part of the territory. It wasn't that
I was trying to hide from further visitors, now that I knew I could be
found. I was never lost—to those who know how to see. But I had lived
in this place long enough. There is something in the Rom soul that will
not let us live in the same place for very long.

In the old days when Earth existed, most of us were nomads. Wanderers. We lived in caravans and roamed wherever we pleased. At night
we slept under the stars unless the weather was foul. In winter we might
pull the wagons together and hole up for the season; but as soon as
spring arrived, off we went again. In at least a dozen of the languages
of Earth the word "Gypsy" came to mean "wanderer." Poets would say
things like, "I must down to the seas again, to the vagrant gypsy life."
Which is bullshit, of course, I have to point out, with all due respect
to the literary folk. A real Gypsy would no more go to sea than he
would grind his horse up into sausages. The sea, the sea, the stinking
fishy sea—it's never been a place where any Gypsy cares to find himself.
Live by the seashore, yes, that's fine. Nice breezes, good eating. But go
and toss about on the waves? No, never. Better the broader seas of
space, calm and—well, you get the general idea of what those old
misguided but well-meaning poets were trying to say. At least they were
thinking about us.

For some reason our wandering ways were tremendously bothersome
to the Gaje. Whatever they can't control gives them an itch on the
inside of their skulls. Sometimes they tried to pass laws requiring us to
settle down. Hah! What good could that do? We used to say that
making a Gypsy live in one place was like harnessing a lion to a plow.
To be tied all your life to the same four walls and a roof, the same little
plot of ground, the same dusty street—why, that was torment, that was
slavery. We were meant to wander.

Well, things change, more or less; but the more things change the
more they remain the same. (I can't take credit for that line. It's Gaje
wisdom, spoken by one of their wise men a thousand years ago. Don't

look so surprised. Even the Gaje have their moments of wisdom.) There aren't any lions any more and there are no more plows and Gypsies stopped living in caravans a long time back. But we still have trouble with the idea of being tied down. We may live in houses for a while, but only for a while. Sooner or later we move on. And when we move on it isn't from one little country to another on the same continent of the same small planet. It is by great leaps across thousands of light-years.

(There wouldn't be an Empire today, but for us. The Gaje can't deny that. They may have built the starships, but we were the ones who piloted them to the far reaches of the sky. And all because we are a restless people; and all because we can never call any place home, except our true home that was cruelly taken from us ten thousand years ago. Other places aren't home. Just shelter. Places to wait.)

So. Moving day. Blue-green clouds scudding across a lemon sky. The air crisp and triple-cold. Not even any ghosts hovering around. A good day for taking to the road, Yakoub Rom. Take yourself onward, before the old Devil hangs his weights on your heart and pulls you down. The old Devil, that sly one, o Beng, yes. He may be my cousin too but I won't ask him to dinner.

I emptied out the ice-bubble where I had lived for the past year or so and gathered all my things together and packed them into my elegant little hundred-cubic-meter overpocket, and when I drew the drawstring I sent ninety-nine point ninety-five cubic meters' worth of the over-pocket's contents into a handy storage dimension in a nearby con-tinuum. What was left had negligible mass and no weight at all. I tied it to my sleeve with a string and let it bob along beside me as I went on to my new home base.

It was on the other side of the Gombo glacier and about a hundred kilometers to the north. That was a good little walk. I sang to myself in Rom the whole way, not bothering always to make sense, for who was listening? And when my toes began to grumble I stopped and put my head back and yelled my name into the wind and grabbed my crotch and flung out my arms and lifted my knees to my chin and stomped them down again and capered around like a lunatic, doing one of the old dances. Hoy! Hootchka pootchka hoya zim! And then I went for-ward, laughing, with the sweat running around and down and through the tangled black jungle on my chest and belly. Hoy! Yakoub of the Rom is on the road again!

It started to snow an hour after I set out. The sky turned white and the horizon disappeared and there were no longer any landmarks to guide me. From then on there was snow flying in my face all the way. I drank it in and spit it back out. Even in the whiteness and the blankness I kept to my course. Long ago on a planet called Trinigalee Chase that I would otherwise rather not talk about I was taught a trick for keeping on course with no instrument other than the one between my ears, and it stood me in good stead now. It's the one thing I remember from Trinigalee Chase that I'm glad not to have forgotten.

Wherever you go on Mulano the scenery is the same: ice, snow, ice, snow. The place has no tilt to the plane of the ecliptic, so it has nothing much by way of a change of seasons, and even though it has two fancy suns that give it plenty of lively light it's too far from them to enjoy any real warmth from them. So both hemispheres of Mulano are winter-bound all the time. I hadn't had a day without snow since I had arrived.

But that was all right. I'd spent enough of my life on tropical worlds. Generally speaking the planets where humanity has chosen to settle are ones where the climate is easy; maybe a little wintry around the poles on some, but usually balmy everywhere else all the year round. Soft translucent surf, powdery beaches, green fronds waving in the gentle breeze: that's your basic Gaje world. If they colonize any nastier ones —Megalo Kastro, say, or Alta Hannalanna—it's because there are raw materials on it that are too valuable to pass up. Otherwise, considering how many millions of planets there are just in our one galaxy, the Gaje don't see much reason to settle on the uncomfortable ones. Can't say I blame them, either.

The one exception to that is the world they all started from, Earth. Of course they didn't colonize Earth, they simply evolved there. And got away from it as quickly as they could. As any sensible being would have done. Ah, the climate of Earth! A hellish cantankerous thing, that climate. I know that from my studies and my occasional little ghosting trips. Aside from a few really sweet places not very well suited for large blocs of population it was all either too hot or too cold, too wet or too dry, too barren or too lush. Where you had a decent climate you usually got earthquakes or volcanic eruptions or hurricanes as part of the package.

(The Gaje like to argue that natural adversity of that sort is what makes a race great, and maybe so. But I have to point out that according to the account in the Swatura the climate on Romany Star was absolutely perfect, and we nevertheless managed to create a pretty impressive civilization there, thank you.)

(On the other hand, Romany Star got hit by two lethal solar flares within six thousand years of each other. You win some and you lose some, I guess.)

Anyway, a little chilly weather has never bothered me much. And Mulano, being outside Empire control and not totally unlivable even at its most blustery, was just the sort of planet where I could take a quiet little sabbatical from the cares of government. I wasn't likely to be bothered by tourists or slave-traders or synapse-peddlers or body-farmers or agony-mongers or census-agents or stockbrokers or encyclopedia salesmen or prospectors or tax-collectors or any of the million other piffling distractions of 32nd-century life. The snow was piled so deep that even the archaeologists stayed away. Maybe the occasional ghost would turn up, but those were my own people, so no problem. And I knew I could live comfortably enough in an ice-bubble, because I had spent a couple of years once on Zimbalou, which is one of the Rom nomad worlds. Ice-bubbles are standard lodging there for anybody living at surface level. Zimbalou as it wanders here and there around the galaxy is never allowed to get within thawing range of any sun, because its major cities are nestled way down deep in tunnels far below the ice, and anything approaching warmth would mean total disaster. It's a dark and dismal place but its people love it. I almost came to love it myself. At any rate I learned the art of constructing ice-bubbles there.

So I walked up the side of the glacier and over the top and down the other side and headed north until I came to the right place. It was a special place on a planet that doesn't have many special places. I had found it and marked it for myself a few days before Chorian had turned up.

Though Mulano is basically nothing but a huge glittering empty white ice-field, this part of it was different. It had one astonishing feature, something truly strange. God, how I love a good strangeness! And this was a strangeness so strange that even from ten kilometers away I could feel it emanating toward me, and the force of it was like the roaring of a tremendous pipe-organ whose music filled half the heavens.

What it was, you came over a low snubby hill out of the whiteness and suddenly there was green in front of you, stretching ahead as far as you possibly could see, across snow-blinking valleys and hills and up the side of a distant glacier. And what the green was, was thousands upon thousands of fleshy sea-green tentacles as thick as your arm above and as thick as your thigh below, jutting up through the snow every few meters apart to a height of five or ten or twenty meters and ever so slowly waving and twitching about like heavy cables. There was a voluptuous music in their slippery sinuous movements. I imagined those wriggling waving things whispering to me, saying, Come here, Rom baro, come here, come here, come let us stroke your pretty black beard. Let us give you joy, Rom baro.

The first time I saw that scene I thought they might be the exposed limbs of some enormous herd of strange animals trapped and buried by some tremendous blizzard. The ghost of Valerian was with me that day and I said that and he said, "That's a smart guess, Yakoub," which was his usual way of telling me that I was full of shit.

(Valerian's never tactful. He's the black sheep of the Rom, an old space-pirate. Once he was a commander in the Imperial navy until he found that he preferred piracy and now there's a bounty on his head, though it would surprise me extremely if anybody ever manages to collect it. As a nation we Rom deplore piracy, at least publicly, and so we deplore our cousin Valerian, but he practices his trade as if it were poetry and you have to admire him for that.

"Have you ever seen anything like that before?" I asked him. But he was gone. I made a fist and shook it at the place where he had been glowing in the air. "Hey, you Valerian! Hey, this is the place for me, this place! You watch and see!")

That was a week or two ago. Now I was back, and meaning to stay. The tentacles were all waving away as before, wiggly as worms, green as grief. The nearest ones were close enough so that I could have reached out and tickled them. Or they me. They were puckered and pockmarked and they had rows of small darker-green nubbins sprouting all over them.

I unloaded my Riemann projector, so handy for dumping unwanted tangible matter into intangible places, and made ready to carve me a new ice-bubble. But first I had to be sure that I wouldn't be trying to build a nest for myself in the flank of some buried mountain, or some other equally unpromising submerged feature of the local geography. And I wanted to know more about those tentacles anyway. So I switched the projector to scan intensity, which lined up the molecules of the local geography in a convenient way and turned the subsurface more or less transparent for five hundred meters all around me. That was when I discovered that the twitchy rubbery things that were sticking out of the snow were in fact the branches of trees. The little green nubbins were their leaves. I was standing right on top of an enormous forest buried practically to its tips in snow.

Trees, yes. Weird, slender, seductively curved, undulating like lovely many-armed dancers mysteriously rooted to their places on stage. Maybe they were even intelligent. I suppose they didn't mind being buried like that, snow being a fine insulator and the air temperature being disagreeably low at that time of the year. Perhaps they emerged from their snowy tomb only once every fifty or a hundred years, I thought—during what might pass for summer on Mulano, if there was any such thing as summer here. Or—more likely—they lived perpetually under snow like this, the way the spice-fish lived so happily in the ice of the glaciers. You travel around enough, you get to see everything, and then some.

Well, I didn't seem to have anything to fear from them, and they broke the monotony. So I tuned my projector up to compaction level and burrowed a hole in the ice for myself, long and deep, slanting downward just at the place where the forest began. I built this bubble a little bigger than the last one, with shining walls and a lovely luminescent floor and a long window running across one side. I spent half a day fashioning an elegant door out of a slab of ice mounted on a thick dowel of the same useful substance. On its inner surface I hung the little shining Vogon sphere that would maintain light and power and a perpetual globe of sweet warm air between me and the wintry world without.

Then I went inside and closed the door and said the word that activated the Vogon sphere. Everything turned bright and cheerful. Hoy! Yakoub has a roof over his head again!

Now I set about hauling my possessions back from the various adjacent dimensions where I had stowed them.

My treasures. The things which root me to myself and remind me of who I have been and who I must yet become. The deep-piled rug, two Yakoubs long and three Yakoubs wide, woven in wondrous red and green and blue and black on lost Earth itself by a sultan's fifty castrated slaves. The three brass lamps, fat-bellied and squat, with the names of my fathers inscribed on their sides. The necklace strung with Byzantine gold coins that had belonged to that wondrous whore Mona Elena, and which I meant to return to her if ever I saw her again. The silken scroll of office, spun for me by nine blind eye-beaters of Duud Shabeel, which I should have surrendered upon my abdication but did not because I

could not bear to part with anything so ingenious: look at it long enough
and you begin to know with complete certainty that you can never die.
The starstone, plucked from a sand-dragon's bloody throat on
Nabomba Zom, in whose depths the red light of Romany Star shines
with wondrous warmth. The wonderwheel. The shadowstick. The Rom
scepter, bareshti rovli rupui, the chief's silver wand, with its eight-sided
red-tasseled head engraved with the five great symbols, nijako, chjam,
shion, netchaphoro, trushul: axe, sun, moon, star, cross. The statue of
the Black Virgin Sara, our patron saint. The veil that had belonged to
La Chunga, the Gitana dancer. The set of tinsmith's tools, worn and
bent. The frayed and tattered bearskin, last of its kind in the universe.
The golden candlesticks. The Tarot cards. The scythe that was dipped
in my bath-water when I was born, to drive the demons away. The
amulet of sea-urchin fossils. The dear little prickly niglo, the hedgehog that we brought with us from Earth into half the worlds of the
galaxy, carved from the fiery yellow jade of Alta Hannalanna. And
more, much more, the treasures of a long life, the gatherings of all my
great odyssey.

These things I arranged in the ice-bubble in the ways that I liked to
arrange them. Then I stepped outside and saluted the writhing green
arms rising from the snow just before me, and called out my name three
times, and cried the words of power, and waved my manhood in the
frosty air and made water in front of my door, slicing a hot yellow track
through the snow in the home-sealing patterns. And laughed and
danced one more quick dance, arms and legs flying, hootchka pootchka
hoya zim! Yakoub! Yakoub! Yakoub!

It was almost like being in my house of power again, my shining
palace on Galgala where I lived when I was King of the Rom and
shaper of the destinies of worlds. I lit the lamps and grasped the scepter
and stood upon the carpet and once again they came to me, the chief-
tains of the Rom, one by one, saying, "I am Frinkelo," "I am Fero,"
"I am Yakali," "I am Miya," bringing me their disputes and their
sorrows and their dreams. Wherever I am, that place is my house of
power, my palace. That is one of the great Rom secrets, the reason why
we can be wanderers. It is not that we have no roots, but that all places
are one to us and we put down the same roots wherever we may be,
for every place where we may wander is the same place: it is the place
known as Not-Romany-Star. And therefore any place can be home for
us, since no place is home.

So in the silence and the solitude of this new place beside the strange

forest I lived and was happy in the company of myself. The ghost of
Polarca came to me, and Valerian, and several of the others, misty
figures drifting through time to show me that they still loved me.
Shrewd old Bibi Savina came once or twice, that wise and cunning
woman who has given me so much good advice over the long years, not
only while I was king but even before: for she was the one who had gone
ghosting back to my childhood to tell me that I would and must be king.
"This is the right place," she said now, and winked. "Stay here until
it stops being right." It was good to see a woman again, even an old
one like Bibi Savina. She was bent and withered, was Bibi Savina, and
looked at least twice my age, though I was almost old enough to be her
father. She had never been the sort to go in for remakes. Hard to
imagine, Bibi Savina with a remake, prancing around like a giddy girl.
Would I have desired her, if she had had herself made young and
beautiful? Of course I have never felt any such feeling toward Bibi
Savina: how could it have been otherwise? Aside from everything else
there would have been a fantastic scandal, considering her high role in
the government, if I had ever laid a finger on her. Not that I wasn't glad
to see Bibi Savina, and more than glad, but I would have liked to be
visited while I was on Mulano by someone for whom I felt a little more
passion, too. When you're living in an igloo in the middle of an ice-field
a couple of pretty breasts and a few sleek thighs provide a wondrous
amount of warmth and light. (You think that's disgusting, a man my
age talking like that? Just you wait. Except you won't be as lucky as
I am; you won't still have the juices flowing when you get to my age,
if you do, the way they flow in me.)

Of course it isn't possible actually to make love to a ghost, but as I
say, there's a certain delight in having a beautiful woman around, even
if she's intangible. I would have enjoyed a visit from the elegant and
supple and perpetually beautiful Syluise, for instance, that extraordinary woman who has haunted me for many too many years; but Syluise
paid me no visits. It would have astounded me if she had. That would
have been too loving a thing for her to do. Still, I had my hopes, such
as they were. She rarely left my mind. I found myself remembering her
in a thousand ways. How she used to plunge into a tub filled with that
luminescent blue protozoan from—where? Iriarte? Estrilidis?—and rise
from it like Venus, glowing, dazzling. And I would lick it off her, all
over. The taste of it still with me. Ah! The bitch. How I loved her. I
still do. I always will. Every man is fated to have a Syluise in his life,
I think. Even a king.

The ghosts came; the ghosts went. And sometimes when I was alone I closed my eyes and I was on Galgala at my court with clouds of gold all around me, or I was drifting in the pleasure-sea of Xamur, or I was at the Capital and advancing to the sound of a hundred trumpets up the broad crystalline steps of the throne-platform of the Fifteenth Emperor, who rose to welcome me and offer me a cup of sweet wine with his own hands. Me, Yakoub, born a slave and three times sold, and there was the emperor, and Sunteil beside him, and the Lords Naria and Periandros not far away, bidding me welcome! Sweet dreams, true dreams, happy dreams of a life without regret. And I told myself that I could go on this way for a hundred years more, a thousand, living in the bright glow of my memories and completely content.

2.

THEN SYLUISE TURNED UP AFTER ALL. OR HER GHOST, rather. I can't say she came just when I had given up hope, because I had never had any real hope of seeing her, just wistful softheaded fantasies that I knew were foredoomed. And then there she was, Syluise the golden, Syluise the glorious, hovering in the air right in front of me.

"You haven't missed me at all, have you?" she said.

Dear Syluise. Always opening with a jab.

"I've thought of no one else the whole time," I told her. Sounding romantic and sarcastic both at once. Which was it? How would I know?

Billowing waves of electromagnetic splendor surrounded her like an aurora, shooting off a halo of emerald, scarlet, violet, gold. She looked gorgeous within it. I have never seen her looking anything but gorgeous, no matter the season, the time of day, the geophysical or emotional weather. That's her specialty: beauty so intense that it's unreal. She is like her own statue.

"It's been a long time, hasn't it, Syluise?"

"I've been traveling."

"Polarca tells me he saw you in Atlantis."

"Did he? What keen eyes he has. I looked for you there, but you weren't around."

"I'm not ghosting these days," I said.

"No. You're burrowing down in the snow and holding your breath until your face turns blue. Isn't that what you're doing, Yakoub?"

I could hardly bear to look at her, she was so beautiful. An alien beauty, not Rom at all, cascades of shining golden hair, intense blue eyes, long slender legs. She *is* Rom, that I know, but long ago she had herself changed into this Gaje form. Which never alters: I have known her eighty years and she has not aged by a day. She is her own statue, yes.

But there is more to her than her glittering beauty. She poses as a woman for men, a grand courtesan; and God knows she plays the role magnificently. But it's all a game to her, these tempestuous passions. Something else burns inside her, unknowable, untouchable, some deeper ambition than making men kneel to her beauty. The beauty is synthetic, after all. She might have been squat and coarse and bestial, dull-eyed and thick-waisted and mud-faced, before she had herself remade as a goddess. For all I knew she might even have been a man, before the remake.

"I've given up the kingship," I said.

"Yes. I know. You've abdicated. But why spend your retirement in a place like this?"

"Because there were things I needed to think about. This is a good place for thinking."

"Is it?"

"My mind works well in cold weather. And stark scenery like this helps me get down to essentials."

Essentials. I wanted to reach for her and pull her down against me. Those breasts, those lips. *Those* were essentials. Her perfume filling the air. Mulano ghosts were clustered around her, dazzled by the energy coming from her. My throat was dry and there was an ache in my balls. Maybe it would have been better if she had never come here. You can't make love to a ghost but you can certainly lust after one.

"Which essentials do you mean, Yakoub?"

I have outlived all my wives. Syluise will not have me. I want no others. There's something hard and contrary about her that mesmerizes me. But perhaps I have had enough wives for one life. Probably I would not take Syluise if she ever were to accept me. But still I ask her, from time to time. And always she refuses.

I said, "The future of the Kingdom is the only essential, Syluise."

"But what concern is that of yours now?"

"I still am king."

"Are you? Make up your mind. You say that you've abdicated. You can't be king and not be king at the same time."

"I'm taking a holiday from the kingship, is all."

"Ah, is that what it is? A holiday?"

"A time for reevaluation. For thinking things over. A tactical move. I could have the throne back in a minute if I asked for it." She smiled: a flicker of the flawless lips; a faint gleaming of the matchless eyes. "You doubt that?" I asked.

"I don't doubt that you believe it."

"But you don't believe it."

"You *do* think you can be king and not be king at the same time. I should have realized that from the start. If anybody knows how your mind works, I do."

"What are you trying to say, Syluise?"

"I knew you in Cesaro o Nano's time, before you were king. I remember how you used to insist that you would never accept the throne in a million years, that the whole idea disgusted you, that you'd fling it in their faces if they ever tried to offer it to you. You said that again and again, and then when they did come to you you grabbed it as fast as you could and you didn't let go for fifty years. You think I take anything you say at face value, Yakoub? You're the only man I know who can hold six contradictory ideas at once and feel perfectly comfortable about it."

"I didn't want to be king. I did refuse the throne. Again and again, until I saw that I had to be king, that there was no option about it. And then I let them give it to me."

"And the abdication? Why did you do that?"

There was a sudden astonishing softening in her tone. For an instant she wasn't just dueling with me. She seemed actually to care. I felt myself melting with love. Like a boy, like a Chorian. Like a ninny.

"Do you really want to know?" I asked.

She came closer. The aurora around her died away and she descended until she was almost at ground level and almost within my reach. Just one kiss, I thought. Those rosy nipples hardening against my palms.

"I want to know, yes." Still soft, her voice.

"A tactical move," I told her.

Hot in my mind burned the memory of those last days before I had gone before the great kris to resign. That time of despair and turmoil in my soul, when wherever I looked I saw chaos and decay. The prancing young men and women decking themselves out to look like Gaje, the intermarriages, the star-pilots taking their little detours to do their little smuggling operations, and all the rest: the final decadence of an ancient great race, so it had seemed to me. I had tried to tell myself I was exaggerating, that I was growing crochety and conservative with age. But at last it had all exploded within me, suddenly, uncontrollably: a sense that everything was falling apart and that some desperate measure had to be taken. That was when I called the krisatora together and told them I was abdicating; and if I live ten thousand years I will never forget the looks of utter astonishment on their faces as I gave them the news.

She frowned. Like a cloud crossing the face of the sun.

"A tactical move?" she said. "I don't understand."

I took a deep breath. I had never spoken explicitly about this before, not with Polarca, not with anyone. But I had never been able to withhold anything from Syluise. "It seemed to me that things were going wrong in the Kingdom, that we had lost our direction, that we had forgotten our purpose. I needed to upset people. To shake people up. In order to get the Kingdom back on its course."

"Its course?"

"I'm speaking of Romany Star," I said.

"Oh, Yakoub!"

She sounded sad and loving and patronizing all at once. But more patronizing than anything else.

"Where are the Rom of Romany Star?" I demanded. "Do we want our true world again, or are we willing to live in exile forever? Do we even think of such things any more? The One True Place, Syluise: does that mean anything to you?"

Her aurora flared up again. I could no longer see her face.

"A fat, complacent people, rich and settled: is that who we are, Syluise? Piloting our ships, serving the Gaje, snuggling up to the Imperium? No. No. Once we lose sight of what really matters, we lose sight of our own selves. We become no better than Gaje. Is that what you want, Syluise? Maybe it is. Your beautiful Gaje hair. Your narrow Gaje waist." I felt anger mounting suddenly, rising and rising. "Do you understand? I saw my own people losing their way. And I their king, presiding over the whole catastrophe."

A sharp gust of wind cut across the ice-plain, lifting drifts of snow and hurling them at us. The hard white swirls went through her without her seeming to notice.

"And abdicating, Yakoub?" she said gently. "How is that going to make things better?"

"They need me," I said. "They've already sent one messenger out to urge me to come back. There'll be more. They'll beg me. They'll ask to know my terms. I'll tell them, then. And they'll have no choice. I'll be king again, Syluise. But this time they'll have to follow me wherever I lead them. And where I lead them will be Romany Star."

"Oh, Yakoub," she said again. Her aurora grew dense as the heart of a sun. I could no longer see her, but I heard her. Was she weeping, within that searing blaze of energy?

No. That was laughter, that sound.

Syluise! That heartless bitch. The force of the hatred I felt for her just then could have driven a fleet of starships from one end of the galaxy to the other.

3.

SOMETIMES WHEN I WAS ALONE I COULD FEEL THE PRES-ence of the Gypsy kings of centuries gone by, crowding close within my soul. I felt Chavula close by, that little hard-edged man who had forced the Gaje to let us aboard their ships. And Ilika, with the flaming red beard, the one who showed how the leap was made, the quick conversion of Rom mind-force into the power of spanning the light-years. Claude Varna the great explorer, the finder of worlds. Tavelara, Markko, Mateo, Pavlo Gitano, all jostling within me, sharing their spirit with me, urging me onward. And there were other kings too, dark figures without names or faces, the kings of time immemorial, kings of the old world, the rough kings of the roads of Earth; and even older kings, kings of Gypsy Atlantis, kings even of Romany Star. On the day I became the high Rom baro they all had entered me and still they rode with me and I felt them within. And was grateful.

And who were these, these others lurking in the mists? I was unable to see them but I could feel them, mysterious, unknown. I had an idea who they were. Kings yet to come is who they were, Yakoub's successors, the kings of the unborn future, stirring in my soul. I knew that I would have to die in order to set them free to live out their destinies, and I felt some pain, knowing that; but it would have to be. That was all right. Give me a chance to live out my destiny, all you kings to come, and then you can have your own!

Syluise had laughed at me. Well, let her laugh. I knew why I had been given the kingship and I meant to accomplish what I had been chosen to bring about. They had chosen me because the vision was stronger in me than in anyone else; and even if all the others had lost sight of the vision now, I had not. I asked only one thing, that I would be allowed to live long enough. That was all I asked. One thing that I feared was that I would die without having given Romany Star back to my people. But what of it, you ask, if I did die too soon? I would be dead: what would anything matter to me then?

If you ask that, you understand nothing.

The power was within me, to achieve what must be achieved. If I had the power and I failed to make use of it, that was contemptible. My people would curse me forever. If there is a life after this life, I would blister and blacken there forever in their scorn. And if not—well, no matter. I must live as though all the Rom yet to be born are watching me. As though I dwell each day in the beacon glare of their scrutiny.

4.

YOU MIGHT THINK I'D HAVE HAD A CHANCE TO ENJOY A reprieve from all this socializing. But it wasn't long before I had company again.

This next visitor was confusing, because he was the Duc de Gramont.

Or his doppelganger. I wasn't sure which, and that was what was confusing. And disturbing.

Julien de Gramont is an old friend who has managed to tread a very neat line between the overlapping spheres of authority of the Rom Kingdom and the Empire. That's a measure of Julien's cleverness. By way of a profession Julien has set himself up in business as the pretender to the throne of ancient France, France having been one of the important countries of Earth around the year 1600 or so. France got rid of its kings a long time back, but that's all right; I can't see any real harm in claiming a lapsed throne. What I don't exactly understand, even though Julien has tried to explain it to me seven or eight times, is the point of claiming the throne of a country on a planet that doesn't even exist any more. It has something to do with grandeur, he said. And gloire. That word is pronounced *glwahr,* approximately. French is a very strange language.

(Just in passing I want to point out, since the notion is not likely to occur to you on your own, that the Duc de Gramont's beloved France was a place no bigger than a medium-big plantation would be on an average-size world such as Galgala or Xamur. Nevertheless France had kings of its own, and its own language and laws and literature and history and all the rest. And in fact was a very considerable place, in its time. I know that because I was there once—right around the time they were getting rid of their kings, as a matter of fact. It's an odd and somehow endearing thing about the Gaje of Earth that they found it necessary to divide up their one little planet into a hundred little separate countries. Of course that arrangement was a great pain in the buliasa for us when we lived among them. But all that came to an end a long time ago.)

The first couple of years I lived on Mulano I had had a doppelganger of the Duc de Gramont living here with me. Julien had had it made up for me as a going-away gift when he heard of my abdication, because he knows I am fond of French cuisine, a field in which he has great expertise; so he thought I might like to have my own private French chef while I was living in my self-imposed exile.

But doppelgangers generally last only a year or two, or maybe a little longer in a cold climate like Mulano's. Then they fade away. They don't come back to life, either. My Julien doppelganger had vanished in the usual way at the usual time, several years back. When I saw what I took to be the doppelganger of the Duc de Gramont picking his way toward me between the wiggling arms of my forest—pausing once or twice to pull off a leaf and pop it into his mouth, as if tasting it to see if it was worth using in some sauce—I couldn't make sense of it at all.

"Alors, mon vieux!" he cried. "Mes hommages! Comment ca va? Sacre bleu, how cold it is here!"

I gave him a blank look and backed away a little. Ghosts I understand, doppelgangers I understand, but the ghost of a doppelganger?—No.

In a ragged shred of a voice I said, "Where did *you* come from?"

"Ah, is this the best greeting you can manage, mon ami?" Speaking to me coolly, from on high, ultra-French, miffed, deeply wounded. "I spend half a dreary interminability in the capsule of relay to get to this dreadful place, and you show no jubilation upon the sight of me, you evince no delight, you merely ask me, brusquely, without the littlest shred of courtesy, Where did I come from? Quel type! Where is the embrace? Where is the kiss on the cheeks?" He threw up his hands and burst into a crazy flurry of random French, like a robot translator gone berserk. "Joyeux Noel! Bonne Annee! A quelle heure part le prochain bateau! J'ai mal de mer! Faites venir le garcon! Par ici! Le voici! Il faut payer!" And went capering around like a madman.

After a little while he subsided, as though his gears were winding down, and stood there sadly watching his own breath congeal in front of him.

"So you are not in any way glad to see me?" he said very quietly.

I studied him. Doppelgangers sometimes look a little transparent around the edges. This one didn't. This one didn't really seem like a doppelganger at all. It had Julien's quick darting piercing eyes, Julien's elegant movements. Its little dark mustache and small pointed beard were trimmed precisely in the right way, not a fraction of a hair askew, just as Julien's always were. Doppelgangers lose those small fine touches quickly. Entropic creep sets in and their definition starts to blur.

"You really are you, then?"

"Oui," he said. "I really are I."

"Truly Julien?"

"Sacre bleu! Nom d'un chien! Truly, truly, truly! What is the matter with you, cher ami? Where has your brain gone? Is it that this terrible cold—"

"The doppelganger you gave me," I said. "I couldn't figure out how a doppelganger could come back."

"Ah, the doppelganger! The doppelganger, mon vieux—"

"It faded away long ago, you know. So when I saw it again—when I thought I saw it—"

"Oui. Bien sur."

"How could I know? A doppelganger returning after it had faded? That isn't supposed to be possible. Some kind of trick? Some way of slipping an assassin past my guard? The devil's hairy hole, man! What was I supposed to think?"

"And what do you think now?"

I gave him another long close look.

He grew upset again when I didn't say anything. Waving his hands around, tossing his head in that stylishly frantic way of his. "Cordieu, cher ami! Mon petit Romanichel. Gitan bien-aime. Dear Mirlifiche, esteemed Cascarrot. It is only me! The true Julien! Vraiment, I am not a doppelganger. Nor an assassin. I am merely your own Julien de Gramont. N'est-ce pas? Can you believe that? What do you say, Gypsy king?"

Yes. Of course. How could I doubt it? He was the genuine item. No doppelganger could possibly generate so much heat, so much frenzy, so much exasperated passion.

I felt embarrassed.

I felt contrite.

I felt like a damned fool.

To mistake a man for his own doppelganger may not be a dueling offense, but it certainly isn't much of a compliment. And to do it to poor Julien de Gramont, with his royal pretensions and his excitable Gallic temperament—

Well, I apologized most profusely and he insisted that it was a harmless mistake and I invited him into my bubble and brewed up a batch of steaming coffee for him, the ancient Rom coffee, black as sin, hot as hell, sweet as love, and in five minutes it was all a forgotten matter, no offense intended, none taken. Julien had brought presents for me, two overpockets' worth of them, and he proceeded now to conjure them out of the storage dimension and stack them up in heaps on my floor. Sweet old Julien, still worrying about my gastronomic comfort! "Homard en civet de vieux Bourgogne," he announced, pulling out one of those cunning flasks that will prepare and heat your meal just so if you merely touch your finger to the go-button. "Carre d'agneu roti au poivre vert. Fricassee de poulet au vinaigre de vin. Pommes purees. Les filets mignons de veau au citron. Everything is labeled, mon ami. Everything is true French, no grotesque dishes of the Galgala herdsmen, no foul porridges of Kalimaka, no quivering monstrosities from the swamps of Megalo Kastro. Here. Here. You like kidney? You like sweetbreads? Fricassee de rognons et de ris de veau aux feuilles d'epinards. Eh, mon frere? Coquilles Saint-Jacques? Pate de fruits de mer en croute? Bouillabaisse Marseillaise? I have brought you everything."

"You're much too good to me, Julien."

"I have brought enough so that you can eat like a human being for two years, perhaps three. It is the least I can do for you, in this terrible savage solitude. Two years of the fine French cuisine." He gave me a sly look. "How long more do you think you stay here, mon cher? Two years, is it? Three, four?"

"Is that what you came here to find out, old friend?"

Color rose to his cheeks.

"It is of concern to me, your long absence from the worlds of civilization. I sorrow for you. Your people sorrow for you. You are a man of importance, Yakoub."

"Among the Rom," I told him, "we say 'important' when we mean 'corpulent.' Did you know that? 'A man of importance' means to us a man with a big belly." I looked at the flasks stacked all over the bubble, dozens of them, with any number of their cousins still tucked away in the storage dimension. I patted my middle, which has become kingly indeed in these my later years. "So that's why you brought all this stuff, Julien? You want me to be even more important than I already am?"

"The worlds call out for you, Yakoub." His stagy French accent suddenly was gone; he spoke in the purest Imperial. "There is great chaos out there, because there is no king. Ships are lost in the star-lanes; piracy increases; quarrels of great men are left unresolved. Your people have a great need for you. Even the Empire has a need for you. Do you realize that, Yakoub?"

"I intend no offense, Julien. But I want to know who told you to come here."

He looked uncomfortable. He toyed with his little pointed beard. He fiddled with his flasks, he fooled with the labels. I left the question lying there in the air between us.

"What do you mean, who told me to come here?" he said finally.

"It's not a very complicated question, is it?"

"I came here because you are missed. You are needed."

"Don't hide behind passive verbs, Julien. *Who* misses me? *Who* needs me? Who paid you to stick yourself in a relay-sweep depot and come out to talk to me?"

Glumly he said, after a bit, "It was Periandros."

"Ah. The grand surprise."

"If you knew, why did you ask?"

"To see what you would say."

"Yakoub!"

"All right. So Periandros sent you. Does that mean Naria's man will be here next?"

He frowned. "What do you mean?"

"The three lords of the Imperium is what I mean. Sunteil's man left here a little while ago. Now you're here on behalf of Periandros. It stands to reason that Number Three will want to touch base with me too, and maybe the archimandrite as well, or even, God forbid, the emperor himself. If the emperor's still alive."

"The emperor is still alive," Julien said. "What's this about Sunteil?"

"He sent a Rom boy named Chorian."

"I know Chorian. Extremely young, but very competent. And very tricky, like all you Rom."

"Is he? Are we?"

"What is Sunteil troubled about?"

"That my abdication is some kind of hoax, and that I'll be coming back to the Empire when I'm least expected, to cause the greatest amount of trouble."

Julien beamed serenely. "Of *course* your abdication is some kind of hoax. The question that should be in Sunteil's mind is why you have perpetrated it, and what can be done to persuade you to give up the game you are playing." To that I made no response, but he didn't seem to have expected any. He watched me for a moment and then, with only the smallest knowing twitch of his exquisite eyebrow, he turned away and began to wander around my bubble, picking up this thing and that, handling my dearest possessions with the practiced touch of a flea-market antiquities dealer, which is one of the professions he has practiced in his time. I let him. He would do no harm. He fondled a bright yellow silken diklo, a Rom scarf that someone had worn in the lost and fabled land of Bulgaria fifteen centuries ago. He caressed the veil of La Chunga. He tapped out a quick rhythm on my ancient tambourine and then he laid his hands reverently on my lavuta, my Gypsy violin, passed down from Rom to Rom like all the rest of this stuff since the time when Earth still was.

"May I?" he said.

"My guest."

He fitted it in place under his chin, strummed its sounding-box a moment with his fingertips, reached for the bow. And made that old fiddle laugh, and then he made it weep, and then he made it sing. All in eight or nine measures. He looked at me, eyes bright, triumphant.

"You play like a Rom," I told him.

A self-deprecating shrug. "You flatter like a Rom."

"Where did you learn?"

He fiddled off another measure or two. "Years ago, on Sidri Akrak, there was an old Rom who called himself the Zigeuner Bicazului. He played in the marketplace outside the Palace of the Trierarch and Periandros sent one of his phalangarii to invite him in; and for a year and a half this Bicazului was court musician. He played the lavuta, the cithera, the pandero, everything. I asked him to teach me a few of the old tunes."

"There are times I have to remind myself you are not Rom, Julien."

"There are times I have to do the same," he said.

"What happened to him, that Bicazului of yours? Where is he now, do you think?"

"It was long ago," Julien said, gesturing vaguely. "He was very old." He put the violin down and walked to the window. For a long while he stared out. The yellow sun was low in the sky and clouds were thickening; a storm was coming on. The tentacles of the trees were moving more slowly than usual. After a time he said, "You like it here, Yakoub?"

"To me it seems very beautiful, Julien. I'm at peace here."

"Vraiment?"

"Yes. Vraiment. I am truly at peace here."

"A strange place for you in the autumn of your life, Yakoub. These fields of ice, this tempestuous snow—"

"The peace. Don't forget the peace. What does a little snow matter, if you have peace?"

"And those repellent green things? What are they?" There was distaste in his voice. "Les tentacules terribles. Les poulpes terrestres, the octopus of the land?" He shuddered, a precise, elegant motion.

"They are trees," I said.

"*Trees?*"

"Trees, yes."

"I see. And these trees, do they seem beautiful to you as well?"

"This place is my home now, Julien."

"Ah. Oui. Oui. Forgive me, mon ami."

We stood together by the window. The sound of his fiddling was still in my ears. And also I heard the last words I had spoken just now, echoing and echoing and echoing, *This place is my home, this place is my home.*

For a moment I thought I would ask him to go outside with me so I could show him the place where on a clear night the red fire of Romany Star glowed in the sky. Julien, I would say, I did not speak the truth. *There* is my home, Julien, I would say. And then I thought, No. No. He is dear to me but he could never understand, and in any case I must not say such things to him, for he is Gaje. Truly, he is Gaje. I thought again of the music he had made with my fiddle; and I told myself, There are times I have to remind myself you are not Rom, Julien.

5.

HE SEEMED ABASHED FOR HAVING SPOKEN SO HARSHLY against Mulano, and after a time he asked if we might go out for a stroll, so that I could show him the beauties of the landscape. I knew that he had already had more than enough of a taste of the beauties of the landscape when he came through the forest from whatever place the relay-sweep capsule had dropped him; this was his way of making amends. But we went out anyway and I showed him the trees at close range, and pointed out the great sweeping flow of the glaciers, and told him the names I had given to the mountains that rose like a jagged wall on the horizon. "You are right," he said finally. "It is very beautiful in its way, Yakoub."

"In its way, yes."

"I meant that truly."

"I know, Julien."

"Dear friend. Come: it is time now for the lunch, do you think?"

We went inside. He peered for a long while at his flasks and selected one finally, and flicked his thumb against its go-button. The inner surface of the flask grew misty as it heated up. Reaching into one of the overpockets, he brought forth a bottle of red wine and popped the cork with his thumbs. "Le dejeuner," he proclaimed. "Cassoulet en la maniere de Languedoc. It has been a long cold afternoon, but this will heal me. Do you wish bread?" He rummaged in the overpocket and drew out a baguette that might have been baked three hours ago in Paris. For a few moments he busied himself with the task of serving our lunch.

Then he said, continuing our earlier conversation as though there had been no break in it at all, "I don't believe Sunteil is afraid of your returning. I think it's your *not* returning that he fears."

"Polarca has the same theory."

"Polarca? Has he been here too?"

"His ghost. Still is. Perhaps hovering right over your shoulder as we eat." I shoveled down the cassoulet in silence for a while, washing it along with splendiferous gulps of the wine, and belched him a belch of great resonance and grandeur to show my appreciation. "This is truly fine, Julien. If I had to come back in my next life as a Gajo, I would want to be a Frenchman of France, and eat like this three times a day."

"The King of the Gypsies does me great honor by such lavish praise, Yakoub."

"*Former* King of the Gypsies, Julien."

"You hold the title until your death, or until the judges of the great kris formally depose you. Your abdication is not binding on the Rom government. As you well know."

"Are you a lawyer now as well as a chef?" I asked.

"You also know that matters of succession are of deep importance to me, Yakoub. It is my great passion, my overwhelming obsession."

"I thought your great passion was for food," I said, maybe too sharply. "And your overwhelming obsession was something to do with women."

"Don't mock me, Yakoub."

I had stung him that time. I was sorry, and I said so. Perhaps he did have his little pretensions. But he was an old friend, and a dear one.

He said, after a while, "No one understands your abdication. They see it as a betrayal of all that you have worked for during a long and honorable life."

I could have explained myself then, I suppose. Did he think, did any of them think, that there had been no reason for my going away, that I had simply tossed my crown away for the sheer spiteful fun of it? I will admit to you here and now that there had been times on Mulano when I woke up in the night in a sweat, convinced of my own utter idiocy. But generally I didn't think that was the situation and I certainly didn't want them to, neither the high lords of the Imperium nor those who were now the big Gypsies. Did they believe I was that flighty, that capricious, that irresponsible? *Me?* Speak, Yakoub, explain yourself, defend yourself. Here's your moment.

But Syluise's laughter rang in my ears. And also I reminded myself yet again that this old and dear friend of mine was a Gajo, and a confidante of the emperor and in the direct pay of the Lord Periandros besides, and all I said was, "Power kept too long goes flat, Julien. You know, when you leave a bottle of champagne open too long, what happens to it?"

"I cannot believe that any such thing has happened to you, mon ami."

"How long was I king? Forty years? Fifty years? Enough."

"So this is what you will do? Will you sit here in all this ice and snow —forgive me, I truly cannot like this place, my friend—will you watch these unpleasant green tentacles writhe and quiver at you for the rest of your days, and do nothing else?"

"For the rest of my days? I don't know that. This is what I have been doing. It pleases me to do it. This is what I intend to continue doing, Julien, until it stops pleasing me, if it does. If."

"This I do not understand. A moment of boredom, a fit of mere pique, Yakoub, and you allow yourself to throw away everything that you—"

"Let me be, Julien. I know what I'm doing."

"Do you?"

"I know that I'm done with being king. Isn't that sufficient for you? Damn it, Julien, let me be!"

I pushed my plate aside and walked to the door of the bubble and stared out at the gently undulating arms of the forest. I listened to my breath go in and out, in and out. I sent little messages of greetings to my liver, my pancreas, my alimentary canal. Hello there, old friends. And my bodily organs sent friendly little messages back. Hello there, you. We know each other so well, my organs and I. I basked in their admiration. The high regard in which they held me pleased me very much. We had a good thing going. If we played our cards right we could stick together another two hundred years. Maybe even more. I thought about that and it felt good. I thought about tonight's dinner. I thought about the wine. I thought about the snow that was starting to fall in counterclockwise swirls. The one thing I didn't want to think about was being king again. I wanted to think about not being king. The presence of the absence of my power was what gave me life and vigor these days.

Into my mind came lovely lascivious thoughts that had nothing to do with anything Julien had been saying. Watching the forest's green limbs writhing voluptuously about, I felt strange stirrings within myself. I could go out there, I thought, and lie down naked in their midst, and then they would embrace me like a lover. I imagined all those myriad tentacles caressing my body, slithering here and there in all the sensitive places, knowing just what I liked best. Sucking, stroking, tickling, poking. Ooh. Ah. Oh, yes, good! Very good! Gently I drifted into profound eroto-botanical fantasies, odd but pleasing floral delights. There was fine food in my belly and good red wine in my brain and now my loins were coming alive with these delectable new yearnings. At my age, still capable of responding to something strange and new! Pay heed to that, all of you. Hearken and learn. You might think the old fires die down, but they don't. No. Not even on this chilly world. Not at all. Ever.

Julien came up behind me. His voice drilled cruelly into my reverie.

"And your people, Yakoub? You will leave them kingless forever? You will allow the guild of pilots to disintegrate?"

The vision of tentacular delight shattered and popped like a punctured balloon. I was furious with him for breaking in on me. He should have known. A moment of solitary reflection, a sacred interlude. Private and sacrosanct. And he had smashed it without a thought. And him claiming to be French, too.

But I held my wrath in check. For ancient friendship's sake.

Sourly I said, "The krisatora know what to do. If they want another king, they can declare the office vacant and elect someone. Otherwise the Rom can manage well enough without a king for five years, for fifty, for five hundred if necessary. The French have managed without one, haven't they, for something like *thirteen* hundred years."

"And there are no more French," said Julien bleakly.

"What do you mean?"

"We are nowhere. We are nothing. We are a memory, a book of recipes, and a difficult language that scarcely anyone understands. Is that what you want for your people, Yakoub?"

"We are Rom. We have been since before there were French or English or Germans or any of the million tribes of Earth. We will go on being Rom whether we have a king at this moment or not." I found my wine and took a deep draught of it. That calmed me a little. It was splendid stuff, and when my temper had cooled I told him so. The French might be an extinct culture, but *someone* still understood how to make a decent Bordeaux. After a moment I said, "Why am I in the thoughts of the Lord Periandros?"

"The emperor is old and feeble."

"That is hardly news, Julien."

"But now the end seems to be in sight. A year or two, perhaps, but he can't last much longer than that."

"So? The Rom won't be the only ones with a succession problem, then. What else is new?"

"This is serious, Yakoub. There are three high lords and the emperor has shown no strong inclination toward any of them."

"I know that. Let them draw straws to see who gets it, then."

"They are very strong men, and very determined. If the emperor dies without indicating a preference, there could be a war for the throne."

"No," I said, with a fierce shake of my head. "That's completely inconceivable. What do you think this is, the Middle Ages?"

"I think this is the year 3159 A.D., Yakoub, and there is an Empire of many hundreds of worlds at stake, and nothing essential has changed in the human soul since the time of Rome and Byzantium. Periandros won't sit idly by and see Sunteil have the throne, nor will Naria step aside gracefully for Periandros, nor—"

"There won't be any more wars, Julien. Humanity *has* changed. Going to the stars is what did it."

"You think?"

"War is an outmoded notion," I told him grandly. "Like the appendix, like the little toe. Another five hundred years and nobody's going to be born with an appendix any more, and good riddance to it. A thousand years beyond that and there'll be no more little toes either. And war is already gone. You know that as well as I do. It's an obsolete concept in this age of galactic empire." I was getting heated up by my own rhetoric. That's always a danger sign. But I went steaming right on. "There hasn't been a real war since—since I don't know when. Hundreds of years. A thousand, maybe. Not since Earth went down the drain and all its petty little garbage went with it." I was wondrously worked up now. "Wars are unthinkable in today's galactic society! Not just unthinkable but logistically impossible!"

"Don't be so sure of that."

"Why are you such a pessimist, Julien?"

"Only a realist, mon ami." There was a sudden wintry bleakness in his eyes that I could hardly bear to see. He had given much thought to all this. Not that I hadn't; but I had been away from it for five years. Had I let myself get too far out of touch with reality? No. No. No. He said, "I think the idea of war might be all too easy to revive. Perhaps some entirely new kind of war, a war between stars, but bloody and horrible all the same."

Yes? No. This is all nonsense, I thought. I laughed in his face. Poor gloomy Julien, lost in these morbid apocalyptic fantasies. Scared shitless by phantoms. War? Between stars? If wine did this to him, maybe he ought to stick to water. He was starting to annoy me now.

"Come off it," I told him. "I'm too old to be frightened by this sort of stuff."

"Then I envy you. For I myself am greatly frightened."

"Of *what?*" I shouted.

He kept calm. Calm as death. "It is too great a vacuum, this absence of a clear line of succession. A vacuum can engender disruptive forces, my friend, and the greater the vacuum the greater the disruptions."

I couldn't argue with that. It was verging across the line from politics into physics. I never argue with physics.

"They'll work it out," I said, more quietly and without much confidence. I think I was beginning to experience a slow confidence leak. "An agreement among themselves. A rational division of authority. Maybe even a partition of the Empire, who knows? Would that be such a bad idea?"

"There is not one vacuum but two," he went on, as if I had not spoken at all. "For what also is absent is the King of the Rom."

"Don't start with me again on that, Julien."

"Just tell me this, Yakoub: putting aside the question of your resuming authority again, what if you were to return to the Imperium and request a meeting with the emperor—he'll see you, whether you're king or not—and make the nature of the crisis clear to him?"

Now I saw his real game. I didn't like it.

I said, "And advocate the naming of the Lord Periandros, perhaps, as his successor?"

Julien reddened. "Do you think I am so clumsy as to ask that of you?"

"You do favor Periandros, don't you?"

"I favor stability. I am close to Periandros. But I would rather see

Sunteil wear the crown, or Naria, than have the Imperium shattered by civil war. What matters is that there be *some* succession. You might be able to bring that about. No one else would dare to speak of such things with the emperor."

"I've abdicated, Julien."

"The system is out of balance with you gone."

"Polarca said the same thing in virtually as many words. Polarca's ghost. Let it be out of balance, then. A rat's ass for the balance of the system, Julien."

"Yakoub—"

"A rat's ass!"

"The possibility of war—"

I waved my hands around impatiently as though his words were farts and I was trying to clear the air.

"If you would only consider, Yakoub, the risk of allowing such instability to—"

Again I cut him off. "No," I said. "Enough of this." And then I said, "What did you say this thing we were eating is called, Julien?"

With a sigh he answered, "Cassoulet, mon ami."

"And how is it made?"

You can always distract a Frenchman by asking him for a recipe. "It is the garlic sausage, and the breast of lamb, and the filet of pork, to which one adds the white beans, and—"

"It's superb," I said. "Absolutely superb. I must have some more."

6.

NIGHT CAME. WE SAT QUIETLY. OLD FRIENDS HAVE THE privilege of being silent with one another. Sleet beat furiously against my window for a time. Then the storm moved on and the sky began to clear. Stars cut their way through the thinning storm-clouds, sparkling with fierce intensity against that deep backdrop of blackness that is seen only on a world where no one dwells.

I sat quietly, yes. Feeling the fullness of my belly, feeling also a certain pressure on my shoulders that I knew was the weight of all the universe moving above me. That immense inconceivable clockwork mechanism, the billion billion soundless stars gliding on their tracks in the heavens, whipping their billion billion billion worlds along as they turned on the unknown axis that was at the center of it all somewhere. Everything interwoven, everything connected by invisible rods and struts that we imagine we understand.

And then I thought of our own little corner of it all, that speck, our few hundreds of worlds within our one galaxy—the galaxy that seems so vast when we are out traveling in it, but which is only one small stitch in the whole colossal tapestry. The worlds of men, of Gaje, of Rom. Kingdom and Empire. All our intricate struggles and maneuverings: they were so tiny against that great sky. Tiny, yes, but not trivial, for what was the universe, after all, except one atom and another and another and another, each one as important as any other in the structure of the whole thing? No, not trivial. Nothing is trivial. Subtract one atom from the universe and all is lost.

So they would need a new emperor soon, in this little corner of the universe that is everything to us? Well, I knew what that situation was like. I was around when the Fourteenth Emperor was dying and I am even old enough to remember the last days of the Thirteenth. To be close to a dying emperor has its perils, as it is perilous to be close to a star about to burn out. The star has been blazing away for nine billion years and now its course is just about run: in a little while the wild dance of the hot little nuclei will be stilled forever and there will be only a sphere of cold blackness where there had been ferocious light. Then it happens and in that moment of the birth of void a great whistling inrush of air comes bellowing in from every corner of the cosmos at once. You can get swept willy-nilly to the ends of the universe if you happen to be in the way when that wind goes rushing by.

(Of *course* I know that there's no air in the space between the stars. Don't be a literal-minded fool. Just try to understand the sense of what I'm telling you.)

The Fifteenth was dying and mighty tornados would spawn in his wake. And afterward, when the roaring had stopped and a deathly stillness was setting in, they would have to anoint someone as the Sixteenth and give the universe into his hand. Sunteil, Periandros, Naria, those were the choices. The three lords of the Imperium. Well, no surprises there. I knew them all. I had seen them come up and I had watched them move themselves into position. Year after year of subtle jostling and maneuvering until power came within reach; and just one more maneuver left to go. And everybody's nerves cranked to the breaking point until the outcome was settled.

(How much easier for everyone it would have been, I suppose, if we had set the Empire up as a hereditary monarchy in the first place. The heir apparent known to all, well in advance. None of this nasty fear of a chaotic interregnum. Plenty of time for the bureaucrats on whose shoulders the whole system really rests to scope out the new man and get some sense of how to keep him under control, so that everything would go purring along the right way after the shift in power.)

(Easier all around, yes. But very stupid, too, and in the long run catastrophic. The history of hereditary monarchies tells us that it's just like rolling dice—you can get hot and have five or eight good throws in a row, but you can't do it forever, and sooner or later you're absolutely certain to crap out. History is littered with the rusting wreckage of dynastic monarchies. *Gaje* history, that is. Since the beginning of time we Rom have had sense enough to rely on elected leaders only.)

Among the contenders in the struggle coming up in the Imperium, Sunteil was most to my liking. There was the old devil in that man. You could see the wickedness in his eyes, the shine, the sparkle. Sunteil was a man of Fenix in Haj Qaldun, Chorian's home world, a place of tawny desert sands and steady unremitting heat. If the heat of Fenix doesn't drive you crazy, it makes you sharp and glistening. Among the Rom of the Kingdom there is a saying, Count your teeth three times when it's a Fenixi that you kiss. Sunteil was of that sort. Dark and devious. My kind of man. He could almost have been Rom, that one.

Julien had chosen to throw in his lot with Periandros. I couldn't see it. That drab little bookkeeper! Not Julien's sort of person at all. What had Periandros done to buy him—promise Julien that he would construct a new France for him somewhere, and set him up as its king?

Sidri Akrak was Periandros' native planet, a world where shaggy monsters with nightmare faces run screaming down the streets of the cities, things with black fangs and red wattles, with bulging fiery eyes the size of saucers, with horns that branch a thousand times and turn into devilish stinging tentacles at their tips. Visitors to Sidri Akrak, if they aren't warned, sometimes have total nervous breakdowns in the first fifteen minutes. And yet the Akrakikan take their monstrosities utterly casually, as though they were nothing more than dogs or cats. That's how they are: souls of bookkeepers. Nothing reaches them. They have no blood and no balls and nothing in their heads but some kind of clicking chattering arrangement of gears, or so it seems to me. How I despise them! And Periandros was an Akraki of the Akrakikan, the pure item. I have known robots with greater passion in a single swivel-joint than he had in his entire body. Yet he had been favored by the Fifteenth Emperor and lifted up out of obscurity within reach of the throne. Now it seemed he might actually attain it. I don't know: maybe something like Periandros is the sort of creature best suited to reign in the Gaje Imperium. There have been Akraki emperors before and they were not the worst. I suppose the Gaje get the kind of emperors they deserve.

And Naria. The youngest; I knew him least well of the three. A man native to Vietoris who wore his skin in the deepest of purple hues and his hair a flaming scarlet, cascading to his shoulders. He appeared too cold and calculating for my taste. Don't misunderstand me—a little calculation is all right; we are all calculating; but coldness is another matter. Perhaps I was prejudiced against him because of his Vietoris origins, my own home world, in a manner of speaking, except that it was never "home" to me, simply the place where I happened to be born —into slavery—and where I was taken from my father and sold again before I knew anything of anything. It's hard for me to think of Vietoris or any of its Gaje folk without shuddering, though they tell me it's a gentle lovely world. Lord Naria of Vietoris might have many kindly traits glinting like buried treasure somewhere deep within his soul, but I had never seen evidence of them, and I wished him chilly luck in the contest that lay ahead.

Sunteil, Periandros, Naria. If I returned to the Empire, could I influence the choice? Should I? Would I? Julien de Gramont was right that I should care about the coming struggle. Who rules the Imperium is a matter that concerns Rom as much as it concerns Gaje: we share one galaxy, after all. And only a fool would think that it is possible to separate the interests of the Rom in any real way from the interests of the Gaje; the two races are interdependent, and we know that all too well. Which is why we Rom set up the Empire in the first place.

(Try to get a Gajo to believe *that*! But why would we want to try?)

"Well, and in the end will you return?" Julien asked.

We had eaten and eaten and we had eaten some more, and now he had drawn a flask of fine old gold-flecked cognac of Galgala from the overpocket and it was sliding into us with no difficulty at all. But I had learned when I was not much more than a boy, living in the elegant palace of Loiza la Vakako, how to keep my brains from flowing out as the alcohol flows in.

"Votre sante," I cried, lifting my glass to him.

He lifted his. "Horses and wealth," he said in good Romany.

We drank. I signalled that he should fill the glasses again.

"Splendor and grace," he said.

"Joy and mischief," I responded.

"Delights and delicacies!"

"Deviltry and debauchery!"

"At your age," he said. "You are a rogue, Yakoub!"

"Ah, no. I am a very prosaic person, within myself. I am as dull as your Lord Periandros, my friend. Shall we drink one more and say that the feast is over?"

"*Why* won't you go back to the Empire?" he asked one more time. "You've been away five years. Is that not enough?"

"It doesn't seem that way to me."

"Chaos will descend when the emperor dies. Can you allow that to happen?"

"How can I prevent it? Anyway, sometimes chaos is a thing to be desired."

"Not by me, Yakoub."

"You are a sweet man, Julien, but you are a Gajo. There are many things you don't understand. I will stay here, I think."

"How much longer?"

"Until it is time to go."

"The time is now, Yakoub."

I shrugged. "Let the chaos come. It's not my affair."

"How can you say that, Yakoub? You, a man of honor, of responsibility, a *king*—"

"Former king, Julien." I rose and stretched and yawned. "We've been eating and drinking half the night. The stars come and go in the sky. Shall we say this is enough, and say goodnight?" It was not like me ever to say that anything was enough; but perhaps I was changing. Perhaps I was starting to grow old. Could that be? No. No, I didn't think so. Perhaps it was simply that I had grown weary of defending myself against Julien's persistence.

He stared at me for a long while without answering.

Then he said in a soft voice, and in Romany without flaw, "I forgive you and may God forgive you."

I was stunned by that. Those are words that are spoken among us at the time when consciences are settled, words that are said to a dying man or by a dying man by way of clearing all accounts. Did Julien know that? He must. He had been close to Rom much of his life. Surely he knew what we meant when we said those words. Te aves yertime mandar! I forgive you! He frightened and troubled me with those words as I had rarely been frightened or troubled in my long life.

"One last drink?" he said, after a time.

"I think we have had enough for one night," I replied.

7.

JULIEN STAYED WITH ME ANOTHER THREE DAYS, FIVE, ten, something like that. He could have stayed a month, or forever, if he had wanted to. We were very careful about what we talked about. Mostly we talked about food, which was always a safe subject. We went out hunting or fishing every day and came back with sleds laden with the creatures of Mulano, and in the evenings Julien prepared whatever we had caught in the classic French manner, explaining every step to me as he worked.

He was a chef of miracles. I caught a spice-fish for him and instinctively he knew it needed nothing more than poaching in its own broth; but with the other things he worked wonders using only the little collection of herbs and spices I had brought with me from the Empire. It was astonishing, the effects he achieved. On a wintry world like Mulano where there isn't much in the way of vegetation the animal life is pretty sparse also. Except for the ghosts, of course, which feed on electromagnetic energy and don't give a damn whether there's any grass. Such creatures as there are to be had had never seemed to have much flavor to me. The spice-fishes are splendid, certainly. But the other things were bland at best. Even so, Julien made something spectacular out of a netful of ice-runners. Flat little beastly things, with half a dozen bright blue eyes on the top of their round bodies and an infinity of scuttling legs underneath. He made a ragout of them; and it was awesome. He turned a basket of leopard-snails into something fit for the gods. And what he was able to do with cloud-eels defied belief. I think he might have been seriously thinking of trying his hand at cooking snow-serpents, too. Until I told him that I wouldn't countenance the hunting of scavengers. Julien probably would have cooked up a batch of ghosts if he could have figured out some way of catching them. Once when I was busy elsewhere he went out and snipped some young tender tendrils from the trees near my bubble to use in a salad. That bothered me. I imagined the wounded trees whipping about in pain beneath the snow. But the salad was amazing.

Now and then we spoke of the old times we had spent together on this world or that, Xamur, Galgala, Iriarte. We talked of women, Syluise, Esmeralda, Mona Elena. And women of his. That was pleasant enough. Julien made all his women sound like goddesses. I imagine he made them feel like goddesses, too: there are men with that skill, though there should be more. He talked of feasts of years gone by, sweet friends also gone by, the changes that time brings. But never again did Julien mention the imperial succession or the problems that my abdication had caused. I loved him for that, his willingness to relent. He had relented too late, though. That first night he had put something under my skin with his Romany prayer of forgiveness, and it was burrowing through my flesh without mercy.

I thought he was going to make one last effort to get me to end my exile on the day he left Mulano. The words were there, just behind his teeth, I could tell; but he kept them caged and would not release them.

For a long time we looked at one another without saying anything. And I felt a great rush of pity for him. I saw in his burning eyes the piercing desperate loneliness of the man whose race is gone, whose nation is a fantasy. For Julien it was all la cuisine, la belle langue Francaise, la gloire, la gloire; but France was no more likely to come again than a river is to flow backward to its source, and what a secret crucifixion that knowledge must have been to him! So he busied himself in the affairs of realms that were, and perhaps it seemed to him that by his diplomatic shuttling about he was somehow maintaining the memory of the realm that had been. Poor Julien!

We embraced in silence and in silence he went away, trudging off due east through the forest of tentacles toward the rendezvous point where he would wait for his relay-sweep. The last I saw of him he had paused by one of the trees and was patting its rubbery trunk, as though commending it for the sweet flavor of its succulent tips.

8.

I WAS ALONE A LONG WHILE AFTER THAT. I WENT QUIETLY
through my days and my evenings, thinking more of the past than of
the future. Death was on my mind much of the time. That was strange.
I had never given much thought to death. What use is that, to ponder
death? Death is something to defy, not something to think about. I had
been close to death many times but never once had I believed that it
would take me, not even that time when the mud of Megalo Kastro,
which is alive and loves to eat life, was sucking at my skin. Perhaps that
is because there have always been ghosts about me, telling me my own
future, though telling it in their tricky ghostly way. Not in the way we
used to use fool the Gaje, no cards, no crystal balls. When a ghost tells
you your future, you taste the certainty that you will have one. Through
much of my early life one of those protective ghosts that sometimes
visited me was my own. He never said so, but I came to recognize
myself in him, for he was booming and uproarious with a laugh that
could shatter worlds. That is me; that is how I have always been, even
when I was young, constantly unfolding toward that kind of overwhelming vigor. How I relished seeing him, that big barrel-chested
wide-shouldered man with the thick black mustache and the fiery eyes,
drifting toward me out of the fog and mist of time! As long as he was
with me what did I have to fear?

But there were no Yakoub-ghosts visiting me now, nor had I seen any
for a great long while. I began to wonder why. Was my time almost up?
The devil it was! Still, I let myself imagine it. It is a dirty pleasure,
imagining your own death. I saw myself coming in from a day on the
ice, sweating and struggling under the burden of some animal I had
caught. And lying down just a moment, and feeling something within
my body seeking suddenly to get out. They teach us the One Word
when we are young, and the One Word is: Survive! But to everyone and
everything there comes a time when that word no longer applies and

the striving no longer is proper, and when that time comes it is folly to oppose it. Even for me, that time must come, try as I do to deny it. It maddens me, knowing that it must come even for me. Yet here in my imaginings I felt calm as it arrived. What is this, the death of Yakoub? Here on this bleak snowy world? Ah. I see. I see. Well, then, this is the time. No more struggling against it. What a philosopher a man can become, suddenly, when he knows at long last that he has no choice! So then I rose and went outside, and dug a grave for myself in the snow, and lay down under the light of Romany Star. And buried myself, and said the words over myself, and wept for myself, and danced and got drunk for myself, and spilled my drink out on the white breast of the ice-field as a libation, and at the very last I sang the lament for the dead over my own grave, the mulengi djili, the tale of my long life and magnificent deeds. And as I played all this out in my head I heard the voice of Yakoub the Rom asking me, What is this nonsense, Yakoub? Why are you playing with yourself this way? But I could give him no answer, and again and again I found myself letting such thoughts as these invade my mind, and I confess I took pleasure in it, a dirty pleasure, pretending that I no longer cared, that I no longer held life by the balls in a grip that could not be broken, that I was ready to lie down, that I had had enough at last.

Then I had the third of my visitors. This one came at noon, which for all Rom is the strange time, the dark time, the most mysterious moment of the day.

This was noon of Double Day, you understand, and so a doubly strange moment, when both the suns of Mulano are at their highest at once and the light of one erases the shadows of the other. A shadowless instant, a dead moment in time. When that moment comes I halt wherever I am and seal my nostrils against the air, for who knows what spirits travel freely in that instant?

On the day of the third visitor the air was curiously warm—warm for Mulano, I mean—as though a springtime might actually be on its way. There was a faint glaze on the surface of the ice, a sort of millimeter-thick melting, and indigenous ghosts by the thousand clustered overhead, crackling and buzzing with peculiar excitement.

I had been out for a long walk that Double Day morning, to the edge of the glacier and halfway up its slow fluid side, carving my way with an ice-axe like some prehistoric huntsman. There was a cave I liked on the glacier's slope. It was deep and low-roofed, with glassy walls that glowed with vermilion fire when the light of both suns came striking down through its ceiling, and far in the back was a spiraling tongue of ice that ramped up from the cave floor as though it were some sort of ancient altar, though I doubted that it was anything more than an accidental formation. I would often go to it, lay my gloved hands on its sleek curves, and close my eyes and feel all the stars in their courses go spinning through my brain.

On my way back from this place the moment of noon overtook me, and I stood still with my openings sealed. In that moment between moments a deep rich voice spoke:

"Sarishan, cousin."

The surprise of it came with the force of a kick. I would have started and perhaps even fled instinctively. A sudden spontaneous flood of primeval fear-hormones came pouring into my blood. But I reacted just as quickly to regain control, turning off the flow, instructing the cells of my blood to devour that wild flow before it could reach my brain.

"Damiano!" I cried. "Cousin!"

As if he had materialized out of a snowbank. A lean long figure who bore himself with the tense powerful force of a coiled whip. All Rom are my cousins but Damiano is my cousin truly, the son of the son of my father's youngest brother. His eyes are Rom and his heavy sweeping mustache is Rom but he has lived most of his life under the baking white sun of Marajo of the sparkling sands, and for protection's sake he wears his skin in thick leathery folds that to me look neither Rom nor Gaje but like something not even human.

Holding himself at a distance from me, he looked around and shook his head. "What a place, cousin! The boy said it was forlorn but I never imagined anything like this!"

"There is great beauty here, cousin. There is wondrous peace. Stay here a week or two and you'll come to see it."

"I'll take that on faith," said Damiano. "Do I disturb you, cousin?"

"Disturb?"

"I think you are not glad to see me."

"Devlesa avilan," I said, the old formula of welcome. "It is God who brought you."

"Devlesa araklam tume," Damiano responded. "It is with God that I found you. The boy said this place was all ice, but I didn't believe him. He didn't tell me the half. Is there nothing alive here but you?"

"There are frozen rivers where shining fish swim as though through water. There are ghost-creatures of pure energy all around us as we talk.

There are little animals that scamper over the ice and eat invisible plants, or one another. And on the far side of that hill there is a great forest, cousin, although I think you will not recognize the trees to be trees."

"And you're happy here?"

"I have never been happier."

"I am only Damiano, cousin. No need for dancing around the truth with me."

My eyes blazed. "You come five thousand light-years to call me a liar?"

"Yakoub, Yakoub—"

"Did the boy say I seemed to be happy?"

"Yes. He did."

"And I say it now. Shall we ask the ghosts for affidavits too?"

"Yakoub."

"Damiano—cousin—" Then we were laughing, and then finally we were embracing, and pounding each other on the back, and doing a little dance of gladness on the shining thin-crusted ice. "Come," I said, and led him, half-running, back over the hills and valleys to my ice-bubble.

He gaped at the forest.

"Chorian said nothing about this!"

"He never saw it. I was living on the other side when he was here."

"These are your trees?"

"I could show you how they grow, beneath the ice."

He shivered. "Another time, perhaps."

I opened several of the flasks that Julien de Gramont had left me, and gave him a meal such as I think Damiano had not dared to expect from me on Mulano; the wine flowed freely and he gulped it in the manner of any wandering Rom, a whole goblet in a single swallow. I think that would have turned Julian apoplectic, to see wine of such rare vintage poured down my cousin's gullet that way. But Julien was far away and we didn't feel any need to honor his French niceties in absentia: I matched Damiano guzzle for guzzle, until we were easy and loose with each other and his strange leathery skin was glowing like a charcoal fire.

I knew he hadn't come here to see the sights. Damiano is a great man on Marajo, with rich business interests of every kind, fire-egg plantations and magnetic farms and a vast slave-breeding establishment and much more, and if there had been nine of him he still would not have time to oversee everything properly, so he had often declared. Yet he had made the journey to my bleak little hiding-place, and he had come alone and in the real self, sending no mere ghost, no doppelganger. That was a great compliment. Well, and so he wanted to add his voice to the chorus urging me to give up my exile. We drank and ate and ate and drank and I waited for him to make his appeal, but instead he talked only of family things, the cousins on Kalimaka who were pulling trans-uranic elements out of their sun and selling them to all comers, and the ones on Iriarte who had gambled away five solar systems on a single toss of the dice and then had won them all back before dawn, and those of Shurarara who without even bothering to ask permission of the Imperium had yanked their world out of orbit and were taking it off into nomadry, telling everyone that they were going to leave the galaxy entirely. That last astounded me. "Are they serious, Damiano? What will they use for a sun, as they cross those hundreds of thousands of light-years?"

"Oh, they have a sun, cousin. Or its equivalent: enough to keep themselves warm, at any rate. That part's no problem. But nobody believes that they'll actually leave the galaxy. They're just putting that story around to cover their disappearance, when all they mean to do is head for the Outer Colonies and live as pirates, eight or ten thousand light-years beyond the Center. Strike and run, strike and run."

"This is not the Rom way," I said gloomily.

"Valerian?"

"One pirate, yes. But a whole world of them?"

"These are strange times, Yakoub. With both the Empire and the Kingdom headless—"

Ah. Here it comes, now.

He held out his glass for more wine. I filled, he guzzled.

"Is the emperor still dying?" I asked.

"They give him six months, a year."

"And then?"

"Sunteil, I think."

"It could be worse."

"It could. I think he's manageable. But the question is, Will the new king be able to manage him?"

"The new king."

That sounded strange in my ears. More than strange. I felt the echo of those words go clanging and clamoring through my soul and my bones began to ache.

"The new king, yes." Again he extended the glass to me. The devil! He had his hook deep into me now.

I poured for him.

"There is a new king?"

Damiano shrugged, nodded, shrugged again. Then he rose and strolled around the bubble, fingering this old Gypsy artifact and that one, taking in the immemorial past through his fingertips. I boiled and bubbled with eagerness to know. The devil! The devil! How beautifully he had caught me!

I said, working at indifference, "Chorian did say that the krisatora were thinking of holding an election, since I seemed to be sincere about my abdication. But Julien de Gramont—you know him, the French pretender?—was here a little while afterward. He was still working on me to go back to Galgala and reclaim the throne."

"You told him you weren't interested, cousin."

"You know that already? Julien was in touch with you too?"

"Julien has been in touch with everyone," said Damiano. "In particular the krisatora. He reported what you had told him."

"Ah."

"And so there has been a new election."

"About time," I said. Casually. Keeping tight control, though I was on fire inside. I allowed myself a little more wine, and forced myself to drink it as Julien might have done, savoring its bouquet. "So we should rejoice that the Imperium is saved from chaos and there will be no more worlds turned pirate. The Rom again have a king and Sunteil will be emperor soon, and all is well."

Curiosity was raging at my gut. But I wasn't going to ask.

Damiano smiled in an angular, off-center way. "It isn't certain yet, about Sunteil, you know. And we have no reason to think that all will be well for the Rom, either."

"Because of the new king, you mean?"

"Because of the new king, yes."

I sat absolutely still, staring at him. And Damiano, for all the flush of wine burning in the deep-hued folds of his heavy skin, sat just as still, stared back at me just as stolidly. I felt the great strength of him. Truly he had the blood of my fathers in his veins. Was *he* the new king? No, no, he could never have gone so far from Galgala this soon after the election, if that were the case.

"All right," I said. "Who is he, Damiano?"

"You care?"

"You know I care."

"You have taken yourself far from it all. You live beyond the Imperium now, in a place of ice and ghosts and shining fishes."

"Who is he?"

"Why did you do this to us, Yakoub?"

"A time comes when a change is needed."

"For the Rom, or for Yakoub?"

"Yakoub is who I was thinking of," I said. "I had to leave, or I would have choked on my office."

"Well, so you left, and there has been a change. Not only for you but for all of us."

"Who is he, Damiano?"

He gave me a terrible look.

"Shandor," he said.

"My son Shandor is King of the Gypsies?"

"Shandor, yes."

It was like a giant blade twisting and churning through my entrails, that one simple statement. I could feel rivers of my own blood rising and surging and spewing forth. It was with the greatest effort of my life that I kept myself from leaping across the table and digging my hands into Damiano's throat, to throttle the words back into him and make him not have said them. But I did not move and I did not speak. It was a calamity beyond all measure, and I had been its unwitting architect.

Into my stunned and shattered silence my cousin Damiano said, "Well, Yakoub?"

"I never foresaw that. In all my dreaming and planning I never foresaw that." I shook my head again and again. "How long ago was it done?"

"Very recently."

"If any of this is untrue, Damiano, what you have told me here today—"

"Shandor is king. May my sons die within this hour if I have told you any untruths."

"My God. My God."

Wild angry Shandor, the one man in the universe I had never known how to control! Shandor the red, Shandor the murderous. Him? King? I should have taken him from his cradle and hurled him down into the dark sizzling heart of the Idradin crater. There might still have been the chance to halt him, back then. How could I not have seen that this would happen?

"And are the worlds accepting him?" I asked.

"They flock to him. They rush to him. There is such hunger to have a king again, Yakoub. Even a king like Shandor."

"My God," I said again. "Shandor!"

"Is this what you wanted when you went away, Yakoub?"

"They are not supposed to give the kingship to the son of a king." My voice was leaden. "It is against the custom. It is not hereditary, the kingship."

"He asked. He forced them."

"Forced the krisatora?"

"You know what Shandor is."

"Yes," I said. "I know what Shandor is." I felt an earthquake beginning in my soul. Great boulders were breaking loose from my spirit and tumbling down upon me, and I was being crushed by them. Now I saw the full immensity of the mistake I had made by leaving Galgala. I had left an open place for him, never suspecting the reach of his ambitions, or that he could ever realize them. And he had rushed in to fill that place. What a fool I had been, and telling myself all the while that I was being supremely clever! To be shrewd and invulnerable for a hundred seventy-two years, and then to play one final card, thinking it was the shrewdest play of all, and in that way to destroy in one moment of misplaced cleverness all that I had worked to build—

I have never known such shame as I did in that moment.

Damiano must have seen it in my face, some outward show of the horror and anguish I felt, for it was reflected in his own; he looked into my eyes and he seemed startled and shaken by what he saw there. I could not face that. I turned my back on him and went to the door of my bubble and kept on going, out into the bitter night. Double Day had ended while we talked, and the searing light of the stars bore down on me from every corner of the heavens. It was about to start snowing again. The first few flakes spiraled past my head. I stood alone in the midst of the ice-field, aware that there were ghosts around me everywhere, Mulano ghosts and perhaps Polarca's or Valerian's also: their chilly laughter was everywhere in the night. But I knew I would not be hearing that laughter much longer. The game was up for me here, sooner than I had thought, and without my winning what I had hoped for. The question now was one of salvage, not one of victory.

Damiano stood behind me, saying nothing.

"Give me a day and a half to pack my things," I said.

THREE:

I Am Come as Time

Krishna:

> I am come as Time, the waster of the peoples
> Ready for that hour that ripens to their ruin.
> All these hosts must die; strike, stay your hand—no
> matter.
> Therefore, strike. Win kingdom, wealth and glory.

—Bhagavad-Gita

1.

I NEVER EXPECTED TO BE KING OF ANYTHING. THAT'S THE truth, no matter what Syluise thinks. Of course the prophecy was on me practically from the time I could blow my own nose, but it was years —a lifetime, really—before I came to understand what Bibi Savina's ghost had been trying to say to me, back there in my infancy on Vietoris. Only by hindsight did I finally penetrate the mysteries of her chanting and magicking. I suppose I could tell you that from the start I was full of the passion to be top man and tell everyone what to do and have my boots licked daily, but it would be a lie. I wasn't like that at all when I was small. Maybe I got that way later, a little, but remember that being king does strange things to otherwise modest men. All I wanted in the beginning was just to live until tomorrow, and then to live until the tomorrow after that, and to make my way down the narrow path between pain on the one side and the end of all pain on the other side, living each day in joy. Even though I might be a slave, even though I was condemned to everlasting exile, yet what I wanted was as simple as that: not a kingdom but only joy.

My father was Romano Nirano, a Rom among Rom, a man who had kingliness in his smallest fingertip. As you know I was sold away from him when I was seven, but I can see him now as if he were standing right beside me, the broad face with heavy cheekbones, the powerful brooding eyes deep in their hoods, the heavy flowing mustache, the grand sweep of black hair streaming across his forehead. It is my face too. We have borne that face down through all the thousands of years since we were driven forth from Romany Star and I think it is a face that will endure to the end of all time. As will we.

He was already a slave when I was born. From *his* father he had inherited such a grand catastrophe of debts that there was no question of paying it off in five lifetimes. The old man had been a speculator in moons and was caught short in the Panic of 2814 when all the heavy metals completely lost their value; and after that we were destined to be paupers for centuries. My father could have wiped it all off by a bankruptcy, but my father thought bankruptcy was cowardly.

So he sold himself and my mother and my five brothers and sisters and me in return for a quit-claim. The family debts were wiped off the books and we became the slaves of Volstead Factors, a great interstellar corporation that was itself an imperial fiefdom.

"There's no disgrace in being a slave," my father told me. I was five years old and I had just discovered that I was different from most other children. I belonged to someone else. "It's a business arrangement, that's all. It may be an inconvenience but it's never a disgrace. It's an arrangement that you want to alter as soon as you can, of course, and if you have the chance and you don't take it then *that's* a disgrace. But aside from that there's no shame involved in it."

He was referring to modern slavery, you must realize. The institution was very different in ancient times. But then everything was. We may use the same name for a thing today that the ancients did—"slave," "king," "emperor," "ghost"—but the meaning that the word contains is not at all the same. The distant past is not simply a foreign country, as someone once said, but another universe altogether.

I learned that I was a slave before I learned that I was Rom. Or to put it more accurately I always knew that I was Rom but it wasn't until I was six that I came to know that most other people were not.

We spoke Romany at home and Imperial outside and we shifted from one to the other without difficulty. I thought that everyone did the same. My mother told us old Rom tales, stories of gods and demons, of sorceries and witchcraft, of heroic journeys by caravan across strange far-off lands. I thought that everyone knew those tales. We kept Rom treasures in our house, gold pieces, musical instruments, brightly colored scarves, sacred icons. I never entered the houses of my playmates and so I never knew that they had no such possessions.

When I was six I went out one day to carve a gloryball from the gloryball tree on the riverbank and when I got there I found my sister Tereina being attacked by a band of other children. Tereina was twelve then and her attackers, both boys and girls, must have been eight or nine years old, so that she towered over them; but there were half a dozen of them and they were tormenting her. "Rom trash, Rom trash, Rom trash!" they were chanting as they circled round and round her. "Rom, Rom, Rom, Rom!"

They were trying to snatch away the necklace at her throat. It was a chain of gleaming wind-scarab shells that my father's brother had brought back as a gift for her from Iriarte and it was the most precious thing she had, pulsing with light of a hundred subtle colors. Tereina slapped frantically at the clutching hands. She was too tall for them, but they had managed to rip open her blouse and her breasts were showing, and I saw long red scratches on her skin.

"Rom trash, Rom trash, Rom trash—"

She saw me and cried my name. And asked me in Romany to help her, and then said in Imperial, "Yakoub, give them the evil eye! Put the spell on them, Yakoub!"

I was only six. But I was big and strong and I had no reason to be afraid of them. And my mother had told me the legends of the evil eye, the black magic that the drabarne, the old Gypsy witches, had used to make their enemies suffer. Some of those legends are pure fantasy and some are real, though at that age I had no way of knowing which was which. To me everything was real then and I thought I could hurl my sister's tormentors into the heart of the sun if only I said the right words and made the right gestures. I think they thought so too; for I made my eyes change and puffed out my cheeks and crooked my arms above my head and marched toward them, chanting, "Iachalipe, iachalipe, iachalipe!"—enchantment, enchantment, enchantment!—and they turned and fled, squealing like frightened pigs. I roared with laughter and screamed curses at them and squirted my urine after them to mock them.

Tereina was weeping and trembling. I comforted her the way a man comforts a woman, reaching up and putting my arms around her, though I was only a child. Then I asked, "Why were they doing that? Because we are slaves?"

"Why would they care that we are slaves? Half of them are slaves too."

"Then why—"

"Because we are Rom, little brother. Because we are Rom."

So that evening it was necessary for my father to explain a great many things to me that I had never known, and after that evening life would always be different for me.

"We call them Gaje," he told me. "Which means, in Imperial, a fool, a bumpkin, a clod-hopper. Their minds are slower than ours and they think in a clumsy plodding way. We go from one to five to three to ten while they are moving slowly along, one two three four. Of course some of the Gaje are quicker than others. The emperor is a Gajo and so are his high lords, and they all have very quick minds indeed. But most of the Gaje are simpletons and we have had to put up with their stupidity ever since we came to live among them. And they know how much quicker we are than they. Which is why they once persecuted and oppressed us, and why even now they fear us and mistrust us, though most of them would deny that they do."

"And are there many of these Gaje?" I asked.

"Ten thousand of them," my father said, "for every one of us. Or maybe more. Who can count the Gaje? They are like the stars in the heavens. And we are very few, Yakoub. We are very few."

My head was swimming with these surprises. My father, when he walked down the street, carried himself like a king; and I had thought we were people of great worth indeed, even though just now we might happen to be slaves. And now to learn that I belonged to a sparse and insignificant race, that we Rom were like scattered flecks of white foam in a vast sea of Gaje, came to me with stunning impact. In the eye of my mind I saw now my father's face and the faces of my father's brothers standing out in a crowd of Gaje and I understood for the first time how different they were, different in the set of their jaws, in the fire of their eyes, in the black luster of their thick strong hair. A race apart, an alien people—more alien even than I could suspect—

"You know there once was a place called Earth, Yakoub?"

"Earth, yes."

"Destroyed long ago, ruined, shattered by Gaje idiocy. We lived there, we and the Gaje, before we all came out into the worlds of the stars. They called us Gypsies then. And a great many other names, Zigeuners, Romanichels, Gitanes, Tsigani, Zingari, Mirlifiches, Karaghi, dozens of names, because they had dozens of languages. Because they were too stupid and quarrelsome to speak only one, and so they befuddled themselves with tongues. We wandered among them, always strangers. Never staying in the same place for long, for what was the point of that? No one wanted us. They despised us and always schemed to harm us; so we stayed put only until we had earned a few coins by begging or telling fortunes or sharpening their knives, or until we had stolen enough to eat for a few days more, and then we moved along."

"Stolen?" I said, shocked.

He laughed and put his huge hands on my shoulders, gripping me in that firm loving way of his, and he gently rocked me back and forth as I stood before him. "*They* called it stealing. We called it harvesting. The fruits of the earth belong to all men, eh, boy? God gave us appetites and put into the world the means to satisfy those appetites; when we take what we need, we are simply obeying God's commandment."

"But if we took things that didn't belong to us—" I said, thinking

of those clutching Gaje fingers reaching for my sister's precious necklace.

"This was long ago and life was harsh. They would have let us starve,
so we took what we needed, grass for our horses, wood for our fires,
some pieces of fruit from the trees, perhaps a stray chicken or two. How
could they deny us the things that were in the world to use when we
were hungry, when we were thirsty?"

And my father sketched a picture for me of Rom life on the Gaje
Earth that left me dazed and chilled. A race of shabby unkempt people,
vagabonds, charlatans, beggars, thieves, weavers of spells, charmers of
snakes, dancers and blacksmiths and tinkers and acrobats, traveling in
rickety caravans from land to land, making their camps on the outskirts
of towns amid terrible filth and squalor, keeping themselves together by
an endless juggling act of trickeries and improvisations. Forced into a
life of lying and cheating, of begging, of all manner of desperate struggles. Scorned and despised, feared, whispered about. Even put to death
—put to death!—for no crime other than that of being unlike the dreary
settled folk among whom they roamed. I began to see this lost world
of Earth as a kind of hell where my ancestors had undergone a torment
for thousands of years.

As he spoke I began to cry.

"No," he said, and he shook me, hard. "There's nothing to sniffle
about. They made us suffer but they never broke our spirit. We had our
life and the Gaje had theirs, and perhaps theirs was more comfortable,
but ours was truer. Ours was the right life. We were kings of the road,
Yakoub! We soared on the high winds. We tasted joys that were altogether unknown to them. And we still do. Look what has become of
us, Yakoub: the former thieves, the former beggars, the raggle-taggle
Gypsies! Kings of the road, yes, and now it is the road between the stars!
Down through the years we have kept to our ways. Maybe some of us
slipping away from them now and then, sure, but always coming back,
always bringing the Rom way back to life. And that way has brought
us great comfort and goodness, with even greater things yet to come.
We speak the Great Tongue. We live the Great Life. We travel the
Great Road. And always the One Word guides us."

"The One Word?" I said. "What is that?"

"The One Word is: *Survive!*"

2.

OF COURSE I STILL UNDERSTOOD VERY LITTLE OF THE full tale. He had told me nothing of how the Rom had led the way into the stars, of how the Imperium had come into being, or how we founded a Rom kingdom and wove it betwixt and between the fabric of the Imperium to become the true force that governed mankind. Pointless to try to explain all that to a child of six, even a Rom child. Nor did he tell me then of Romany Star and why it was that the Rom were a people apart from the Gaje; for it would have been cruelty to have me know so soon that we were set apart from the Gaje in a secret way that could admit of no compromise, that there was no kinship at all, that we were of a wholly alien blood. Not just different by customs and languages, but by the blood itself. There would be time for that dark knowledge later on.

All this took place in the city of Vietorion on the world Vietoris. I have not set eyes on that planet since I was taken from it by my second owners, more than a hundred sixty years ago, but it is forever bright in my memory: the first home, the starting point. The dazzling sky streaked with gold and green. The great sprawl of the city like a black shawl across the crumpled ridges of the vast plain. The astounding jagged red spear of Mount Salvat rising with the force of a trumpet-blast in an overwhelming steep thrust above us. Perhaps nothing was as immense as I remember it but I prefer to remember it that way. Even our house seems palatial to me: white tiles flashing in the sunlight, rooms beyond rooms, soft music far away, heavy musky-scented yellow flowers everywhere in the courtyard. Was it truly like that? On Vietoris we were slaves.

There is slavery and slavery. My father had sold us to Volstead Factors but not so that we would be chained and whipped and left to make a dinner out of crusts. Our slavery was, as he so often said, a business arrangement. We lived the way other people, ordinary free people, lived. Each day my father went to the staryard where the great bronze-nosed ships of the company lay in their hangars and he worked on them like any other mechanic, and at night he came home. My mother taught in the company school. My brothers and sisters and I went to school, a different one. When we were older we would work for the company, too, in whatever jobs were chosen for us. We ate well and dressed well. Because we were slaves we were bound to the company, and could never work for anyone else, or leave Vietoris to seek a new life for ourselves; that way the company was certain to recover its investment in our educations. But we were not mistreated. Of course the company could choose to sell us if it felt it had no need for us. And in time it did.

I would watch the starships sailing across the night, lighting up the northern sky like flaring comets as they raced up toward wink-out speed and the interstellar leap across the light-years, and I would tell myself, "That ship flies because my father's hands were on it in the staryard. My father knows the magic of starships. My father could fly a starship himself, if they would let him."

Was that true? I suppose not. Even then I knew that all the starship pilots were Rom: I often saw them swaggering through the city, big black-haired men with Rom eyes, in the puff-shouldered silken blue uniforms that pilots of the Imperium affected in those days. But that didn't mean that all Rom were starship pilots. And I suspect that I didn't comprehend, at that time, the distinction between a starship mechanic and a starship pilot. Pilots were Rom; my father was Rom and worked with starships; therefore my father knew how to pilot a starship as well as any of the men in blue silk. In truth my father had great skill with tools of all sorts—the old Rom gift, coursing through our blood since the days when we had been wandering coppersmiths and tinsmiths and workers in iron and repairers of locks—he could do anything with his hands, fix anything, fashion miracles out of a scrap of wire and a bit of wood—but even he probably would have found it a challenge, I think, to take the controls of a starship in his grasp. And then again perhaps he would have known what to do: intuitively, automatically. He had great skills. He was a great man.

He taught me the names of the tribes of the Rom. We were Kalderash, and then there were the Lowara, the Sinti, the Luri, the Tchurari, the Manush, the Gitanos. And many more. I suspect I have come to forget some. Old names, names springing out of our wandering-time on Earth. Later, when I learned about Romany Star and the sixteen original tribes, I decided that the names my father had taught me were names that went back to the time of Romany Star. Now I know that that is wrong, that those are names we took when we were scattered among the Gaje of Earth only a few thousand years ago, in that time when we roamed in wagons, living as outcasts. Those names have lost meaning now, for we are spread very thin over a great many worlds and the only tribe that can matter to us is the tribe of tribes, the grand kumpania, the tribe of all Rom. But yet the names are a part of the tradition that we maintain and must maintain. And so Kalderash parents tell their children that they are Kalderash, and Lowara Lowara, and Sinti Sinti, even if it is a distinction without distinction.

My father taught me, also, the Rom way as it had been handed down from generation to generation over the centuries and through all the migrations. Not just the special customs of our people, the folkways, the rites and festivals and rituals and ceremonies. Those things are important. They are the instruments of survival. They unite and preserve us: the knowledge of what is clean and unclean, of how birth and marriage and death must be celebrated, of how authority is apportioned within a tribe, of how the invisible powers are to be dealt with, all those things which we know to be true beliefs. We must be tenacious of such things, or we will be lost; and so I was instructed in them as all Rom children are. But the rites and rituals are not the essence of the Rom way; they are only the devices by which that way is sustained and nurtured. My father took care to teach me what lay underneath them, that which is far more significant, that is, a sense of what it is to be Rom. To know that one is part of a tiny band of people, driven by misfortune from its homeland, that has clung together against a swarm of enemies in many strange lands over thousands of years. To remember that all Rom are cousins and that in one another is our only safety. To consider at all times that one must live with grace and courage but that the primary thing is to survive and endure until we can bring our long pilgrimage to its end and return to our home again. To realize that the universe is our enemy and that we must do whatever we can to protect ourselves.

At first I felt very little connection with the wandering Rom in their caravans, those ragged old mountebanks and jugglers who wandered the roads of medieval Earth. To me we seemed nothing much like those ancients, we of the far-flung Imperium who live in cities and fly between the stars. They were curiosities; they were folklore; they were *quaint.*

Then came the night when my father took me up the side of mighty

Mount Salvat to the lookout point five thousand meters above the city, and there, in the air that was so thin and piercing that it stung my nostrils, he showed me Romany Star in the sky and told me the last piece of the story. And then everything came together, and I knew that I was one with those far-off Kalderash and Sinti and Gitanos and Lowara of vanished Earth, that we were truly of a single blood and a single soul, that they were part of me and I was part of them.

Now at last I understood the stealing of chickens and apples in the wandering-time long ago: hunger kills, and we must go on living if we are to reach our goal, and if the Gaje will not let us eat then we must help ourselves. Now I understood the contempt for Gaje law: what was Gaje law to us, except a weapon held at our throats? I understood the lies and casual deceptions, the six conflicting answers to any prying Gaje question, the refusal to be swallowed up in the Gaje world in any way. The Gajo is the enemy. We could not let ourselves be deceived in that. They are the ancient foe; and all our striving must be aimed toward leaving them behind us, not toward entering into any union with them. For as surely as a river of fresh water is lost in the sea we would be lost forever if we let the Gaje once engulf us. So my father taught me when I was very young.

3.

ONE AFTERNOON WHEN I WAS SEVEN A PRETTY WOMAN IN a yellow robe came into the classroom where we were learning about the emperor, how he labored night and day to make life better for every boy and girl in the Imperium. She glanced quickly around the room and pointed to half a dozen of us, saying, "You, you, you, you, come with me." I was one of the ones chosen.

We went outside. It was a mild misty day and rain had fallen a little while before: the leaves of the trees were gleaming as if they had been polished. A car was waiting in the street, long and low and sleek, a silvery metallic color with the red comet-tail emblem of Volstead Factors on its hood. I remember all this as if it happened the day before yesterday.

I didn't mind leaving school. To tell you the truth I had never cared much for it anyway. Me, a schoolteacher's son. And that day's lesson had seemed foolish to me: the poor silly emperor, working night and day! If he was so powerful, why didn't he have people doing his work for him? And they had showed his picture on the screen in the classroom, a small frail man, very old and thin, who looked as though he might die at any minute. This was the Thirteenth Emperor, and actually he lived a surprisingly long time after that, but I doubted that anyone so wizened and feeble could manage even to take care of himself, let alone look after the needs of every boy and girl in the Imperium. School seemed nothing but Gaje nonsense to me: already I was dismissing anything I didn't like as Gaje nonsense, you see. In this case I was probably right, although I have learned over the years that not everything that is Gaje is nonsense, and now and then that not everything that is nonsense is Gaje.

I was the only Rom boy in the car. There was a Rom girl, too, one of my sisters' friends. The other four were Gaje. The Rom girl was a slave like me, and so was at least one of the Gaje boys. I wasn't sure about the rest. It wasn't easy to tell who was a slave and who wasn't. But in fact all six of us had been picked from the classroom because we were slaves. The company was undergoing an economy drive. A certain percentage of its slave-holdings was to be sold off, particularly young slaves still in school, who would not begin to provide a return on investment for many years. We were being taken to the marketplace to be sold, right then and there. I would never see my home again, my father, my mother, my brothers, my sisters. I would lose my little collection of music cubes, my storybooks and my playthings. I would never have my share of the old Rom treasures from Earth in our house. None of this was explained to me as they drove us to the marketplace. There are some ways in which even modern slavery is very much like the ancient kind.

In the vestibule of the marketplace they looked me over, tapped me here and there, ran me in front of some kind of scanner. No one wanted to know my age or name or any other information about me. A robot stamped my arm; it stung a moment and left a circular purple mark.

"Lot ninety-seven," I heard a hoarse bored voice say. "A boy."

"Move on inside, ninety-seven," said someone else. "That line over there."

It was a short bit of business to dispose of us, there in the slave-market of Vietorion. There was something dreamlike about it for me. When I think now of that afternoon I feel the roaring in my ears that I sometimes feel in dreams, and everything moves very slowly, hardly moving at all, and there are fierce shadows everywhere.

We stood on a circular dais beneath a glaring globe of hot bright light in the center of an immense drafty bare room that looked like a warehouse. There were hundreds of us up for sale at once, most of us children but not all. Some were quite old and I felt sorry for them. We were all naked. I had no trouble with being naked but some of the others huddled miserably with their hands over their middles or their arms folded across their breasts, trying to hide themselves. Much later, when I understood more about the way slave-markets worked, I realized that the ones who try to hide themselves usually are bought last, for the lowest prices, by the stingiest masters. The theory is that a slave concerned with such matters as privacy and shame is bound to be troublesome in other ways too.

A snub-nosed metal housing that looked a little like a neutron cannon descended from the distant ceiling and started to turn. A red warning light on the wall began to glow. Medical scanningbeams now were playing over our bodies. If the beams found any sort of defect, some internal sore or ulcer, a badly healed bone fracture, a weakness of the heart or lungs, it would instantly be picked up and entered on the sales screen where prospective buyers could take note of it.

Meanwhile the bidding was going on, click click click. The buyers had electromyograph terminals fastened to their cheeks and the auction was conducted at the speed of thought. A certain twitch of the facial muscles indicated the choice of a slave, a different kind of twitch registered the offer. A quick voltage spike gave the buyer a yes or no and the next round began until bidding closed. The whole process took no more than three or four minutes.

Of course I understood nothing of this or of anything else that was going on. It all drifted past me in a strange serene way. Like a dream, yes. Sometimes the most frightening dreams are the serene ones.

"Ninety-seven," a little robot said. I turned around and it stamped me on the forehead with the code number of my purchaser, and that was that.

Before night had come I was on board a starship bound for Megalo Kastro.

"What price did you go for?" a tall flat-faced boy asked me.

There were ten of us in the cabin. I was the youngest. I simply blinked at him.

"He's too young," said one with strange limp orange hair. "He can't read."

"I can too!" I cried. "You think I'm a child?"

"I went for sixty-five cerces," the flat-faced boy announced.

"Eighty, me," came from one who had a bright green jewel set in the center of his left cheek.

The flat-faced boy glared at him. I hoped maybe they would fight.

"How can you tell the price?" I asked one of the other boys, a small quiet one.

"It's in your forehead code. You need a mirror to see." He peered close at me. "You went for a hundred."

"My price was a hundred," I told the flat-faced boy. "How do you like that?"

They all swung around to look, crowding in around me. They looked skeptical, and then they looked angry, and then awed. I pulled my shoulders back and clapped my hands and laughed. "A hundred," I said again. "A hundred!"

To this day I'm proud of that. Someone must have seen merit in me even then.

4.

I HAD BEEN BOUGHT BY THE GUILD OF BEGGARS, MEGALO Kastro Lodge 63. My lodgemaster's name was Lanista, and I shared my cabin with four boys named Kalasiris, Anxur, Sphinx, and Focale. I put their names down here because all of them have been dead for many years and it is a kindness to mention the names of the forgotten dead, even if they were no members of your clan. Lanista was Rom and my four cabinmates were not. I think I fetched such a high price because anyone could see at a glance that I was Rom. The Guild of Beggars is a Gaje enterprise but they get all the Rom they can for it because they regard us as superior beggars. Begging is in our genes, they believe. Not far from the truth, you know.

Although I can remember names and faces and places and all these other details of my being sold away from my family I can't tell you how long it was before it first dawned on me that I was never going to see my home again. Sometimes the very big patterns escape a child's notice completely while the fine ones stick fast. I don't know what I thought of all that was happening to me. Taken out of school, yes; sold, yes; put aboard a starship, yes; going somewhere far away, yes. But forever? Never to return? No more mother, father, brothers, sisters? I don't remember being troubled by any of that, then. All I felt was a wonderful strange sense of floating free. Seed on the wind, drifting in the gusts. Go wherever the wind goes.

But I am Rom, of course. When we stay too long in one place we begin to rust. The slavemasters were simply doing me a favor by plucking me away. Setting me free by sending me off into new slavery. They were the ones who put me on the road I was meant to travel.

There's no world anything like Megalo Kastro in the known—that is, the human-inhabited—part of the galaxy. The name means Great Fortress in Greek, one of the ancient languages of Earth, and indeed there is a great stone fortress there, looming like a colossal crouching beast at the top of a rugged cliff overlooking the sea. But it wasn't built by Greeks. It wasn't built by anyone who could claim kinship to either of the two human races.

You don't have to walk more than a dozen paces down the Equinox Hall of the fortress of Megalo Kastro to realize that. The hall gets its name because twice a year the pulsing golden-red light of the sun comes through an archway and strikes the pommel of an altar at its western end, precisely at the equinoctial moment. Nothing extraordinary about that; paleolithic men were setting up altars like that on Earth twenty thousand years ago.

But the geometry of Equinox Hall takes your breath away. I mean that literally. Walk a few paces along that twisting corridor of rough-hewn green stone and you begin gasping a little. It's like walking on the deck of a heaving ship. Everything is disorderly and unstable. You expect the walls to start gliding back and forth. A few paces more and you start to sweat. The vaulted roof twenty meters overhead is undulating, or seems to be. Your eyes are throbbing next, because they can't quite follow the lines of the architecture and keep going in and out of focus. The whole structure is like that: alien, oppressive, fascinating.

No one knows who built it. There it stands, gigantic, terrifying, mysterious, half in ruins, telling us nothing. The archaeologists think it's five or ten million years old. It can't be much older than that, they say, because Megalo Kastro is a young planet and tremendous geotectonic stuff is going on all the time; at the rate continents rise and fall there, the fortress can't be enormously ancient. But it looks a billion years old. In one of the cellar rooms there's the outline of a single large hand in what looks like chalk, but isn't, on the wall, and that hand has seven fingers of equal size and a pair of opposable thumbs, one on each side. Perhaps one of the builders amused himself by sketching it in during his lunch break. Perhaps it was put there as a joke by some member of the exploration team from Earth that first found the place. Who can say? If we could dig up some alien artifacts in the vicinity, that might tell us something, but the only artifact we have is the fortress itself, brooding at the edge of the sea.

And that sea—that nightmare of a sea—

There are many life-forms on Megalo Kastro, nearly all of them large, predatory, and nasty. It's a young world, as I say: this is its Mesozoic that's going on now, and everything has fangs and scales. But the biggest life-form of all is one that is, thank God, unique to Megalo Kastro. The sea itself, I mean. Not a true sea at all, but a horrendous vast pudding of pale pink mud, warm, quivering, sinister, unfathomably deep, that stretches across an uncharted gulf ten thousand kilometers wide.

That sea is alive. I don't mean that it's full of living things. I mean that it *is* a living tning, a single malign entity with some sort of low-level intelligence. Or, for all anybody knows, intelligence on the genius level. It thinks. It perceives. You can actually observe its mental workings: questing ripples on its surface rising in little interrogative quivers, short-lived protuberances like exclamatory worms, puckered bubbling orifices that come and go. God knows what evolutionary process brought it into being. God knows, but no one else does. Scoop a section out to study it and all you have is a lump of watery mud, rapidly growing cool. And the thing from which it was taken lies there with its feet basking in the warmth of Megalo Kastro's subterranean magma and its arms resting on the shores of the far-flung continents, laughing at you. And it will eat you if you give it the chance.

Believe me. I know.

The crust of Megalo Kastro is loaded with all manner of valuable elements that were consumed long ago on older worlds, and a dozen different mining companies operate there. Most of them are looking for transuranics, which fetch a good price in nearly every solar system, but there was also a Rom outfit at work hunting for rare earths, especially the scarcest of them, thulium, europium, holmium, lutetium.

(Those who rarely leave their home worlds are forever surprised to learn that all the planets of the galaxy, no matter how far away or how strange they may be, are composed of the same general bunch of elements. I think they believe that alien worlds ought to be made up of alien elements, and that there's something improper—boring, even —about finding such things as oxygen and carbon and nitrogen on them. As though an atom with the atomic number and weight of hydrogen could be something else besides hydrogen on some other world. Only an idiot would think that every planet has its own periodic table. There's only one set of building blocks in this universe: did you think otherwise?)

Mining on Megalo Kastro is an unpretty business, considering the heat, the humidity, the toothy monsters lurking behind every toothy bush, the frequency of devastating volcanic eruptions, and the various other disagreeable qualities of the place. Nevertheless it's a profitable industry, to say the very least, and the whole planet has a wild boomtown atmosphere where money flows freely from pocket to pocket. Which makes it a fertile sphere of operations for the Guild of Beggars.

It was Lanista who taught me how to beg. Our lodgemaster. He was of the Sinti Rom, twenty years old or maybe thirty, with strangely pale skin and cool eyes set very far apart in his head. "You smile at them," he said. "That's the key thing, to smile. You make your eyes shine. You make yourself look pathetic and appealing all at once. You put out your hand and you break their hearts."

I began to see why the guild had paid a premium price for me. I had the shine in my eyes. I had the smile. I was a choice urchin, winsome, irresistible, clever.

"What if they won't give?" I asked.

"When they say no and shake their heads, you look them right in the eyes. You smile your sweetest smile. And you say with a voice like an angel's, 'Your mother sleeps with camels.' And then you move along as though you have given them your greatest blessing."

I liked the idea of being a beggar. It didn't offend my sense of pride. It was a challenge; it required technique. I wanted to be good at it. By o Beng the Devil, I wanted to be the best!

Later when I went ghosting forth on Earth and saw the Rom of the old days I watched them at their begging with the eye of one professional for another. They were good. Very good. I saw the Gypsy mothers in the street whisper to their little ones, four years old, five, "Mong, chavo, mong"—beg, boy, beg!—and send them out among the Gaje. To train them, to develop their skills early. Begging helps to teach you not to know fear. Fear is a useless luxury when it is the Rom life that you live. A little of it gives you the spice of wisdom, any more than that and you are made helpless.

Begging is useful in another way. It makes you invisible. Most people don't want to see a beggar, because the sight of him stirs guilt and anxiety and niggardliness and other negative feelings. So a beggar can move among a crowd practically unnoticed except when he insists on being seen.

(I should make it clear that the prime activity of the Guild of Beggars isn't begging. Begging pays the company's expenses, more or less, but the main work of the guild is espionage. No one spelled that out for me when I came to Megalo Kastro. But it became obvious as time went along.)

When he was finished instructing me Lanista furnished me with the accoutrements and regalia of my profession. My alms bowl, into which money could be dropped but out of which money could not be taken without setting off an alarm. (The bowl would also sound its alarm, loud enough to shake a comet from its orbit, if it ever wandered more than three and a half meters from my body.) My staff of office, signifying that I was a licensed beggar and that all funds I took in would be put to pious uses. My red neckerchief, which all guild beggars wear so that they can recognize each other at a glance and keep a proper distance. And my holy amulet, a small flat plaque of silvery metal chased with intricate coruscating patterns in some scintillating darker substance, which I was to hang about my throat under the neckerchief to protect me from unspecified perils of the soul. The amulet contained a recorder sensitive enough to pick up anything spoken within a five-meter radius of me, but Lanista saw no need to tell me that.

"You are all ready now, Yakoub," he said. A car was waiting outside the lodge to take all the beggars to town for the morning's work. Gently he shoved me toward it. I turned and looked back and he made a secret Rom sign at me and winked. "Go," he said. "Mong, chavo, mong!"

5.

IT WAS A HIDEOUS TOWN, NOTHING MORE THAN SHACKS of corrugated tin splotched with purple mud from the unpaved streets. Light rain fell about six hours out of every ten and the air was so thick with mildew and mold that it had a greenish cast. White furry things sprouted in your lungs every time you drew a breath.

But the begging was good. The miners would come back from their shifts and draw money from their pay accounts for a quick holiday, and they thought it was bad luck to let the money stay in their pockets too long. Mainly they spent it on gambling, drink, drugs, and whores, as men in such towns have done since time began. But there wasn't one of them who wouldn't toss a handful of obols into a little beggar-boy's bowl, and when you happened upon one at just the right moment of exuberance he'd grandly fling you fifty minims, a tetradrachm, even a cerce piece or two, whatever happened to be in his purse. It added up.

Though I was the youngest and cutest and probably the cleverest, I was also the newest and maybe the most innocent. That cost me at first. You had to have a territory; and of course the established boys of the guild already had staked out the most lucrative zones for themselves. As for the other boys who had arrived with me, they were anywhere from two to five years older than I was, and were quick to grab the best of what was left for themselves. The best I could do was lurk around the edges of the town. I was lucky to bring in five obols a day.

That was bad. We were credited with a percentage of our take toward the price of buying our freedom, and if I kept on at that rate I'd still be a slave to the guild when I was a hundred years old. I didn't want that and neither did the guild: a beggar older than about twelve was useless to them and they *wanted* us to be able to buy our writs and clear out when we were no longer efficient producers. Often they would ask the most capable ex-beggars to sign on as freedmen in the upper hierarchy, though.

Once I realized what was happening I found a niche for myself that the other boys hadn't bothered to notice. Instead of soliciting the miners I solicited the whores.

Their guild had the same buy-out deal that ours did, but they were bound by a minimum ten-year indenture and so they didn't feel the same pressure that we did to earn and save, earn and save. And quickly I found how easy it was to wheedle the coins from them. Just bring out the maternal in them, that was the ticket. Let them mother you. And they'd pay and pay and pay.

Good God, how I wish I'd been older! I spent my working days in this perfumed crib and that, letting them hug me against their shining jiggling breasts or nuzzling up with my cheek to their plump jewel-socketed bellies. Even after all this time I still remember them vividly, even their names: Mermela, Andriole, Salathastra, Shivelle. The fragrance of their bodies. The silken sheen of their thighs. Those rosy nipples, that rippling resilient flesh. Every one of them was beautiful. (Perhaps it wasn't really so, but that is how I remember them, at any rate, and so be it: they were all beautiful.) They let me touch them everywhere. They giggled, they laughed, they loved it. And they loved *me*. When the customers showed up I quickly went out the back way, though some would let me stay, hiding behind the curtains and listening to all the panting and groaning. I would watch now and then, too. I learned a great deal very young. And into my begging bowl went the obols and tetradrachms and once in a while a gorgeous five-cerce piece shining with all the colors of the rainbow.

In the whorehouse district I was everybody's mascot, everybody's toy. Some of the younger ones—they weren't more than thirteen or fourteen years old themselves—were even willing to give me a little first-hand instruction in the mysteries of love. But of course I was only seven and that would have been not only an abomination but a waste of their time and mine besides. I was content to learn by observing, at least for another couple of years.

How the money rolled in! There were days when I could barely carry my bowl back to the lodge, it was so stuffed with coins. (My recorder was stuffed, too, with the intimate chatter of the whorehouses. I still had no idea that the senior members of the guild were miners of sorts themselves, that they spent hours every night processing our tapes, filtering the idle noise and panning for the data that we beggars were being paid to collect, such nuggets of information as whether the men in the mines were cheating their employers by withholding the locations of rich lodes of ore.)

In short order I was the star of the guild. The big producer: the number-one beggar. I knew that because Lanista and the other senior brothers of the lodge treated me with great warmth and respect and also because of the obvious envy and even coldness of my fellow beggars. Well, I could handle that part of it. When my cabin-mate Sphinx tried to cut in on my bordello territory I took him aside and beat him bloody. I was eight and he was eleven; but I had my career to look out for.

Now for the first time ghosts were beginning to visit me with some regularity, too. That was the most exciting thing of all, even more than the games I was beginning to play with the whores in the cribs, even more than the occasional sight of some snarling giant reptile looming outside the force-field that protected the town.

I knew a little about ghosting. There had been that old witch-ghost in my earliest boyhood, though I had never spoken of her to anyone. But when I was a little older I heard something concerning ghosts from my father, who had strived with such skill to prepare me for everything that was coming in adult life, and I came to suspect that a ghost was probably what that old woman had been. But though she must have visited me five or six times when I was very young, I had not seen her since I had left Vietoris, or anyone like her. And so it was a little startling, years later, when the ghosts began to come to me on Megalo Kastro.

"It's something that only the Rom can do," is what my father had told me. "And not every Rom; for it takes training, it takes will. And you must have the power in you in the first place. To leave the body, to split yourself off and go wandering across time and space—"

When the first ghost came I thought he was my father. He hovered by my side: big, powerful body, blazing eyes, black mustache, somehow transparent and solid both at the same time. There was an aura around him. His laugh was wondrous: like the rolling thunder that descends from the mist-plateaus of Darma Barma, where great lightnings crackle every moment of the day. Anxur was with me, and Focale, but the ghost didn't let them see him. Nor did they hear that splendid laughter.

He looked liked my father but something was wrong, something about his face was a little off. Of course. The ghost wasn't my father: he was me. But he didn't tell me that. All he did was grin and touch my shoulder and say, "Ah there, you Yakoub. How big you're getting!

How well you're doing! Keep it up, boy. Everything's moving in the right direction!"

That ghost came three or four times a year, and that was about all he ever said to me. There were two other ghosts I sometimes saw, a youngish man and a very beautiful woman, who never said anything to me, simply stared and stared as if I was some kind of curiosity or freak. I had no idea who they were and it was a long time before I found out. But I came to welcome their very infrequent visits. It was a warm, secure feeling, knowing they were near. I thought of my ghosts as guardian angels of a sort. And so I guess they were.

It was all right, those first few years on Megalo Kastro. I was growing fast and getting shrewd. I was putting money aside for my freedom. I had vague thoughts of buying my writ by the time I was ten and going swaggering back to Vietoris as a freedman to work at my father's side in the staryard.

But then everything started to change, very quickly and very much for the worse.

First there were shifts in the top levels of the guild lodge. Apparently this was a custom of the guild, to keep anyone from building a private power base. The preceptor-general was transferred to some other world and a new man came in from one of the Haj Qaldun planets, and then the procularius was replaced, and soon afterward we got a new abbot-principal. The last to go of the original guild officers was Lanista, the lodgemaster, the only Rom in the hierarchy of our lodge and my particular ally; and once he was gone I felt suddenly very alone. Especially since the new hierarchs proceeded to impose a set of startlingly cruel new regulations upon us.

I never learned whether they instituted their "reforms" because orders had come down from the high command of the guild to tighten the expenses of the lodges or simply because they were persons of cold and astringent spirit. Perhaps it was some of each. But we were informed, a week after Lanista's departure, that from then on our share of our daily take would be cut to one fifth of its former amount, and that the calculations would be adjusted retroactively for the past eighteen months. Also daily begging hours were to be extended and we would be expected to contribute ten obols a day toward our meals, which until then had been provided by the lodge without cost. There was a sudden sharp drop in the quantity and quality of lodge food, too —not that it had ever been anything extraordinarily fine.

None of this made much sense to me then nor does it now. Starving your workers is not a good way to increase production. Making it virtually impossible to buy our freedom not only went against the stated guild policy of trying to clear us out by the time we were twelve, but completely removed our incentive to fill our begging bowls. (But of course it was the conversations we were taping, not the coins we were wheedling, that the guild was really interested in. Even so, our earnings were far from trifling.) The best explanation I can give is that they were trying to turn us into malcontents so that they would have a pretext for selling us off while still under indenture rather than letting us work our way free. A petty policy and a self-defeating one, but human history is full of such things.

Did we protest all this, you ask? To whom? And for what purpose? We were slaves.

I still felt such joy at going forth among my voluptuous ladies—and now I was nearly ten; I was daily being initiated into new mysteries—that the changes at the lodge made little difference to me at first. But I was growing swiftly and I felt hungry all the time under the new rations, which made me furious. And at the monthly accounting I discovered that I was now hopelessly far away from my writ of freedom, my return to Vietoris, my family, my father. So when my fellow beggars began to agitate and conspire among themselves, I found myself very willing to throw in my lot with them.

Focale was the leader. He was the tall flat-faced boy who had asked me my price on that first day of our journey to Megalo Kastro. I had disliked him then. But we had become friends, more or less, afterward. He was taller now and even less lovely of face, with strange tiny features and little washed-out eyes.

"We should escape," he said, one day when we were in the baths. Because we were not wearing our amulets, his words would not be recorded for our masters. "They can't hold us. We'll make our way to the starport and smuggle ourselves on one of the outbound ships."

It was complete foolishness, of course. But you must remember we were still only children.

All the same we gave it a try, not once but four times. We slipped out of the lodge and went on foot through town and to the port, hoping to stow away. We were caught every time. The proctors suddenly looming up before us and behind us, the hands clamping down on the backs of our necks, the kicks and slaps, the days of bread and water:

it happened that way every time. We never had a chance of getting away. There were televector transmitters in our holy amulets that constantly broadcast our locations, but we didn't know that. One time they actually let us get within sight of the port. We stared at the great ships standing nose to the sky and tried to imagine what worlds they might be bound for. "Galgala!" cried Focale. "Where everything is golden." And Anxur whispered, "No, Marajo! There's a desert there that has sand bright as diamonds." Sphinx spoke of the lush glistening forests of Estrilidis, where the cats had two tails. And then the proctors rose up and seized us and beat us until we whimpered for mercy.

That was our third attempt. We never saw Focale again after that. We assumed he had been sold off the planet, for he was the worst troublemaker in the lodge.

Even without him we were determined to escape. I more than the others; I became the ringleader in his place, though I was one of the youngest. My slavery, which had rested comfortably enough on me during the first few years, now was an intolerable burden. I was furious all the time. I bubbled with wrath and impatience. Why should I spend my boyhood on this miserable sweaty world, nibbling on dry crusts and begging in grimy whorehouses for small coins? I lived day and night only for the moment of attaining freedom. As I made my way through the town I studied the maze of alleyways and covered passages, plotting a course that I imagined would allow me to give the proctors the slip. My friends the whores would help me. I meant to scramble from crib to crib, hiding behind their skirts and under their beds, zigzagging across the town until I reached the place where I could run for freedom. Then I'd have to take my chances with the winged and beaked horrors of the jungle outside, but I had a plan. I would go west, away from the port, and seek refuge for the night in the great fortress overlooking the sea. They would never expect that; they would think I was terrified of going near that place. Everyone was. But I was Rom; why should I fear a pile of old stones? I would hide there and let them believe I had been eaten by some monster of the wilderness, and after a time I would slip away, bypassing the town entirely. When I reached the spaceport I would cry sanctuary to the first Rom I spied and that would be an end to my slavery. Or so I thought.

They caught me before I got halfway across town and this time they beat me without pity. I thought all my bones would break, and perhaps they would have, except that I was young and limber. Then they took me before the procularius. That bleak and frosty man glowered at me and asked the lodgemaster, "How many times does this make for him?"

"His fourth attempt, sir."

"Where did we get such trash? Do with him as you did with the other. The ugly one."

So they would ship me wherever they had shipped Focale. I didn't care. It couldn't be any worse than staying at the lodge.

A guild proctor with a beefy red face and thick hulking shoulders ordered me into a land-car and we drove north and then west for half an hour or so. It was a sweltering day and the sun had a heavy gray-green veil over its face. After a time I saw the dark looming bulk of the ancient fortress outlined against the sky ahead.

Despite all my bravado I caught my breath sharply and shrank back into my seat. Why were we going *there?*

But we weren't. The proctor turned off on a side road that led straight to the sea. We halted at a turnoff and he ordered me out. The road here ran along the seaward side of a steep cliff made of some soapy-looking soft green stone, badly chipped and cracked. The sea lay twenty or thirty meters below; it was a straight drop down from the shoulder of the road. I looked over the edge. I had never had a close look at the sea of Megalo Kastro before. It was nothing at all like water; it was pink and stiff-looking, like some kind of disgusting custard, and steam was rising from it. The surface of it was rough and gritty. There was nothing like surf or waves. It lay almost inert, pressing up against the shore, making small, sinister rippling motions.

The proctor seized my amulet and pulled it away from my neck.

"You won't be needing this any more, little Rom."

I saw what was about to happen and tried to break free. He was too quick for me. He seized me by the waist and lifted me high overhead in one swift motion and hurled me far out into that loathsome sea.

6.

I WAS DEAD. I HAD NO DOUBT OF THAT. IF I DIDN'T BREAK my neck as I hit the surface of the sea I would be devoured in an instant by it. As I soared and plummeted I was sick with fear, knowing that this was my end. For years I had heard tales of this strange sea, how it was one giant living organism thousands of kilometers deep and broad. How it fed on the creatures of the land that tumbled into it, how sometimes it even would extend a sticky tendril of itself onto the shore to snare something passing by.

I was a long time falling. It seemed to take an hour. It went on so long that my fear left me and I grew impatient to know what would come next. I felt the warmth of the sea rising toward me and its strange odor, sweet and not unpleasant, struck my nostrils. Hot wind-currents played over the surface. I thought of my father and my sister Tereina and of the plump little whore Salathastra. Then I hit.

Despite the height from which I had fallen my landing was soft and easy. The sea seemed to reach up to catch me and it drew me down into itself. Quietly I lay just beneath the surface, unmoving, not even bothering to breathe, cushioned by the density of the strange warm fluid.

Was this what being dead is like? How restful!

I floated. I drifted. The sea took me and carried me. I felt my clothing dissolve. Perhaps my skin and flesh were gone too and I was nothing but bones glistening in the steaming pink mud. I kept my eyes closed. I felt fingers of the sea caressing me everywhere, my thighs, my belly, my loins, unseen slithering serpents sliding over my body. There was a kind of ecstasy in that. The sea made soft sucking noises. It burbled and squeaked and hissed. I stretched out my arms and I could touch the fingertips of one hand to the shore and the other to the shore of the distant unknown western continent ten thousand kilometers away. My toes dangled down to the roots of the planet, where hidden volcanoes poured forth fiery lava.

It is digesting me, I thought.

It is making me part of itself.

I didn't care. I was dead. I loved the sea and I loved being eaten by it. Being absorbed by it. Becoming part of it.

Then a deep voice said, "Swim, Yakoub."

"Swim where?"

"To the shore. This stuff can't hold you."

"It's eating me."

"It will if you let it. But why let it?"

"Who are you?"

"Open your eyes, Yakoub."

I didn't. I went on drifting. Warm, safe, sleepy.

"Yakoub." The deep voice again. More insistent. "Wake up. Wake up, you coward!"

That stung. "Coward? Me?"

"You heard me."

"Why coward?"

"Because you are selling your whole life to this thing, and for a foolish price. Are you afraid to live? Are you afraid to do all the great things that destiny holds for you?"

I opened my eyes. There was purple haze all around me. I saw a ghost above me in a shimmering golden aura. Blazing eyes, black mustache. My father's face, almost. Almost. Not my father, but close kin all the same, someone I knew well. Knew better than my father, even. He looked angry but he was smiling also. "Yakoub," he murmured. Gently, now. "Swim, Yakoub. You must. This death is not for you."

"What death is, father?"

"I am not your father."

"What is it you want me to do?"

"Swim."

"How?"

"Lift your arm. Good. Now the other one. Kick. Kick. Kick. Good, Yakoub. Kick. Kick."

The wriggling fingers of the sea danced about me like worms standing on their tails. Sea-stuff was in my mouth, my eyes, my ears. A strand of it held me around my throat. Another stroked my genitals, and I grew stiff there, and thrust with my hips, driving against the resilient warm mud. Now and again I opened my eyes. Colors flashed everywhere. The shore was far away, a black line against the sky. The ghost still hovered over me, eyes bright with encouragement. He said nothing.

But I could hear his booming laughter every time I swam another stroke. I saw other ghosts now, too, five, six, a dozen of them. The beautiful woman again. Beckoning to me, urging me on. Images flickered in the air, throngs of people, grand robes, glittering headdresses, strange planets, awesome ceremonies. Was it the sea that was throwing up these scenes, or my guardian ghosts? Swim, Yakoub. Swim. Swim! What a struggle it was! I yearned to let go, to relax, to give myself to the sea, to allow myself to slip down into that vast warm caressing body. That great mother. But the ghosts were unrelenting. Swim, they insisted. Swim. Swim. Swim!

And I swam.

I discovered how to pull energy from the sea, to draw on it instead of letting it draw on me, and I swam toward shore with steady strokes now. Never pausing. Never faltering. I gained in strength with each stroke. How could I let myself die here? There was so much for me yet to do! Life was calling to me. Swim, Yakoub! Live, Yakoub!

I saw a colossal tree growing right at the edge of the sea. Its roots were deep down in the sea-bed and its trunk, a vast white shaft streaked with strands of pale purple, rose swift and straight for a hundred meters or two, not branching at all except at the top. I think the tree was sea-stuff too, for its enormous crown, spreading like a huge umbrella and casting a giant blue shadow, was in constant metamorphosis. Eyes, faces, coiled serpents, long fluttering leaves, fiercely beating wings, cool flickering flames, everything swarming, writhing, changing, nothing the same for two seconds in a row. I thought that one of the faces I saw was that of Focale, but it came and went too quickly for me to be certain.

That tree was life to me. It throbbed and surged with the vigor of constant transformation that is life. I swam toward it. I knew it was my sanctuary. I could hear it singing to me, and as I neared it I sang also.

I saw the gnarled roots rising above the sea-surface, and I seized one and clung to it and pulled myself hand over hand across its smooth slippery sides until I was up out of the sea entirely. I lay there for a time, gasping. Then I rose and walked down the narrow ridge of the root's upper face until I came to the trunk itself, and I embraced it, stretching out my arms as wide as they would go, which was scarcely enough to reach a fiftieth of the way around that trunk.

And then I was ashore. I was naked and my skin was glowing with the warmth of the sea. Nothing could frighten me now. It was like a birth, coming forth from that sea. Under a glowering sky I began to walk eastward, not caring if I had to walk across half a world. I would make it.

I walked for days. No creature molested me. A bird-like thing with rubbery wings the width of a house flew above me much of the way, enfolding me in its purple shadow. Sometimes I saw familiar ghosts. At last I came to a place where the belly of the earth had been split open and the pistoning arms of huge dark machines rose and fell, rose and fell, sending up clouds of white steam and black geysers of mud. Some men standing beside one of the machines pointed at me. I went to them.

A smiling Rom face looked down at me.

"Sarishan, cousin," I said in Romany. "I am a runaway slave and I cry sanctuary, for my masters have treated me wrongly." I felt calm and strong. I had come into my manhood in that sea.

7.

THE OUTPOST I HAD REACHED WAS THE ONE WHERE ROM miners were at work excavating for rare earths. They fed me and clothed me and kept me with them for a month or two. Then they put me aboard a starship that was heading into the arm of the galaxy known as Jerusalem Spill, where the worlds are packed thick and close. I would have gone home to Vietoris if I could, but no one at the mining camp had so much as heard of Vietoris, and when I tried one night to show them, in what was probably a completely wrongheaded and incorrect way, where in the sky Vietoris was located, they said that there never were any ships out of Megalo Kastro that headed in that direction. Perhaps that was so. In any case it was probably best for me that I ultimately went where I did, for that was where I was meant to go. The gods had decreed that the Vietoris part of my life was over.

The ship I did take was a third-class freighter with a Gaje captain but a Rom pilot and crew. They found out quickly that I was Rom too and I spent most of my time in the jump-room, watching them gear the ship up to wink-out. They even let me stay there for the leap itself, when the pilot grasped the jump-handles and poured his soul into the soul of the starship and sent it across the light-years. I watched the pilot's face in the moment of leap, when he did that special thing that only the Rom of all mankind are capable of doing properly. I saw the ecstasy in it, the sudden beauty that came over him—and he was not a beautiful man—and in that moment the yearning awoke and burned in me to grasp jump-handles myself, to give my soul to a starship's soul, to be one of those who pilots the great ships in the enormous void.

"My father works on starships," I said. "You probably know him. His name is Romano Nirano. He fixes the ships that come to Vietoris."

But they had never heard of Romano Nirano, and they had never heard of Vietoris. Because they liked me, they opened their big star-tank for me, a black sphere in whose swirling opal-hued depths all the stars of the galaxy were shown, and they tried to look up Vietoris. But they had trouble finding it because I was unable to tell them the name of Vietoris' sun; it had always been just "the sun" to me, and that wasn't good enough. Finally someone keyed into a planetary atlas and located Vietoris for me and they showed it to me in the star-tank. It was off in an unimportant corner of the galaxy and we were getting farther and farther from it with every leap. So I would not get to go home.

It saddened me that none of these Rom starmen knew of my father. I had thought he was famous from one end of the universe to the other.

"Here's where you'll get off, boy," the pilot said. He picked up the pointer and showed me a star-system midway across Jerusalem Spill, where five worlds whirled around a mighty blue sun. "The end of the line. There are Rom aplenty there, but beyond these worlds you won't have a chance of finding your own kind."

That was how I came to live on the kingly planet of Nabomba Zom, in the palace of Loiza la Vakako, who would be like a second father to me, and more than a father. I was twelve years old, or perhaps thirteen. On Nabomba Zom I grew and blossomed. On Nabomba Zom I became who I was meant to become.

8.

LOIZA LA VAKAKO WAS LOWARA ROM, OF FABULOUS
wealth and legendary shrewdness. Lowara are always good at amassing
money and shrewdness is their second nature. The entire planet of
Nabomba Zom belonged to him, and fourteen of its twenty moons. He
ruled this great domain and its kumpania of many thousands of Rom
like a Gypsy king of old, without cheap pomp or foolish pretension but
with complete strength and assurance. Much later, when I was king,
I patterned my style more than a little after that of Loiza la Vakako.
At least in superficials. Of course he and I were really very different
sorts. He was a natural aristocrat, cool and self-contained, and I—well,
I am not like that. Kingly, yes. Cool, no.

I was covered from head to toe with the bright crimson manure of
salizonga snails on the day he and I first met.

My friends the starmen had dropped me off at Port Nabomba as part
of a cargo of agricultural implements: the cargo manifest listed so many
tractor drives, so many rotary aerators, so many ground-effect harvest-
ers, and "one Yakoub-class agricultural robot, humanoid model, one-
half standard size, expandable, self-maintaining." I stood in the midst
of all the crates with a yellow cargo tag dangling from my ear. The
customs inspector stared at me a long while and said finally, "What the
hell are you?"

"The Yakoub-class agricultural robot, humanoid model." I grinned
at him. "Sarishan, cousin."

He was Rom, but he gave me no greeting in return nor did he seem
amused. Scowling, he checked through the cargo manifest, and his
scowl grew deeper and blacker when he found the entry in question.
"You're a robot?"

"Humanoid model."

"Very funny. Expandable, it says."

"That means I'll grow."

"*Expendable* is more like it. How old are you?"

"Almost twelve."

"That's pretty old for a robot. What the hell are they doing dumping obsolete machinery on us?"

"I'm not really a—"

"Stand over there and keep quiet," he said, checking me off. "Item twenty-nine, one crate tractor drives—"

So I entered the kingly planet of Nabomba Zom as a unit of agricultural machinery and that was almost exactly how they treated me at first. Still wearing my tag and clutching the little overpocket containing the gifts from the starmen that were my only possessions, I was unceremoniously loaded on a truck a few hours later, along with a crate or two of the other newly arrived farm gear, and taken out to a plantation in the heart of a wide, lush valley somewhere in the interior of the continent. I spent the next six months there, shoveling the precious manure of the salizonga snails.

You would quiver in your boots if you ever saw a salizonga snail bearing down on you in its inexorable way, snorting and snuffling and dropping tons of vivid excreta in its wake. The salizonga snail is the biggest gastropod in the known universe, a ponderous creature eight meters long and three or four meters high, encased in a domed shell of overlapping glossy yellow plates thick as armor. Terrifying as it looks —the great waving eye-stalks, the tremendous rubbery pedestal of a foot—the worst it can do to you is trample you to death, which it certainly will do if you don't get out of its way. It won't eat you, though. It won't eat anything except a certain red-leafed moss that will grow only in the interior of Nabomba Zom, which by not much of a coincidence is the only place in the universe where the salizonga snail is to be found.

No one would give a shit—so to speak—about this bulky monstrosity, if not for the fecal matter which it deposits with irrepressible zeal and in astonishing quantity as it thunders through its favorite pastures. This brightly colored stuff contains an alkaloid from which a perfume is distilled that is desperately coveted by the women of five thousand worlds. Only the *male* salizonga secretes the valuable alkaloid, and unless the manure is collected and refrigerated within a few minutes of excretion the alkaloid will break down and become worthless. Therefore it is necessary for human workers to follow the snails around— robots don't seem capable of distinguishing between male and female salizongas, the distinction being an extremely subtle one—and hastily shovel the newly dumped male-snail dung into refrigeration tanks before it loses its commercial value. This was the job that I was given on my second day on Nabomba Zom. It did not strike me as an enormous improvement over panhandling in the fleshpits of Megalo Kastro.

Well, it is the decree of God that man born of woman shall work for his daily bread, and woman born of woman likewise; but nowhere did God specify that anybody was entitled to *pretty* work. At that moment of my life shit-shoveling seemed to be my assignment, and at that moment of my life I saw no immediate alternative at hand. I will not pretend that I came to enjoy the work, but in truth it was less unpleasant than you might imagine, and without any effort at all I can think of eight or ten far less delightful professions, though I would rather not. In astonishingly short order I stopped thinking entirely about the nature of the commodity I was handling and simply kept my mind focused on staying alive out there in the manure-fields. (There was some risk involved because the huffing and puffing of the snail you were following would drown out the sound of any other one in the vicinity, and it was all too easy to be crushed under one of those massive whopping ambulatory mountains if it came up behind you while you were concentrating intently on the snail just ahead.)

Nabomba Zom is one of those worlds that has no seasons. Night and day are of precisely equal lengths and the climate is nothing but delightful all the year round. So I am merely guessing when I say that six months went by while I was on that plantation. During that time my voice grew deeper and my beard began to sprout. And one day there was much excitement at the far end of the plantation—cars, shouts, people running back and forth. I wondered if some careless soul had been fatally flattened by a snail. Then the foreman buzzed me on my ear-phone and told me to head for the plantation-house that minute.

As it happened I had suffered a little accident just a few moments earlier. The snail I was following had suddenly gone into high gear, and in my effort to keep up with him I had slipped on a patch of the red-leafed moss and gone skidding belly-down into a mound of dung the size of a small asteroid.

"I need to wash first," I told the foreman. "I'm all covered with—"

"Now," he said.

"But I'm—"

"*Now.*"

They brought me before a man of astounding presence and power, who might have been fifty years old, or eighty, or a hundred fifty. I never knew, and he never seemed to grow a day older in all the years I was with him. He was slender for a Rom, almost slight, with narrow sloping shoulders and a shallow chest, and he wore no mustache. In his left ear were two silver rings, an ancient style just coming back into favor among us then. There was wondrous shrewdness in his face: a quick sly smile, just a wry twitch of his cheek, really, that warned potential adversaries to beware. He was no one you would want to try to best in a bargain. To say he looked shrewd was like saying that water looks wet. His eyes were ferociously penetrating. I felt transparent before those eyes: he was seeing my guts and my bones. As I stood before this formidable regal man all splattered and plastered and encrusted with snail-slops, he reached out his hand toward me.

"Closer."

"Sir, I—"

"Closer, boy. What's your name?"

"Yakoub. My father is Romano Nirano of Vietoris."

"Romano Nirano, eh?" He seemed impressed, or so I imagined. "How old are you?"

"Going to be thirteen, I think."

"You think. Runaway slave, are you?"

"A traveler, sir."

"Ah. A traveler. Of course. The grand tour of the universe, beginning with the celebrated snail-honey farms of Nabomba Zom. What are you, Kalderash Rom?"

"Yes, sir."

"Are you good with machines, as all the Kalderash are supposed to be?"

"My father is the greatest mechanic in the staryard of Vietorion."

"Your father is, yes." He nodded and pondered a moment. Then he turned and beckoned into another room. "Malilini? Is this the one you meant?"

A woman came out, or a girl; I was never sure. She might have been sixteen, or twenty-six, or thirty-six. Her age would always be her secret. She was unusually beautiful, and beautifully unusual. Her hair was an azure cloud, her eyes were warm and dark and set very far apart, her lips were full and inviting. I had seen that face before, but where? One of the whores in the mining town? No, none of them had been as beautiful as this. Some passenger on the starship? No. No, I remembered now: it was the face of the lovely ghost who had come to me several times on Megalo Kastro, both at the beggars' lodge and when

I lay drifting on the living sea. She had never spoken to me, only stared and smiled. We looked at each other now as though we had known each other a long while.

"Yakoub," she said. "At last."

I was bitterly ashamed, standing before such beauty in my dung-stained work-clothes.

"My daughter Malilini," said the kingly man. "I am Loiza la Vakako." He gestured to his robots. "Clean him. Dress him." They stripped me naked in an instant. I felt less ashamed being naked before her, before him, than I had been in my dreadful filth. They sprayed me and dried me and trimmed my hair and to my amazement they even ran a shaving-beam over my downy cheeks, and then they wrapped me in a pearly gray robe with a red sash and a high collar of deep rich blue. One of the robots spun a mirror out of air molecules in front of me to let me inspect myself. I was lovely. I was lost in admiration of myself. All this had taken only minutes. Malilini was glowing with pleasure at my transformation. Loiza la Vakako came close and examined me. He was scarcely any taller than I was. He studied me, nodding, obviously satisfied.

Then he took my elegant collar in both his hands and with one quick yank he ripped it halfway loose on the left side. I was stunned and appalled.

Loiza la Vakako laughed, a great whooping Rom laugh.

"May all your clothes rip and wear out like that! But may you live in health to a great old age!"

I realized that he was speaking to me in Romany. It was one of his Lowara customs, this ceremonial tearing of my new finery. He clapped me on the back and led me outside. By this time I understood that he was the Rom baro here, the great man of this planet, and I was going to live with him. I was not allowed to go to my hut for my things; but when we arrived at his palace after a three-hour flight across the shimmering wonder of that magnificent continent, my few pitiful little possessions were waiting for me in my suite of rooms, along with a host of lavish new belongings whose uses I was barely able to comprehend.

Now did I truly come to learn the meaning of splendor. The palace of Loiza la Vakako stood on the shore of a sea nearly as strange as the one that had come close to claiming my life on Megalo Kastro, for its water was red as blood, and throbbing heat came from it, almost at boiling temperature. Then there was a beach of pale lavender sand sloping steeply up toward a broad ridge where, amid a dense garden of shrubs and trees from a hundred worlds, the palace rose in airy swoops and arabesques. I never knew how many rooms it had, and very likely the number changed from day to day, for the palace was a thing of billowing fabric and sliding struts, light as a spider's web, forever transforming itself in new and ever more lovely ways as the rays of the hot blue sun waxed and waned through the day. Here I would live as a young Rom prince, dressed in the finest of robes, a new one every day, and dining on delicacies such as I had never imagined before and have never tasted since; here I would discover the meaning of wealth and power and the responsibilities that such things bring; I would have my first understanding of the mysteries of ghosting; here too I would learn a thing or two about the nature of love. But the greatest lesson of all that I would learn on Nabomba Zom had to do with the impermanence of grandeur and pleasure and comfort: for after having lived in the greatest of luxury until I had come to take such things utterly for granted, I was to see it all snatched from me in a moment. And snatched from the lordly Loiza la Vakako as well; but that was far in the future just then.

9.

HE HAD EIGHT DAUGHTERS BUT NO SONS. DAUGHTERS ARE a delight—I have had many of them myself, and would gladly have had more—but there is a way that a man feels about his sons that is quite different from the way he feels about daughters, and it has to do with the fact that some day we must die. When a man sees his son he sees the image of himself: himself reborn, himself regenerated, his own replacement, his claim on the future. Through his sons he marches onward into the centuries to come. They bear his face; they have his eyes, his chin, his mustache, his heart and balls. I love my daughters with all my heart but they cannot do that special thing for me that a son can do, and there is a difference in that, and any man who says it is not so is lying to you or to himself or both. At least this is it how it is among the Rom, and has been since the beginning of time. It may be otherwise for the Gaje; I have no way of knowing and no great concern about it.

I would not make too much of this matter. But when a man is as powerful as Loiza la Vakako, and has no sons, and takes in an unknown little dung-splattered boy to live in his home, there might be significance in it. Six of his daughters were married and lived in the far reaches of Nabomba Zom or on its major moons. He treated their husbands as princes but not, I think, as sons. A seventh daughter—Malilini—lived with him at the palace. Nothing was ever said of the eighth, though her portrait hung beside the other seven in the great hall; she had quarreled with her father long before, over what I will never know, and had taken up residence in some far corner of the galaxy.

Loiza la Vakako also had a brother, who ruled two of the outer and less blessed worlds of this solar system. Pulika Boshengro was his name and Loiza la Vakako rarely spoke of him, though he too was in the family portrait gallery, a dark man with a narrow forehead and a long dour face. In the portrait he looked so little like Loiza la Vakako that it was hard for me to believe that they had sprung from the same womb; but when I finally met him, many years later, I was able to see the resemblance instantly: in the bones beneath the flesh, in the soul behind the eyes.

Grand though his palace was, Loiza la Vakako allowed himself surprisingly little time to take joy of it. Even in him, that settled and contemplative man, the Rom restlessness dominated. He was constantly on the move, forever setting forth on journeys of inspection across his far-flung domain. He had to know what was going on everywhere. Though all the overseers of his plantations were capable and loyal, Loiza la Vakako could not allow himself to be a mere absentee master. And also he was Rom baro here, he was head of the Gypsy kumpania of Nabomba Zom, which meant that he had all manner of judicial and ritual responsibilities to carry out among his people.

From the beginning I often rode beside him when he made these tours. And learned more of the art of governing in a single afternoon than six years at a university could have given me.

Nabomba Zom is one of the nine kingly worlds of the galaxy. That is, it is a planet that was especially chosen by the Rom as their own, when the first settlement of the stars was carried out nine hundred or a thousand years ago. The rulers of the kingly worlds—the others are Galgala, Zimbalou, Xamur, Marajo, Iriarte, Darma Barma, Clard

Msat, and Estrilidis—hold their power, technically speaking, by direct grace of the King of the Rom, and each has the privilege of nominating one of the nine krisatora, the judges of the highest Rom court. Of course I knew very little of all this when I first came to live with Loiza la Vakako, but gradually he educated me in the intricacies of the system by which we hold our sprawling realm together.

As I traveled with him I came to comprehend something I had never suspected as a schoolboy on Vietoris or as a slave on Megalo Kastro: that to rule is a burden, not a privilege. There are certain rewards, yes. But only a fool would accept that burden for the sake of the rewards. Those who hold power do so because they have no choice: it is God's decree that has descended upon their heads and they must obey. Even if Syluise thinks it is not so.

I watched Loiza la Vakako, then, making decisions about the planting of crops or the damming of streams, about the price of grain, about trade with other planets, about taxes and import duties. I watched him holding court and settling the bewildering disputes of petty people in outlying provinces. And I thought of the lesson they had been trying to teach me on my last day at school, about the Thirteenth Emperor and how hard he worked. I had wondered then why an emperor would want to work so hard, when supreme power was his. Why not spend all your days and nights in feasting and singing and sipping fine wine? Now I understood that there was no choice about the work. It was the price of supreme power. It was what supreme power was: the privilege of toil beyond the comprehension of ordinary beings. There had never been any ruler, I realized—not even the famous wicked tyrants, not even the murderous monstrous villains—who had not found himself harnessed to the plow the moment he ascended the throne of office.

Still, there were comforts if you wanted them. A bit of compensation, I suppose. Loiza la Vakako toured his realm in an air-car that was a little palace in itself, a sleek teardrop-shaped vehicle bright as fire that moved with the speed of dreams. When you were aloft you had no sense of motion: you might have been drifting on a magic carpet. And there were soft wondrous draperies fashioned from the black-and-scarlet mantles of the great clam of the Sea of Poets, there were cushions upholstered in the shining leather of sand-dragon skin, there were floating globes of pure cool light. When we dismounted we were greeted by bowing officials who had strewn carpets of petals for us, and servants were waiting with fresh robes, bowls of fragrant juices, ripe fruits, smoked meats of mysterious origin.

Yet despite all this magnificence Loiza la Vakako's private quarters, both aboard the air-car and wherever he stopped to spend the night, were always strangely austere: a thin mattress on the floor, plain white wall-hangings, a pitcher of water by his side. It was as if he accepted the grandeur as something necessary, a requirement of office, but gladly put it all aside when he could be alone. If you would see the truth of a man, look at the room where he sleeps.

Nabomba Zom is a world that lends itself to magnificence. I have never seen any place more beautiful except for Xamur the matchless, which no world could surpass. But Nabomba Zom comes close. There is the amazing scarlet sea, which at sunrise reverberates as though struck by a hammer when the first blue rays of morning fall upon it. There are the pale green mountains soft as velvet that run down the spine of the great central continent, and the chain of lakes known as the Hundred Eyes, black as onyx and just as glistening, that lies east of them. The Viper Rift, that serpentine chasm five thousand kilometers long, whose walls shine like gold as they descend an unmeasurable distance to the fiery river in its remote depths. The Fountain of Wine, where invisible creatures carry out natural fermentation in a subterranean basin and a geyser sprays their delightful product into the air every hour. The Wall of Flame—the Dancing Hills—the Web of Jewels —the Great Sickle—

And all the fertile fields, from which every manner of crop pours forth. There is no world more bountiful. Even the dung of the giant snails, as I had already had occasion to discover, was of no little value.

Of course I didn't spend all my time touring this planet of wonders in Loiza la Vakako's air-car. There was the rest of my education to consider. I could read and write, more or less, but that was all the formal learning that I had arrived with. Loiza la Vakako had reasons —sound ones, as I would discover—for wanting me frequently to travel by his side as he carried out his official functions, but he also brought in tutors for me at the palace and he required me to take them seriously. Which I did; I have many appetites, and one of them is for knowledge. There is more to life than belching. I applied myself to my studies with zeal and dedication.

And then there was Malilini.

I didn't know what to make of her. She moved through the palace like a sprite, a goddess, a ghost—like anything but an ordinary mortal. I don't think I spoke six words to her, or she to me, in the first three years I lived there. But often I saw her watching me—she had her father's sly eyes—covertly from a distance, or simply staring frankly at me when we were in the same room.

She terrified me. Her beauty, her grace, her strangeness. I knew that she had come ghosting to visit me on Megalo Kastro—staring at me then too, never saying a word—and that she had watched over me as I lay adrift in that warm quivering sea into which the guild's man had thrown me. Why? Why, when they had summoned me from my dung-shoveling duties, had she said "Yakoub. At last," at our first true meeting?

I didn't dare ask. Shyness has never been part of my character; but in this one instance I was afraid to seek explanations, for fear I would shatter some fragile spell that was binding the two of us together. I told myself that in time I would know. Until then, wait. So I waited. I grew tall and broad and strong, and I let a mustache grow so that when I looked in the mirror I began to see myself with my father's face, and I learned languages and astronomy and history and many other things, and at dawn I would ride across the plateau behind the palace on the supple six-legged Iriarte horse that Loiza la Vakako had given me for my last birthday. Sometimes I would see her far away, glowing in the blue sunrise, riding an even swifter horse. Though I grew daily deeper into manhood, she never seemed to change: always a girl at the edge of woman's estate, radiant, without flaw.

Sometimes it wasn't Malilini that I saw, but Malilini's ghost. I saw her aura. And her ghostly smile, flickering only a moment out of that aura before she vanished, could set me ablaze with strange and troublesome emotion.

In those days I understood very little about ghosting, nor was there anyone I could turn to for information: it has never been something that we discuss easily even among ourselves, let alone care to set down in books. I had known since my days on Megalo Kastro that it is somehow possible for certain people to split their spirits loose from their bodies and go roaming around in far places, apparently invisible to most people but capable of making themselves seen—in a strange not-entirely-there way—whenever and to whomever they chose. These ghosts had an aura, an electrical crackling about them.

I realized now that one of the ghosts that had visited me on Megalo Kastro was Malilini's. And—now that I was beginning to wear my adult face—I became aware that one ghost, the one with the long mustache and the great roaring laugh, was very likely my own. Even now I saw him from time to time. Hovering for a flashing instant in the air in front of me, winking, grinning, amiably slapping my cheek in a lusty greeting.

If that man was me, I reasoned, then I must be capable of going ghosting. But how was it done? How? How?

Sometimes I would sit by myself for hours at a time on a great throne-shaped green rock at the edge of the scarlet sea and try to do it. I imagined myself driving a wedge down the side of my brain the way a stonemason would split a block of marble with a chisel, and spalling off a part of my soul that would be free to go floating to other worlds, other times. It never worked. I gave myself monumental headaches, as though someone really was hammering at my brain with a mason's wedge, but nothing else ever happened.

And then one day I found Malilini suddenly sitting beside me on that great green throne. I hadn't noticed her approaching at all.

"You'd like to know how to do it, wouldn't you?"

"What?"

"Ghosting. That's what you're trying to do. I know."

My cheeks flamed. My eyes would not meet hers. "What makes you think so?"

"Yakoub, Yakoub—"

"I'm simply trying to review my quadratic equations."

Her hand came to rest on mine. Her fragrance dizzied me. "Let me show you how," she said.

10.

*THE FIRST TIME YOU GO GHOSTING IS THE MOST FRIGHT-*ening experience you will ever have in your life. I think even dying must be a trifle, compared with that.

Your soul breaks in half. Part of you drops like a leaden turd to the ground and the other part bursts free, soaring up wildly, a starship out of control making random leaps across the cosmos. But it isn't just the cosmos you're traveling through. It's the river of time. That river flows from past to future, and you are heading upstream.

You see everything that ever was in all of time and space and none of it makes any sense to you. Whatever you see you are seeing for the first time. A chair explains itself to you, or a flower, or a fish, and you are incapable of understanding. You walk down a highway and you are not sure whether you are going east or west, until you realize that you are going in both directions at once. You are lost beyond hope. You choke on your own bewilderment. You wish you could cry but you have no idea what crying is like, or wishing.

A primeval terror takes hold of you, a fear that shakes you like a hundred earthquakes at once.

People you have never seen before smile at you and greet you—or are they saying goodbye? You take five steps up the hill and discover that you are descending. There are no landmarks. The world is water. The horizon bends. The stars fall like rain and make hot golden splashes all around you. You hear the sound of weeping; you hear laughter; you hear nothing. Silence tolls like a great bell. The world is a whirlpool. You begin to drown. Some creature is lodged in your throat. Your eyes are spinning in your head. That primeval terror intensifies and now you begin to understand what it is. It comes from the heart of the universe. The fear that you feel is the force that binds the atoms of the universe together. It is the fundamental substance. What makes all those particles cling to one another is terror: the dread of chaos. Of loneliness. Of loss. And with that understanding the fear begins to ebb. All bonds are loosened and it does not matter. You can learn to love chaos. Everything is streaming away from the center and all is well.

When the fear goes and the atoms lose their grip on one another, then at last you find your footing. You are floating freely in utter void. There is no way for you to fall because nothing exists. And in that emptiness you are able to make any choice you desire.

Here, you say. I will go here. You get there just like that. No one can see you unless you want to be seen. You don't collide with anything that's already there because you're surrounded by a thing called an interpolation zone that pushes everything out of the way. So you want to go to Megalo Kastro. Sure: there you are, Megalo Kastro. And you hover in the air over a steaming bowl of warm pink mud that spans half a world. A naked boy lies bobbing on the breast of that quivering fluid mass. He seems asleep. Dreaming. You smile at him.

"Yakoub?" you say. Your aura crackles. He opens his eyes. They shine with strength and fearlessness. Your ringing laughter enfolds him. "Swim, Yakoub. Swim. Swim."

How easy this is, now that you know the way!

11.

HER HAND WAS STILL RESTING ON MINE. WHEN SHE MADE a small movement as though to draw it away, I held it, and she did not resist.

I said, "Why did you want to go ghosting on Megalo Kastro in the first place?"

"To look at you."

"But you couldn't have any idea I existed!"

"Oh, yes," she said. "Of course I knew you existed."

"How could you?"

"Because you were going to come here."

"And how could you have known that?" I asked.

"Because you are here now," she said. And then she laughed. "Don't you understand? There is never any *in the first place.*"

FOUR:

People, Places, Worlds

Consider, for example, the times of Vespasian. Thou wilt see all these things, people marrying, bringing up children, sick, dying, warring, feasting, trafficking, cultivating the ground, flattering, obstinately arrogant, suspecting, plotting, wishing for some to die, grumbling about the present, loving, heaping up treasure, desiring consulship, kingly power. Well, then, the life of these people no longer exists at all. Again, remove to the times of Trajan. Again, all is the same. Their life too is gone. In like manner view all the other epochs of time and of whole nations, and see how many after great efforts soon fell and were resolved into the elements. But chiefly thou shouldst think of those whom thou hast thyself known distracting themselves about idle things, neglecting to do what was in accordance with their proper constitution, and to hold firmly to this and to be content with it. . . .

What then is that about which we ought to employ our serious pains? This one thing: thoughts just, and acts social, and words which never lie, and a disposition which gladly accepts all that happens, as necessary, as usual.

—Marcus Aurelius

1.

I THOUGHT OF MALILINI NOW AS I STOOD IN A BROAD GLIT-
tering field of Mulano's crusted ice, waiting for the relay-sweep to carry
me into space. How she had brought magic and mystery into my life;
how I had loved her; how she had been swept away from me down the
river of time. What if she had lived, and I had been able to take her
to be my wife? An idle thought. Meaningless. Useless. Like asking
myself, What if rain were to fall upward, What if gold grew on trees,
What if I had been born a Gajo instead of a Rom? On Galgala gold
does grow on trees. But I am Rom and the rain falls as it has always
fallen and Malilini is long dead and will be dead forever more.

I was alone. Damiano had already gone on ahead to make his own
plans and preparations. We would meet again later. It was nearly the
last moment of Double Day. The two suns of Mulano hovered on the
horizon, about to plummet from view. The sky was dark green, quickly
deepening into the gray of the momentary twilight. I narrowed my eyes
and searched the heavens for Romany Star, as I had always done at that
moment of the day.

And in that moment the dazzling radiance of the relay-sweep aura
burst high into the air and a roving tendril of the sweep found me and
caught me up and flung me far out into the Great Dark. Goodbye,
goodbye, a long goodbye to my quiet life on Mulano! Yakoub's on his
way again.

Only a madman could enjoy traveling by relay-sweep. And if you
aren't a madman when you set out, there's a fair chance that you will
be by the time the sweep turns you loose.

For some people it's the sheer peril of the process that sends them
around the bend, or the absurd implausibility of the whole thing. What
you are doing, after all, is going out by yourself into space without a
starship around you or anything else except an invisible sphere of force,
and dropping in free fall through hundreds or even thousands of light-
years, which is one hell of a drop. The sweep picks you up and flicks
you out into nowhere, and there you stand, neatly cocooned in the little
sphere of safety that your journey-helmet has woven about you, plum-

meting across the universe with nothing but empty space at your elbow. It's vertigo to the fiftieth power for anyone who allows himself to buy into the notion that he's actually falling from one end of the galaxy to the other.

That part of it has never bothered me at all. When you have held the jump-handles in your hands as often as I have, when you have lifted starships through wink-out and hurled them across the sky, a little bit of relay-sweep travel doesn't seem like much of a challenge.

Gypsies were born for traveling, anyway, and any means of transportation that takes you from one place to another is all right with us. It isn't as though you see stars and planets flashing by all the time: you aren't in realspace at all, but in this or that adjacent auxiliary space, taking zigzag shortcuts through wormholes in the continuum. Which is why the journey doesn't take you thousands of years and why you aren't in any danger of getting tossed into some star or crashing into a planet that happens to lie in your path. So there's no serious risk in it. Oh, maybe one traveler in a hundred thousand gets caught in a shunt malfunction and spends the rest of his life out there in his sweep-sphere, hanging suspended in the middle of nowhere for ten or twenty thousand realtime years. That's a miserable kind of fate but the odds against its happening to you are pretty favorable ones. Practically every relay-sweep traveler gets where he wants to go. Eventually.

No, what troubled me wasn't the risk: as I've already said, it was the boredom. The stasis. The utter inexorable inescapable solitude. The mind going clickety-clack while the body rests in metabolic slowdown. The clamor of your thoughts. No one to talk to but yourself as the random search of the space-time lattice goes on and on and you wait for the shunt that will bring you out on an inhabited world reasonably close to the one you intended to reach. A starship's wink-jump is *fast*. Relay isn't. You dangle out there and you wait. And you wait.

I am, God knows, enormously fond of my own company. I can amuse myself thoroughly and consistently. All the same, enough can sometimes be enough, and maybe even a little more than that.

What the hell. Nobody had *forced* me to go creeping around in remote worlds that didn't have regular starship service. Of my own free will had I chosen to go to Mulano. Now, of my own free will—more or less—did I choose to return, and the only way to get back was by relay-sweep, and so be it. I would simply be patient until my patience was exhausted, and then I would find some more patience somewhere.

As it happened, I was lucky this time.

I braced myself for the long haul and muttered a bahtalo drom for myself, and off I went. I took a deep breath as the stars winked out all around me and I dropped into auxiliary space. And in that gray dreary nowhereness I sang and told myself jokes and laughed loud enough to bend the walls of my sphere. I recited the whole Rom Swatura from beginning to end, the entire ancient chronicle starting with the departure from Romany Star and running through all that had followed it; and when I ran out of that I dreamed up a fanciful continuation of it that stretched over the next ten thousand years that are to come. I made a poem out of the names of all the Kings of the Rom spelled backwards. I drew up lists of all the other kings and emperors I could think of out of Earth history. I made a list of every woman whose breasts had ever felt the touch of my hands. Oh, yes, I passed the time.

On and on I plummeted, toppling through space. I don't know how long the journey took. It didn't matter at all. You have no real way of telling anyway. Once I made a relay jump that covered a mere fifty light-years and cost me a full year of elapsed realtime time. On another jump I crossed from Trinigalee Chase to Duud Shabeel, which is about as far as you can go and still remain in the known part of the galaxy, in less than an hour. There's never any way of knowing how it will turn out.

But this time the time passed very swiftly for me. Maybe my body was in suspended animation but my mind was throbbing and pulsing with eager plans. I had been in cold storage on Mulano too long; now I was impatient to get back into the Empire and set to work at the heavy tasks that faced me. Sometimes impatience can make a long journey seem a thousand times as long as it is, but this time it had the opposite effect for me. I was keyed up. I was charged. A hundred seventy-two years old, me? Up your buliasa! I felt like a boy again. Not a day over fifty, me.

Going back, taking charge. Setting straight all that had become snarled during my absence. Doing something about the state of the Empire, the state of the Kingdom, the antics of the high lords, the maneuvers of my terrible son Shandor—oh, yes, there was plenty waiting for me! I loved it. I swam in it all the way back. It was the shortest swiftest jolliest relay-sweep journey I had ever undertaken.

Ah there, you worlds of the Imperium! Remember me?

Hoy! Yakoub! Yakoub! Yakoub!

On my way back at last!

2.

IF THINGS HAD BEEN DIFFERENT I WOULD HAVE BEEN Loiza La Vakako's son-in-law and in the fullness of time I would probably have come to inherit the rich overflowing bounty that was Nabomba Zom. Certainly things were heading in that direction. And then someone else would have become King of the Gypsies, most likely, because why would I have let them talk me into leaving my real and glorious domain and my true and splendid palace to take up all the heartaches and struggles of the Kingdom?

But that was not how things worked out. Maybe in some other universe Yakoub grew rich and fat and old and sleepy and died happily in the arms of his beautiful Malilini years ago by the shores of the scarlet sea. And the crown of the Rom went to some dazzling brilliant leader whose cleverness was far superior to mine and who has already reclaimed Romany Star for his people and done many other wonderful things. But in the universe where I live everything has turned out in quite another way.

I regret all those splendors and happinesses that I might have had but lost, I suppose. And I suppose I should lament all the hardships that came my way after the downfall of Nabomba Zom. All the same, though, do I have any real complaint? I've eaten well and lived well and loved well. I have been given great tasks to do and unless I am greatly fooling myself I think I have done them well. Take one thing and another and it seems to me that the life I have lived hasn't been anything to lament about, bumps and bruises notwithstanding. We need a few bruises, and worse than bruises, to teach us the real meaning of happiness. And in any case this was the life I was meant to live: not the other. That one was only a dream.

Strangely I am unable to remember when Malilini and I first became lovers, I who remember so much and in such fine detail. But it was a gradual process and maybe there was no first time. Perhaps we always were lovers. Perhaps never.

We went riding together and swam together in the warm streams that fed the hot scarlet sea and sometimes we went ghosting together, now that I had learned the trick of it. We slipped away in our ghostly way to most of the other kingly worlds, Marajo and Galgala and Darma Barma, Iriarte and Xamur. I had never dreamed such richness could exist, as I saw on those noble planets. The universe seemed to me to be like a great hymn of joy, crying out in beauty from a thousand throats at once.

We went far in space when we ghosted but we never went any great distance in time. A year or two back, five, ten, that was all. I think she feared breaking away into the deeper realms of time. And in those days I never knew that it was possible, or I would have raged hungrily for it: to see old lost Earth, to visit the pyramids of Egypt and the temples of Babylon, to ghost on backward in time into Atlantis itself. Even to visit Romany Star! But none of that did I do, for lack of knowing that it could be done.

I was a man now and Malilini still was whatever Malilini was: beautiful, unchanging, ever young. I suppose we kissed, finally. I suppose we clasped hands and held them that way for an hour. I suppose we came laughing out of the crimson stream and shook our naked bodies dry under the powerful blue sun and turned to each other and embraced. And then I suppose a moment came when the embrace went on and on until there was no longer any boundary between her and me, and we fused into one, her long slender thighs clasped about me, her pale supple slender form and my thick-muscled shagginess joining at last. And then that fiery spurting moment of pleasure. But I have lost the memories of it. I suppose thinking of these things was too painful.

I knew her but I never knew her. She never said much. She was sparkling and airy but also she was elusive, remote, always an enigma. Why hadn't she ever loved before? Why did she love now? I never looked for answers. I know I would never have received them. I would have done as well turning to the stars in the heavens and asking why this one burned with a blue fire and this one with a red, this one yellow and this one white.

Even so, it was understood after a time that we were betrothed. I began calling Loiza la Vakako "father" and it seemed completely natural. Vietoris and my real family were as forgotten to me as yesterday's dream. When I rode out across Nabomba Zom in the air-car of Loiza la Vakako I knew that I was being groomed to take his place some day as the monarch of this resplendent world. By now I had met the husbands of his other daughters and I could tell that each of them had failed in some way to fulfill the hope that Loiza la Vakako had placed in him. That was a wound and a sadness to Loiza la Vakako, but he would never let it show. They were good men, they ruled their provinces carefully and well, but there was some last measure of depth and breadth missing from them, it seemed, and none of them would inherit the domain, only that part of it that was his own fief.

And I? What did I have that they lacked?

I didn't have the foggiest idea. But Loiza la Vakako saw it. Somehow he saw the kingliness in me when I myself felt not a trace of it. I had been a little slave boy and then I had been a snotty street-begging urchin and now by some flukish turn of fate I was living the life of a rich young prince, but rich young princes are generally not very profound characters and neither was I. What I wanted most to do was ride on the moors and swim in the scarlet ocean and plunge into the shimmering depths of the Hundred Eyes, and then to turn to Malilini and slide my trembling hands along the insides of her thighs; and somehow Loiza la Vakako saw in me a king. Well, there was a king hidden inside me, all right. But it took Loiza la Vakako to perceive him there.

To celebrate our betrothal he gave a grand Rom patshiv, a ceremonial feast. And that was the one mistake he made in all his serene and rich life of wisdom and foresight, and it brought his ruination and mine.

The patshiv was months in the planning. Word went out to all corners of Nabomba Zom that the cream of every harvest was to be set aside for it; and the agents of Loiza la Vakako on all the kingly planets and half the worlds of the Imperium were instructed to ship wondrous foods and wines to us. Loiza la Vakako's six married daughters and their six princely husbands were to be there, and even Loiza la Vakako's brother, the dark and somber-faced Pulika Boshengro, would come down from his realm on one of the neighboring worlds.

A great pavilion was built in the courtyard of the palace, and long tables, Rom-fashion, were set up under an arbor of arching glimmervines that would cast a sweet tingling radiance over the feast. Now came the cooks, platoons of them, legions of them, to set to work at mincing meats and chopping garnishes, seasoning the game birds with sage and thyme and marjoram, flavoring the beasts on the spits with peppercorns and rosemary, preparing the huge platters of beans with cream and lentils, mashed peas in vinegar, cucumbers rich with yogurt and dill, the olives, the horseradishes, the meatballs spiced with nutmeg, all the dishes that have been beloved of the Rom for so many thousands of years. And the casks of wine! The flagons of brandy! The barrels of beer!

And when everything was ready and the whole clan had assembled Loiza la Vakako came forth from the palace in robes of such majesty and opulence that it was hard for me to remember the simplicity of his private rooms, the austerity and even asceticism of his inner life. I was in robes of the same magnificence, walking beside him. And Malilini, shimmering with her own beauty and gowned in something that seemed to be nothing more than spun air, against which her dark glowing loveliness burned all the more brilliantly.

Loiza la Vakako had intended this feast to be one such as Nabomba Zom had never seen before. That would go down in the legends of the Rom as unsurpassed in all our history and unsurpassable by the generations to come. Well, there is no denying that it was a feast such as Nabomba Zom had never seen before. But not in the way that Loiza la Vakako had in mind. And as for being unsurpassed and unsurpassable—no, that was not to be.

We took our seats at the high table: Loiza la Vakako in the center, his brother Pulika Boshengro at his left, Malilini to his right, me on Malilini's other side. All about us were lords and ladies of the realm, the six daughters, the six sons-in-law, the local archimandrite and three of his thaumaturges, the imperial consul and a bunch of his hierodules, assorted high vassals from the outlying plantations, and a host of others, including a cadre of nobles that Pulika Boshengro had brought with him from his own court, all garbed in swirling costumes of the most startling brightness.

Loiza la Vakako stretched forth his arms in benediction, inviting everyone to sit.

The servitors poured the first round of wine. They heaped the salads and smoked meats on our plates. We all waited. The guest from the most distant land must taste the first morsel.

That was Pulika Boshengro. He rose—a small, compact man like his brother, full of coiled energy and passion. His eyes gleamed with a chilly sort of intelligence.

Beside him on the table lay his lavuta, his violin, a good old Gypsy fiddle. This Pulika Boshengro was said to be a musician of high attainments, who would open our feast with one of the ancient tunes, a quick fiery melody to start the festivities the right way. A great silence fell. Pulika Boshengro ran his fingers lightly up and down the fingerboard of his fiddle and reached for his bow. All around the pavilion people were smiling and nodding and closing their eyes as if they could already hear the music.

Pulika Boshengro drew the bow across the strings. But what came forth was no sweet old Gypsy tune. It was three harsh fierce discordant scraping notes.

A signal. A cue for action.

The henchmen of Pulika Boshengro moved with astonishing speed. Before the third note had died away I was pulled roughly to my feet and I felt an arm tight across my throat and a knife in the small of my back. All along the head table the same thing was happening to Loiza la Vakako, to Malilini, to the six sons-in-law and their wives. Sharp gasps went up from the guests at the lower tables, but no one moved. In a single instant we were all hostages.

I turned my head to the left and stared across Malilini at Loiza la Vakako. His face was calm and his eyes were untroubled, as though he had seen this coming and wasn't at all surprised, or as though the strength of his soul was such that not even being seized at his own feasting-table could disturb his balance. He smiled at me.

Then one of Pulika Boshengro's men grunted in alarm. He pointed at Malilini.

If I live to be a thousand this moment will blaze furiously in my mind. I looked toward her; and I saw her face going strange. Her eyes were clouded, her nostrils were flaring, the corners of her mouth were pulled back in a grimace that was not a smile.

I knew the meaning of that expression. She was summoning her power so that she could go ghosting.

Pulika Boshengro knew what that face meant too. And saw at once what I was too dense to understand in that first wild moment: that what she intended to do was slip away a short distance into the past, a week perhaps or even less, and warn her father that his brother must not be admitted to the feast.

Now that coiled energy of his came into play, and that chilly intelligence. An imploder leaped into Pulika Boshengro's hand, a little steel-jacketed frog-nosed weapon. He fired once—a soft blurping sound—and Malilini seemed to rise and float away from him, up and back and across the feasting-table. She lay sprawled face upward amidst the wine-flasks and the platters of meat and she did not move.

For a moment Loiza la Vakako seemed to crumple. His face dissolved and his shoulders heaved as if he had been struck by an enormous mallet. Then his great strength reasserted itself and he stood straight again, unmoving and seemingly unmoved. But I saw that winter had entered his eyes. And then for a time I saw nothing at all, for my tears came flooding forth and with them came such an eruption of fiery anger that it blinded me. I let out a tremendous cry and tried to swing around, giving no thought to the blade that was pricking my back or the arm pressing with choking force against my throat. My hands were still free; I clawed for eyes, lips, nostrils, anything.

"Yakoub," said Loiza la Vakako quietly. *"No."*

Somehow that voice cut through my madness; or perhaps it was the powerful arm tightening on my windpipe.

I subsided all at once, and stood slumped, looking at my feet. It was over. We were prisoners and Pulika Boshengro had captured Nabomba Zom with three screeches of his fiddle. A whole world had fallen and there had been but a single casualty.

He had brooded in secret for years over what he imagined to be the injustice of the family inheritance that had given Nabomba Zom to his brother, and nothing but two bleak and stormy little worlds to him. All this time Pulika Boshengro had pretended love and fealty, waiting for his moment. No one but a brother could have overthrown Loiza la Vakako; for he was well guarded and even the armies of the Imperium would have been hard pressed to take Nabomba Zom. But who looks for treachery at his own feasting-table? Who places armed guards between himself and his brother? Certainly not a Rom, you would say, not anyone in whose heart the true blood flows. Our family bonds come before all else. Yet we are not all saints, are we? For Pulika Boshengro there was a stronger force than love of family.

It was done and it could not be undone. No matter that there had been hundreds of witnesses, high officials of the Imperium among them, and judges and senators of Nabomba Zom. To the Imperium this was purely an internal matter, a squabble among the Rom lords of Nabomba Zom; there was no reason to interfere. And the judges and senators of Nabomba Zom were nothing more than vassals; they owed their allegiance not to some code of laws but to the prince of their world, who was Loiza la Vakako no longer, but now Pulika Boshengro, by right of conquest.

Primitive, barbaric stuff, yes. But we do well to remember that such things still can happen even in our age of magic and miracles. We may live two hundred years instead of sixty, we may dance from star to star like angels, we may wrench whole planets from their orbits and set them spinning through the sky; but even so we carry the primordial ape within us, and the primordial serpent as well. We live by treaties of courtesy and civilized behavior; but treaties are only words. Greed and passion have not yet been expunged from our genes. And so we remain at the mercy of the worst among us. And so we must beware. Only in a village without a dog, the old Rom saying goes, can a man walk without carrying a stick.

I suppose it still might have been possible to overthrow the usurper and restore Loiza la Vakako to his place, if anyone had been willing to lead the way. Pulika Boshengro had come to Nabomba Zom with only a handful of men from his home world. And Loiza la Vakako was wise and good and everyone loved and respected him, while Pulika Boshengro had shown himself to be a man to fear and mistrust.

But there wasn't any uprising of loyal vassals. After the first shock and amazement of the events of the banquet and the coup that had followed it, life went on as usual for the people of Nabomba Zom, both great and small. The family of Loiza la Vakako was in custody—we were all dead, for all anyone on the outside knew—and there was a new master in the palace. A change of government, that was all it was. Within days the vassals of Pulika Boshengro were arriving by the thousands and the spoils were being divided; and that was that. Loiza la Vakako had fallen; his wealth and splendor had passed to his brother; life went on. And I had lost my beloved and all my bright prospects for the future in one terrible moment.

We were kept in cells behind the palace stables, penned in foul little force-spheres like beasts awaiting the butcher. Loiza la Vakako and I shared one cell. I knew we were going to be put to death sooner or later and I started making my final atonements every time I saw the shadow of the jailer outside. But Loiza la Vakako had no such fears. "If he had meant to kill us," he said, when I had voiced my uneasiness for the hundredth time, "he would have done it at the feast. He'll get rid of us some other way."

He was entirely at ease, altogether placid and composed. The loss of his kingdom, his palace, his world itself, seemed to mean nothing to him. I knew that the murder of his daughter before his eyes had seared and withered his soul, but he refused even to speak of her death and showed no sign of grief.

"If only your brother had been a moment slower," I blurted finally. "If only she had been able to get away and give us a warning—"

"No," he said. "It was wrong for her to attempt it."

"Wrong? Why?"

"Because no warning was ever given. If it had been meant for there to be a warning, we would have received it, and none of this would have happened."

"But that's exactly it! If she had managed it she could have changed everything!"

"Nothing can ever be changed," said Loiza la Vakako.

There it was again: the fatalism of the Rom, the cool acceptance of what is as what must be. As though it is all written imperishably in the book of time and for all our power of ghosting we dare not try to alter it. A streak of that fatalism runs through our souls like dark oil on the breast of shining water. A thousand times a day I thought of slipping away myself to the hour before the banquet and giving the warning that would save Malilini; but each time I looked toward Loiza la Vakako I came up against his steely acceptance of what had happened, and I didn't dare. No warning could be given because none had been received. As Malilini had said in a happier moment long before, "There is never any *in the first place.*" Everything is circular and everything is fixed. There is no such thing as prophecy: there is only the giving of reports on the known facts of the future, which is as sealed and unchangeable as the past. When I came to do more ghosting myself I would understand that more clearly. That there is a law—call it a moral law; no monarch ever put it on the lawbooks—that we must not use our power to change the past, lest we tumble everything into chaos. Loiza la Vakako meant to live by that law even though it cost him his daughter and his domain. By daring to break the law that must never be broken Malilini had condemned herself and no one now could save her. I had to abide by that. But inside myself I was screaming against the madness of it, telling myself over and over that it still was possible to save Malilini and to spare Loiza la Vakako from overthrow, if only Loiza la Vakako would permit it. And that he would never do. Why, he seemed almost to be blaming her for her own death!

I waited now for mine. But the days passed and we were left to ourselves, thrown a little food now and then but otherwise ignored. We grew filthy and sour-breathed and our teeth felt as if they were coming loose. I could not believe how far we had fallen. I wondered what depths still gaped for us.

Loiza la Vakako's serenity never faltered. I asked him how he remained so tranquil in the face of such grief and he shrugged, and said that everything was part of God's plan: who was he to debate strategy with the Master of All? It is God who orders events and we who obey, no matter how strange or wrong or even evil the shape of those events may seem to us.

I tried to accept his wisdom and make it part of me. But my despair was too great. I could abide the loss of the comforts that my life on Nabomba Zom had brought. Those things had come to me by pranks of fate; I could accept their departure in the same way. But what kind of God was it who let brother cast down brother? How did it serve the welfare of this world to put the tyrant Pulika Boshengro in the place of the wise Loiza la Vakako? And most bitter of all to me—who could justify the slaying of Malilini? To cast such beauty from the world so soon—no. No. No. No.

Sometimes ghosts came to me as I lay sobbing to myself. They never spoke, but they would hold out their hands to me in gestures of consolation, or smile, or even wink. One who came was the one who I now knew to be my future self, robust and hearty and overflowing with laughter. He was the one who winked. So I understood that I was not going to die in this place. And I saw also, from his wink, that my sense of heavy tragic gloom was one day going to lift, that I would laugh and know joy again. Inconceivable though that was to me in my despondency.

What was happening during all these days or weeks of captivity was that Pulika Boshengro was negotiating our enslavement. He meant to scatter the family of Loiza la Vakako to the far corners of the sky.

"All right, come out of there, you two," our jailer told us finally, and we crept forth into the great blue blaze of day.

I had been sold to a place called Alta Hannalanna, which I had never heard of. Loiza la Vakako's lips quirked ever so slightly when I told him, as if he had to struggle to hold back from me the truth of how dreadful a place that was. He himself was to go to Gran Chingada: again, a world unknown to me. I asked him about it and he said only, with a barely perceptible toss of his head, "They have great forests there, extraordinary trees. Wood from Gran Chingada draws a high price wherever it is sold." Only later did I learn what sort of conditions prevailed in the terrifying forests of that prehistoric world: the men in the logging camps were lucky to last eighteen months on Gran Chingada, where the grass itself would eat you alive if you gave it half a chance. Where vampire lizards the size of your hand came springing up out of scarlet flowers and went straight for your throat. Loiza la Vakako was being sent to his death. And so, I suspected, was I, despite the visits of my ghosts. But Loiza la Vakako would not tell me anything at all of Alta Hannalanna.

In those days there was no imperial starship service from Nabomba Zom to Alta Hannalanna, or to Gran Chingada. And so I discovered for the first time what it was like to travel by relay-sweep. Loiza la Vakako and I were marched out and trussed up and journey-helmets were clapped over us and our coordinates were set for us, so that we would be caught and thrown out into space toward the worlds of our slavery.

He was calm to the last. "Think of it as part of your education, Yakoub," he advised me. "Think of *everything* as part of your education."

And he smiled and blew a kiss to me, and they closed him into his sphere of force. I never saw that great man again, except once, long afterward. My turn came next. I stood there alone in midday sun, half blinded by the glare, not knowing in any way what was about to befall me and trying to tell myself that it was all for the best, that all of this was, as Loiza la Vakako said, simply part of my education. But I was frightened. I would be lying most wickedly if I tried to tell you I was not frightened. I had my whole life still ahead of me and I knew that if I didn't die in this abominable jaunt through space I would surely perish young on Alta Hannalanna, which made me angry but which also filled me with dread. It wasn't being dead that frightened me, but the moments just before dying, when I would lie there knowing that my life was being taken away from me before it had really begun. I did manage to keep my bowels under control, at least; not everyone would have managed that. I waited a long while in terrible fear and then I was yanked aloft and the world vanished about me. I muttered a spell of protection for myself, though I didn't place much faith in its power just then. And I went whirling away into God knows where on my way toward slavery on Alta Hannalanna.

Now, something like a hundred fifty years later, I found myself again and again thinking back to that first relay-sweep journey. How miserable I had been, how terrified, how altogether absurd. But I was very young then and I hadn't yet come to see the world the way a wise man like Loiza la Vakako did. Indeed it *is* all part of your education, everything. You are never taught anything by hiding in the dark and sucking on your thumb. It is in the water, and only in the water, that you learn how to swim.

Once more now was I flying across the void toward unknown adventures and an unknown fate. But by this time I had already had my education, and I was prepared for whatever would come. And so I sang and laughed and let the time glide by, in my journey back to the Empire from frosty Mulano, until I heard the whistling in my ears that told me that final shunt had been achieved and I was about to make my re-entry into the universe of men.

3.

XAMUR.

I knew at once that that must be where I had landed.

There's a moment of serious disorientation when you come out of relay, when your mind feels like it's been turned inside out like a hungry starfish's stomach and you can't tell your fingers from your ears. It lasts anywhere from fifteen seconds to fifteen minutes, depending on the resilience of your nervous system, and while it's going on it feels not tremendously different from the sensations you sometimes feel at the beginning of a ghosting. I went through all that now. This time it lasted about half a minute, for me. But that half minute was enough to tell me that I was on Xamur. More than enough. I knew right away, by the fragrance of the air. By one sweet wondrous whiff of it.

Xamur is listed among the nine kingly planets, but it really deserves some sort of higher designation, though I can't immediately think of one. *Godly* is a little too strong, maybe. But you get my drift. The place is simply paradise. It is a land of milk and honey and even better things.

The air is perfume—I don't mean the air is *like* perfume, it *is* perfume—and the sea might just as well be wine, because a sip of it will make you smile and five sips make you euphoric and a dozen good gulps will lay you out with a case of terminal giggles. The sky is a deep rich blue-green boldly streaked with red and yellow, a fantastic array of colors, and the atmosphere has some electric property that gives every-thing a shimmering halo, a dreamlike aurora. Under that dazzling sky the landscape is serene and orderly and perfect, almost maddeningly restful, every tree placed just so, every brook, every hill. It's all so beautiful you could cry: you stare at it and you feel that beauty in your heart, your belly, your balls. I can't tell you who made the worlds of this universe, but I do know this: that He must have made Xamur last, because all the other planets were the rough drafts and Xamur was plainly His final revised and edited statement on the subject.

Landing there was a delicious stroke of luck. You can't expect seven-decimal accuracy when you travel by relay-sweep, and in dialing up my destination coordinates when I left Mulano I had specified that any of the nine kingly planets would do. Except Galgala, that is. Galgala was in my son Shandor's control, I assumed, and it didn't seem wise for me to walk right into his headquarters alone and undefended before I knew what was going on. Later on I would do exactly that, of course; but that was later on. Right now any of the other kingly planets would have been an acceptable base of operations for me: Iriarte, say, or my cousin Damiano's Marajo, or even wandering Zimbalou. If I could have picked one, though, Xamur is the one I would have picked. And now I had it.

And it had me.

I stood there in that first dizzy moment breathing in the perfume and staring at the swirling colors of the sky and looking across the way at the green and glorious towers of the city of Ashen Devlesa, whose name means "May you remain with God" in Romany. And I felt myself being grabbed by an invisible force and swept into the air. I went soaring across the countryside in a wild swooping ride that ended when I was dumped down like a sack of onions in an open-roofed courtyard.

I picked myself up, blinking and grumbling, and looked around. Towering columns of speckled blue stone walled me in on all sides.

"All right, where the hell am I?" I asked the sky.

And the sky answered me. The sound of my voice activated some sort of responder device and out of mid-air came pleasant synthetic female tones telling me, first in Imperial and then in Romany, "You are in the Ashen Devlesa holding tank of the Imperial Xamur Department of Immigration."

"You mean I'm a prisoner?"

A long itchy silence. What were they doing, looking up "prisoner" in the dictionary?

I breathed perfumed air, in-out, in-out, making little hormonal adjustments to keep myself calm. Vague hissing and buzzing sounds came from overhead.

Then, finally: "You are not a prisoner. You are in detention. You are awaiting normal clearance procedures."

Oh.

That was annoying, sure. But not really surprising. Or very threatening, really. This was just bureaucratic bullshit: I knew how to deal with that. I felt myself easing.

When you land on a non-imperial world like Mulano you are of course completely on your own from the moment you drop from your force-field. But if the sweep puts you down anywhere in the Imperium, your arrival is a matter of record once the immigration scanner of the planet where you are arriving detects your signal, which is usually six to twelve hours before your landing. So there had been plenty of time for Xamur Immigration to get a fix on me and grab me with a tractor beam the instant my sweep-tendril released me. A routine pickup of an unscheduled arrivee from God knew where.

"So?" I said. "Let's get on with it, then. Bring on your normal procedures. You think I came to Xamur to stand around in here and admire the architecture of your holding tank?"

Almost at once someone official-looking poked his nose between two of the stone columns. He looked at me and made a little gleeping sound and went away, and came back with another of his kind. They gleeped and gobbled and honked at each other some more and went back outside for further reinforcements. In a matter of moments half a dozen people in the uniforms of the Imperial Xamur Department of Immigration were staring at me in total wonder and disbelief.

They couldn't have been much more flabbergasted, I guess, if they had reeled in the Emperor Napoleon, or Mohammed, or the Queen of the Betelgeuse Confederacy.

They knew right away who I was, of course. Not only by the face, the eyes, the mustachios. Before setting out from Mulano I had taken the trouble to don my seal of office, which I hadn't worn in maybe ten or fifteen years. Now great pulsing heroic splashes of light were cannoning off my brow in that flamboyant gaudy way which is at once so overwhelming and so absurd. It was like a broadcast going out on every wavelength of the spectrum at once, hammering in the news: KING—KING—KING—KING. I might just as well have come out of the relay-sweep wearing a crown of gold and emeralds and rubies half a meter high.

Two or three of the Immigration people were Rom. They were down on their knees in a flash, making the signs of respect and muttering my name. The Gaje ones did no such thing, naturally. But they were plainly taken aback, and they stood there gaping, goggling, twitching, and yawping.

I knew what they were thinking, too. They were thinking, This sly old bastard has turned up without warning, without bothering to trouble himself about using diplomatic channels at all. We can't send him away without touching off a terrific uprising among his followers, but we can't admit him without dragging Xamur into whatever enormous Rom power-struggle the old bastard's return is probably going to touch off, and no matter which way we go we are very likely to lose our jobs over this. Or thoughts to that effect.

I switched off my seal of office. It was blinding everybody in the holding tank. To the Rom who were groveling at my feet I said in Romany, "Get up, you idiots. I'm only your king, not God Almighty." To the others, those miserable terrified Gaje civil servants, I said in a more kindly way, "I'm not here on a visit of state or on any sort of political mission. I've come here purely as a private citizen who owns property on this world."

"But you are King Yakoub?" one of them stammered.

"Certainly I am."

"I don't think we have a protocol on former kings," said one of the others nervously, and brought up something on a screen that was just out of my direct line of sight. "Officials to notify, appropriate municipal response, parades, light-spikes, sky-banners, display of regalia, pyrotechnic celebrations—no, there's nothing here that covers any such—"

"I'm not a former king," I said quietly.

The Gaje officials looked at me in bewilderment and the Rom officials looked at me in horror.

One of the Rom said, "Sir, the covenant of abdication—"

"Don't worry yourself about it, child. Whatever stories about me that you may have heard coming out of Galgala were highly inaccurate."

One of the Gaje—he seemed to be the highest ranking of the bunch —made a frantic gesture and something else came sliding up on the screen. This time I moved around and got a squint at it. It was the table of reception protocol for a royal visit.

"You are still king, then?"

"When did I say that?"

They looked more baffled than ever.

But I wasn't ready to take up the issue of whether I was or was not still king just now. Especially not in a holding tank in front of a bunch of Immigration Department flunkeys. Let them puzzle over it, I thought. *He denies being a former king—but he doesn't directly assert that he's the* present *king—but on the other hand—and furthermore—nevertheless—contrariwise—*Yes, let them stew.

"The question of the kingship is neither here nor there," I said airily. "I just told you: this is a private visit for me. I'm here to inspect my estates at Kamaviben and nothing more. I don't want there to be any fuss made over me." And gave them my most regal glare. "Is that understood?"

4.

BUT I SHOULD HAVE KNOWN BETTER. OF COURSE THERE was fuss, and plenty of it.

Bureaucrats! Accursed paper-shuffling functionaries! Pettifogging little tenth-echelon panjandrums! I'd sooner have the honest refreshing company of a herd of salizonga snails any day.

In general I am not the sort of person whom anyone is likely to call naive. Not at *my* age. But I would have to agree that I was being naive, and then some, to have entertained the fantasy that they might have just let me walk out of that holding tank without any sort of complication. There was no way that the King of the Gypsies whether incumbent or retired was going to enter Xamur or any other kingly world in secrecy and privacy, no matter how much blustering and storming he did. That I understood. But I did imagine that they would admit me with a minimum of pomp and circumstance, if that was what I seemed to want.

I was wrong.

Kings and even ex-kings may have vast power over this and that, but when it comes to matters of protocol the bureaucrats always get the last word. In this case I had the Rom immigration people to blame as much as the Gaje, or more so. The Rom saw their king—or their ex-king, whichever I was—coming to town unexpectedly and they felt it absolutely incumbent upon themselves to cry hallelujah over me so that I would be properly covered with the appropriate glory.

Therefore they passed the news of my arrival up to the highest levels of the Xamur imperial administration and inevitably from that point on there was no halting the avalanche-like force of the bureaucracy as it swung eagerly into full action. You can't expect governmental functionaries to carry out any sort of useful activities, naturally—the whole concept is practically a contradiction in terms—but give them something meaningless like an official welcome to organize and it's their finest hour. It was all that I could do to head off a full-scale parade along the shining ramparts of Ashen Devlesa. But I did have to go through an interminable reception at the capital, a grand pyrotechnikon that lit up the skies over four continents, a noisy and crashingly boring concert by the Xamur Symphony, and a banquet so ridiculously inept in its overelaboration that it would have sent Julien de Gramont off weeping to light a candle to the memory of Escoffier.

All of this was a nuisance but in one way it also served a worthwhile purpose for me. It served notice on Galgala and to the Empire at large that I had reappeared. But since I had declined to claim the full royal treatment, had turned down the usual parade and the awarding of the usual decorations, my appearance in Ashen Devlesa created more than a little ambiguity surrounding the matter of my intentions in coming back from retirement. Which was fine. Keep them all guessing: that's always a useful strategy. I didn't say a thing. I smiled a lot and waved a lot and looked sublimely radiant while the speeches were going on around me, and when it was all done with I thanked them politely and went on out to Kamaviben, to my grand estate far off in the countryside by the shores of the Sea of Pleasure.

(Actually Kamaviben isn't all that grand a grand estate, as grand estates go. The grounds are of decent size and the location is sublime, but the house itself, while of some architectural interest, wouldn't raise the pulse rate of a small-town magistrate. At no point in my life have I ever been a particularly wealthy man, you know. And perhaps there is just enough of the old wandering Rom spirit in me to make it superfluous for me to live in a really overwhelming place. I am just as content in an ice-bubble or a roamhome or a simple log shanty as I have ever been in the various palaces that I have occupied in my time. Yet I think Kamaviben is marvelously grand in its way, and I would never want to live in any dwelling more splendid. Or even in any other dwelling at all, unless it be on Romany Star.)

In the years of my absence they had maintained it for me in perfect shape, as though I might show up there unannounced on any given afternoon. The stables were swept, the lawns of quivergrass were impeccable, the double rows of blackleaf pseudo-palms down the main drive had been pruned only a week before. A staff of ten took care of Kamaviben for me, the most loyal and devoted robots on any world of the galaxy. They were sweet machines, my Kamaviben robots: they even spoke Romany. (With a Xamur accent, that faint little lisp.) Of course a Rom craftsman had made them for me, the Kalderash wizard Matti Costorari. I have known Rom that were less Rom than those robots.

From Kamaviben I sent word to those who mattered most to me, telling them I was back. And then I waited.

5.

POLARCA WAS THE FIRST TO SHOW UP. NOT HIS GHOST this time, but the true and authentic item. My grand vizier, my good right hand, my companero, my cousin of cousins, my blood brother.

This man Polarca is more dear to me than either of my kidneys. You can get new kidneys if you need them—I have done it—but where would I get another Polarca? I saved his life once, as he never tires of reminding me. I think he regards me as being in his debt because I saved him. That was long ago, on Mentiroso, when we suffered side by side in Nikos Hasgard's foul clutches, which is a story I mean to tell you sooner or later. Since that time we have been brothers. Polarca is small and quick and jittery, a hedgehog sort of man. Like the hedgehog he is very prickly but sweet inside.

He came rollicking in from Darma Barma, where he keeps a grand

and glorious floating villa out in the lightning country. He calls it his vardo, his Gypsy wagon, and sometimes he speaks of it as a roamhome, which is a bit like calling a bludgeon a toothpick. But Polarca has always been fond of exaggeration.

He had had a remake since I had last seen him and that took some getting used to. He was wearing his eyes a deep piercing blue now with bright red rims, and his ears were higher and thicker than before, with black fur on them. He looked strange but he looked healthy and full of fire.

"Yakoub!" he cried. "Oh, there, you Yakoub!"

"Polarca. Is it really you?"

"No, you antiquated piss-in-bed, it's my other ghost."

I grinned. "Don't you call me names, you slippery mirage."

He radiated love and warmth. "I'll call you what I like, you old ball of grease."

"Pig-poisoner!"

"Gajo-licker!"

"Chicken-stealer! Pocket-picker!"

"Hah! Oh, you Yakoub!"

"You Polarca, you!"

We laughed and hugged and slapped each other's cheeks. We grabbed each other, wrist by wrist, and cavorted up and down the hallways in a wild crazed dance, singing at the top of our lungs. Two roaring bellowing old fossils is what we were, with more life in us than any fifty snotnosed boys. We made so much noise that the robots came to see what the matter was. They looked alarmed and dismayed. Maybe they thought an assassin was in the house. But they are Rom robots at heart; as soon as they saw that this was all friendly, that this was my phral here, my brother, my Polarca, they relaxed.

I told them to fetch us a flagon of my rarest and best brandy, a loaf of palm-tree bread, a cluster of Iriarte grapes. We sat down to table and he opened his overpocket and pulled out the gifts he had brought me. Polarca always brings plenty of gifts and they are always things you might have wanted a year ago or perhaps will want next year, but rarely anything you would want at the moment. This time he came out with an ornate pair of double-vented air-shoes, a magnifying pen, half a dozen ceramic ear-spools, and the complete text of the Meditations of Marcus Aurelius inscribed on the eye-tooth of a sanguinosaur. I thanked him most solemnly, as I always did when Polarca loaded me down with oddities and superfluities of that sort. He had also brought with him something that was actually worth bringing: a slab of the wind-dried beef from Clard Msat, which is a delicacy I had longed for with a keen ultraviolet longing during my years on Mulano. Splendid Polarca! How had he known I was yearning for that?

We drank and ate in silence for a time. The brandy was from Ragnarok, a hundred years old, eighty cerces the flagon. You could buy a good slave for less. We talked then of his travels. Incurable wander-itch has afflicted him all his life. Lately he had been to Estrilidis, to Tranganuthuka, to Sidri Akrak. He had ghosted to Earth five times in the last six months, and Mulano on and off maybe a dozen times to check up on me, and some other places besides, an itinerary that would have brought an ox down with apoplexy. There is restlessness in any Gypsy's soul, but Polarca carries it to a lunatic extreme. When he had run through all his travel tales he fell silent again, and we ate and drank some more.

Then he said, "So you came back after all."

"So it would seem."

"What day did you return?"

"What *day?*"

"The day of the month." Patiently, as though to a child.

"I think it was the fifth of Phosphorus," I said.

"The fifth! Good! Good!" His eyes gleamed wildly. "I win a thousand cerces from Valerian, then!"

"How so?"

"A bet," Polarca said casually. "That you'd be back in the Empire within five years. It was a very close thing, Yakoub. You skipped out originally on the ninth of Phosphorus, you know."

"Did I?" I shrugged. "You two had a bet, did you? Did he think I wasn't coming back at all?"

"He said ten years. I said five. There wasn't anybody who felt you'd never come back."

"You yourself said I wouldn't come back. That time on Mulano, when you were giving me all that bullshit about Achilles in his tent. You said that I was going to stay on Mulano, that that was the wisest thing for me to do."

"So I lied," Polarca said. "Sometimes you need to be pulled around a little by the ears, Yakoub. For your own good." He reached into his tunic and pulled out a deck of cards. They sparkled and hummed on the table between us. "A little klabyasch?" he suggested.

"For money?"

"What else? For the exercise? Five tetradrachms a point."

"Make it a cerce," I said. "I'll relieve you of the pile you've won from Valerian."

He smiled sadly. "Poor Yakoub. You never learn, do you?" He put the cards on autoshuffle and they jumped around like frogs on the table. Then he clapped his hands and they formed themselves into a deck in front of me.

"Your deal," Polarca said.

He hunched forward, eyes gleaming crazily. Polarca plays cards like Attila the Hun. I put the deck on manual and dealt them out, and he pulled them in as if each one was the passport to heaven. And of course the game was a rout. Though he is a small man his hands are huge, and those cards came flying out of them like angry mosquitos. He slapped them down with furious zeal, shouting, "Shtoch! Yasch! Menel! Klab-yasch!" and I was done for before I knew it. He took me for a fortune. Well, it makes him happy to murder me at klabyasch, and it makes me happy to make Polarca happy.

As the echoes of the game died away I said, "And tell me how it is, in the Imperium."

"Pah. The usual Gaje lunacy. The Emperor will hang on forever. He's only a shadow. The high lords are behaving like fools and villains. You can see them circling each other, waiting to pounce, and meanwhile the administration goes to hell. The Empire is running on autopilot. Taxes are down. Corruption is up. Whole solar systems are dropping out of the communications and transportation nets and nobody seems to notice. This is an ugly time, Yakoub."

"And Shandor?" I asked, and held my breath.

Polarca looked up at me. His burning red-rimmed eyes held firm on mine a long moment. Then he laughed softly and shook his head and waved his hand, brushing aside my concern the way you might brush aside a mosquito. "Shandor!" he said, chuckling as if he found the name itself amusing. For him, he seemed to be saying, Shandor was a topic hardly worth discussing, a trifle, an absurdity. "He is nothing, Yakoub. Nothing!" Polarca reached for the brandy. The flagon was empty. He tapped its side. "This stuff isn't half bad, you know?"

6.

OVER THE NEXT FEW DAYS THE REST OF THEM SHOWED up. My dear ones, those who had been my rod and my staff in the days when I was king. One by one they arrived on the starships that came to Xamur from every part of the galaxy. My cabinet, the inner circle of my court in the days when I had a court. And two others besides, two unexpected guests.

Jacinto and Ammagante came in together, from Galgala. Those two always traveled together, though they could scarcely have been more unalike: Jacinto small and wizened, like some dark hard nut that could not possibly be cracked, and Ammagante tall, big-boned, with the easy open face of a sunny-souled child. In my reign Jacinto had been the money-man, the studier of trends and the manipulator of forces, the one who guided our investments, patiently spinning the web of Rom holdings that stretches from world to world to world. Ammagante was his wizard of communications, through whose long arms flowed the instantaneous impulses that brought Jacinto the information he had to have. There is strange power in that woman. She speaks in tongues. In his infinite wisdom my son Shandor had dismissed them both, and—so Polarca gave me to understand—Jacinto and Ammagante were scraping along now in private scams of their own, earning the odd cerce here and there, managing to eke out some sort of pittance. I could imagine what sort of pittance it was, knowing them as I did.

The same ship that brought them from Galgala brought that cunning old woman Bibi Savina. Our phuri dai, the mother of the tribe. Who would surely have been a king among us, if things had been otherwise. (We can't have women as kings—it isn't done, it has never been done —but in her way the phuri dai is as important as the king. And sometimes more so. Woe betide the Rom king who ignores her advice or denies her her high place. There have been some who have tried, and they have regretted it.)

I think of Bibi Savina as being incredibly old, ancient beyond measure. That is because of the visits she made to me when I was a trousers-pissing babe and she a ghost, ages and ages ago. But in fact she is younger than I am by thirty years or so, though she elects to look like a crone. I greeted her with deep respect, even a little awe: me, awe! But she deserves it. She is a fount of power and sagacity. Of course the change in government on Galgala had had no effect on her authority: the phuri dai is chosen not by the king but by the will of the tribe itself, and once she is in office no king can remove her. Even rash Shandor had enough sense not to try to butt horns with Bibi Savina. But the fact that she had come to Xamur at my beckoning told me where her loyalties must lie.

Biznaga arrived next: my envoy to the imperial court, my link to the galactic government. Elegant and supple, he was, with a diplomat's grace and poise, and a diplomat's fine wardrobe: I never knew anyone who dressed himself as finely as Biznaga. He came in from the Capital, where he had been living in retirement. Shandor had pensioned him off too. He must not have trusted any of my people. I wonder why.

From Marajo, where he had gone to look after his own business interests after his journey to my snowy world of exile, came my cousin Damiano. With him, to my surprise, was young Chorian—the first of the two uninvited guests.

Polarca didn't like that at all. He drew Damiano and me aside and said, "What in the name of Mohammed is *he* doing here?"

"I thought he would be useful," Damiano said. "He sees things with clear eyes and he has the true Rom fire. And he has served me well on more than one occasion."

Polarca was unimpressed by that fine speech. "He's Sunteil's man, isn't he? Do you want the things we say here to get back to Sunteil?"

"The same sun will rise twice in a single day before that happens," Damiano replied, giving Polarca that coiled-spring look of his. "Maybe he draws his pay from Sunteil, but his heart is with us. May all my sons die in this hour if I have told you anything but the truth."

Damiano will bury you under his Rom dignity and his Rom rhetoric when he wants to win an argument. Polarca threw up his hands in despair. But I was with Damiano, this time. I touched Polarca's shoulder lightly. From a distance, Chorian was staring at me with that puppyish adoration and utter awe that I detested and that I understood so well. I think Polarca was jealous of that. He's human too, as much as any of us can be called human; he didn't want anyone to be here who worshipped me more intensely than he did himself. But of course Polarca shows his adoration in peculiar ways.

"I don't see any risk in having Chorian here," I told him quietly. "The boy is one of us. I came to know him very well when he was on Mulano with me."

"But Sunteil's own private Rom—"

"He isn't Sunteil's. He just lets Sunteil think he is."

"Maybe he just lets you and Damiano think he isn't."

"Polarca," I said, smiling easily, massaging his arm. "Ah, you Polarca. This is nothing but paranoid shit and you know it."

"Yakoub, I tell you—"

"Polarca," I said, a little less gently.

Even then there was another round or two of grumbling out of him. But in the end he had to yield, and he did. Chorian was beside himself with relief and gratitude: he knew that a debate had been going on over allowing him to remain. And he was practically frothing with joy at seeing me again. Yet for all his callow ways he seemed less naive, somehow more seasoned, than he had on Mulano. He was beginning to take on a little swagger. Some of that naivete had probably been just camouflage, anyway; but beyond question he was gaining swiftly in confidence these days and must have felt less of a need to hide behind his boyishness. He was going to be useful. Damiano had done well to bring him. Now and then during the conferences of the next few days I saw Polarca still brooding as though he was still absolutely certain we had invited a spy of the Imperium into our midst; but even he stopped worrying about Chorian after a time.

In due course Valerian appeared. Or rather Valerian's ghost, I should say: Valerian didn't dare set foot himself on any world of the Empire, not with that bounty of ten thousand cerces posted on him. Even a Rom might have gone for that. Valerian has plenty of enemies among us, after all: the Gaje aren't the only victims of his piracies. But Valerian or Valerian's ghost, it made no great difference, for Valerian's ghost has such vigor that it isn't easy to distinguish it from Valerian. Except that the ghost, like most ghosts, has a way of drifting a little above the ground, and of emitting a bit of electrical crackle now and then.

Valerian is an extremely theatrical man. There's an aura of high drama about him that precedes him by a hundred meters wherever he goes. He preens, he roars, he gesticulates, he flashes his eyes and strikes poses. He has tremendous style and presence, but it's a style and presence that come out of some grand opera fifteen hundred years old.

Valerian sees himself as the direct ideological heir of Blackbeard and Sir Francis Drake and Captain Kidd and Robin Hood and any other buccaneer who ever lifted a penny from someone else, and like most of them he has the same fine lofty resounding justifications for his depredations. Of course he's really just a criminal. Get one layer down inside him beneath the idealism and you'll find that what he loves is danger and the thrill of living outside the law. Get below that and you discover that secretly he sees himself as nothing but a businessman, an entrepreneur of the star-lanes concerned mainly with risk-to-reward ratios. If you could get below *that* I think you'd find pure chaos at the heart of his soul.

He is a completely unscrupulous man. But I've never had reason to doubt his loyalty to me. I saved his ass, or at the very least his neck, when he was brought up on serious charges before the great kris of Galgala, and he will always be grateful to me for that.

After him came Thivt, who is the great anomaly in my life and possibly the great anomaly of the galaxy. I regard Thivt as my cousin and at times, like Polarca, a blood brother. He is deeply versed in Rom ways and Rom lore, and I accept him unhesitatingly as Rom. But he isn't Rom, not really. I don't mean that he's a Gajo, either. I'm not sure he's human at all.

He is a changeling, who actually was taken by Rom in childhood and raised by them, just as Gaje folklore would have you believe was our regular custom all during medieval times. An exploration party found him wandering around by himself on a planet in the Thanda Banadareen system. He looked to be five or six years old. The only word he could speak was the one that was assumed to be his name. No parents in sight, no crashed spaceship, no trace of relay-sweep gear to be found, no nothing. Somehow the notion took hold, nevertheless, that he was the only survivor of an unrecorded free-lance expedition. When the explorers left Thanda Banadareen they took him along, back to Iriarte, which is where I encountered him a hundred years or so later. By then he was high in Rom councils and he spoke Romany like a true phral of the blood. He even had learned how to ghost: so far as I know, the only non-Rom who has ever mastered that. Thivt had achieved the rare trick, almost unique in history, of becoming Rom by adoption. There are those who think that he must really be Rom by birth, because he can ghost. I don't know about that. Thivt looks Rom and he sounds Rom and he lives Rom, and Rom trust him like one of themselves; but I sense an aura about him, a vibration, that is something else entirely, something very strange. I'm not the only one who has felt it, either.

Can it be that there are alien beings hiding in the still uncharted wilderness of Thanda Banadareen, and that they sent Thivt to us in human guise as some sort of observer, or even an emissary? No one, so far as I know, has ever returned to the world where Thivt was found to take a second look. It doesn't seem to have been a particularly inviting or useful sort of world. The galaxy is very large and we are very few; the course of exploration has moved elsewhere, to places that are considered more promising. I wonder about that world sometimes. I wonder about Thivt.

Now that Thivt was on hand, the group I had summoned was complete. But then at the last minute Syluise came waltzing in, the second of the two uninvited guests.

Polarca broke in on me while I was in my bath to tell me that she had arrived. The moment he entered the room I knew that something unusual was up, because his blue-and-red eyes seemed to have shifted halfway up the spectrum with anger or surprise, and those weird furry ears of his were twitching like a beast's. It was the fight-or-flight syndrome taking him over. Polarca regards Syluise as nothing more or less than a snake—a snake of the most deadly kind, whose fangs are venomous but who might just opt to strangle you to death for the hell of it.

"Guess who's here," he began ominously.

"Shandor?" I said. "Sunteil?"

"Worse."

"Do we have to play guessing games, Polarca?"

"*She's* here. The great love of your life."

Polarca wishes fervently that I had never become mixed up with Syluise. Even making allowances for his sometimes overprotective attitude toward me, Polarca may have something there. But he also has a little problem with strong-willed women and that may account for some of his dislike of her.

"Seriously? Syluise?"

He was pacing up and down. "I try to tell myself that you're in your right mind," he said. "But to invite a troublesome and totally self-centered cunt like that to a high-level strategy session, Yakoub—"

"What makes you think I invited her?"

"What's she doing here, if you didn't?"

"You didn't try to find out?"

"Christ," he muttered. "You think she'll talk to me? She walks right through me as though I'm not there. She comes promenading in here from the spaceport like the Queen of Sheba, with a dozen robots in her train, installs herself in one of the master suites, unloads six overpockets' worth of gowns and robes and tiaras and God knows what else, starts giving orders to everybody in sight as though she's the new owner of the planet—"

"All right," I said. "Hand me that towel."

Polarca had exaggerated a little, but only a little. Syluise had indeed come with a retinue of robots, and she had set herself up in high style in a choice corner of the house. I went to pay a call on her and she received me as if this was *her* grand estate and I was the recently arrived guest.

One of her robots showed me in.

"I have plenty of robots available for my guests," I said. "It wasn't necessary for you to bring your own."

"I didn't want to be a burden."

"On the robots?"

"I like my own robots, Yakoub. They know how to look after me the way I like to be looked after."

"You really are a bitch, aren't you, Syluise?"

"Do you think so?" She made it seem as if I had complimented her. She looked as splendid as ever, the hair gleaming like the golden forests of Galgala, the blue eyes sparkling playfully, the tall slender body glowing within some sort of magical filmy wrap that emitted faint silvery music whenever she moved. "It's so good to see you again, Yakoub."

"You saw me not long ago on Mulano."

"I was ghosting then. Now I'm real. We haven't been this close to each other in the flesh for six or seven years, do you realize that?" The dazzling smile, a trillion electron volts. "Did you miss me?"

"Why are you here, Syluise?"

"Can't you be romantic even for a minute?"

"Later. First tell me why you came."

"I was worried about you. You sounded very confused, when I visited you on that icy planet of yours."

"Confused?"

"Telling me all that stuff about how you had abdicated so that your people would beg to have you come back. And that you had done it all for their good, so you could lead them on to Romany Star. Did you actually believe that it made sense, what you thought you were doing?"

"Yes."

"And now that Shandor is king, what are you going to do?"

"That's why I've called this meeting," I said. "But I don't remember asking you to attend it."

"I thought I could be of some help."

Sweet Syluise. "I'm sure you did," I said. "But you still aren't answering my question. How does it happen that you're here?"

"I heard you were back from that other place, that Mulano. The news is all over the Imperium. That you had landed on Xamur, that you had gone to your estate. So I decided to come to you and offer you whatever I could. I didn't know about the rest of it. That you were giving a big patshiv, that you had invited Polarca and Valerian and the phuri dai and all the others."

I found it strange, hearing her use those Romany words. Patshiv, phuri dai. Romany words sounded all wrong, coming out of those flawless imitation-Gaje lips of hers. I had a way of forgetting for years at a time that somewhere within the elegant Gaje package that Syluise had sculpted for herself there lurked a Rom soul. Somewhere.

"Just a coincidence?" I said. "That you came right in time for the meeting?"

She nodded. And held out her hands toward me.

Well, what was I to do? Interrogate her? Had Damiano tipped her off, or Biznaga, or even, God only knew why, Bibi Savina? Maybe so; or maybe it *was* only a coincidence. What the hell: she was here and I suppose I was glad to see her.

It had been a long time, a very long time, for Syluise and me. I had never been able to resist her anyway. Not since the beginning for her and me, more than fifty years back, before I was the king, that time when Cesaro o Nano had sent me to make a ceremonial visit to the Rom of Estrilidis, and she had come floating up out of the night, young and golden, a vision of Gaje perfection, cutting through all my defenses and beckoning me into shameful obsessions. Come here, she had said that night. I will make you a king. She said it in Romany with those Gaje lips of hers and I was lost. Rising above me, turning me from king to slave with a single glance. Her head thrown back, her lips parted, her breasts swaying wildly. I had been her slave ever since. An old man's foolishness? No. I wasn't old, fifty years ago. I'm not old now. Something like this would have happened to me at any age. Does everything I do have to make sense? Everyone is entitled to be struck once in his life by a fit of irresponsible passion. Or by a thunderbolt of instantaneous love, if that's what you prefer to call it. Call it whatever you like. Call it madness. Syluise was my madness.

"Come here," she said now.

Yes. Oh, how she sparkled, how she gleamed! Oh, yes, yes, yes!

7.

WE HAD THREE DAYS OF FEASTING AND REJOICING BE-
fore we got down to anything serious. I didn't want to hurry it. I had been away by myself in the snow for much too long, and it was good just to have them all around me, these old dear friends, Valerian and Polarca and Thivt, Biznaga and Jacinto and Ammagante, Damiano and Syluise. Not ghosts this time—except for Valerian—but sweet warm flesh.

So we had a grand patshiv in the ancient traditional style, with all the food and drink anyone might want and then some, and dancing and singing and clapping of hands. Even the robots joined in, stamping their footpads in rhythm until they had caught the beat and finally leaping out into the middle of the floor to cavort and prance with the rest of us. Of course we loved that. At a patshiv everyone must be happy, everyone must feel like an honored guest, even the robots. God, was it a good time! The great chunks of roast beef, the suckling pigs, the barrels of foaming beer and rich red wine! Each night we sat around a blazing fire of fine aromatic wood, telling old tales of travel and high adventure, the roads we had taken and the joys and mishaps we had had. For a moment out of time we were Rom of the old days, the wanderers, the caravan people, the tinkers and the fortune-tellers, the most serious people in the world and at the same time the most playful, enjoying ourselves in the way that we have always enjoyed ourselves. And in the darkness afterward, by the pale luminous glow of the nightbirds that flitter through the night of Xamur, there was Syluise, smooth and sleek to my touch. For the moment I was able to put aside all thought of what I still must accomplish; for the moment there was only Syluise, and the glowing birds in the darkness, and the silence of the night.

When I was ready to get down to real business I led them all away from the house on the long journey to the far edge of my property, where the Idradin crater throbs and pulses and stews with ferocious passionate energy.

The Idradin is the one blemish on Xamur's fair face. A ghastly pustule, an angry inflammation. There are those who lament the fact that a thing as hideous as the Idradin could exist on beautiful Xamur, but I think otherwise. Without the crater Xamur would seem an intolerably perfect world, unreal, outrageous, almost fraudulent. Xamur is in a way a little like Syluise, masked in a beauty that is too perfect for our flawed universe: it needs some single fault to make it seem genuine, and so does she. I am content that the Idradin is there, and content also that it is on my own land. It serves always as a reminder to me that the dream of perfection is a fool's fantasy, that there is always some loathsome canker in the sweetest bud.

The crater is a great round hole that goes straight down to the boiling magma that lies at the heart of Xamur. Around its jagged rim lie broad concentric rings of old worn black lava, dozens of them, hurled to the surface long ago by the fierce power of ancient eruptions. They form a sort of natural amphitheater, grim and bleak and lifeless. You can walk down to the lowest ring—if you dare—and see wild red shafts of flame spearing through smoky gray clouds, and hear monstrous forces belching and rumbling in the depths. Wisps of sulfuric miasma constantly come drifting up, staining the sky and all the surrounding countryside a bright vomitous yellow.

A hateful ugly place, yes.

But I had lived so close to it for so many years that I no longer could feel any hatred for it. I no longer saw the ugliness. Call it perverse if you like, but the sight of the Idradin had come to be something I found heartening and inspiring. I drew from it a sense of the raw strength of the forces it contained. Which are the forces of creation itself. We live on the surfaces of our planets. There are suns within them.

We gathered on the ninth circle of the crater, far enough away so that the stinking gases would not choke us, close enough to feel the warmth and the deep rumblings. Some—Biznaga, Jacinto, Damiano—seemed repelled and nauseated by the place. Chorian seemed almost frightened. Polarca was tense and taut, and kept glancing back over his shoulder.

As though he expected an eruption any minute. Even Valerian looked a little worried, and he wasn't even actually there. But there was nothing but serenity on the faces of Bibi Savina and Thivt; Ammagante appeared indifferent; and Syluise, to my surprise, looked ecstatic. She stood with her arms flung wide and her head thrown back. She was glowing with a supreme radiance against the somber backdrop of the crater's dark fumes. I felt crazy with love for her, seeing her like that. Like a schoolboy. At my age. I knew it was insane. The crater has that effect on me sometimes. So does Syluise.

I said, scanning their faces one by one, "All right, the business at hand. My son Shandor seems to have set himself up on Galgala as the king. This is absolutely not legitimate and something had goddamned well better be done about it. Will one of you tell me how a miserable thing like this was ever allowed to happen in the first place?"

Silence from all quarters. And some squirming and wiggling.

"According to you, Damiano, he called the great kris together and compelled the krisatora to elect him. Is that actually what happened?"

Nods. Shrugs. From Bibi Savina a flat blank stare.

"Jesu Cretchuno Adam and Eve, can't any of you speak? Explain to me how the krisatora can be forced to take such an action. The krisatora when they are in session have power over any Rom, even the king. Not the other way around. Who were they, these krisatora? Nine puppy dogs? Nine robots? Did he threaten them? With what? How can an election under duress be considered valid even for a minute?"

Biznaga said, "There is no record of what took place at the kris, Yakoub. Except that Shandor called the krisatora together and when they emerged from the hall of judgment he was the king."

I looked toward Damiano. "You told me he forced them."

"That's what I assume."

"Who were these krisatora?" I asked.

"You know them all," Damiano said. "The same who were in office when you were king. Bidshika, Djordji, Stevo le Yankosko, Milosh—"

I cut him off in mid-list. "They should have known better. The son of a king has never been king before. And with the old king still alive, too. Oh, the bastard, the bloody bastard! He walked in there and told them what to do, and they did it, and nobody dared say a word against it. Even you. You all just smiled and nodded and let it happen."

"And you take no responsibility at all?" Valerian said.

"Me?"

"You, Yakoub. But for you none of this would have happened. You set the whole thing up, didn't you? Who told you to abdicate in the first place?"

"I had my reasons."

"I bet you did."

"You think my abdication was a whim? You think it was just some cockeyed impulse that took hold of me? Do you? Do you? Don't you think that I had a plan, that I was acting in accordance with my long-range strategy, when I walked out of Galgala?"

They were all looking at each other. Suddenly I realized what they must be thinking. The old man has taken leave of his senses, is what they were thinking. I saw now that they might have been thinking that for quite some time.

I glared at them.

"You bastards, have you been humoring me?"

"Humoring you how?" asked Polarca.

"You think I'm crazy, don't you?"

"Did I ever say a thing like that, Yakoub?"

"You didn't say it, no," I agreed. "But you've been thinking it. Haven't you, Polarca?"

"Absolutely not."

"Valerian?"

"Crazy? You?"

"Damiano? Biznaga? Come on, you pigs, put up your hands! Everyone who thinks Yakoub is somewhere around the far bend into senility, wáve your goddamned hand in the air!"

No hands went up. Their faces didn't show a flicker of emotion. Did I have them cowed? Or were they determined to go on hiding what they thought of me, no matter what?

The crater roared and gargled. There was the sound of colossal masses of rock moving about somewhere deep within it. A plume of yellow smoke came burping up to the surface and spread a rank rotten stink everywhere, like the fart of a giant. No one reacted. No one moved. They were staring at me like a bunch of robots and there was no way I could read what was behind their eyes.

After a time I said in a quieter voice, under the tightest control I could manage, "I want to assure you that I'm still very much in my right mind. Just in case any of you happen to doubt that. My abdication may have been a tactical mistake, though I'm not yet convinced of that, but it wasn't the arbitrary and capricious action of a crazy old man."

And I launched into the full explanation: how I had come to feel that we were slipping away from our underlying nature, how we were being drawn more and more deeply into the Gaje Empire when in fact what we needed to do was to begin preparing ourselves for the return to Romany Star that had been our goal for so many thousands of years, and which was now perhaps just a couple of hundred years away. I told them how I had felt the need to do something dramatic in order to shake people up. That I had decided to go away for a few years and leave them leaderless, so they could ponder the error of their ways. And how I had planned to return and resume the throne, stronger than ever, once the full impact of my absence had been felt.

They listened to me soberly, almost grimly. Ammagante seemed to be engaged in some abstruse set of interior calculations. Damiano was scowling, Chorian looked astounded, Biznaga almost in tears. The others seemed puzzled or bothered or dismayed, all but Syluise, who had heard all this before and merely seemed bored. And Bibi Savina, whose invincible serenity remained unbroken. It occurred to me that the old woman might not even be listening to me, might not even be here, might be off ghosting somewhere at the far end of time.

When I was finished Jacinto said, softly, coolly, "And did you imagine that we could run a caretaker government for you forever, Yakoub? That five years or maybe ten would go by with the throne vacant and there'd be no pressure to elect a new king?"

"I thought there would be attempts made to get me to come back, before that happened."

"There were," Damiano said. "Do you know how many men I had out searching for you, starting the year after your disappearance?"

"I left my patrin behind me all over the place."

"So you did. We picked your signs up eventually. It still took three years for Chorian to find you. But we were at it constantly all those years."

"As were various lords of the Imperium," I said. "Julien de Gramont was sent after me by Periandros. And of course Chorian was working not only for you but for Sunteil. Well, I expected to be found a little sooner than I was. And I never dreamed that Shandor, of all people, would make a grab for the throne."

"But he did," said Damiano.

"And it serves you right," Valerian said. He is never gentle with me. "You created a vacuum and that son of a bitch moved right into it.

Does it get us any closer to Romany Star to have Shandor as our king?"

"Shandor is not the king," said Bibi Savina suddenly, in a voice that seemed to come from another solar system.

Everyone turned toward the phuri dai.

"The election was not an election. The abdication was not an abdication. Yakoub is still the king."

"Of course he is!" Chorian shouted, and instantly looked shamefaced at having dared to speak.

"And the other king on the throne on Galgala?" Biznaga said. "What is he, a figment?"

"Some figment!" Valerian boomed. "He saw his moment and he reached out and grabbed. And now we're stuck with him. Unless you want to set off a civil war, Rom against Rom. While the Gaje sit back and laugh at us."

"That must not happen," Thivt said.

"Are we supposed to accept Shandor as king, then?" Damiano asked.

They all began to talk at once. Then Polarca's dry sharp voice came cutting through the babble:

"Bibi Savina is right," he said. "We can simply ignore Shandor. Yakoub's abdication didn't mean a thing. There was never any such custom as abdication among us in the first place. A king is king until he dies, or until the krisatora depose him. I haven't heard anything about an act of deposition. And even if there was, we can claim that it was done under duress, and is therefore invalid. Yakoub is our king."

Biznaga shook his head violently. "But Shandor holds the seat of government. Shandor is recognized by the Imperium as the head of the Rom people. What legal means do we have of displacing him now?"

They started to babble again. This time I held up my hand for silence.

"I have a plan," I said. "I brought this whole mess down upon us all by myself when I chose to leave the throne. And now I intend to clean it up. All by myself."

"How?" Valerian demanded.

"By going to Galgala. Alone, without any sort of escort. In person, not a doppelganger. And walking all by myself into the king's house of power and telling my son Shandor that he has to get his ass out of the place inside of five minutes, or else."

"That's your plan?" Valerian asked, looking amazed.

"That is my plan, yes."

"Go to Galgala?" Jacinto said. "Go before Shandor alone and give him an ultimatum?"

"Yes," I said. "Absolutely."

I saw them looking at each other again. Gaping, staring. General disbelief. Their faces saying that they knew now beyond any doubt that I had lost my mind.

"And what happens then?" Valerian wanted to know. "He smiles politely and says, Of course, daddy, right away, daddy, and clears out? Is that what you expect, Yakoub?"

"It won't be that simple."

"I think it'll be *very* simple," Valerian said. "You'll make your speech, and when he recovers from his amazement he'll take you and toss you in a dungeon nine miles deep. Or do something even worse."

"To his own father?" Ammagante asked.

"This is Shandor we're talking about. He's an animal, he's a wild beast. You remember what he did that time on Djebel Abdullah, when the stardrive failed and the food ran out? This is a civilized man? This is a son to be trusted? Authorizing the use of the bodies of his own passengers for food, for God's sake?"

"Valerian—"

"No," he said angrily. "You want me to pretend it never happened? This Shandor is our king! This is the man whose sense of tradition, whose mercy, whose benevolence, you plan to appeal to! How do you think those passengers got to be dead in the first place? And what do you think he'll do to you, Yakoub, if you put yourself within reach of him?"

"He will not harm me," I said.

"Madness. Absolute madness."

"He may try to imprison me, yes. I don't believe he would dare to harm me. Not even Shandor would do that. But if he does imprison me he'll forfeit whatever support he may have among our people. I can wait out a little time in a dungeon. At my age you learn to play the waiting game."

"But this is crazy, Yakoub!" Valerian said. "Why not send a doppelganger, at least?"

"You think that would fool him? The first thing he'd do is test me to see if I'm real."

"And when he finds out that you are—"

"I mean to risk it."

"And if he does kill you? Can we do without you?"

"He won't. But if he does, I become a martyr. A symbol. The instrument of his overthrow."

"And who will be king, then?"

"Do you think I'm the only man who can be King of the Rom?" I shouted. "Jesu Cretchuno, am I immortal? Some day you'll need another king. If that day is sooner instead of later, what of it? Shandor has to be cast down. No matter what the cost. I made it possible for him to seize the throne—by the Devil, I made it possible for him to be alive—and I will be the one to pull him down from the place he has grabbed. I will do it by going to Galgala. Alone."

"This is very rash," Jacinto murmured.

"If it will avoid a war between Rom and Rom—" Thivt said.

"No. I'm with Valerian," said Polarca. "We can't afford to lose you, Yakoub. There's got to be some less risky way of pushing Shandor aside. Proclaim the abdication null and void, ditto the election of Shandor, set up a legitimate government here on Xamur, remind Rom everywhere of their loyalty to Yakoub—"

"No," I said. "I don't intend to recognize Shandor's usurpation even to the extent of establishing a rival government. Our capital is on Galgala. I will go to Galgala."

"God help us all," muttered Valerian.

Then they all began yelling again at once, and in no time the meeting was reduced to absolute hysteria. I tried to quiet them down and couldn't do it. When a king can't get the attention of his own advisers there's real trouble in the commonwealth. I watched them rant and scream for a while and I did a little ranting and screaming myself and none of it was any use. So I just walked away from them. I went around to the far side of the crater and climbed up a couple of circles and sat with my back to them, listening to the screeching and bellowing of my best and my brightest.

After a long while I heard the sounds of someone climbing up behind me. I didn't look around. I was pretty sure who it was, because even with my back turned I sensed the strangeness of him.

Thivt.

I waited, saying nothing. Feeling his alien spirit getting closer and closer to me.

We have never satisfactorily settled, you know, the question of whether there are other intelligent races in the galaxy. Certainly there must have been some, once—the ancient fortress on Megalo Kastro is just one of a number of indications of that. But there aren't any living alien cultures to be found. The only intelligent species we know about are ourselves and the Gaje, the two basically identical human races that evolved on different worlds thousands of light-years apart. As our ever-widening expansion carries us outward into the galaxy we have come across any number of interesting and complex creatures, but none that have the traits we think of as intelligence. You might want to count such things as the living sea of Megalo Kastro as an intelligent life-form, but that isn't intelligence as we understand it.

(The presence of two separate but identical human races is a different but related puzzle. A lot of heavy thinkers among the Rom say that it's statistically unlikely and probably biologically impossible for any species to have evolved independently in virtually the same form on two different worlds. They suspect that Rom and Gaje must have had a common ancestor on some other world entirely, far away. That we are all the descendants of colonists who were left behind in prehistoric times. As for the differences that do exist between the two races—the Rom ability to ghost, say, and the related ability to propel starships into leap mode—those are explained away as mutations that crept into our branch of humankind during our thousands of years of separate existence on Romany Star. These are Rom speculations, remember. There aren't any Gaje speculations on these topics. The Gaje, of course, don't have any inkling of our alien ancestry. If they did, they probably would have lynched us all long ago, back on Earth in the years of persecution. It was tough enough for them to handle our wandering ways and our disdain for their laws. Knowing that we were spooks from some other planet would certainly have set off some kind of giant pogrom, a holy crusade against the evil witch-things from the stars. Maybe it still could.)

Thivt, at any rate—Thivt, I am convinced, is something else. Neither Rom nor Gaje, I think. But I doubt that I will ever know the truth; for Thivt is my friend and my cousin, and courtesy forbids me to ask him to tell me whether or not he is human.

He stood behind me, giving off waves of strangeness. He let his hand rest lightly on my arm. I felt warmth coming from him, tenderness, sympathy. That is the most alien thing about him: the way he can touch your mind, the way he can make a sort of communion.

"Yakoub," he said.

"Listen to them, Thivt. Screeching like chickens in the barnyard."

"They will be quiet soon."

"They're all against my plan, aren't they?"

"Is that important to you?"

"If they think I've gone crazy it is. I'll need their support if things don't go well for me on Galgala, and I doubt that things will. How can I ask them to come in there and risk their lives for me, if they think I've deliberately put my neck in danger against all their advice?"

"They will do whatever you ask of them, Yakoub."

"I don't know about that." I was wavering. In the face of such concerted opposition I was starting to think I should abandon my idea. Maybe it *was* crazy. Maybe it was imposing an unnecessary risk not only on me but on everyone. "They aren't fools," I said. "If they think I shouldn't go, then perhaps—"

Thivt's fingers continued to press lightly against my arm. I felt love flowing from him to me, concern, support.

"Follow your own judgment, Yakoub. It never leads you astray. If you think that what must be done is for you to go to Shandor, then you must go to Shandor. You are the king. You will prevail."

I turned toward him.

"You think so, Thivt?"

His dark solemn eyes were close to mine. At this moment he seemed more mysterious than ever to me. I wondered what lay behind that bland serene brow, what sort of brain, what alien corrugations and furrows. He was sending comfort to me. He was sending strength. Whatever he might be, offshoot of whatever unknown species that had taken on human form, he was my friend. He was my cousin.

"I think so, yes," he said. And said it in Romany.

"All right. So be it."

I walked back around the crater to the others. They had fallen silent by this time, and they were all staring at me.

"You aren't going to do it, are you?" Polarca said.

"My mind is made up."

"Put it to the phuri dai, at least!" Valerian cried. "For God's sake, Yakoub, let her decide!"

"The phuri dai!" Polarca chimed in. "The phuri dai."

Once again they turned to Bibi Savina, crowding around her. They were still all against me, all but Thivt. They really did think I had lost my mind.

"All right," I said, beginning to feel fury rising. "Let's listen to the phuri dai. Tell us, Bibi Savina. What should I do?"

There was an eerie light in Bibi Savina's eyes and her withered and shrunken body seemed to blaze with an inner flame. For a moment she appeared to stand straight again, and from her there emanated a kind of beauty that far outshone that of the magnificent Syluise.

"You must go to Galgala, Yakoub," she said in a strange voice like that of one who is in a trance. An oracle's voice. "Stand before Shandor and tell him he is not king. It is the only way. It is what you must do."

FIVE:

Into the Mouth of the Lion

What had this prophet done? What did he tell us, above all to do? He told us to deny all consolations—gods, fatherlands, moralities, truths—and, remaining apart and companionless, using nothing but our own strength, to begin to fashion a world which would not shame our hearts. Which is the most dangerous way? That is the one I want! Where is the abyss? That is where I am headed. What is the most valiant joy? To assume complete responsibility!

—Kazantzakis

1.

DESPITE BIBI SAVINA'S DECREE THERE WAS STILL PLENTY of uproar. By twos and threes they came to me and worked at changing my mind. Think of the risks, they said. Think of the danger. Think of the loss to our people if Shandor harms you, Yakoub. Think of this, think of that. You are indispensable, they told me. How can you simply hand yourself over to Shandor like this?

He is my son, I said. He will do me no harm.

Polarca told me flat out that I was crazy. I had never seen him so exasperated. He ranted, he stormed, he threatened to resign his office. I pointed out that he had no office to resign from, just now. He wasn't amused. He started ghosting around almost uncontrollably, leaping back across space and time in an altogether hysterical way. He was in a frenzy. I thought he would begin frothing at the mouth.

The person of the king is sacrosanct, I insisted. Even Shandor will recognize that, when I come to him on Galgala.

Valerian wanted to go to Galgala in my place and end Shandor's usurpation by force. He would gather up his entire pirate fleet and descend on him and march to the house of power and evict him from the throne. Biznaga remarked on the improbability of that, asking if Valerian seriously thought Shandor would let him get within a light-year of Galgala with his ships. At the first sign of his approach, Biznaga suggested, Shandor would simply let the imperial government know that the notorious pirate Valerian was in the vicinity, and an armada of the Imperium would be waiting for him when he arrived.

Biznaga too urged me not to go: calmly, quietly, in his best diplomatic manner. Jacinto, Ammagante, the same. Damiano was more volatile, and ranted and stormed almost as fiercely as Polarca. There was talk of finding one or two of my other sons, wherever they might be—my children are scattered all over the universe, God knows where —and bringing them to Xamur to plead with me. Or sending them to their brother Shandor as my ambassadors. Small mercy they would have had from him, too. Someone, I forget who (and just as well that I did) suggested appealing to the aged emperor for help in deposing

Shandor, the most laughable thing I have ever heard. And so on for several days. The only allies I had were Thivt and Bibi Savina. And possibly Syluise, though she held herself aloof as usual from most of the discussions and it wasn't easy to know where she stood. But I looked into her cool blue eyes and seemed to find support in them. In her remote and unfathomable way she appeared to be telling me to do as I pleased, accept the risks, reap the reward.

So I simply lied to them. Be calm, I told them, I know what I'm doing. Everything is written in the book of the future, and all will be for the best.

Somehow that settled them down. I let them think that I had received some sort of privileged information out of the future: an obliging ghost, possibly my own, coming to me and letting me know in the customary oblique ghostly way that my gamble had paid off somewhere down the line, that Shandor indeed had backed off when faced with the live and legitimate King of the Rom, that I would be restored to the throne and we would once more be traveling the path toward Romany Star. And they bought it.

But the truth is my ghosts were keeping away. Sometimes I saw a little flicker out of the corner of my eye that might have been some ghost hovering near, but I never was sure. That could have bothered me, if I had allowed it to. I told myself that the reason I was getting no ghosts was that I was being tested, my resolve, my courage: those who might have ghosted me, even my own self, were making me go through this thing unaided. I was on my own in this thing. Well, that was all right. I would simply proceed into the future at a rate of one second per second, with no hints of what was to come, the same as everyone else. Shandor was a wild man but there was logic to my strategy and I felt that no harm ultimately would come to me. Still and all, it would have been pleasant to get a little visit from some future self of mine, just a quick little reassuring flash, a wink, during those days when I was getting myself ready to walk into the mouth of the lion.

2.

SO IT WAS AGREED, IN THE END. YOU CAN'T REALLY ARGUE
with a king once he's made up his mind. I would go to Galgala, I would
confront Shandor, and then, well, we would all see what happened after
that. I made only one concession to my friends' fears. My plan had been
to go to Galgala alone, but Damiano talked me into taking Chorian
along as an escort. Chorian was, after all, a servant of the Imperium,
and Shandor might just think twice about laying violent hands on him,
regardless of what he might feel like doing to me.

I could see a little logic in that. Chorian could come to Galgala with
me. But I let it be known that even so I was going to enter into the
presence of Shandor alone, unescorted, not cowering behind the shield
of the Imperium and some boy still wet with mother's milk. And I
dared them to give me any further argument.

I am, basically, a very cautious man. You don't get to live as long
as I have by being reckless. My father drilled the Three Laws and the
One Word into me when I was very young, and the fact that I have
survived as well as I have for as long as I have ought to be sufficient
proof that I was a careful student at least of that much. Those who live
by common sense, my father taught me, are righteous in the eyes of
God. So they are. I would live no other way. Still and all, there is
common sense and common sense, and some kinds of common sense
make more sense than others. Time and again I've discovered that the
conventional "safe" ways of doing things are often wildly risky. And
that what looks impossibly crazy to conventional people is really the
only reasonable course to take.

For example, that time when I was living in slavery on Alta Hannalanna. Do you think common sense has any value in a place like Alta
Hannalanna? Common sense would have gotten me killed there, that's
what common sense would have done.

What a foul brute of a world that was! How I detested it, how I suffered, how I toiled in misery! A thousand times a day did I curse the soul of Pulika Boshengro, he who had sent me there in slavery to get rid of me after overthrowing his brother, my beloved mentor and foster father, Loiza la Vakako. That planet could well have been the end of me, if I hadn't been willing to take a crazy chance.

They shipped me there, as you know, by relay-sweep. It was my first taste of that dismal mode of travel and it was like a nightmare for me, those hours and weeks and perhaps even months—who could tell?— a prisoner in my little sphere of force as I hurtled across the galaxy. I raged and screamed until my throat felt like rags, and still the journey went on and on. Still I hung, suspended between life and death. For the second time in my life there was a slave-mark on my forehead and there was no way I could rip it off, not even by tearing at the skin. I was helpless. I was, I think, twenty years old, twenty-five, something like that. It all seems the same from this distance. I was very young, any-way. My life had hardly even begun and now it seemed all over. When I had been a babe in my cradle the wise old crone had come to me and whispered great prophecies of kingship and glory, and where had they gone? The little Gypsy boy on Vietoris, the beggar-slave on Megalo Kastro, the shoveler of snail-shit on Nabomba Zom: this was glory? This was kingship? Indeed for a time only a little while before I had lived the life of high privilege, when I was the heir to kingly Loiza la Vakako. I was the future husband of his lovely daughter. The gentle world of Nabomba Zom would one day be my domain. And then suddenly it all had been torn away from me and I was a slave again, stuffed into a relay-sphere and flung into nowhere, heading for a world so dreadful that Loiza la Vakako had not been able to bring himself to describe it to me—

I don't remember my landing on Alta Hannalanna. It must have been a bad one, though. I had lived in my relay-sphere for so long that it had become like a womb to me, and when I was dumped out onto the surface of that sickening planet I think the shock of it separated me from my sanity for a while. The first thing I can recall is crouching on my knees with my head down, sweating and puking and trembling, while a tall man in a gray uniform jabbed me again and again in the kidneys with a truncheon. I didn't know where I was. I didn't even know who I was.

"Get up," he said. "Slave."

The air was hot and dank and the world was quivering like a trampo-line beneath me. I wasn't imagining it. There was no solid surface, only a bewildering grotesque lacework of interwoven rubbery yellow vines thick as a man's thigh that stretched from horizon to horizon. The texture of the vines was rough and sticky, with warts and humps rising everywhere. They quivered like the strings of a fiddle. I thought I could feel the planet breathing below them, heavy groaning exhalations that set the vines in motion, and then long slow sighing inward draughts. A dense clammy rain was falling. The gravity was very light, but there was nothing exhilarating about that; it simply made everything seem even more unstable. I was dizzy and sick.

"Up," the guard said again, and prodded me without mercy.

He shoved me aboard a weird kind of vehicle that had no wheels, only peculiar spiderleg-like limbs that ended in huge hand-shaped clamps. It made its way across the face of Alta Hannalanna like some sort of giant bug, grasping and then releasing the strands of the planetary vines as it pulled itself forward. In time it came to a place where the vines parted to create a vast dark hole, and it plunged down into it, and down and down and down, until I was somewhere deep within the heart of the planet.

I was not to see the surface of Alta Hannalanna again for many months. Not that there was much virtue in being up there, for the whole place is an impassable maze of those evil sticky vines; a veil of thick gray clouds perpetually hides the sun; and the rain never ceases, not even for a moment. But down below is even worse. It is all one great solid spongy mass, hundreds of kilometers thick. Wide low-roofed tunnels run through it, crossing and crossing again. The walls of those tunnels are moist and pink, like intestines, and a sort of sickly phosphorescent illumination comes from them, a feeble glow that breaks the darkness without giving comfort to the eyes. The whole planet is like that, from pole to pole. Afterward I learned that the spongy underground of Alta Hannalanna is the substructure of the vines, their mother-substance, a gigantic mass of vegetable matter that completely engulfs the entire globe. The vines that spring from it are its organs of nourishment. They bring moisture to it, and by exposing themselves to the foggy light of the surface they allow some sort of photosynthetic processes to take place below. Apparently the whole thing is one vast organism of planetary size, the vegetable equivalent of the living sea of Megalo Kastro. The real surface of Alta Hannalanna lies buried somewhere beneath it, far down. It shows up on sonar probes, an underlying layer of solid rock, but no one has ever seen any reason to penetrate deep enough to find it.

By God, it is an awful place! I blush to think that it was a Rom who discovered it, that great Gypsy spacefarer Claude Varna, five hundred years ago. To his credit Varna thought it was a horror not worth further examination; but something in the report he filed aroused the curiosity of a biologist in the employ of one of the huge Gaje trading companies a century later, and a second expedition went forth. Alas that it did.

The tunnels are inhabited. Indeed the tunnels were created by their own inhabitants. For they are nothing more than colossal worm-holes, excavated by enormous sluggish flat-topped creatures whose bodies are three times the width of a man's and extend to unbelievable lengths. Slowly, patiently, these things have been gnawing their way through the underground world of Alta Hannalanna since the beginning of time. They are mere eating-machines, mindless, implacable. What they devour they digest and excrete as thin slime that runs in rivers behind them, gradually to be reabsorbed by the tunnel walls.

There are other life-forms in those tunnels, comparatively insignificant in size, that live as parasites on the great worms or on the surrounding vegetable matter. One of them is a kind of insect, a creature the size of a large dog with a savage beak and huge glittering golden-green eyes, repellent to behold. It is because of these creatures that I spent two years of my life in terrible torment in the tunnels of Alta Hannalanna.

The insects live within the worms. They use their beaks to inject the worms with their gastric juices and actually tunnel into their bodies, where they feed on their tissues and in time lay their eggs. Huge as the worms are, I suppose they would eventually be completely consumed by these little monsters within their bodies if they were not capable of defending themselves. The worm's defense is a chemical one: when it becomes aware that it has been entered—and it may be years before that news penetrates to its dim brain—it secretes a substance that trickles toward the zone of irritation and causes its own tissues to harden into a stony mass. Thus it forms a cyst around the invader, which is trapped within it until it starves. The stony material that forms these cysts is a rich lustrous yellow in color, smooth to the touch, and can be polished to a high gloss. In the commerce of the starways it is sold as Alta Hannalanna jade, although in truth it is more akin to amber. And it fetches a very high price indeed.

The filthy trick of collecting this jade was taught to me by one of my fellow slaves, a gaunt white-haired man named Vabrikant. He was a native of one of the Sempitern worlds; he said he had been on Alta

Hannalanna five years; and he looked at me with such appalling pity when I was handed over to him for instruction that I felt my soul beginning to curdle.

In silence he handed me tools: a sort of curving scimitar, a pick, a two-pronged thing with a spring attachment. "All right," he said. "Come on with me."

Together we set out from the slave dormitory, an oval antechamber where several of the tunnels met. Quickly the path narrowed and the ceiling grew lower, until we had to walk with knees bent. Though there was barely light enough to see by, Vabrikant moved from intersection to intersection with the ease of long familiarity. The atmosphere was damp and close and the air had a nauseating sweetness.

We went forward for hours. I couldn't begin to see how we would ever find our way back. Now and then Vabrikant halted and hacked a chunk from the tunnel wall to eat. The first time he offered some to me I refused, and he shrugged; but later he said, "You might as well. It's all you're going to get today."

I nibbled it warily. It was like eating a sponge; but there was a faint residue of musty flavor in my mouth afterward, and the hunger-gripings that I had been feeling were allayed at least for a little while.

Vabrikant smiled. "Better than starving, eh?"

"Not by much."

"You get used to it. Gypsy, are you?"

"Rom, yes."

"I knew a Gypsy once. A woman. Sweet, she was. The most beautiful little thing, dark eyes, the darkest hair you ever saw. I wanted to marry her, that's how I felt about her. I chased after her across six worlds. She was always kind to me. Married one of her own sort, though."

"We seldom marry outside," I said.

"So I discovered. Well, makes no difference now, I guess. I'm in this fucking place for life." He straightened up, sniffed, nodded. "Come on. We're almost there." He shook his head. "You poor bastard. Shipped here so young. You sure must have done something really shitty to have been sent to Alta Hannalanna."

"I—"

"No. Don't tell me what it was. We don't ever talk about what it was that got us sent up." He pointed ahead. "Look there, Gypsy-lad. There's worm-waste. We've got our worm."

Indeed I saw a stream of pale fluid spreading toward us on the tunnel floor, the worm excretion that I was to get to know all too well. Soon we were moving thigh-deep through it, sliding and slipping with every step. Vabrikant shined his helmet-light ahead. A worm was in the corridor.

We came up behind it. It filled the tunnel nearly from wall to wall, so that we had to walk sideways, our backs to the wall; and even so we could barely get through. We crept on and on for what seemed like miles, stooping so low that I thought my back would crack. The reek of the worm's fluid made me gag at first, but I began to get used to it. Its body was soft, almost buttery. It would have been easy to put my hand right through the yielding skin, deep into its flesh. Vabrikant said nothing for perhaps half an hour. Then he halted and tapped my shoulder.

"You see? Jade-light."

"I don't—"

"There. The yellow fire."

Yes. The worm's skin seemed to be blazing just ahead over a patch bigger than I was. When we were closer I saw the strange transformation of the giant creature's flesh within that patch: something dark and hard was visible deep within, and all about it was the fiery glow of inflammation that Vabrikant called jade-light. He went to work unhesitatingly, hacking open the side of the worm with the pick, then using the scimitar to widen the incision. He inserted the two-pronged device as a clamp. With steady even strokes he cut his way inward. The worm showed no reaction to what he was doing.

"That's the critter in there," he said. "This is the jade, growing around it. Reach in and touch it with your hand."

"In there?"

"Reach in, boy."

I crawled forward, shuddering, and thrust my arm deep within the quivering incision until I touched something hard and smooth as glass. It was the wall of the cyst that surrounded the trapped parasitical insect.

"I feel it," I said. "What do we do now?"

"We cut it out. The danger is that the critter won't be dead. If it isn't, it's going to be awful hungry and not in a real good mood. When we open the wall it's likely to jump out at us. It's got one hell of a beak."

"How can we tell if it's dead?"

"By opening the wall," Vabrikant said. "If it don't jump at us, then it's dead. If it do, we're in trouble. We lose a devil of a lot of jade miners every year."

I stared at him. But he simply shrugged and set to work.

It took half an hour, working with a drilling-bit and chisel, to cut the jade cyst from its matrix in the worm's soft flesh. When I pointed out that a laser knife would have done the job a lot faster he looked at me in sorrow, as though I were mentally defective. "Give us lasers, sure. The overmasters would really go for that idea." I felt worse than foolish. We were not merely slaves but prisoners.

Luck was with us this time. The worm had done its job of self-defense; when we lifted the jade slab that Vabrikant had cut free we saw the husk of the insect dead within, dry and empty. "There are days I almost hope one of them will pop out and kill me," he said. "But I guess I don't really want that or I'd go looking for it, I guess. Here. Take hold with me." He caught the inner face of the jade cyst and pulled it free, dumping the shell of the dead insect back into the depths of the worm's flesh. As we stepped away, the wound was already beginning to close; we got our tools out just in time. And the worm moved on.

That was how jade was mined on Alta Hannalanna. You'd trek endlessly for hours down the clammy tunnels searching for a worm, scan up and down the length of its immense body for the jade-light that marked an entrapped parasite, start cutting and hope for the best. Hours of numbing boredom relieved only by a few minutes of terror, followed by hours of boredom again. With that revolting sickly-sweet stench in your nostrils all the time. And then try to find your way back to the dormitory. Vabrikant always knew the way, but I wasn't always paired with Vabrikant; sometimes I went out with younger men who didn't have much more of a sense of the tunnels than I did, and we got lost, and then after a while I was often the senior member of the mining team, for new slaves arrived all the time, and it became my job to try to find the way. Sometimes we wandered for days trying to return, and there was nothing to eat but the stuff we carved from the walls of the tunnel.

About one worm out of three carried an encysted parasite. Maybe one parasite out of three was still alive when we cut into the jade. You had to be ready to bash it with your pick if it came charging out; that was why we traveled in pairs, one to cut, one to stand guard. Even so slaves died all the time. Sometimes you met a free parasite that was wandering the tunnels looking for a worm. That was always bad. They came charging at you like demons. When we did manage to find our way back to the dormitory after filling our quota of jade it was cold comfort indeed. All we did was rest and brood until it was time to go out again. It was a bleak, hopeless existence. Life at the dorm was so grim that after a little while we started looking forward to our next tour out in the tunnels. We talked constantly about escaping, of somehow getting on board one of the relay-sweep capsules that periodically took the jade away to be sold. To do that we'd have to mount an attack on the overmasters who guarded us when we were at the base. The overmasters were slaves themselves; no one would work for pay alone on a planet like this; but they set themselves up as our enemies and there was no hope of conspiring with them. They were armed with truncheons and with sensory-whips and they went swaggering about glowering at us as though we were troublesome dogs. Usually the truncheons were enough to keep us in line, but once in a while some miner went seriously berserk and then the sensory-whip would come into play. Those who had felt its lash never risked it a second time. But I did.

3.

TO KEEP FROM GOING OUT OF MY MIND I GHOSTED OBSES- sively, compulsively, all over space and time, taking the big jump fifty times a day. Sometimes I even did it when I was crawling down a tunnel toward a worm, although you aren't supposed to ghost in dangerous circumstances because it diverts your attention for a fraction of a moment, and sometimes that can be fatal. Maybe I didn't give a damn; maybe I was feeling a little suicidal, or just reckless. Or maybe I thought that if I jumped often enough, one time I just wouldn't return to Alta Hannalanna at the end of the trip. But of course it doesn't work that way. You always come back.

My present was a nightmare and my future promised nothing but more of the same. So I went ghosting back into my own past most of the time, a special torment, sweet and prickly. I ghosted Nabomba Zom and I saw myself out riding with Malilini, and it broke my heart. But as I hovered invisible above that young happy pair I didn't dare make myself known to them; I remembered Loiza la Vakako's admonitions about interfering with the past, and I feared making the attempt, much as I longed to. I told myself that one ghostly word from me on the eve of Loiza la Vakako's fatal banquet could save Malilini's life and spare me from this hell of Alta Hannalanna, and yet I held my tongue. Crazy? Maybe. But my fear was even greater than my pain.

I ghosted Megalo Kastro and watched myself begging among the gentle kindly whores. I saw myself swimming for my life in that strange ocean. I went back even farther, to my life on Vietoris. I had never ghosted that far back before. I looked down at myself standing beside my father on the slopes of Mount Salvat, with Romany Star blazing in the sky.

Then I wanted to see my father again, to find out how things had gone for him after the company had sold me away into slavery. But I couldn't find him, though I roamed Vietoris from end to end. My whole family had disappeared. I thought perhaps there was something missing from my ghosting skills, that I didn't yet know all there was to know about locating particular people in space and time. That was the easy thing to believe, that it was my own fault if I couldn't find my father anywhere.

I grew bolder. I went to worlds I had never seen, Duud Shabeel, Kalimaka, Fenix, Clard Msat. They became real to me and Alta Hannalanna was only a dream. I would be right inside a worm, hacking away at its flesh, and between one second and the next I would disappear for hours on Estrilidis, Iriarte, Xamur. When I came back nothing had changed: I was still in mid-stroke, the scimitar descending. Sometimes I went away again in that very moment. It was as easy to go back a hundred years as it was to travel back a month. I swung in wider and wider loops, hurling myself backward without giving a damn about the consequences.

One day I summoned the ghosting force and sent myself out without pausing to think about where I might be going. What did it matter? Any place would be better than Alta Hannalanna. There was the familiar disorientation and dizziness and then I was looking at blue sky, heavy fleecy white clouds, a yellow sun. What place was this? Short wide-crowned trees with brown trunks and green leaves, and a meadow of thick green grass, and tents in the meadow, and men and women gathered around a huge cauldron. The men wore plush waistcoats, velvet riding-breeches, long black coats, gleaming boots that came up to mid-calf. The women had satin dresses loose and open on top to show their breasts, colorful shawls, plumed turbans. Three or four of the younger ones were singing and beating on tambourines. The men were clapping and stamping their feet. A great shaggy brown animal tethered to a pole was dancing too, comically, lurching from side to side on its powerful heavy legs. I knew at once where I was and the knowledge stunned me. Where else but lost dead Earth? Who else could these people be but a band of traveling Gypsies? How handsome they were, how vital and strong! I floated through their encampment, listening to them shouting to one another in a language that I could only understand in snatches but which beyond any doubt was some ancient form of Romany, and I felt a joy and a wonder that lifted me entirely out of my misery and swept me off into exaltation.

Now that I knew I could ghost as far back in time as Earth, I went there often, hoping to find my people again. And very often I did; but it was a long time before I saw them in such merriment again. Instead I saw them huddling in leaking lean-tos under a cold rain, wearing nothing but ragged scraps of old clothing. I saw them cooped up in prisons, living a filthy life in squalid wooden huts while grunting bailiffs strode among them with whips. I saw them living on roots and leaves in the forest. I saw them marching on dry dusty roads, looking fearfully back over their shoulders. I saw their dark eyes peering out through barbed wire fences. Again and again and again I went to Earth and sought out my people and whenever I found them I found them suffering and hungry. That was when I knew that for the Rom old Earth had been Alta Hannalanna all the time, when they lived as homeless strangers, despised and hungry among the uncaring Gaje. It was then that the resolution was born in me to devote the rest of my life to setting right that ancient wrong, to end the years of wandering at last. I would bring my people home to Romany Star.

But first I had to get myself free of this hideous place where I was trapped.

4.

ONE DAY THEY BROUGHT VABRIKANT BACK BADLY wounded from the tunnels. He had gone out a couple of days before with a novice, a long-legged boy from Darma Barma—that was what they mostly used Vabrikant for, the training of novices—and this time he had been imprudent or too slow or he had simply not cared; and when he opened the cyst the insect was alive and waiting. It sprang out already fighting and laid him open from side to side with a single swipe of its beak.

I give the boy from Darma Barma credit: he struggled with the thing and killed it, and staggered back all the way to the dormitory with Vabrikant in his arms although he had been seriously cut and gouged himself. A couple of the overmasters came out to see what had happened. Vabrikant was a horrifying sight and he seemed close to death. He was unconscious, breathing slowly and hoarsely, his mouth slack. His eyes were open, but they looked like little slits of glass. The overmasters studied him a moment, shrugged, walked away.

The merciful thing would probably have been to help him die as quickly as possible, but I was too young to understand that. I went running after the overmasters, shouting, "Hey! Are you just going to leave him lying there?"

One of them didn't even look back. The other turned and peered at me in disbelief. Nobody spoke to overmasters here unless they spoke to you first.

"You said something?"

"He's still alive. He's in pain. For God's sake, aren't you going to do anything for him?"

"Why is that your problem?"

"That's *Vabrikant* there. He's the best man in this whole godforsaken place."

The overmaster stared at me as if I had gone insane and made a quick offhand gesture with his thumb, telling me to get back where I belonged. I wasn't having that. I came up close to him, practically nose to nose, and pointed angrily at Vabrikant. "He doesn't have to die! Get him into surgery, will you? At least give him a pain-killer." A chilly stare was the only response I got. "God damn it, aren't you human? A man's lying there on the ground with his guts hanging out and you won't even do anything?"

The overmaster had his truncheon in one hand and his sensory whip in the other. I saw the blaze of irritation and fury in his eyes and I knew that if I didn't back off in another moment he was going to jab me. But I didn't care. I went on pointing and shouting and then, when that seemed to do no good, I grabbed him by the arm and swung him around.

He didn't give me the truncheon. He gave me the sensory whip.

I wasn't prepared for that. Not that you could ever be; but the sensory whip was a weapon that ordinarily was used only in extreme jeopardy. It could kill. I thought it had killed me. I had never known such pain as that in my life. I felt as if I had been speared in the skull with a mining pick. My head rolled until it almost fell off my shoulders and my heart stopped beating and my feet went out from under me and I fell down, choking and gagging, biting at the spongy flooring.

When I came back to consciousness the walls seemed to be spinning. The roof of the dormitory was gone and the hundreds of kilometers of sponge-stuff above us had blown away and I saw the open sky, and it was all bright yellow swirls of lightning dancing up and down. Gradually my vision cleared and I saw the overmaster against the blare of yellow light. He was standing over me, waiting to see what I would do next.

The sensible move would have been to get myself away from him fast. To forget all about Vabrikant and creep or crawl or drag myself back into some dark quiet corner of the dormitory, if indeed I had enough strength left in me to do anything like that, and lick my wounds, if I could remember where my tongue was. Otherwise, if I made any sort of further trouble at all, the overmaster was going to lash me with the sensory whip a second time, and the second time would almost certainly kill me. I was young and I was very strong, but I had just taken a tremendous jolt of force through my entire nervous system. A second hit of that magnitude and I was done for.

Any sensible person would have known that. And I was a sensible person. Usually.

But I also knew that Vabrikant was going to die very soon if I didn't do something. And that I was probably going to die before long too, for I had grabbed an overmaster's arm in anger, and that marked me as extremely dangerous. Slaves were not supposed to tell overmasters what to do. They certainly weren't supposed to lay hands on them. The next time I got out of line the overmasters would finish me off.

Feebly, numbly, I got to my feet. I was shaking like a man with the palsy. My arms dangled as though they had no bones. I was a thousand years old. The overmaster watched me smugly. He held the sensory whip cocked and ready, but he knew I was going to shuffle away in defeat. A man who has been hit like that doesn't come back for more. It's only common sense. So when I took a couple of shambling steps in his direction he understood that I was simply disoriented. I must have meant to go the other way. Yellow lightning was still crackling through my brain and I could barely focus my eyes. A moment went by before he realized that I had no common sense at all and that I was about to do a very foolish thing; and by then it was too late for him. He raised the whip and started to squeeze off the fatal hit, but I came in smoothly underneath his arm, moving much more rapidly than I had any right to, surprising us both. And I took the whip away from him and told him what I was going to do to him; and then I turned the whip's force down to its lowest level and I lashed him with it.

I didn't want to kill him. I didn't even want to make him lose consciousness. I just wanted to hurt him, again and again, until he groveled, until he begged, until he screamed. I wanted to give him as much torment in five minutes as I had absorbed in two years on this world. So I lashed him at the lowest setting and I lashed him again, and then again. His sphincter control went on the third hit. He fell down and scrabbled about, sobbing, moaning, biting the ground, slapping his hands and feet against the floor in desperate pain. Begging me to stop. I enjoyed not stopping.

Other overmasters came running, of course. With one foot on the fallen one's back I faced them down. "Keep back or I'll whip him again. I won't kill him right away. I'll just go on whipping him."

They looked at each other, bewildered. Maybe they didn't even give a damn what I did to him. But no one was going to take responsibility for it.

"Call out the med-robot," I said. "Take Vabrikant inside and have him sewn up."

"He's dead," one of the overmasters said.

"Take him in anyway. Try to resuscitate him. Do whatever you can."
I waggled the sensory whip menacingly in their direction. "Go on. Do
it!"

Nobody moved. I gave the overmaster on the ground another jolt.
"Do it," he screamed. "Do it!"

"Vabrikant is dead."

"Do it anyway!"

They sent for the med-robot. It gathered Vabrikant up, holding him
like a doll that was losing its stuffing, and went clanking away.

Now what? Keeping the overmaster as a hostage wouldn't protect me
for long. He might die any minute from the effects of the lashings, even
at the lowest setting, and then I'd have no leverage at all over the rest
of them. Or else the others would decide not to worry about him and
they'd simply rush me from every side. By now they must be thinking
that if they didn't get me under control fast they could have a full-scale
slave rebellion on their hands. They had sensory whips, sure, but there
were a lot of us and not very many of them.

I had to get out of there.

"Get up," I said to the overmaster at my feet.

"I can't."

"Get up or I'll kill you."

Somehow he managed to do it. He was trembling and whimpering.
I could smell his fear. He was the prisoner of a crazy Rom and he
expected me to do almost anything now. He was right.

"Start backing out of here," I said.

"Where are you taking me?"

"Just get moving. One step at a time, very carefully. The sensory
whip is just behind your neck. If you do anything wrong I'll scramble
you up so much that you won't be able to remember to take it out of
your pants before you pee. We're going out into the tunnels."

"Please—"

"Come on."

"I'm afraid. I hate it out there. What are you going to do to me?"

"You'll find out when you find out."

I edged him out into one of the eastern tunnels, keeping him between
me and the other overmasters. They followed us a little way, but they
had no rules to cover this situation and they hung back uncertainly. In
ten minutes we reached a place where seven or eight tunnels intersected.
I had had two years now of roaming these tunnels and I had a pretty
good idea of how they ran; the overmasters didn't. Entering the inter-

section, I grabbed my shivering shit-stinking hostage and shoved him with all my might back down the corridor toward the dormitory. The last I saw of him he was hurtling toward the other overmasters like a boulder tumbling down a mountainside. I turned and disappeared into the maze of tunnels.

They hunted me for days. But they came close only once, when I was slithering along the flank of some fat worm and I thought I heard the sounds of pursuit from both directions. There was jade-light just ahead and I went for it. With my bare hands I tunneled into the worm's flesh at the glowing place until I reached the shining stony cyst within. It was a new one; I could see the furious giant insect glaring at me through the still transparent walls. I slipped down underneath the cyst with that terrible beak only a finger's breadth from my belly on the other side of the thin jade wall, and there I huddled, smothering and nauseated, for what felt like a hundred years. It was crazy, taking refuge right inside a worm. I might have been encysted myself, if I stayed in there very long. But I stayed as long as I dared; and when I could stand it no longer, I burrowed my way out. There was no sign of overmasters at either end of the tunnel. For days more I wandered in that hellish maze until by some miracle I came to one of the passages that led to the surface. When I reached the upper level, the vine-level, I found myself at the relay-sweep station where the jade was shipped out. A little persuasion with the sensory whip and I had myself shipped out instead. It was a crazy escape from beginning to end. But if I'd relied upon prudence and sober judgment, I might still be slicing open jade-worms in the tunnels of Alta Hannalanna. Or dead a long time by now.

5.

THEY DIDN'T EXACTLY HAVE PARADES AND PYROTECHNI-kons waiting for me when Chorian and I landed on Galgala. But there is no question that I was the center of everybody's attention. This was a situation that had no parallel in all our thousands of years of history.

A former king of the Rom was coming to visit the Rom capital world. Who ever heard of such a thing, a *former* king of the Rom? And the former king's own sinister and dangerous son was on the throne. That was a new concept too, a second-generation king. It was all brand new. Everyone was waiting to see what I was going to do. And what Shandor would.

We took the starship *Jewel of the Imperium* from Xamur to Galgala. It was one of the new ones, the so-called Supernova-class starships. I thought *Jewel of the Imperium* was a dumb name for a ship, flat and obvious and clunking, and I didn't think a lot of that Supernova-class label either. In my day starships had the names of people—*Mara Kalugra, Claude Varna, Cristoforo Colombo*—and we didn't need to call the models Comets or Supernovas or Black Holes. But I will say this for these new ships: they certainly are elegant. It had been a decade or so since I had last been on an actual starship, though I had done plenty of running around the galaxy by relay-sweep in that time. Maybe it's a mark of the decadence of our era, the luxury of modern-day starships. The *Jewel of the Imperium* was like the finest hotel you could imagine: immense, palatial, pink polished marble everywhere, huge and fantastically costly statuettes in Alta Hannalanna jade looking down at you from a million recessed niches, plasma lighting that changed color according to your mood, six passenger levels with a gravity-well dining room on every one, and so on and so on. The captain was a very slick young Gaje named Therione, a Fenixi, probably one of Sunteil's proteges. I was invited to dine at his table, naturally. The pilot, a fat grizzled old Tchurari Rom from Zimbalou named Petsha le Stevo, sat there too, though I could tell that Therione wasn't happy about that. With a Rom ex-king on board, the captain could hardly snub his own pilot. But Petsha le Stevo had table manners of the old school. He was a snorter, a guzzler, a belcher. He gloried in it. And each time he patted his belly and let a good one fly I could see Therione cringe. He was a dapper one, that Therione, absolutely up to the mark. Pink skin glowing, his nails gleaming, his little mustache trimmed every day. After every belch Petsha le Stevo would look across the table at me and wink and grin, as if to say, Ah there, you Yakoub, wasn't that something! Compared with him I felt positively fastidious, myself. I wondered what a primordial fossil like that was doing aboard a starship of the Supernova class. But in fact he was right on top of his skills, a totally state-of-the-art pilot. I found that out when I paid a ceremonial visit to the jump-room.

I couldn't make any sense out of it. Everything sleek, metal and tile, like a lavatory. An empty-looking room, some little nozzles here, some shining metal plates there, not much else. You have to understand that I am no stranger to starship jump-rooms. I put in fifty or sixty years behind the handles myself, you know. But here was neither rhyme nor reason. Where was the star-tank? Where was the wink-wall? Where in the name of two-headed Melalo were the handles themselves?

Petsha le Stevo beamed like a proud father as I stared around in bewilderment.

"This is a jump-room?" I said.

"New. Everything new. You like it, huh?"

"I hate it. I can't understand any of it."

He grinned. "Very simple. Even a Gajo could jump here. Of course we do it better. For them, always, sweating, struggling. For us, as easy as taking a shit. You want to see?"

"See you taking a shit?"

"See me make a jump, king."

"We've already jumped."

"No problem, king. We jump again." He laughed and went lumbering forward. Held his enormous deep-seamed hands high like Moses announcing the Ten Commandments. Suddenly there was blue light dancing from his fingertips. He made a gesture. I saw stars suspended in mid-air, as though he had a star-tank in front of him, but there was no tank, only blue light and flecks of brighter light gleaming within it. He wiggled his left index finger. "There," he said. "You feel it?" Yes, I had: the sense of slipping a leash, of sliding free down the secret alleyways of space-time, that was wink-out. Nothing else in the universe feels like that. "No longer heading for Galgala," Petsha le Stevo said gleefully. "Iriarte, now. You see, how easy?" He held up his hands again and again he summoned the blue light. A movement of his right thumb. "Sidri Akrak, now! No problem! Just like that! Here, you try. You stand here, on the foot-plate—"

A chime went off. The face of Therione appeared on the viewscreen. The captain's finely groomed Fenixi features were livid and his voice sounded oddly strangled as he demanded to know what the hell was going on. Petsha le Stevo urged him not to worry. "Course correction, is all," he said, telling me with frantic waves of his hand to step back out of viewscreen range. "A little routine stuff, boss. We got to do the triangulum, is all."

I thought Therione would have a stroke.

"The *triangulum*? What triangulum? I don't know what the fuck you're talking about."

"Five seconds more, boss. Everything's all right." Petsha le Stevo grinned and held up his hands once more. Blue light; wink-slide; we were heading for Galgala once more. Therione started to say something; Petsha le Stevo pointed to some indicator I couldn't even find; Therione muttered and the viewscreen went blank. Turning to me he said, "You see? Nothing to it. You make any jump you like, and you don't like it, you just jump right over it. Even a Gajo could do it, maybe. Easier than before. Though still not very easy, for a Gajo."

Of course it has always been possible for Gaje to operate starships. They invented them; they would not have built something they were totally incapable of using. But up till now it has been real toil for them to carry a ship through wink-out. They needed fifty different computers operating at once to tell them what to do, and even at that they would tremble and quail at the difficulty of the task, and six times out of a dozen they had to abort the jump at the last instant and start it all over. And those were the gifted ones, those few who could touch the handles and have something happen, maybe one out of a million. They burned out fast, those Gaje pilots. Three jumps, five, ten, and they were through forever. They would go cross-eyed with shock if they went near a jump-room after that. It was hardly worth bothering to learn how, was it? Just to make three jumps? For us it has always been much easier. Those of us who have the gift, which for us is about one out of ten, we walk up to the handles and we grasp them and we feel the force flowing through us, and we add our power to the power of the ship and give it the force that carries it up over the brink into wink-out, and away we go. I tell you, I did it fifty, sixty years, and I never grew weary. It is in our blood, by which I really mean in our nervous systems, in our brains. We are different: but of course we are of different birth. Which is why, after the first years of star travel, the Gaje stopped trying to drive the ships and left all that to us. They figure we have the gift, something passed down in our genes, like a natural sense of rhythm; and they are right. Not that they understand the real reason why we have these skills that they don't have. If they only knew. Our true birth, our nativity on Romany Star. There is so much they don't know about us. Even our ghosting is something we have kept hidden from them.

I wondered, though, about these changes in the technology of starship piloting. If the Gaje were designing new ships that made it reasonably possible for them to operate them themselves, there were going to be consequences for the Rom. If not now, then in ten years, twenty, fifty. It was something the Rom king ought to be giving some thought to. But the Rom king was Shandor, and all that Shandor had ever given thought to was Shandor.

As I stood there trying to figure out this strange new jump-room, Petsha le Stevo said, "Maybe I shouldn't have put the course back the right way, huh, king? Maybe we should keep going to Iriarte instead? Sidri Akrak?"

"What do you mean?"

Gloomily he said, "You go to Galgala, there'll be big trouble for you there. I hate to see it, it isn't my business, but I don't like what's been going on. And you going to Galgala, you walking right in on Shandor—"

So even he knew. And was wondering what was going to happen. And was worrying about me. Good.

I knew what was going to happen too, and it didn't worry me at all. It was what would happen *after* what was going to happen that I wasn't so sure about. But all I could do was wait and see, just the same as anyone else.

6.

*IT WAS GOOD TO SEE GALGALA AGAIN. ALL THAT WONDER-*ful gleaming gold everywhere, all the throbbing yellowness of the place.

Considering our ancient love for the yellow stuff, it's not amazing that we chose Galgala to be our capital world when we went out into space. Gold may be meaningless nowadays, but it continues to gleam just as brightly as it did in the days when whole nations went to war over it. So the headquarters of the Rom monarchy lies smack in the middle of Aureus Highlands on Galgala the golden. And the house of power of the King of the Gypsies is bedecked with enough gold to choke an army of Renaissance popes. Golden walls, golden banners, gold dust suspended in clouds to give the air that glittering, glimmering look of richness and warmth.

I thought Shandor's first moves when I landed on Galgala would give me some clue to the pattern of things, but Shandor didn't make any first moves. I was traveling on a diplomatic passport, and I half expected to find that he had had the gall to revoke it—for of course he knew I was heading his way; the whole universe probably knew it—but no, I got the full V.I.P. treatment when I arrived. On Xamur the immigration officials hadn't had any protocol for dealing with former Gypsy kings, but by now the word had gotten around that I was back in circulation, and I was waved right through the customs barriers, and three limousines were waiting for me and my entourage, and there was a suite set aside for me at the Hotel Galgala. Not the royal suite, because there is no royal suite at the Hotel Galgala; when the King of the Rom is on Galgala he stays in his own house of power, naturally. But it was good enough. I didn't need the three limousines, since my entourage consisted entirely of Chorian, but I accepted them anyway. And spent a week living it up in the hotel, hot baths and masseurs, glorious feasts, much bowing and scraping from the staff. Everyone stared at me as though I were some kind of sacred monster. Hardly anyone spoke to me except in tones of greatest reverence. They even backed in and out of my presence, which was bullshit. Such abject obeisance to a Rom king? What did they think I was, some Gaje lord who required that sort of pomp?

I waited for Shandor to acknowledge my arrival in some way, but I didn't hear from him. The little turd. Nor were there any ceremonial visits from the great Rom nobles of Galgala, which I might reasonably have expected. After all, I was the one who had raised most of them to the nobility, wasn't I? But nobody came to see me. Evidently Shandor had them all cowed. Well, it must have been tough for them, choosing between the king and the ex-king. Especially when the king was someone with Shandor's lethal reputation. I wondered what I would have done if I had been in their position.

But I wasn't in their position. I was in my position, and the time had come to set things in motion. At the end of the first week I told Chorian to stay there and wait for me and by no means to follow me inland, which was an order that he accepted with very ill grace indeed; and then I sent for one of those limousines and I had myself taken from the city of Grand Galgala out into Aureus Highlands to the royal house of power. And went the last stretch of the distance on foot, up the golden steps, to beard Shandor in his lair, to tell him that I wanted him to get his tail off my throne this very instant.

I didn't expect him to react positively to that. I figured, in truth, that he would hesitate only slightly before clapping me in one of his dungeons.

Good old Shandor. He so rarely disappoints.

7.

I STOOD ON THE STEPS OF THE HOUSE OF POWER AND THE light of Galgala's sun, reverberating off all that gold leaf and gold chain and gold plate, hammered me like a gong. I came close to flinging my arm across my face to shield my eyes when I turned the corner and that fantastic radiance started banging away at me.

But I didn't. I stood tall and met the glare and glitter with a glare of my own. You can't show up at a king's house of power and start things off by cringing on the front steps. Not if it's your intention to knock that king off his throne, and that was what I had come here to do. In a manner of speaking, that is.

There were armed guards out front, wearing fancy tunics of cloth-of-gold. I had to laugh at that. Guards! At the house of power of the King of the Rom! Since when did the King of the Rom need to cower behind a bunch of guards? God knows it hadn't been like that when I was king.

But I wasn't king now. Shandor was. And Shandor did things differently.

The guards faced me down. They looked swaggering and arrogant and mean, but I could see them sweating behind their arrogance, because they knew who I was and I frightened them. I *terrified* them.

"Identify yourself," said the guard in front, flat-faced and beady-eyed.

"You damned well know my name," I told him.

"Nobody gets up these steps without identification."

"My face is my identification."

His face went green. He was starting to look sort of sick.

I put my nose close to his. "You see these eyes? Hey? You see this mustache?"

The guards exchanged troubled glances. A second one, tall and swarthy with a classic Rom face—he could have been one of my grandsons, or maybe great-grandsons—stepped forward and said, "Sir, the rules require—"

"Screw the rules. I'm here to see Shandor."

"There are formalities—"

"For *me?* You ought to be down on the ground kissing my boots, and here you are telling me about formalities!"

The second guard sighed. "Put it down in the records. His Former Majesty Yakoub—"

"His Excellence and Beneficence," I added.

"His Excellence and Beneficence His Former Majesty Yakoub—ah —seeks audience with King Shandor, is that it?"

"Seeks audience with Shandor, yes."

"Put it down. Seeks audience with King Shandor at the house of power on Galgala, the fourteenth day of Beryllium, 3162—

And on and on with their precious formalities. I barely paid attention. My mind was a million parsecs away. Leaping from world to world, remembering old glories, hatching new plans. A bad habit of mine. I'm too old to break bad habits, I think. I don't even want to. But after a minute I got hold of myself and tuned in on the palace guards again and discovered that they were on the intercom to some functionary in the interior of the building, setting up an appointment for me for a time two or three weeks hence. I don't make appointments. I reached out and broke the contact and said, "Tell Shandor that Yakoub will see him right now."

"But—"

I was already in motion. They would have had to stop me forcibly to keep me out. For a moment they actually considered that, I think; but they didn't quite dare. Instead the two who had been speaking with me came up beside me, one on each side and clinging close like busy fluttering wings, and the others ran on ahead to spread the word that something unusual was happening. I went up the steps at a hard stride, steaming past the banners of kingship, past the clouds of gold dust in their magnetic pinch-containers, past the emblems of all the worlds that Rom voyagers have discovered, past the rest of the host of regalia and memorabilia that I knew so well from my own fifty years or so of residence in this building when I had been King of All Gypsies. And then I was inside.

It isn't much of a palace, really. Nobody ever meant it to be. It's all flash and gleam on the outside, but that's because of the gold. Inside it is a very humble sort of building. That's intentional. We want to honor our humble origins, when we lived in little rickety horse-drawn wagons and went roaming around old Earth sharpening knives and telling fortunes and picking pockets. So we deck our house of power out with a lot of superficial glitz—a king has to be at least a *little* kingly—but the building itself basically isn't much of an advance on those old wagons. We leave the grand and imposing edifices for our colleague the emperor, far away at the Capital, as the Gaje call that exceedingly grand and imposing world of theirs at the heart of the Imperium.

They need that sort of stuff, those people. It makes them feel important, and God knows they need that. A house of power doesn't need grandeur. It *is* grandeur, just by being.

Our own royal throne room, to give it a name it doesn't deserve, is hung with dark carpets and lit with ancient smoky lamps. Shandor was sitting practically in the dark, scowling at me, when I walked in. I think one of his Gaje women was lurking somewhere in there too, but she vanished when I entered. The unmistakable whiff of her remained behind in the air.

I almost didn't recognize him. He must have had a remake not long before and he looked no more than thirty or forty years old. Smooth olive skin, black hair, even a nose job. But underneath all the changes that his vanity had dictated I could still see Shandor's hard bright eyes, his broad cheekbones, his full lips. The Rom features. Like mine. Like my father's. Ineradicable. The tyranny of the genes.

"What the hell are *you* doing here?" he snapped. Then he shook his head. "But you aren't here, are you? You're just his doppelganger."

He was trying to look fierce, and by and large he was succeeding at it. Shandor was a fierce man, all right, and a dangerous one. The blood of innocents was on his hands. Don't forget that The Butcher of Djebel Abdullah is what people used to call him, before he got himself absolved of that revolting atrocity. But he was fidgety also. He has always had fidgety moves. He was different from me in that respect, and from all my other sons. We know how to keep calm, at least on the outside. There was something wrong about Shandor right from the start.

"No doppelganger," I said. "The real thing. The genuine item. I thought I'd pay you a little visit."

"Don't try to play games with me. We've known each other too long. What gives you the right to barge in here like this?"

"The right? The *right*? I have to ask permission to greet my own son?"

"The king," he said.

I stared at him. "You little bastard," I said. "You snot. How do you come off setting yourself up to be king? You know who the king is, Shandor."

I thought his eyes would pop from his head. Nobody had spoken to him like this in ninety years, probably.

His face twitched. He did twitchy things with his fingers too. He moved his lips but nothing came out except little hoarse croakings. I wanted to think that it was fear that was clamping down on his voice, and maybe it was, a little. But mainly it was anger. It took him a moment to regain control and when he did manage to speak it was a ragged squeaking blurt, almost pathetic:

"You abdicated!"

"So? You believed me?"

"You stormed around telling everyone on fifty worlds that you had had it with being king. You disappeared and no one heard a peep out of you for years. You hid yourself away on God knows what uninhabited planet somewhere outside the Imperium, walking out flat on your responsibilities, letting your own beloved people shift for themselves, ignoring the—"

"Shandor."

"Don't interrupt me."

"What? Who the hell do you think you are?" I almost went up the wall in a wild fit of wrath. Telling me to shut up? Me. *ME.* "You viper. You miserable shit."

His face was white. "I won't hear crap like that. I'm your legally anointed king—"

"My king? *My* king?" I started to rant and rave. I wanted to throttle him. He saw it in my eyes and I think this time he really was afraid of me. And if he was, it was probably for the first time in his life.

I looked back across the years, across what seemed like geological eons, and I saw him at his mother's breast. My sweet and comforting Esmeralda, first of my wives, holding little red-faced sniveling Shandor, first of all my sons, and he was biting her breast. Really sinking his fangs in.

King? Him? I wanted to swat his behind.

"The abdication was conditional," I said. "It's invalid."

"Conditional? Conditional on what?"

"On my continuing to stay abdicated. I voluntarily gave up the kingship and now I voluntarily take it back. The throne was never vacant. The alleged election that allegedly put you where you think you are was illegal."

"You're out of your mind—"

"You need your mouth washed out," I told him.

You have to bear in mind that this Shandor I was berating was no kid. I figure he must have been something close to a hundred years old, which once upon a time was considered a ripe old age. Even now it's a little past the prime of life, though the easy availability of remakes makes it hard to say when the prime of life really is.

But to me Shandor had always been a snot, a shit, and a worthless treacherous villain. That's a hell of a thing to have to say about your own first-born son, I know.

I gave him some three non-stop minutes on the subject of laws and customs and the kingship and filial obligation, and he was so stunned that for once he listened to me without saying a word. He was frightened and angry at first, and then troubled and angry, and then annoyed and angry, and then the anger disappeared and I saw him starting to look crafty. I could read every emotion as though he was sending up beacons. Shandor might be dangerous but he wasn't really smart. He just thought he was. Now that everyone lives so long, you see false wisdom all over the place. Just because someone has lived a long time doesn't make him a sage. You accumulate smarts up to a point, and then you stop, and often you start to slide backward.

(Except me, that is. I'm always the exception. Does that sound to you like I'm kidding myself? All right, then I'm kidding myself. Go ahead and fuck around with me because you think I'm senile. You'll find out.)

I paused for breath finally and he said, "Are you finished?"

"More or less. I'm calling a session of the krisatora to have you deposed and me reinstated. I just wanted to give you the courtesy of knowing that ahead of time."

He didn't react. He didn't even seem mildly irritated. Now he *was* being crafty.

"You have nothing to say to that?" I asked.

"I have plenty to say."

"Go on."

He sat there looking at me. I saw my own face staring back at me, except his was dark and bleak and joyless, my face with all the true essence of my soul burned out of it.

After a time he said, very quietly but with a really ugly, menacing undertone in his voice, "I say that you're a crazy old fool. I say that if I have to listen to any more of your garbage it's likely to start seriously bothering me. I say that if you bother me in any serious way you're likely to make me do something that you'll regret. I may even regret it too. Now get your ass out of here or I'll have you thrown out."

"You say that to me?"

"I say that to you. If I didn't think you were insane I'd have you locked up. And maybe brainburned to keep you harmless. But you *are* harmless."

"You know who I am, Shandor?"

"I know who you were, yes. But that was a long time ago. I feel sorry for you. Now get out of here. Shoo, old man. Shoo. Beat it."

I took a deep breath. It was time to make a real move, I saw. Things were starting to slide off in the wrong direction. It wouldn't do anybody any good for me to go slinking away from Shandor like a whipped dog. Getting thrown out of the house of power like some grubby panhandler might be marginally more useful, but it still wasn't what I had had in mind.

Glowering, fuming, I took a couple of steps toward him.

"You pig, Shandor. You unmentionable stench. You loathsome offense in the eyes of God."

He looked really troubled. He didn't have any idea what I was likely to do.

"Keep back—"

"You need a lesson."

"I warn you—"

"Discipline, that's what you need." I brought my arm swooping up on a sharp curve and slapped him hard in the face. My hand left red marks on his cheek. He stared at me, amazed. Utterly astounded.

"I don't believe this. Laying hands on God's anointed—"

"You wish," I said. I slapped him again. This time his lower lip, the fat one, started to bleed.

"Guards!" he yelled.

Alarms were going off all over the room. Just like Shandor to have filled the room with all these alarm systems, too. In his own house of power, cowering with fear, hiding behind electronic nonsense.

"Guards. *Guards.*"

They came running, and paused, panting, baffled, looking at us. Shandor waved his arms wildly. He was crazy with rage. Suddenly he was six years old again and Daddy was beating the shit out of him, and he couldn't stand it.

"Grab him! Take him out of here! Lock him up! Put him in chains! Throw him in the bottom dungeon! The one with the snakes! With the riptoads!"

"I am your anointed king," I said calmly.

They were paralyzed. They didn't know what to do. Afraid to touch me, afraid to disobey Shandor. They gaped like fools. There was a long ugly moment of absolute stillness. I felt a certain sympathy for them. In the end Shandor had to call for his robots, and they had no compunction at all about dragging me out of the room. Down to the bottom dungeon, yes, the foulest and smelliest hole on the entire planet. I was in for it now. I was really going to suffer, that was absolutely certain. At my age. After all that I had achieved. Well, I was pretty sure I could take it. I wouldn't be the first wise and venerable old relic to get himself locked up and tormented in the name of some high cause. And in fact that was precisely what I had come here to accomplish. All I hoped was that I hadn't underestimated Shandor's ferocity and overestimated his political savvy. I had really pushed his buttons just now; he might really make me suffer for it, regardless of the cost to himself. He might even have me killed.

Ah, well. Even that would be worth it, in the long run. Or so I told myself.

The last thing I heard as they took me away was Shandor, starting to sound as though he was getting control of himself again, saying in a venomous voice, "I'll fix you, old man! I'll have you brainburned! I'll have you disconnected! When I get through with you you'll be too stupid to drool! Be sure you put him in chains. *Tight* ones."

In chains, no less.

You might think that your own first-born son might show more respect for you. But then again, this was Shandor. He was always a bastard, my son Shandor.

8.

BY THE TIME SHANDOR WAS BORN I WAS ALREADY SEV-
enty, eighty years old or even more, what used to be considered a full
long life. And he was my first son, remember. But of course people live
a lot longer than they used to and it's considered a little gauche to start
your family too young, even if you like kids, which I suppose I do.

Even for the modern era I was late in getting married, though. That
wasn't my fault. I would gladly have settled down on Nabomba Zom
with Malilini when I was only in my twenties, but as you know marrying Malilini wasn't in my cards. After that came the small detour of
Alta Hannalanna, and when I had made my escape from that particular
holiday camp I needed a few years to relax and enjoy life a little, which
I did, though I'm damned if I can tell you where I spent those years,
or who with. Anyone is entitled to lose a few years in simple amuse-
ments after he's had an experience like Alta Hannalanna. Somewhere
along the way I realized I needed to earn a living, and, since knife-
grinding and horse-trading no longer hold much glamor for a promising Gypsy lad, I took up the trade of starship-piloting instead. I knew
I had the gift; I had never had any doubt of that.

But a pilot, being even more of a traveling man than your usual
Gypsy, generally doesn't tend to establish really sound marital arrangements. He—or she, if that is what she happens to be—simply moves
around too much. In my case I went into the service of one of the
exploration companies, which meant I was out there on the remote
reaches most of the time, finding planets that no one had ever visited
before. Doing that gives you a good sense of the diversity of geography
in our universe but you don't meet a lot of nice girls in those places.
Then, too, my career as a jump-room jockey was interrupted for a while
by the minor matter of my third tour in slavery, the unfortunate Mentiroso episode, out of which came my enduring friendship with Polarca
but which was not otherwise a real joy. So it was a considerable time

before I finally took a wife and set about the task of replicating my invaluable genetic heritage.

Her name was Esmeralda, a fine old Gypsy name if there ever was one. I didn't pick her. She picked me, or to be more precise her family did, her brothers and cousins. The reason why they picked me apparently was that they knew I was the one who was going to marry Esmeralda, so they had to find me and make sure that I did it. It was one of those typical upside-down inside-out deals that ghosting brings about, where causes and effects get all tangled up, past and future all come out of the same stew-pot in the same dip of the ladle, and there never really is any clear sense of the beginnings of things. You go along and you go along and suddenly you realize that you're already hip deep in a complicated situation that you didn't even know existed.

Esmeralda was all right. I didn't love her at first—how could I? I didn't even know her—but I think I came to. Or at least to feel fond of her. So long ago I have trouble remembering. Certain things I remember in absolute detail down to the last syllable, others get a little blurry.

The way she looked, for instance. A fine-looking woman, that's what I remember, but I have some difficulty about the details. A big woman, yes, long strong legs and powerful hips, child-bearing hips. Dark sparkling eyes, lustrous hair. About her other features, the nose and lips and chin, I'm not so sure. I think she was pretty. She gained weight after a time, mostly from the waist down: it anchored her, it was a kind of ballast. Didn't have to put it on, could have taken the treatment, but she didn't care. I think she liked being heavy. Might have been a tradition in her family, the women being heavy.

She was an Iriarte woman. That's a good world, Iriarte. I have always liked spending time there. It has a small yellow sun very much like the one that Earth used to circle, and broad blue seas. A lot of Iriarte is dry and mountainous and cool, but there are splendid vineyards that produce some of the finest wine in the galaxy, and its cities have the rich, throbbing feel of life and power about them. The population is mostly Rom, and in the main a tough brawling kind of Rom, a mercantile sort of people, entrepreneurs, traders, shippers. The Rom of Iriarte are the craziest gamblers I know: they'll bet any amount on any kind of deal, and usually they don't have cause to regret it.

Esmeralda came from a wealthy family. Not wealthy in the Loiza la Vakako sense, owning whole worlds, but wealthy enough. And in a sense they *did* own whole worlds, though they were uninhabited ones.

They were dealers in reconditioned planets. That was a fine Rom thing to be. In the old days on Earth a lot of us were dealers in reconditioned livestock, of course. This was the same thing on a larger scale. Take an old horse with worn-out teeth and fill the crowns with tar so they look like a young horse's teeth with black centers, yes. Touch up the gray hair with ink or permanganate of potash. Make a cut above the eye and use a straw to blow air in, so the horse seems healthier. Prick him with a hedgehog just before he goes to market to make him look livelier, or put a piece of ginger in his ass so he struts like a cavalry charger. Yes, yes, good old tricks, a grand tradition, deceive the Gaje every time. What choice did we have? We had to eat. And the Gaje made it so hard for us.

Esmeralda's people were in a similar line of work. They sent out explorers—I was one—looking for planets with reasonably habitable specs, an oxygen atmosphere, a manageable gravitational pull. A reliable water supply was desirable but not always necessary. A decent climate helped. There are plenty of such worlds around, waiting to be found. Of course some of them need a little retouching before they can be sold off to developers and colony-promoters. Unfriendly native lifeforms? Chase them far out of sight. Problems of chemical incompatibilities? It isn't that big a deal to make local adjustments before showing a world to potential buyers. Amazing what a few tons of nitrogen or ammonium sulphate can accomplish. Dismal scenery? Do some quick landscaping. Every planet can use some handsome new native shrubs and ground covers. Shortages of raw materials? Plant some trees, salt the ground here and there with useful minerals, set up fish hatcheries to improve the quality of the rivers and lakes. It sounds complicated but they had it all down to a science and they could polish a scruffy planet to a high gloss in an astonishingly short time. They didn't believe in carrying a big inventory: fast turnover, that was their secret. Fix it up, put it on the market, move it quickly. And start all over somewhere else.

They offered me a job while I was visiting Iriarte. It sounded good to me and I became one of their scouts, remained one for years. My home base was on Xamur—I had already begun to buy the land that would eventually become my Kamaviben estate—but I didn't mind commuting to Iriarte to pick up my assignments. I led a number of expeditions to the outer regions and among my discoveries were such worlds as Cambaluc, Sandunga, Mengave, La Chunga, and Fulero, all of which were sold eventually by Esmeralda's family for pleasant profits. You probably haven't heard of most of them. For some reason nearly all the worlds I found turned out to be much less congenial to human colonization than they had seemed to be at the time the original explorers' reports and brokers' analyses were filed. The great exception is, of course, Fulero, which you certainly have heard of and where you probably have spent some highly pleasurable holidays. Frankly, we thought Fulero was worthless and we were happy to sell it for the pittance we got for it, but that was one case where the buyers had the last laugh, since it took only the most minor of planetary refurbishments by its new owners to transform it into the lush garden spot and delightful resort world it has become today. Well, even a Gypsy gets fooled now and then, as the saying goes. And in the long run it was very helpful to Esmeralda's people in other transactions to be able to say, "This is the most promising world we've handled since Fulero. And you know what a bargain *that* was."

I'm not sure how long the family was scouting me while I was scouting for them. It may have been quite a while, since they were methodical people in their way, and they weren't going to marry off their prize daughter to any scamp. It isn't clear to me what good it would have done them to disapprove of me, since in the book of the future it was written that I *had* married Esmeralda, but they checked me out in great detail all the same. I was pretty slow in realizing this. Esmeralda had a great many brothers and cousins, and one of them, Jacko Bakht, looked so familiar to me at first meeting that I asked him if he had ever done time in the tunnels on Alta Hannalanna or belonged to the Guild of Beggars on Megalo Kastro. He gave me a peculiar look and said, No, no, never. Of course it was impossible: he was a lot younger than me, and not just from remakes. There was no way I could have met him before. A couple of years later I suddenly clicked on who he was. He was one of the two ghosts who had lurked around silently watching me on Megalo Kastro so often when I was a boy. The other had been Malilini. I decided it had been some kind of employment review, checking back along my time-line. It began to seem to me that I had been ghosted now and then by various other members of the family on other occasions, but I wasn't sure; of Jacko Bakht I was positive. I ghosted back to Megalo Kastro myself, one day, and saw him there with my own eyes, haunting my childish self.

Then came the day when I was on Iriarte for reassignment and the company dispatcher, a clever bright-eyed young Gajo, said to me out of the blue, "Yakoub, have you ever thought of getting married?"

He was very young, that dispatcher, not much more than a boy. But his manner was slick and amazingly self-assured and he carried himself like a born aristocrat. Which he was. His name was Julien de Gramont, and when you asked him where he came from he didn't say Copperfield or Olympus or the Capital or any place like that: he said France. I didn't have any idea then where France might be, but in the ninety-odd years of my subsequent acquaintance with Julien de Gramont, some of which you know about, I certainly have heard a great deal about it from him.

It was Julien who let me know that the lovely and voluptuous Esmeralda was of marriageable age, that the family was looking for an appropriate Rom husband for her, and that I would not be treated with disdain if I were to go courting her. The notion had never even crossed my mind. She seemed far beyond me, a rich prize for some interstellar tycoon: why would they want to marry her off to an obscure space pilot with no family background at all, someone who had been born into slavery and who had managed to get himself sold three more times in his first seventy years? I didn't know and maybe they didn't know themselves; but what I came to see after a little while was that it was a done deal, that my fate had been sealed somewhere in the mysterious coils of time, that I was going to marry Esmeralda because somewhere down the line I *had* married her, and that was that.

I went to Polarca and asked him what he thought I ought to do.

He just laughed. "Is she a good lay?"

"How would I know?"

"And you don't stand much chance of finding out, do you?"

"After the wedding patshiv, I do. Not before."

"Well, let's say she isn't. She's still rich. And if she's rich *and* she's a good lay, you've got yourself a bonus. If not, well, you travel a lot. And you'll still be rich."

"Oh, you Polarca," I said. "You bastard."

"You asked me, didn't you?"

It wasn't so bad. Esmeralda was sweet and kind and although I have trouble remembering the shape of her nose I do remember what she was like that first night, when the endless patshiv finally had ended and she and I staggered off to our marital bed. That says a great deal in her favor, that I can still remember that night, after something like a hundred years. Of course, there's more to being married than a terrific wedding night. Still, Polarca's advice was wise, as it usually was. I could have done a lot worse than marrying Esmeralda. I liked being with her. I can't say she ever really excited me in any way, but she was a warm and good person, very solid and stable, what you might call an old-fashioned kind of woman. I continued to scout for the family; I was away from home something like three quarters of the time; being married to Esmeralda was in some ways pretty much like not being married to Esmeralda, except that I was rich now. When I came home she was always glad to see me and, truth to tell, I was glad to see her. I would sink down gratefully into that big strong body of hers and she would enfold me like a sea.

I bought more land on Xamur. Between my voyages Esmeralda and I went there often. We talked of living there all the time, on my estate, when I gave up the exploration business. As if I could ever live in one place all the time. But I thought I could, then. One time we spent close to a year there. That was when Shandor was born. I don't even have the excuse, with Shandor, of trying to pretend that he wasn't my true son, because I was with Esmeralda all during that year. Not that I think she ever fooled around while I was away, but there have been times when I would have been glad to declare myself cuckolded for the sake of not having to take the blame for Shandor's existence. Alas, alas. Gene of my genes is what that little bastard truly was and there's simply no getting away from it.

I loved him inordinately. That's true too. See how he repaid me; but I loved him.

He was wild from the start. A small fidgety child, always screaming and kicking and biting. I don't know where it came from, that nervousness of his. I certainly don't have it and God knows Esmeralda never did. But Shandor was always a bundle of wires.

I didn't notice that, at first. I thought he was just like me, my absolute duplicate. That was because he had my eyes, my mouth, my face exactly, that classic Rom face that rides like an invincible surfer on all the wild tides of evolutionary change. I expected him to have my big mustache too by the time he was six months old. I loved him for that look of me that he had about him, I suppose. My father and all my father's fathers. Looking at my firstborn son, I came to see myself in a new way: as a link in the great chain of Rom existence that stretched across the eons from the time of Romany Star. How had I dared wait so long to forge that next link in the chain? What if I had died without playing my part in joining the past and the future? Well, now I had done it, and I was proud; and I felt grateful to Shandor for having made it possible for me to fulfill my responsibilities to the race. That was before I discovered what a louse he was.

How did he turn out that way? Was it because I was away from home too much and Esmeralda, bless her, was too gentle, too indulgent, to discipline him in the way that any boy must be disciplined? I don't know. I think it must not have had anything to do with the way that he was raised, that there had simply been some curse on the seed that spawned him. These things happen. Whenever I was home—we lived mainly on Xamur now—he always had my fullest attention. I taught him the things my father had taught me and when it seemed necessary for me to bring him into line I brought him into line the way a father must. When I was away there were other men in the family, his uncles and cousins, to show him the right way. From Esmeralda came love and kindness, constantly. Could there have been a better mother? And yet I began to hear Shandor stories, each time I came home from the stars. I suspect the worst of them were withheld from me, but what I did hear was bad enough. The pets that he mistreated and even mutilated. His haughtiness with the servants. The damage he did to our household robots, who were not, after all, completely without feelings. His callous abuse of his playmates and, eventually, of his younger brothers and sisters. "Shandor is a problem," is the way people put it to me. Nobody seemed to have the courage to say, "Shandor is a monster."

I never would have accepted that word for him. I was still blinded by my love for him. I knew he was bad, but I told myself it was just boyish mischief. He would change. He laughed at me to my face, and I told myself he would change. I struck him, because I had to, and still he laughed. I actually admired him for that. How strong he is, I thought, how unafraid even of his own father. But he will be a good boy one of these days. I would not see the rottenness that ran through him from front to back. By the time I understood what he was like, it was too late for me even to try to do much about it. And then I lost all further opportunity to do anything about Shandor; for history repeated itself, as it seems to try to do whenever you look the other way for a moment. Bankruptcy, family breakup, exile, the loss of the woman I loved, the separation of a father and his children: I got all those things all over again, as if I hadn't managed to learn the full lesson from them the first time around. None of what happened was particularly my fault. So what? When the time comes for you to bear the brunt, fate doesn't give a crap who is at fault.

What happened was that Esmeralda's family sold one phonied-up planet too many. This was a place called Varuna in the solar system of a star known as Corposanto, somewhere out by Jerusalem Spill. Esmeralda's people really did a job on this one. It was a planet so miserable that the rivers ran salt water and the butterflies had poisonous stings. But they redecorated it inside and out, magically transforming it until it was the prettiest thing this side of Xamur, and sold it for an enormous sum to a bunch of eager hotshot Gaje developers who were going to subdivide it into incredibly costly estates for lords of the Imperium.

There must have been really dizzying overconfidence involved in this deal all around. Not only did the buyers pay us a spectacular amount for Varuna, but when they made their own arrangements with the imperial purchasers they worked out low-and-slow payment schedules, in accordance with the age-old tradition that you should always give aristocrats favorable terms, far better than you would give ordinary people. They are flattered by the apparent subservience implied in your generosity and they don't mind being flagrantly overcharged, so long as they don't have to pay the bill right *now*.

Then the various fraudulations that had been performed on Varuna began to unravel ahead of schedule and the planet reverted to its original deplorable state much sooner than we were figuring on. The developers had not yet realized any income on their resale deals and the lords of the Imperium canceled their purchases in droves. When the developers came around to Iriarte to get their own money back, Esmeralda's people waved the bill of sale in their faces. See, here, clause 22A, they said. We assume no responsibility for environmental changes after the transfer of title. The developers protested that they were going to go bankrupt. Esmeralda's people offered their sympathy, as they had done on various such occasions in the past, and then they shrugged and went about their business. They figured the Gaje developers would take them to court, which would not have been the first time, and the Gaje would lose their case—See, here, clause 22A—and that would be that. Tough shit, greedy Gaje.

But instead of going to court, the Gaje developers simply hired an army of mercenaries and invaded Iriarte. That must have seemed like a more productive tactic than trying to sue. I was off on a year-long expedition when it happened. When I got back I discovered that the kumpania of Esmeralda's people had been totally wiped out, their assets and lands confiscated by force, many of the members of the family killed and the survivors scattered in every direction. Esmeralda and all our children had been on Iriarte when the army landed. Where were they now? A shrug. We think they are dead, I was told. Yes. Yes, all dead.

I went away in despair and I was a long time recovering. All I had left was my place on Xamur. I hid there for a while and then I did some traveling. I made attempts to locate Esmeralda and the children, but nothing came of them. After a time I married again, and then yet again. They weren't good marriages, but they were marriages. I wasn't meant to live alone. There were other children, many of them. My first family began to fade from my mind; the wound healed.

In the end I did find Jacko Bakht living under another name at the Capital, earning a meager livelihood running pathetic minor scams at the expense of the less perceptive imperial princes, and he confirmed that Esmeralda had indeed perished when the first implosion bombs went off. My children? They had died too. Jacko Bakht seemed like a dead man himself. I left him by himself and I didn't see him again. I suppose he was telling the truth, because though I made some further inquiries I never heard anything more about any of them, Esmeralda, the children. Nobody ever vanishes completely, in this galaxy, unless he's dead. So they must really all be dead, as Jacko Bakht had said.

All but one, that is.

By some monstrous malfunction of karmic justice Shandor had survived the cataclysm of our family. Twelve years old, and cunning as ice. It was years later that I began hearing stories about a daredevil starpilot, Shandor by name. He was Rom, of course, although he seemed to be mixed up with a lot of glamorous and celebrated women and they were always Gaje women. That's a bad sign right there, a Rom who fools with Gaje women. The stories they told about him were horrifying stories but I didn't pay close attention. I had begun to forget my firstborn son. It didn't occur to me that this man Shandor could be *my* Shandor. The stories kept cropping up, though. Shandor this, Shandor that, this lunatic pilot who did things that anyone else would have been severely punished for. Somehow he never was. People seemed only to admire him for what he did. As I had admired him for laughing in his own father's face when I tried to discipline him. In his boldness, in his ruthlessness, this Shandor made a habit of taking unacceptable risks, and on one occasion—the infamous Djebel Abdullah affair—he had actually lost an entire starship, causing it to be wrecked on one of the nastiest planets known. He denied any negligence. Worse, there were monstrous charges that there had been cannibalism among the survivors and that he, as the senior surviving officer, had not only condoned but even had organized that. He denied that too.

Now it came to my attention that this man was named Shandor son of Yakoub and that he had been born on Xamur. I was stunned. I tried to reject the whole idea. But there could be no coincidence in that, Shandor son of Yakoub. I remembered the red-faced babe screaming and biting Esmeralda's breast. I held high posts in our government now —Cesaro o Nano was getting old and sick and they were beginning to talk of me as the next king, though I discouraged the mere thought— and the deeds of this Shandor were hard to hide from, and after a time I had to acknowledge that he was my son. It was a great shame to me, though all my friends stood by me when he was brought before the kris and charged with the crimes of Djebel Abdullah. And found guilty and expelled from our nation. Although even there he managed to exonerate himself somehow, later on. I don't know how. He was charming, I suppose. Or just wicked. I had as little to do with him as possible. And he with me. It is the only good thing I can say for him. At least he kept far out of my way, when I was king.

9.

THE DUNGEON THAT SHANDOR PUT ME IN WAS ABOUT what I would have expected from him. I hadn't forgotten it was there and I was entirely unsurprised that he had chosen it to keep me in. It was the species of dungeon known in the dungeon trade as an oubliette, the name of which comes from Julien de Gramont's lost and beloved France and is derived from the verb *oublier,* which means "to forget." That is, an oubliette is a hole where you dump a prisoner that you want to forget about.

This particular oubliette was six or seven levels down below the ground, deep in the dark bowels of the royal house of power. It isn't one of the building's famous features. Not something that they show you when they take you on the guided tours. I had been king myself for ten or twenty years before I discovered it one day while I was wandering around in the lower levels trying to find one of the archive chambers. But then, by its very nature an oubliette isn't supposed to be conspicuous.

Since the whole concept of dungeons and oubliettes sounds medieval as hell, you may be wondering how it came to pass that such up-to-date people as we modern high-tech stargoing Rom happened to include one in our royal headquarters. The answer is that I don't know; and the secondary answer is that we are not as modern and high-tech and up-to-date as some of us like to pretend we are. In fact we really are medieval types, when you come right down to it. We live by all sorts of traditions thousands of years old. We are tribal. We have kings. We cast spells. We say ancient prayers in an ancient language. We sing out loud when something moves us and we are not too shy to dance on the tops of tables in the fine old uninhibited manner at our tribal celebrations. We believe in things like duty and family and the sanctity of oaths. We are a people of fierce loyalties and strong passions. In short, we are absolutely medieval, triumphantly medieval. Even me. Even you, for all your modernist pretensions. Why not have a dungeon or two? You never can tell when a dungeon might be useful, even in this modern era. *Especially* in this modern era.

I settled into mine as though it was the finest hotel suite on any of the kingly worlds. It felt almost like coming back to an old, familiar nest. The very first time I had laid eyes on it, decades earlier, it had seemed that way. I had known right away, all the way back then, that this dungeon was going to be my home one day. A presentiment. A little leap, not unusual among us, across the boundaries of time. So when I found myself at long last taking possession of the premises it was with a sense of closing a transaction that had been carried on the books unfinished for a long time.

Not that my dungeon was a great place to live. Dungeons rarely are. This one was about two and a half inches above the water table, and appropriately moist and clammy. An underground stream runs below the king's house on Galgala. The oubliette had its feet right in it. A slick little trickle of water ran across the stone floor at the lower end of the room. Even in the dimness the water had a nice shimmer to it. It was shot through with dissolved gold, like everything else on Galgala. The very walls of my little prison cell were full of gold. I suppose that if this were medieval Earth instead of fantastic futuristic Galgala I might have been able to bribe my way out of the dungeon after spending thirty years or so extracting the gold from the walls by the heat of my candle, or something like that. But this was, after all, fantastic futuristic Galgala where gold is everywhere, and my guards were no more likely to be bought with the pretty yellow metal than they would be with a cupful of air.

Shandor had promised me snakes and riptoads as my companions down there. He didn't deliver on the riptoads, which was just as well. They have unpleasant little barbed teeth and they make nasty room-mates. But I did get a family of snakes, as promised. They were slender and green with large golden eyes—the Galgala touch—and they lived in a niche in the wall, coming out now and then to glide around. They didn't look dangerous or even unfriendly, though I suspect that the rats who lived in the passageways behind the walls thought otherwise about them. Once in a while one of my snakes would show up with a rat-shaped bulge in his belly. The rats, in fact, which Shandor *hadn't* threatened me with, were a considerable nuisance. They had six little jointed legs like some sort of crustacean and beady little black eyes and nasty luminous needle-shaped teeth that gleamed blue-violet in the dark. Occasionally one would go scuttering across me while I was trying to sleep, and I would open an eye to see that hideous tiny glow piercing the blackness. I figured that if I was friendly enough to the snakes, they would discourage the rats from coming around, and that worked pretty well most of the time. I stroked and tickled them, offered them bits of my dinner, told them tales out of the Swatura, sang mournful ballads to them in my most beautiful voice. Even so, my nights weren't totally rat-free and there were a few disagreeable moments.

I also had insects of assorted shapes and sizes and something that I think was an ambulatory slime mold and what may have been giant protozoa that ran in furious circles over the walls and sometimes over me. I have marvelous vision but I could barely see them, and sometimes I thought I was imagining them. And sometimes not. They were transparent, with wheel-like limbs. They made me sneeze. I didn't imagine the sneezing.

Food came something like twice a day—it was hard to reckon the passing of time, there being no windows—brought by robot jailers who never said a word, just slipped the tray through the slot in the door. It was not outstanding food. On the other hand, I didn't starve. That's the best I can say for it: I didn't starve. Later on in my imprisonment the quality of the food improved considerably, as I will shortly describe.

I wasn't tortured. No racks, no thumbscrews, no visits from threatening inquisitors. No visits from anyone at all, in fact. Maybe that was supposed to be my torture. I am nothing if not a sociable man. Of course I had my snakes to talk to, and even the bugs and the slime mold, if I got really lonely. There was also the option of ghosting around, which Shandor was powerless to prevent. I did a lot of that. I spent as much time out ghosting as I did in my cell. That helped.

Chorian, I assumed, had gotten himself off Galgala as soon as he realized that I wasn't going to return from my interview with Shandor. He knew that I was most probably going to be detained, and I had made him swear a terrible oath to keep him from launching any crazy rescue schemes. "I have come here to get myself imprisoned," I told him. "Not to get myself killed, or to get you killed. Your job is to get out of here and spread the word that the vile usurper Shandor has incarcerated his father Yakoub, the dearly beloved Rom king. I want everyone in the Imperium to know what the bastard has done. Do you understand me, Chorian?"

Chorian understood, all right. Unfortunately, he didn't succeed in getting away from Galgala to spread the word, because Shandor had been keeping tabs on him, and Shandor had other dungeon cells available. This I discovered much later, and it explained why the public reaction to my jailing was so slow to build. Sooner or later, of course, Polarca and Damiano and the others realized what had happened to us both, and they started to get the news around. But it took time.

Well, I had time. But even I can get impatient eventually.

10.

ONCE LONG AGO I FOUND MYSELF LIVING ON DUUD SHA-bell, which is a fairly backward place populated by a curious colony of strange religious fanatics. An anthropologist surely would find their habits of self-flagellation and, indeed, self-mutilation altogether fascinating, but to me they seemed more sickening than anything else. On the other hand, they are wondrous craftsmen and their weavings are in great demand throughout the galaxy, which is what I was doing there. For the sake of filthy profit I spent two or three years among them, building up a stock of their merchandise to sell on Marajo and Galgala and Xamur.

After a time I could no longer stand living in their city and watching them go through their rituals of torment and austerity. I left my partner in charge of our trading post and went off to live for a few months by myself in the vast desert that lies to the west of the habitable zone on Duud Shabeel. And there I witnessed a remarkable thing.

There is in that desert a small amphibian whose scientific name I do not know, but which the Duud Shabeel folk call a mudpuppy. It is a blue-green creature with radiant fluorescent red speckles, about the length of a man's hand, that stands upright on sturdy little legs and a long thick tail. It has a large mouth and four bulging eyes at the very top of its head.

Since mud is something infrequently encountered in a desert, and this desert was even more bleak and parched than deserts normally are, you may be wondering why this creature is called a mudpuppy. Sandpuppy might be more accurate. There is a reason. The mudpuppy spends almost its entire existence burrowed deep down in the desert sand, far below the scorching heat of Duud Shabeel's remorseless sun. It lies asleep in its tunnel, scarcely even breathing. Once every five years—or ten, or twenty—rain comes to that desert. Sometimes it is the merest light shower, but more often, when it rains there at all, it rains a deluge. Trickles of water make their way between the grains of sand and awaken the mudpuppies. Hastily they begin to dig toward the surface. If they are lucky, they emerge while it is still raining. The torrential downpour turns the sand to mud and creates short-lived ponds and pools in the low-lying places. In a single frenzied night of mating the mudpuppies dance wildly around, choose their partners, and copulate desperately until dawn. The males die at the break of day; the females lay their eggs in the pools and ponds and then they die too. Forty-eight hours later the tadpoles begin to hatch.

The childhoods of these creatures last about two weeks. That is all they can possibly get, for after the rain comes the heat again, and the desert begins to dry. Within a couple of weeks the little ponds and pools have vanished. The tadpoles, if they have reached maturity before that happens, hastily begin burrowing into the sand, digging themselves down far below the surface. There they rest, slumbering, dormant, until the next time it rains, years hence, when it will be their turn to arise and dance and mate and die.

It rained while I was living in the desert of Duud Shabeel. I watched the mudpuppies emerge, I saw them do their dance. And I wondered: What is the virtue of such a life? What merit is there in sleeping under the sand for years and years in order to have a single night of joy? What purpose can there be in it? These poor creatures are victims of nature's blind impulse toward self-perpetuation. The only purpose they serve is to create the next generation, whose sole purpose it will be to create the next.

And then I thought, Is it not the same with us? Are not we just a more elaborate kind of mudpuppy, arising and going through our little mating dance and dying so that our places can be taken by those who follow after?

I confess that these thoughts threw me into the deepest despair I have experienced in my life, worse even than when I lay imprisoned with the overthrown Loiza la Vakako, worse than when I suffered in the passageways of Alta Hannalanna. For suddenly I saw life as purposeless, and that was terrifying to me. I saw us as mere prisoners throughout all our days, as the mudpuppies are in their burrows in the sand: hoaxed and deceived by nature, filled with philosophical nonsense designed to keep us working at our task of replacing old life with new. If I had been less sturdy and resilient of soul I think I might have wanted to kill myself, thinking these thoughts, alone in that melancholy desert.

And then I thought: What does it matter if we are nothing but mudpuppies? How does it change anything, knowing that? We still must rise in the morning and go through our days and do what is required of us. And if there is no point to it, why, then there is no point to it: but we must go on, and we must do the best job of it that we can. The mudpuppies understand that. They waste none of their strength in weeping and wailing and railing against their destiny. No, they wait and sleep, and then they arise and dance. Let it be the same with us. Let us live as though there is purpose, and go through each day joyously and with vigor, doing the task that is our task. For there is no alternative. This is the only road. Therefore it has to be the right road. Even if everything seems meaningless, nevertheless there must be some meaning beneath that meaninglessness; and even if we are no more able to see that meaning than are the mudpuppies of Duud Shabeel, yet it is better to go onward than not to go onward. So live. Seek. Learn. Grow.

I found great comfort flooding in upon me when I came to understand the truth of that conclusion. My despair lifted and I returned
from the desert and went about my business on Duud Shabeel, and I
have gone about my business, whatever it has happened to be, without
doubts ever since. From that day onward I have known no despair.
Anger, yes, and dismay, and anguish, from time to time; but never
despair. For despair means the loss of hope, and I am no longer capable
of achieving a loss of hope, now that I have absorbed and understood
the lesson of the mudpuppies. The memory of their joyous dancing in
the desert rain has carried me through many a black hour ever since.

I thought of these things again as I lay imprisoned in Shandor's
oubliette. Waiting for the endless hours to pass, waiting for the moment
when I could rise once more to the surface and begin my dance.

11.

GHOSTING. MY ONE AMUSEMENT, MY ANODYNE. THE SOLE
consolation of the hapless prisoner in the clammy cell. Once again it
became my joy and my escape, as it had been for me long ago on Alta
Hannalanna. And on many another occasion after that.

It was a long time since I had done any serious ghosting. You pass
through giddy phases, especially at the beginning, where you do it all
the time. The whole vast range of the past lies open before you and you
can't get enough of it. You go everywhere. Mars. Venus. Atlantis. New
Jersey. It's like being a god. That freedom, that sense of omnipotence.
But eventually you *do* get enough. Everyone who ghosts grows sated
sooner or later, except maybe Polarca, who seems insatiable. Even I did.
I wasn't bored with it. How can you get bored with infinity? But after
you have been everywhere and a half, there are times when it seems as
if you don't need to go anywhere else. Maybe gods come to feel the same
way now and then. Do they get weary of godding, I wonder? Envy the
lowly humans their tedious toil?

You may go without ghosting for years at a time, but you don't ever forget the knack of it. You know it's there, whenever you need or want it. And then you find yourself cast into somebody's dark oubliette and you give thanks to the Holy Spirit that you can do it. Off you go. Up and out, far and away.

12.

I LIKED BEST OF ALL TO DO MY GHOSTING ON EARTH. BACK to my roots, back to the solid terra firma, land where my fathers died. The old Rom blood drew me like a magnet. Again, again, again— Earth, any epoch, any of its myriad nations.

13.

WHERE AM I NOW? A WALLED CITY, PROTECTED ON TWO sides by two great ramparts, on two sides by the sea. The sky is fair, the sun is strong. Who are these dour thick-bearded men in armor? Ah. They wear the emblem of the Cross. These must be Crusader knights. Within the city are Saracen defenders. And here, these darker men and women in tattered white robes and gowns, at the edge of the camp? I hear them chattering in Romany. Or something that sounds as if it might have been Romany once, long ago. They go among the warriors offering services. This man is a blacksmith who carries his own forge on his back. Three stones for a hearth, a bellows that he works with his toes, charcoal for fuel. A file, a vice, a hammer. Sharpen your sword, good knight? Mend your armor? And this one here, the coppersmith. And the old woman who looks like our phuri dai, doing the dukkeripen, saying the future. You will be a great lord, immense estates will be yours, your sons will be dukes and your grandsons will be kings.

We help the good Christian warriors fight their war. We build a great four-story machine for them to invade the Saracen city. The first story is of wood, the second of lead, the third of iron, the fourth of bronze. But it catches fire and the defenders rejoice. So we build for them a stone-catapult that they call the Evil Neighbor, and a grappling ladder called the Cat. And two catapults that fling stones night and day against the besieged city.

I float over the wall and discover that there are Rom within. In this war we work for Christian Gaje and we work for Saracen Gaje. The work is what matters. The issues for which they fight are absurd to us. For the Saracens we mix pots of Greek fire—naphtha and other substances, a monstrous weapon that sticks to your skin and burns you alive—and they hurl them over the walls at the Crusaders. "Allah is Great," the defenders cry. They look at us expectantly and we cry it too, "Allah is Great." Why not? Allah *is* great. God is great under any of His names. These foolish Gaje will kill each other to show the superiority of their name for Him. And they will kill us too, unless we say the words they love. Very well. Allah is great. And Christ is our savior. Whatever they want. The One Word is: *Survive.*

14.

ANOTHER LEAP. WHO SURVIVES HERE? A FLAT HIDEOUS landscape. Mounds of dirty snow, bare trees. Barbed wire. This is a prison. I see Gypsies in prison uniforms, stripes, a brown triangle on the left breast. But some of them carry violins. They stroll from building to building, playing: prisoners of special privilege, wandering entertainers. There are other prisoners here, peering out hopelessly from their dismal shacks. Gaunt hollow faces, dark tragic eyes. Staring, weeping. Listening to the Gypsy violins.

I drift down beside one of the violinists and make myself visible. He gives me a strange look but goes on playing. A sad wild tune. You could sing to it, or you could break into tears. He plays me the sound of a question.

"Sarishan," I say. "I am Rom."

"Are you?" Cool, distant, barely seeming to care.

"Yakoub son of Romano Nirano. Kalderash. And you?"

A shrug. "Daweli Shukarnak. You are new here?"

"A visitor."

"A visitor," he says, as if the word has no meaning for him. "Well, enjoy your holiday."

He turns away and fiercely strikes his bow across the strings of his violin, making a terrible noise. I am reminded of the grinding sound of Pulika Boshengro's fiddle as he gave the signal for his henchmen to attack his kinsmen, and for an instant I feel like cringing. Like screaming.

"Wait," I say. "Is this place a prison?"

"What do you think?"

"And those half-dead Gaje over there?"

"Jews. This is a prison for Jews."

"But there are Rom here too?"

"There are some Rom, yes. They treat us a little better than they do the Jews. They feed us, and we play music for the other prisoners on Sundays. And for the Hitlari."

"The Hitlari?" I ask.

"The prison-camp keepers. The Nazis." He begins to play again, sweetly, a melancholy tune that tears at my heart. "They hate us and they hate the Jews, but they hate the Jews a little more. When they are finished killing the Jews, they will kill us. They want to kill everybody, the Hitlari, everybody who is not like them, and they will, sooner or later. They think they are being kind to us, killing us later. But what sort of life is this for a Rom, inside a prison camp? They have killed us already, penning us up in here." He looks at me as though seeing me for the first time. "You are really Rom?"

"You doubt me?"

"You speak the Romany strangely."

"I come from far away."

"Well, go back there, wherever it is. If you can. Fly away and forget this place. This place is hell. This place is the house of the devil."

"Tell me its name," I say.

"Auschwitz," he says.

15.

IT'S VERY MISTY HERE. I MUST BE FAR, FAR BACK IN TIME. But through the thick white fog I see a great blazing sun overhead. The air is moist and hot. This is a marketplace. In its center grows a gigantic tree with a thousand trunks, and a bewildering tangle of roots and vines descending from its myriad limbs. All around it flows the throbbing life of the market, peddlers, holy men, thieves, mule-carts, children, scribes, magicians.

The people are slender and they have dark skins and sharp bony faces. Their eyes are very bright. They speak a language I don't understand, though I hear a word or two that sounds almost like Romany. At first all these people look Rom to me. But then I see that most of them are not. I see the real Rom among them. They look very much like the others, but the difference, though barely perceptible, is real. They have the Rom glow.

I watch the Rom moving through the marketplace. A juggler here, a team of acrobats there. Five who have mounted a little stage and are acting a play. One is playing a pipe. One who grins and waves a box of dice, and invites passersby to game with him. And one who has trained an elephant to dance: I see the great beast lumbering from side to side like a clown.

Some sort of turbaned prince advances solemnly through the marketplace. Servants with gilded pikes precede him, scattering the crowd. One of the Rom runs up to him, nut-brown, agile as a monkey. All he wears is a white cloth twisted at his waist. He turns handsprings; he shouts and laughs; he makes intricate fortune-telling signs. He holds out the palm of his hand. One of the servants puts a coin in it. Then he pushes the Gypsy roughly away with the flat of his pike. He has come too close to the prince. We are outcasts here. We follow the forbidden trades. It would be a disgrace for these others to juggle in the market-place or to offer to foretell the future. We do what the decent folk may not do, and we do it with much skill.

Where am I? The mist is so thick. It is so very long ago. The heavy air is rich with spices. This must be history's dawn. We are newly come out of our lost and ruined land of Atlantis and we are refugees here. Perhaps this place is Babylon. Perhaps it is one of the island kingdoms of the Mediterranean Sea. I think it is the land that was called India, though. Where we lived so long after we left Atlantis. That elephant, the heat, the vines dangling from the many-trunked tree. It is the same in this India as everywhere else, for us. Somehow we are jugglers and acrobats, tinkers and soothsayers, wherever we go. Outsiders. Outcasts.

I allow myself to become visible. I am by far the biggest man in the marketplace and my clothing is strange and my skin is too light a color. Yet only one person seems to notice me. He is the agile Rom boy who was turning handsprings for the prince. Our eyes meet across nearly the entire width of the marketplace, and he grins at me. That warm grin shines like a beacon in the mist.

Does he take me for some Gaje prince from a far-off land, newly arrived and foolish enough to pay him a fortune in gold for a quick dance and a bit of prophecy?

No. No. He grins again, and winks. It is a wink of recognition and kinship. He sees the Rom in me.

I wink back, and grin. My lips shape a word for him: *Sarishan.*

And back through the mist from him comes an answering word: *Sarishan, cousin.*

Did he truly say that? *Cousin?* He laughs and nods. And turns, that unknown ancient cousin of mine, and disappears into the crowd. And I am alone, separated from him by five thousand years of white fog.

16.

I KNOW WHERE I AM, HERE. THIS IS JULIEN DE GRAMONT'S
lost and beloved France, and I am at the shrine of Sara the Black Virgin.
Festival time for the Rom: we have come from all over Europe for it.
I have been here before, many times, many different years. I may even
be here now, another ghost of me. Or perhaps many of me. So be it.
I look around. A familiar sight. The Gypsy women in long swirling
skirts of a thousand hues, with masses of gold gleaming on their throats
and breasts, the men in dark suits and brilliant scarves, everyone carrying lighted tapers down the gentle slope to the beach. And around them,
as always, surging throngs of Gaje spectators, elbow to elbow. Pressing
close, trying to catch a glimpse of the Gypsies at their rites. Always
watching us. And we are splendid in our alienness. Men on white
horses, priests in black cassocks. Hooves clopping on cobblestones.
Violins and guitars ringing with liquid melodies. The long lines of Rom
winding through the narrow streets to the church where the black
statue of the saint is displayed. Sweet incense on the air and the thick
smell of candle-tallow. Laughter, singing, men, women, children, pick-
pockets and policemen, Rom and Gaje.

"Do you want to know how we steal chickens?" Rom boy teases
wide-eyed Gajo. "Use a horsewhip, that's best. A quick flick of the whip
and you lift her right out of the yard, not even a squawk out of her.
Or else tie a bit of corn to a string and dangle it where the hen can
swallow it. One yank and you have her."

"You still do these things?"

"Oh, that and plenty more!"

"Tell him how to drab the bawlo, Hojok!"

A blink, a smile. "What's that?"

"It means poisoning the pig. A sponge dipped in lard: feed it to some
farmer's pig. The lard melts, the sponge gets big, the pig dies of the
blockage in his gut. Then go to the farmer. Will you give us that dead

pig? We can feed the meat to our dogs. Farmer doesn't know why the pig died, doesn't dare use the meat. Gives it to us. Roast pork at the feast!"

"Is that how it's done?"

"We steal small children, too. Bring them up as Gypsies."

"I think you're just having fun with me."

"Oh, no, sir, no, no. Authentic tales of Gypsy folkways. You spare a hundred francs, maybe? Fifty?"

Sara-la-Kali in the church, the black image. Servant-girl to the sisters of the Virgin Mary, Mary Jacob and Mary Salome, when they fled the Holy Land. A Gypsy girl, devout and good, daughter of a great Rom long ago. The sea cast the sisters up on the coast of Julien's France and Sara, because a vision had told her to do it, made a raft from her dress and went out to save them. And afterward the sisters baptized her and she taught the gospel among the Gaje and the Rom. "You know of the Black Virgin?" I once asked him. "Our Gypsy saint? Her statue in an old church in France?" But no, he knew nothing about her. Not a Catholic saint, I explained. Just our saint. But they kept her in a Catholic church all the same. Visited regularly—a big pilgrimage every year. He knew nothing. I didn't have the heart to tell him that I had been there, to his France, to see the pilgrimage of Sara-la-Kali. More than once, even. Poor Julien, almost a Rom at his soul, but ghosting will always be beyond his abilities. And so I have seen the very France, that burns so brightly in his dreams, that he will never see.

The long night's vigil in the crypt. On the left the old pagan altar, on the right the statue of Sara, in the center a Christian altar almost two thousand years old. All gone now, of course, all vanished when Earth ended. Not a trace left. But I can still go there, ghosting. To see my forefathers at their devotions. Put pieces of clothing on the hooks as offerings to Sara. Rub the holy medals and photographs and be healed, if you are sick. Then the march to the sea, carrying the holy images into the surf. Dip yourselves in too, pour the water over each other's heads, even dip your fortune-telling cards in the water to make them holier. Guitars. Violins. Candle-smoke. Crowds. All of us Rom marching together, and the Gaje looking on, awed and frightened. So long ago. I go there and I march with them. No one questions my right to be there.

"Mandi Angitrako Rom?" someone asks me. "Are you an English Gypsy?"

"No," I said. "Not English. Much farther away."

"Ah, yes. From America. From New York! From Romville in America! Sarishan, cousin! Sarishan!"

Just names to me. America. New York. All so long ago. My people. And I their king to be, walking among them, the man from the stars, laughing, weeping, singing.

17.

THIS CASTLE IS GREAT IDA. STONE BATTLEMENTS, LOFTY arches, deep moat green with age. I see a ghost myself on an earlier visit glimmering on the far wall as the cannons boom. Here and there other Rom ghosts flicker in and out of sight like candleflames along the ramparts. There must be as many ghosts here as there are defenders.

Down in the trenches at the foot of the hill the invading Austrians roar insults at us. From on high in the castle the Gypsy defenders roar right back. The Austrians roar in one language and the Gypsies in another, but to me it is just noise. Hootchka! Pootchka! Hoya! Zim!

Polarca appears at my elbow. "Some fun, eh, you Yakoub?"

"But it always ends the same way."

"Still, how brave we are, yes?"

Yes. How brave. A thousand Gypsies in the service of Ferenc Perenyi, the Hungarian lord of the keep. When the Austrian army came he couldn't find any of his own people to defend his castle; but there were the Gypsies. Look at them! Twenty days under siege, and how they battle! We are always loyal when we are asked to fight. We never run away under attack. Except, of course, when it would be crazy to stay. Perenyi is long gone, out the back gate and fled, leaving his castle to its fate. So it is a Gypsy castle now. If we save it, we can keep it. But of course we have no way of saving it. The Austrians are unrelenting.

"Keep on fighting!" Polarca yells. "You're going to win!"

Sweaty men in grimy rags load the big guns and touch lights to them. Far below, the landscape erupts in flame and the Austrians scatter. The Gypsies reload. I would take a hand in it myself if I could. Reload, aim, fire. Reload, aim, fire. Polarca capers from battlement to battlement. The other Yakoubs run madly about, grinning, shouting, encouraging the fighters. We will save Ferenc Perenyi's castle from the Austrians for him, and if Perenyi never comes back the castle will be ours. Fire! Fire! The Austrians are fleeing!

But the cannons of the castle begin to fall silent.

"Shoot! Why don't you shoot?" Polarca screams.

No one can understand what he says. The din of the battle blots him out. The howling of the wind, the cries of the wounded. And who would understand the Romany of a Rom of the Kingdom, anyway, here on Earth sixteen centuries in the past? But still he tries to rally the fighters.

"Shoot! Shoot!"

"They're out of gunpowder," I say quietly in his ear.

So they are. The Gypsy leader stands on the battlements, shaking his fists. "You bastards!" he cries at the Austrians. That must be what he's saying. "You bastards! If we had any more powder we'd finish you off!"

The attackers are starting to realize, now, that the firing has stopped.

"Come on!" Polarca screams. "Bare hands! Knuckles and fists!"

The Austrians come racing up the hill. We can do nothing against them. Here and there a rifle fires a single shot; but our powder is gone and they sweep over the rim of the castle walls. The battle is lost. The castle is lost.

One lovely moment right at the end. The Austrian troops close in on the brave Gypsies, who are fighting to the last, clubs, knives, fists, anything. And the attackers see that there are no Hungarians here, that only Gypsies remain to defend the castle. The Austrian general appears. He makes a sweeping gesture with both his arms. And calls out. "Run, Gypsy, run as fast as you can!" There will be no attempt to take prisoners. The defeated Gypsies quickly slip away, and the Austrians let them do it, and Great Ida is lost. Only a few Rom ghosts remain. There is Polarca, far off up there. There is another Yakoub, and yet another, high in the battlements. And there? Valerian? Familiar faces everywhere. It was a glorious defeat and we have all come to see it. Some of us many times. That is what all our history is like, I suppose. One glorious defeat after another. Always defeats, alas. But always glorious.

SIX:

A Candle Is All Flame from Tip to Tip

Sit on the bank of a river and wait. Sooner or later the corpse of your enemy will come floating by.

1.

YOU UNDERSTAND THAT DUNGEON LIFE WASN'T ALL SIM-
ply a lot of merry ghosting around. You can ghost only so much, and
then you start getting sick of it. Up and out, far and away, enough and
too much: the ectoplasmic life has its joys but eventually they can pall
on you.

Of course, life in a dungeon palls too, and faster. But it's less strenuous. Ghosting takes a lot out of you at any age. (I think it took more
out of me when I was twenty than it does a hundred fifty-odd years
later.) So the trick is to hold a balance between the boredom of not
ghosting at all and the exhaustion of doing too much of it. That's the
trick in every aspect of life. You commit this excess and then you
commit that excess and everything averages out in the middle, if you're
lucky. If you survive long enough you can say that you've led a nice
moderate life. The theory of countervailing excesses. In the long run all
forces come into balance and all extremes cancel out. This is known as
the process of regression to the mean. It makes for a very happy life,
in the long run. Of course, in the short run you can go out of your
fucking mind.

Nothing as drastic as that happened to me in Shandor's oubliette. I
ghosted here, I ghosted there, and in the intervals between ghosting I
counted the flagstones in the floor, I counted the stones making up the
walls, I calculated the quantity of gold that must be scattered atom by
atom through the floors and the walls, I played with my snakes, I told
stories to my slime mold, I tried to catch my protozoa by their whirling
tails, and when the rats came out to dance I made speeches to them in
several languages and dialects.

All in all it was much like taking a very long relay-sweep journey,
but somewhat more interesting, because on a relay-sweep journey you
don't get snakes and slime molds and protozoa and rats to divert you
from the colossal boredom of the journey. Or anything else. On the
other hand, you *are* on a journey, and you will eventually get somewhere. One thing that was beginning to occur to me as the hours turned
into days and the days tied themselves into skeins of indeterminable

length was that I might not get anywhere at all down here. This was an oubliette, after all. And what is the traditional use of an oubliette? Why, to file away and forget an inconvenient prisoner. Forever, if necessary.

My intuition had said that it would be a useful move, politically speaking, to allow Shandor to incarcerate me. Ordinary people wouldn't think so. They would say that it's lunacy to hand yourself over to a monstrous wicked villain like Shandor. Well, of course it is. Any simpleton can see that. But I'm not a simpleton and I'm not ordinary people, and I perceive life as a chess game. The good player learns to look five or six moves ahead. Which is what I had done. And thereby had landed myself in this dismal oubliette, precisely as I expected. Now I was starting to think that I might just have outsmarted myself.

Fortunately, I'm not given to long spells of brooding and despair. Instead I gave myself long spells of counting flagstones and making speeches to rats. And ghosting hither and yon on any number of worlds in all accessible eras. It passed the time.

And one day Shandor paid me a visit.

There was the usual clanking and creaking outside that told me that one of the robot jailers was bringing me the evening tray of mush and weak tea. Then I heard some *un*usual clanking and creaking and the front section of the wall began to slide back. Shandor stood there, glowering in at me. He was wearing a preposterous red robe and a yellow scarf, and he had the seal of office mounted on his breast, going full blast all up and down the spectrum.

"You're too early for dinner," I said. "But sit down anyway and make yourself at home. Would you like some champagne?"

He didn't smile. He looked tense and mean, even more so than he generally did. Pulling himself up tall in what he must have hoped was a kingly way, he stalked around the cell like a conqueror.

The seal of office was blindingly bright in the dimness of the cell. "Do you mind turning that thing off?" I asked. "You're scaring the snakes. You aren't entitled to be wearing it anyway, you know."

"Don't start in with me, Yakoub."

"Who started with whom? I was sitting down here minding my own business when you barged in. Scattering all that goddamned noisy light around. I have a right to peace and quiet in my own cell."

Sourly he said, "You're really a madman."

"I don't think so."

"Why are you making this much trouble for me?"

"Me? Trouble?"

"And for the entire Rom nation."

I sat up, all attention. "What's this? Strange words out of Shandor's mouth! You express concern for the welfare of the Rom nation, my son? You?"

"You are determined to make me angry, aren't you?"

"Am I?"

"This time you're not going to succeed. I've come to offer you a deal, father."

"*Father.* When did I last hear *that* word from you?"

"I will not let you goad me." He sat down on the stone bench facing me, close enough so I could grab him and slap him around again if I felt like it. Slapping him had driven him berserk, that other time. He seemed to be daring me. For a long while he stared at me as though trying to read my mind. Finally he said, "You abandoned the Kingdom. Everyone agrees on that. You announced your abdication and you disappeared, leaving us all in the lurch. For five years there was no king. The whole Rom nation cried out for a new king. Even the *Empire* called for one. You should have heard Sunteil bitching and moaning. The emperor's a zombie, he said, and the Rom don't have a king either. The whole governmental structure is going to disappear down the power vacuum. What's wrong with you people, Sunteil said. Why don't you elect a new king? So finally we did."

"The election was invalid," I said mildly.

His eyes flashed fire, but he kept himself under tight control.

"Why?"

"Because the krisatora never ratified my abdication. A Rom king *can't* abdicate. There's no tradition of abdication."

"I tell you they did ratify. I was there when they did it."

"The day they elected you?"

"Yes," he said.

"You're the son of a king. A king's son can't be king."

"Just because it's never happened before doesn't mean it can't ever be done."

"A convicted criminal has never been elected king either."

A muscle leaped in Shandor's cheek. But still he held himself still. He was doing very well, was Shandor.

"A criminal, father?"

"The Djebel Abdullah business."

"The first trial was a farce. There was perjury from top to bottom.

Afterward I was able to show that I did everything possible to save my passengers and at the second trial I was given a full exoneration."

"None of your passengers testified at either trial."

"That isn't true."

"None of the ones that got eaten for dinner, boy."

"Don't call me *boy!* I am your king!"

"Not mine, Shandor."

"The second verdict—"

"Was every bit as legitimate as the session of the great kris that elected you King of the Rom."

"I *am* king, father. Whether you like it or not. The krisatora have chosen me and the grand kumpania of Rom on all the worlds have accepted me. And I have been to the Capital and the emperor himself has given me the wand of recognition."

"Has he, now?"

"With his own hands. Sunteil and Naria and Periandros right alongside him. And here I live in the king's house of power and my decrees are obeyed throughout the worlds. Face reality, old man. Your abdication really is binding. And you really can't revoke it now."

"You said you came here to offer me a deal," I reminded him.

"Yes."

"Go ahead. What's the quid and what's the pro quo?"

"I want you to give me your blessing. I want you to make a public avowal of me as King of the Rom and to withdraw all claims of your own to the throne. Also, they tell me you took the scepter with you when you left here. That scepter belongs to me."

"Ah. That's what you want, is it? My blessing and my scepter."

"In return," he said, "I'll let you out of here. I'll allow you to go back to Xamur, to your estate, to Kamaviben, and live out your days in wealth and luxury."

"My freedom is my own property, given to me by God, which no man can take away. You'll give me something that isn't even yours, if I agree to support your claim to something else that isn't yours? What kind of deal is that?"

"It's a deal that will get you out of this dungeon, father."

"I like this dungeon."

"I could have it ghosting-proofed. Would you like it so much then?"

"A threat, is that? You want my blessing under duress?"

"I *ask* for your blessing. I don't demand it. Your being a prisoner here is an embarrassment to me."

"Yes. I know. That's why I'm here."

"So long as you continue to claim the throne you damage our entire nation."

"I could say the same, Shandor."

"There was a vacancy in the government. That is no longer the case. By your obstinacy you foment dissension, you cast doubt on the legitimacy of the Rom government, you undermine the stability of the entire—"

"Of course I do. You don't need to tell me that."

"You are a malicious old man."

"No. *You* are." I laughed. "Go away, Shandor. Let me have a little peace."

"If I go away, you'll rot down here until the end of time!"

"You would do that to your own father?"

"*Are* you my father?"

"And you would shame the memory of your mother too, I see. You really are a worthless shit, do you know that? I curse the little tickle of pleasure that brought you into the universe. I curse the joy I felt between Esmeralda's thighs." I said these things calmly, even sweetly. "I won't make you king, Shandor, no matter how much you bluster and rant. You don't frighten me by threatening to keep me in this pretty hotel of yours, either. And—incidentally—there isn't any way that you can make this place ghosting-proof. Don't you realize that? If I can breathe, I can ghost. Wherever I am. Whenever." I closed my eyes and ghosted right then and there, in front of him. Back to Xamur, something like a century ago. To see my loving young wife, to see my lovely firstborn babe. Shandor was smoldering when I returned, a fraction of an instant later. "Your mother was a splendid woman, Shandor. I just paid her a visit. To tell her how much I loved her. And to let her know what a wonderful person her eldest son turned out to be. Why don't you go visit her too? I know she'd love to see you."

"You're going to molder down here forever, old man!" said Shandor venomously.

2.

SHANDOR WAS NEVER ONE FOR KEEPING HIS PROMISES.
Something like a week later his robots came for me and transferred me
without warning to a much fancier cell on a higher level of the building.
Still no windows, but also no rats, no giant protozoa, no slime mold.
No snakes. I missed the snakes, a little. They had some elegance and
they did me no harm. The new cell was warmer and drier and I had
a bigger couch. The floor was a solid slab of gold. There have been
periods in history when you would have been proud to be imprisoned
in a cell where the floor was a slab of gold, I guess. Well, it was okay.
But I never could forget that this was Galgala where gold isn't much
more valuable than cardboard, and that I might have a golden floor in
my prison cell but even so it was still a prison cell. I went about barefoot
on it, mostly. It was soft and almost yielding under my toes, the way
gold can be. I started scratching lines in it to keep track of the time.
Ordinarily, as you know, I don't give a damn about keeping track of
the time and I will blithely jumble up whole decades of chronology
without seeing any big problem about that. But here in confinement I
was starting to wonder about just how much time might be going by.
Considerable, as it turned out.

So much for Shandor's pledge to let me rot in that dank oubliette
forever, at any rate. I wasn't foolish enough to think that he had
relented. The Shandors of this universe don't know what that word
means. No, he had probably just changed his mind about the efficacy
of letting me rot. Maybe he had decided that I was so old and mean
that I had become permanently rot-resilient, like that rare yellow tim-
ber from Gran Chingada that can spend five hundred years submerged
in a mungar-thangar swamp without being changed in any way. Or
maybe he figured it would be bad politics for the Kingdom to find out
that he was keeping his aged father stashed in a den of snakes and rats.
I don't know. It could be that he had come up with some entirely new

strategy that made it look advantageous to put me in a more comfortable cell. I didn't see what that strategy might be, but I didn't mind.

Polarca came ghosting in and said, "Well? You like this one any better?"

"You never saw the last one," I said.

"Sure I did. I came three times. You were asleep every time. Like a baby, snoozing away. You didn't even mind that there was some kind of a rat sitting on your chest."

"You could have said hello."

"You looked so peaceful," Polarca said.

"Oh, you bastard. What's happening out there?"

"When?"

"Right now?"

"How would I know? I'm not coming from right now."

"When are you coming from, then?"

"You know I can't tell you that."

I could have throttled him. "The Kingdom is in jeopardy, whole worlds are tottering, your oldest and dearest friend is sitting helpless in a dungeon, and you decide to be a stickler for the rules?"

"These are important rules, Yakoub. You know that. Do I really need to be telling you this stuff? Once you start abusing ghosting to slip information back in time, the whole universe falls apart."

"It's falling apart anyway. But you can help me."

"No. I don't think I can."

"Then why bother coming here? Just to torment me?"

"I like to see your sparkling eyes. You look so sexy when you're annoyed."

"I'll give you sexy, you infuriating hyena!"

"Ah. Ah. Temper, Yakoub! Your blood pressure!"

"You *will* drive me crazy. Do I deserve this? A son like Shandor and a friend like you?"

"But I *am* your friend. You don't know how good I am to you. And I don't want you to think I'm not helpful." His ghost-mantle flickered through some fancy electromagnetic changes, the ghost-equivalent of a long-suffering sigh. "All right. Listen to me, Yakoub. Your appeal rends my heart. It's against all the rules but I'm going to let you know the future anyway." He drifted up close to my ear and cocked his head and dropped his voice to a confidential, insinuating level. "It's all going to be okay," he whispered.

"What is?"

"*It.* The fundamental curve of our racial destiny. The Kingdom, the Empire, Romany Star. There. Never say your old friend Polarca isn't helpful. You can thank me now."

"This is what you call being helpful?"

"This is what you call being grateful?"

"Grateful for what?"

"Look at you, scowling at me. I told you what you wanted to know, didn't I? Don't you find that comforting to know? Aren't you relieved? What an ungrateful son of a bitch you are."

I scowled even harder at him. "So what good is your big revelation? It isn't the vague ultimate that worries me. It's what happens now. Am I going to live? Am I going to die? Am I ever going to get out of this damned hole? Give me details, will you? I want to know what's on the docket right now, what will happen next, not what's going to happen in a thousand years."

"You want me to commit sins?"

"A sin to help your king?"

"You should be ashamed. Manipulating me like this. And such disgusting laziness. All your life you've figured out things for yourself. Now you want me to hand you a blueprint?"

"All I want is a little hard data."

"This is absolutely shocking."

"You stubborn pig, Polarca."

"*Me* stubborn? Me?"

"A hint," I begged. "A clue. Or else stop coming around to annoy me. I'd rather not see you at all than have you tease me like this."

"Seriously?"

"Seriously."

"All right," he said. "I take pity on you. I violate all the ethics of ghosting. I tell you things that you yourself wouldn't tell yourself—where's *your* ghost, Yakoub, why isn't he here giving you little hints? I tip you off on the shape of things to come."

"Go on."

"The clue will be right on the plate in front of you."

"Right on the plate?"

"Don't say I never give hints."

"What hint? What does that mean, right on the plate?"

He shook his head sadly. "You're supposed to be the smart one, I thought. You're supposed to be the keen far-seeing intelligence. So I give you the hint that you want and you don't even try to figure it out for yourself? You just sit there angling for another one? Oh, no. Yakoub, I gave you your hint. Don't ask me for any more."

"Oh, you bastard, Polarca."

"There you are. Right on your plate."

"*Damn* you, Polarca."

He vanished. When they brought me my first meal in the new cell I stared at my plate for ten minutes, trying to figure it out. The usual warm mush, the usual bowl of tepid tea. The only thing different was a little sprig of some Galgalan salad greens on the side. I studied those salad greens as though they held the secret of the meaning of life. Maybe they did, but it didn't reveal itself to me. After a while I ate them. That still didn't tell me anything. As I have said before, there are times when Polarca makes me feel as dim-witted as a Gajo. And he enjoys it. God has given me a monster for a son and a sadist for a friend.

Well, God is infinitely wise and infinitely loving. Who am I to question His gifts?

3.

GOD GAVE ME POLARCA WHEN I WAS IN REAL NEED. AND also gave me to Polarca, whose need may have been even greater. I think he may have saved my life and I know that I saved his. This was on Mentiroso, long ago. Because we were on Mentiroso together I will take almost any amount of shit from him. Besides, I know that he means well. He genuinely thinks he's amusing me when he plays his little games with me. Most of the time he's right.

Mentiroso is one of those terrible places that God must have created so that we would better be capable of appreciating the wondrous beauty of the rest of His universe. In that respect it is something like the Idradin crater on Xamur. The crater provides just the touch of imperfection that is required to reveal Xamur as the masterpiece that it is.

But the Idradin is a single geological feature and you can spend your whole life on lovely Xamur without ever having to stare down its noisome maw. Mentiroso, though, is an entire world.

That there should be an entire world as dreadful as Mentiroso might make you begin to wonder about the fundamental psychological makeup of the Creator, if you are someone of simple soul, or one who is given to impiety. In order to create a place like Mentiroso, you might argue, a deity needs to have some of the essential quality of Mentiroso within himself. And the simpleminded will say, If God has something like Mentiroso within His soul, then what difference is there between God and the Devil? And the impious will say, Only a really loathsome sick bastard of a Creator could create a Mentiroso.

The truth is that both of them are right, in their way. But they only see the shadow of the truth. The simpleton fails to consider that there *is* no difference between God and the Devil, because the Devil is an aspect of God, just as the Idradin is an aspect of Xamur. The impious one fails to consider that what looks sick to us may not look that way to God. God is infinite. He contains everything, even what we consider to be evil, or ugly, or sick. He doesn't necessarily agree with our opinion. He doesn't have to. That's the benefit of being God. We, on the other hand, are required by the system to try to see things His way, because if we don't we will perish. Trying to see things His way is philosophy. Actually getting to see things His way is becoming wise. No human being since the beginning of time has in fact succeeded in becoming wise, but some have come a little closer to it than others.

You would never suspect, looking at photos of Mentiroso in some travel magazine, that it is one of the most horrible places in the universe. (Perhaps the most horrible, though I think it may be exceeded in that quality by Trinigalee Chase. Since I don't ever want to think about Trinigalee Chase again in any detail, I'm not capable of making the comparison. If you want my advice, stay away from them both. Neither one is any holiday paradise.)

I went to Mentiroso as a slave, but this time, in contrast to my previous two tours of slavery, I had only myself to blame. I wasn't sold there; I sold myself. This was back when I was a free-lance space explorer, a few years before I went to work for Esmeralda's family's kumpania. Just as my grandfather had before me, I had gotten myself overextended financially and went bankrupt. And as my father had done, I saw voluntary slavery as the way out. I was ten thousand cerces in the hole—can you believe that?—and they were about to take my

Xamur land away from me to satisfy the debt. Then I found out that there was this deal, a five-year indenture on a place called Mentiroso, that would exactly cover the amount of my losses. I jumped for it.

Maybe I should have done more research first. Mentiroso had been discovered only a little while before and there wasn't much data available on it. Widely traveled though I was, I had never heard of it, and I didn't bother to find out more than whether you could breathe the air and what kind of climate the place has. I didn't stop to wonder why anybody would be willing to pay me that much for a five-year indenture. Served me right.

I had to pick up the relay-sweep for Mentiroso on Clard Msat. When I handed in my ticket to the technician who was setting up the outbound coordinates at the sweep depot he looked at it a long time and said finally, "Mentiroso? You're kidding, aren't you?"

"Not that I know of."

"You really want to go *there?*"

"That's where my job is."

"You must actually be serious. You poor dumb bastard." He shook his head sadly. "He wants to go to Mentiroso. He has a job on Mentiroso. You poor dumb bastard!"

Nobody had ever called me that in my life before. I don't think anyone has since, either. I started to ask him what was so awful about Mentiroso. Too late. He set up the coordinates faster than a ghost can fart and the sweep came and got me instantly. The last thing I saw was the look of pity in his eyes. The next thing I saw, almost at once, was Mentiroso.

The other horror worlds I have visited—Alta Hannalanna, say, or Megalo Kastro—tell you right away what a nasty piece of work they are. You hate them at a single glance. From the air, though, Mentiroso seems acceptable enough. A standard human-type world: blue oceans, green vegetation, brown soil. A bit on the scruffy side, maybe, nothing much in the way of forests or mountain ranges, mostly a great rolling savannah from coast to coast. No apparent signs of higher life. (There's not much there, in fact, beyond some insects and lizards and a few simple unspecialized mammals. There's a good reason for that, too.) Small ice-caps at the poles, temperate climate elsewhere, breathable air maybe a touch too high on nitrogen, but that isn't serious. The weather is on the dry side. It all seems okay.

Then you land, and you plunge into hell.

You start feeling uneasy with your first breath. With your second the uneasiness begins edging into fear. One breath more and the fear turns into blind terror, and from then on it never lets up. You don't know what it is you're afraid of, and you never find out. It comes bubbling up through your entire body, your skin, your toes, your fingertips. Everything you have ever dreaded is boiling in you all at once. Your worst fantasies. The horned creature standing at your bedside in the dark. The little shining insects that march over your flesh when you're ill. The churning of the earth beneath your feet, and the mouth that opens before you. The silken fabric on the coffin lid that presses into your face as you lie there buried alive. The gust of wind that carries invisible needles. The one red eye watching you from the sky. The whispering behind you. The sudden jaws fastening between your legs.

It is a tangible presence, that fear that comes over you on Mentiroso. You feel it wrap around you like an icy sheet. You see it glimmering in the air like a wall of cold light. Your flesh crawls. Your balls try to climb up into your belly. Your teeth itch and tingle as though they're about to fall out all at once.

There is no escaping it wherever you turn. It pervades the whole planet. No one knows why. The place is haunted. There is a god dwelling there. Not God, but *a* god, and not a friendly one. Perhaps he is Pan, the old Greek goat whose specialty was causing panic. You see it still in his name, *pan*ic. Panic is what you feel on Mentiroso, hour after hour, a constant unending foreboding. Nothing bad ever actually happens to you. None of your dreads materialize. Yet there is never any surcease. You don't adapt to it; you don't grow numbed. You can't talk yourself out of it by telling yourself that it's a quirk of nature, that it's just something in the air. You simply go on and on, trembling with dread, every minute that you are there. Some minutes are worse than others but none of them is ever good. No wonder that there are no higher life-forms on Mentiroso. Wonderfully versatile though Mother Nature is, even she hasn't managed to evolve a complex organism with a nervous system capable of withstanding a whole lifetime of fear and trembling. The bugs and lizards evidently don't mind.

The worst of it is that the dread that Mentiroso inspires can be bottled and sold at a good price. There's a thriving market for it. I don't know which is worse: that there should be such a place as Mentiroso at all, or that human beings should have found a way to profit from the misery that that doleful planet spawns. I detest both ideas. You may wonder why such things should be. Do I know? Go ask God.

The man who found a way to turn the waking nightmare of Men-

tiroso into hard cash was named Nikos Hasgard. I grieve to tell you that
there was Rom blood in him: he was a poshrat, a halfbreed, his father
a Gajo from Sidri Akrak and his mother true Rom of Estrilidis. It was
the Rom side of him that made him clever enough to see how to exploit
a place like Mentiroso and the Gaje side that gave him the heartlessness
to do it.

Hasgard was a small fleshless mean-faced man with eyes like whips
and a mouth so tightly clamped that it was just a line beneath his nose.
You disliked him on sight. Not only was he willing to turn a profit on
Mentiroso, he didn't seem to be bothered by living there for months at
a stretch: that was how mean and tough he was. (Or maybe he was so
twisted that he *liked* the things that Mentiroso does to your soul.)

The Hasgard process involves tapping into the neural discharges of
human brains that have been exposed for prolonged periods to the
anxieties that Mentiroso arouses. You sit there and quiver and cringe
and the machine records your whole output of tension and apprehen-
sion and trepidation and unrest. It gets pumped into a psychoactive
storage battery from which it can be played back at any time.

There are three levels of playback intensity. Level One gives you, so
they tell me, a sort of interestingly creepy chill, the kind of thing that
reading scary stories late at night will do. It's sheer entertainment, of
a type that has always struck me as pretty dumb, but I suppose it's not
my business how people choose to amuse themselves. Certainly Level
One is harmless.

Level Two is not only harmless but is actually beneficial. What the
customer receives at this degree of intensity is a jolt of energizing
motivation that hits him the way a spur in the side hits a mule. A shot
of Hasgard Two will carry you buoyantly through the most difficult and
challenging job on a glorious wave of confidence and strength. It's
strictly fight-or-flight stuff, the old primordial adrenalin lift, and there's
no drug that compares with it. Sales of Hasgard Two activators must
run to a billion cerces a year, maybe more. They say that use of it isn't
addictive but I'm told it's very hard to do without the stuff once you
begin using it regularly. I've tried it once or twice myself.

As for Hasgard Three, the official position of the Hasgard Corporation is that there's no such thing. That it's just somebody's paranoid
fantasy, which has been whispered about so often that it has somehow
taken on a kind of reality even though it doesn't exist. It does exist.
After I became king I saw the reports on it. What Hasgard Three does
is drive people out of their minds. A single dose of third-level Hasgard

is the equivalent of five or ten years on Mentiroso rolled up and jammed into your mind in one stupefying cataclysmic rush. Strong people go crazy and weaker ones simply die. Despite vociferous denials by the Hasgard people and stringent efforts by the imperial customs authorities, this stuff somehow does get manufactured and is shipped all over the galaxy for use by criminals intent on torture, extortion, or murder. I include certain governmental agencies in the criminal category.

All three levels of Hasgard activators are produced on Mentiroso in the same way. You take your seat in what they call the synapse pit and the various electrodes and other recording devices are affixed to you. For the next six hours, as wave after wave of that peculiar and overwhelming terror that Mentiroso engenders in the human mind goes sweeping through you, your sensations are drained off and fed into storage units. That's all there is. The work is more difficult than it may sound—it's the psychic equivalent of giving blood, and you do it six hours a day—but you're highly paid for it, as slave labor goes; the living quarters are comfortable and the food isn't bad; during your off hours all manner of recreational opportunities are available to you. The trouble is that you feel so crappy all the time that you have very little interest in recreation. You just want to slog your way through your five-year indenture, collect your accrued salary, and get the hell out. If you leave before the five years are up you don't get paid at all: that's what being a slave means. Nevertheless a lot of Hasgard employees leave before the five years are up. As I recall the figures, one out of five goes insane in a way that makes him no longer useful in the synapse pit. One out of five breaks down and dies under the unending mental stress of life on Mentiroso or the strain of working in the pit, or both. And one out of ten commits suicide.

That means you have about a fifty-fifty chance of coming through your five years intact. These facts are not widely known, but they aren't exactly kept secret. In a more humane society, I suppose, the production of Hasgard activators by these methods would be prohibited. But you have to bear in mind that Level One activators are tremendously popular everywhere and that Level Two activators are widely regarded by most planetary governments nowadays as essential productivity-enhancing devices. And Level Three—well, there seems to be a steady demand for Level Three also.

When I took my place in the synapse pit that first day there was a little Rom sitting in the stirrups next to me, a small twitchy man some years younger than I with bright, quick eyes.

"Sarishan, cousin," I greeted him.

"You will love it here," he said. "You will bless the day you came to this delightful world. I am Polarca."

"Yakoub," I said. And I would have told him my family and tribe and planet of birth, but at that moment I trembled with sudden uncontrollable fear and I bent over with my head between my knees, working hard to keep from vomiting in my panic. It was as if some great sleeping beast had turned on its side within the depths of the planet and by its mere mindless movements had sent ripples of terror rumbling through my soul, sensations of malaise far more powerful than anything I had felt up to now. I was bitterly ashamed, to be seen in such a state of fear by another Rom, a man, a man younger than myself.

He touched his hand lightly to my shoulder.

"It happens to everyone," he said. "Just wait, ride it out. It only gets that bad a few times a day."

"What is it?" I asked when I could speak again. "What makes me feel like that? I've been here a day and a half and I haven't felt right for a single minute."

"No," Polarca said. "And you won't feel right again until you leave. Five-year indenture?"

"Yes."

"Same as me, then. Settle in and get used to it if you can. But nobody ever does."

He winced. He doubled over. The terror had him, now.

"Ah," he said, finally. "This world is cursed. This world is fucked. You didn't have any idea, did you?"

"None."

"I did. But I had no choice." He laughed. "Not that anyone ever has any choice. But at least I knew what I was getting into." He showed me how to attach myself to the recording equipment. My hands were shaking so much that he had to force them down on the arm-rests and press hard as he strapped me in. "There. You have to fulfill your quota, you know. You should hook yourself up the moment you come in. There's no use wasting time."

"What causes it, the way I feel here?"

He shrugged. "No one understands it. Some say it's an ionization effect. Some say it's something in the atmosphere. Some even that there are invisible and unmeasurable alien intelligences floating around everywhere here that simply like to give us psychic hotfoots. But all that sounds like vapor and bullshit to me. I think this place is simply the

Devil's playground. He comes here for holidays and has a glorious time. It stands to reason that what the Devil loves would make ordinary people feel utterly shitty. And—" He paused. "Oh. Oh, God. Oh, Jesu Cretchuno! Melalo Ana Lilyi!" He doubled over again. I heard him sobbing and retching. After a time he sat up, white-faced, forehead shiny with sweat. His eyes had a haunted look. He managed a grin all the same.

"How much longer do you have to go here?" I asked.

"I've been here three weeks," he said. "Out of five years."

We were the only Rom in the synapse pit and we liked each other at once; and soon we were inseparable day and night. I suppose it was an attraction of opposites. I was big and even-tempered, he was little and volatile. I was Kalderash, he was Lowara. I tended to be hard-working and almost plodding in some ways, Polarca believed in cutting corners wherever he could. But we both knew how to laugh when what we really felt like doing was crying. His laugh was marvelous. If they could bottle Polarca's laugh it would outsell Hasgard Level Two anywhere. I loved him for his laugh alone. And for being Rom in this dreadful place where there were no others of our kind. Not just any sort of Rom, either. We were both of the true blood, which is not only a matter of genetics. You need to know a loyalty to something other than your own skin to be true Rom. Take Shandor. Shandor is a Rom by genetic heritage but I refuse to accept him as being of the true blood even though he is my son. Polarca, now—ah, Polarca is a Rom of the Rom!

It took me some time to realize that he was dying down there in the synapse pit of Mentiroso.

He tried to hide that from me. When the waves of terror rolled through him and made him quiver and sob he snapped back as fast as he could, grinning and winking and telling jokes. I didn't know what a price he was paying for those grins and winks. Mentiroso was wearing him down very fast. Just how fast was something he wanted to keep secret. True, he seemed weary and worn most of the time and seemed to be making an effort to hold his shoulders square, but we were none of us exactly sparkling under Mentiroso's constant psychoactive bombardment. All the same, though I had no way of knowing how bouncy and vigorous Polarca might have been before coming to this place, I could see that the man I had met in the synapse pit must be a badly frayed and weakened shadow of his true self. Over the weeks that followed he grew even weaker. He shook, he fell down in seizures, he had difficulties focusing his eyes or remembering the beginnings of his sentences by the time he came to the end. Plainly he wasn't going to be able to last much longer. I had already seen a couple of men die of exhaustion right in the pit.

Once I knew what was happening I began asking around, trying to find some way of helping him. He was too proud to tell me anything useful himself but there were others to ask. I didn't want to lose him. Without Polarca beside me jabbing away with his irreverence and his sarcasms I would go out of my mind in this place. But I learned what I had to do.

One day I got to the synapse pit a short while ahead of him and did a little improvised rewiring of his equipment. It wasn't hard. I jacked his electrodes into my headset and mine into his; and then I disabled the connector that ran from my transducer coil to the storage cell. And a couple of other minor things. The net effect of these rearrangements was that he would be cut out of the pumping circuit altogether and my output of neural energy would go to fulfill his six-hour daily quota. He would still have to cope with the round-the-clock torment of life on Mentiroso but at least he wouldn't be subjected to the strenuous demands of the Hasgard equipment as well.

Of course, that meant that my own quota would go unfulfilled. Sooner or later that would show up on the company records. So I began slipping back into the synapse pit during my free time to make up the shortfall. An extra three hours in the morning, maybe three more late at night. I could manage it. The chief problem was making excuses to Polarca for my disappearances in the off hours. Some days I was a little too tired to handle the full double shift, but I tried to make up the time somewhere else along the way. A few of the other workers figured out what I was doing and contributed some hours here and there to my account to help out. Even so I was gradually falling behind. But that was all right. Polarca was visibly gaining in strength.

"What the fuck are you up to?" he asked me finally, months later.

"Up to?"

"In the pit. Why don't I feel so tired any more? Why are you starting to look five thousand years old? Are you pulling my shifts, Yakoub?"

"What does that mean?" I said, all innocence.

"It means that someone is doing my work for me, and it has to be you. Don't pretend you aren't the one."

"I—well, that is—" I faltered. "Damn it, Polarca, I couldn't just sit there and let you burn out! I had to do something."

"Who asked you to? Who gave you the right to commit such a miserable lousy sin against my manhood?"

"Listen to him. A sin against his manhood."

"You think I'm a weakling?"

"I'm the weakling, Polarca."

He looked astounded. "What?"

"I need you too much to let you die. You're the only thing that keeps me sane in this filthy place. And you were going to die sure as anything if I didn't do something to help you."

"But you had no right—"

"No right? No right?"

"You didn't even ask my fucking permission. You just went ahead and took charge of my life." He was shouting. A vein was standing out on the side of his head. "You think I'm a child? You think I need some sort of a protector? You think I can't take care of myself? Where did you come off doing that to me?" And a lot more of the same, getting louder and louder as his righteous indignation turned into spitting anger.

I can shout pretty well myself. Louder than he can. And I was even angrier than he was, now. I shouted him down. "Damn you, Polarca, don't give me any more shit about your manhood, okay? Just sit there with both your hands on your goddamned manhood and let this fucking machinery suck all the life out of you. And when you've died a manly death I'll start going crazy because there'll be no one else here I can talk to. But that's all right. You'll have died a manly death, and that's what's important. I'm sorry I got in the way of your manly death. Okay? Okay, Polarca? I'm sorry. Here. Go be a man. Be a hero." I showed him what I had done with his equipment. Then I put it back the right way and plugged myself in and turned my back on him. I was so pissed off that I hardly even felt the usual Mentiroso horrors, though they were rippling along through my mind at the standard pace all the time.

After maybe half an hour Polarca tapped me on the shoulder.

"Yakoub?"

"Don't bother me. I'm working."

"I just wanted to thank you," he said in a very small voice.

I had never heard Polarca sounding humble before. I never have since, for that matter.

There was no question of my continuing to pull his shifts for him after that, of course. If I had done it much longer it would have killed me, anyway. But I had seen him through a tough time, however much of an insult to his manhood it may have been. And he was Rom enough to admit that once in a while you have to forget about your precious balls and your indignation and your manly pride and simply accept help, if you really need the help. Polarca is tough and resilient but a stint on Mentiroso could destroy anybody. It had been destroying him and he knew it. I got him through. Two or three times later on, during the years when we were on Mentiroso together, I had to get him through again. He was furious with me each time, and I don't think he's ever really forgiven me; but he let me do it. When his indenture was up mine still had almost three months to go, because of the various shortfalls I had accumulated, and he volunteered to stay the extra time and contribute three hours a day to my account to get me off Mentiroso sooner. And I let him. I had to, to survive. It has been like that between us ever since.

4.

EVEN DURING THAT ENDLESS TIME WHEN ALL THAT I WAS doing was sitting there in my cell, idly rubbing my bare feet against the golden floor, I had a sense of doing great battle.

I could feel myself waging war. A conscious, merciless war against the shameless seed of my loins that had tried to usurp my place. By my mere existence here as his prisoner I was destroying him. I knew that beyond any doubt. Now and again I would send my soul out roving, upward through this building in which I was kept, and I would touch the tormented soul of Shandor, writhing and sizzling somewhere above me. He didn't know what to do with me and it was killing him. He couldn't set me free. He didn't dare murder me. And he couldn't keep me locked away here indefinitely, not without having the wrath of the worlds come down on his head.

I sent my soul out farther, deep into the night. The darkness was on fire. I saw the stars of mankind. I saw the many worlds we had seized for our own. And there—there—in the forehead of the sky—

I saw Romany Star there, high overhead, pulsing and blazing. How it pulled me! I felt titanic forces focusing on me and playing through me. Drawing me upward.

All these stars—all these worlds!

And yet for us there is only one world. One road.

5.

SYLUISE CAME VISITING. NOT HER GHOST. SYLUISE HER-
self, the first real flesh-and-blood human being that I had seen since the beginning of my imprisonment. Unless you want to count Shandor as a human being. I suppose you have to.

There was no ghost-aura around her, but all the same she didn't seem real to me. Syluise seldom does. But even less so than usual, this time. I thought that this must be some doppelganger of her paying a call on me. Or something worse, some trick of Shandor's, a cunning projection of some kind, a clever new process.

Real or unreal, though, the power of her beauty went to work on me right away. As always. The old attraction. Her fragrance, her eyes, her skin, her lips, her everything. Making me weak in the knees, dry in the throat. That Gaje flawlessness of hers, that golden shimmer.

(It was never easy for me to understand the appeal Syluise had for me. Of course she's very beautiful, but in a Gaje way, and I have never cared much for Gaje women. That's Shandor's specialty. I like mine dark and juicy, in the true Rom fashion. Oh, yes, there was Mona Elena, long ago, my one fling in that direction, that queen of odalisques, that superb professional. But she was in the nature of an experiment. How could I properly appreciate the virtues of Rom women if I hadn't ever dallied with one of the other kind? And Mona Elena looked a little Rom. More than a little. Certainly much more than Syluise. Dark, voluptuous, with shining eyes, and even the necklace of ancient gold coins on her breast—a necklace which, by the way, I still have, because of the rapidity with which Mona Elena left my quarters on our last night together. That time when the bodyguard of the emperor came looking for her, the lusty Fourteenth.)

I stared at Syluise and remembered all the times she had gone to work on me in the past. I remembered what it felt like: the lump in my throat, the throbbing between my legs, the sweating, the yearning. One wink from her now and it would all start again.

But then I noticed something strange, which was that I was still more or less in control of myself. This time I didn't think she'd be able to turn me into a quivering puppy with one sizzling glance. No. It wasn't fully taking, her almost hypnotic command of me. Within the core of my excitement I could detect a treacherous little node of something very much like indifference to her. Which confirmed my notion that she wasn't real, that all I was looking at was some kind of electronic phantasm.

"Well?" I said. Coolly. Brusquely. Staring at her as if she was a fish in an aquarium, something peculiar and unexpected hanging suspended in a tank before my eyes, bobbing slowly up and down, to and fro. "What are you and what do you want?"

She began to frown. It was like the dimming of a sun. She must have sensed that something was wrong.

"You don't sound glad to see me," she said accusingly.

"Am I seeing you?"

"What kind of question is that? Are you seeing me! Don't you know? And asking me what I am. *What* I am? What is that supposed to mean?"

"Well, *who* are you, then."

"Yakoub! I'm Syluise."

"You are?"

"Don't you recognize me any more? Are you all right, Yakoub? What has he done to you?"

"You're actually Syluise? You came all the way here?"

"To Galgala, yes. Is that such a big deal, getting from Xamur to Galgala?"

"And he let you in?"

"Of course he let me in. What are you trying to say?"

"I don't believe it's really you. That you're really standing right in front of me in this cell right this minute."

She was all in gold. Her Galgala costume, a shining golden robe, very sheer, maddening hints of pinkness glowing through. A band of gold through her golden hair. Her eyelids were painted with gold. So were her lips. She looked magnificent. Like the funeral statue of some slender Egyptian queen.

"What do you think I am, then?" she asked. Her voice was unusually gentle. There is always an edge on Syluise's voice, a soft edge but an edge all the same, the kind of edge there would be on a dagger made of the purest gold. "You think I'm a ghost? A doppelganger? Here. Here, touch me." She took my hand and put it on her bare arm. You can't touch ghosts. Your hand goes right through them. Mine didn't now. How fine her skin was. There are silks and satins that are rougher. Smooth and fine, yes, but I thought it would burn my fingers. Ah, here it comes now. She's starting to work on me and I am lost. Can I fight her off? Damn her, I didn't want her manipulating me again! But she was giving it the all-out try. She brought my hand up to her bosom. Her breasts were swaying like bells beneath her robe. When I touched her nipples they hardened. I began to tremble like a schoolboy. I thought of how it had been between Syluise and me on Xamur not long before in those nights of laughter and joy. But even so, something still seemed different. I would be lying if I said that the feel of her flesh had not excited me, but somehow I was able to withstand that excitement. For the time being, at least. "Is that what doppelgangers feel like?" she asked.

"The best ones do."

"I never felt any that were this good." She ran her hands lovingly along her own forearms and laughed. Golden laughter. How she loved herself. "Oh, Yakoub, how much longer are you going to let yourself stay in this place?"

"You'll have to ask Shandor."

"I did. He says you can go any time you want."

"He told you that?"

"You just have to agree to stop being an obstacle to him."

"The only way I could stop being an obstacle to him would be to take a one-way ride into the nearest sun."

"No, Yakoub." She was standing very close to me. Too close. "You don't understand. You think of Shandor as some kind of beast. How can you feel that way about your own son? Don't you have any love for him?"

"What does love have to do with this? He's my blood, my flesh. But he's still a beast. A dangerous one." Her scent was beginning to drive me crazy. She wasn't wearing perfume, that I knew. That scent was Syluise herself. I knew now why she was here and I hoped I could continue to resist. "Did Shandor send you in here to work on me?" I asked.

"I came on my own, Yakoub. To help you get yourself free."

"By giving Shandor what he wants. My formal blessing."

"Is that so much?"

"Getting out that way isn't freedom. It's slavery, Syluise. I've already been a slave four times in my life, you know? I was born into it and then I was sold into it twice and the last time I sold myself into it. I'm not going to be a slave again. Particularly not to my own son."

"He's the king, Yakoub."

"Bullshit. I'm the king."

"You keep saying that. But here you sit in custody."

"What's happening outside? Do people know where I am?"

"They're starting to find out, yes."

"And?"

"There's a lot of trouble."

"Good," I said. "That's what I want."

"How can you want that? People are suffering. Your own people. Commerce is breaking down. The starships aren't going to the right places. If they're flying at all. Nobody is sure who is king, and there isn't really any emperor either. The whole system may be falling apart."

"That's fine with me."

"I can't believe I heard you say that."

"Why are you mixed up in this, Syluise?"

Letting my question pass, she moved closer to me. Prelude to something-or-other. Gave me the full treatment, heaving breasts, flaring nostrils, sultry glares from under half-closed eyelids. She was wriggling. Thighs rubbing together. Hot breath on my cheeks. Her insatiable lips an inch from mine. The works. Her irresistible weapons, her heavy artillery. It was almost comical. Had she ever seemed comical to me before? Had I really found her so irresistible before? Something definitely must be changing in me. Maybe her working on Shandor's behalf had shattered the spell. She had betrayed me. I had never been able to defend myself against her until now but that went beyond the limits, her blatant maneuvering on Shandor's behalf. Silently I offered the Rom prayer for the dead. We were finished, this golden viper and I. Truly.

"Do you know how much I've missed you, Yakoub?"

"Tell me."

"Let Shandor be king. You've had a hundred years of it."

"Not quite that much."

"Whatever it is, you've had enough. More than enough. Let him have his turn. Do you want to be king forever? What for?"

"Not forever. Just long enough to finish the work I still need to do."

"Let Shandor finish it. You and I, we'll go away somewhere. Someplace beautiful. Fulero. Estrilidis. Tranganuthuka. Wouldn't you like to spend a year or two on Fulero with me?"

"How much is he paying you?"

"Yakoub!"

"I have a better idea. Instead of us going off to Fulero, you live here with me. Right here in this cell, the two of us. You won't love the food but otherwise it isn't so bad. We'll wait Shandor out. Sooner or later he'll crack, or someone will overthrow him, and we'll come forth. In triumph. I'll put the worlds to rights again. We'll spend half our time on Galgala and the other half on Xamur. You could call yourself the queen, if you liked."

"What?"

"I know, we don't have queens. But we can make an exception just once. You'd like that, wouldn't you?"

"You aren't serious. You'd make me a queen?"

"Why not?"

I was just playing with her. As she had been playing with me.

"No," she said. "There'd be a tremendous uproar. You can't foist a queen off on the Rom after all this time. And I don't want to be queen. Or you to be king any more. What do you need it for? So much nasty work. Such stupid ugly nonsense. Come away with me and let's just enjoy ourselves and leave all of that to someone else."

"To Shandor?"

"Who cares?"

A wondrous feeling of freedom flooded my soul.

"I care," I said.

"Don't. Give it all up."

I ran my hands over her shoulders. Her skin was fiery hot but nevertheless it was like stroking a statue. I felt nothing. In her little coquettish way she danced back, out of my grasp.

"Come here."

"Come to Fulero with me."

"Some other time." I reached for her again.

"No."

"No?"

"Not here. Not in this awful little place."

"You said you missed me. Not very much, I'd say."

"I'll show you how much when we get to Fulero."

She gave me another round of the hips and the thighs and the wriggles and I smiled and shrugged.

"I think I'll pass on Fulero," I said amiably. "*You* go. With Shandor."

I thought she would explode. Her eyes were supernovas of rage. Something ugly came glinting through all that unbelievable perfection. She wasn't accustomed to seeing me withstand her. I never had before. Fifty years and I never had. It didn't matter that I was king. There aren't any kings in the bedroom. We're all slaves there, not to other people but to ourselves, helpless against the commands that come from within. Every man has a fatal woman. It may be the same for women as well; I suppose it is. But even fatal attractions can shrivel and fade. And die. This time for once I had stood up against her. Maybe I had even freed myself from her for good.

6.

SYLUISE WENT SLINKING AWAY, SMOLDERING WITH anger and souring female juices. Next thing I knew, Valerian was with me. Valerian's ghost, that is. As usual. Bounding around the cell like a berserk rhinoceros. A rhinoceros is an animal they used to have on Earth, weird as hell, very large, not good to eat. Horn on its nose. When a rhinoceros headed in your direction you got politely out of its way. The same with Valerian.

"Look at this place," he roared. "Gold floors! Gold walls! This crazy planet. I never can get used to your Galgala, you know? All this fucking gold."

"You want some? Help yourself."

"What good is it? Who needs it? You ever been on Earth, Yakoub?"

"You're asking me that?"

He kept rampaging right on. "Of course you have. A thousand times, I bet. You know how they love gold there? The women with ten kilos of gold dangling around their necks? A roll of solid heavy coins in your pocket? It meant something, on Earth, gold. You felt like a giant when you had a little gold. Like a fucking king. Now look. The love of gold is gone from the universe. All that good greed, gone. A whole perfectly fine deadly sin shot to hell. You know what they've done to gold? They've turned it into shit, these Galgala people."

"It's a lot prettier than shit," I pointed out.

"But just as worthless. That's a crying shame, what they did to gold. I wish they never had found this planet. Gold was so good, Yakoub. And now it's crap. You know what did it in? Supply and demand, that's what! Supply and demand, supply and demand! The inexorable law of the cosmos." Valerian paused, sending out blue and yellow ghost-flickers and ghost-crackles like a demented electrical appliance. What an exhausting son of a bitch! He looked very pleased with his own profundity. "That sounds nice, don't you think? The inexorable law of the cosmos. I always did have a way with words, hey, Yakoub?" Then he was off again, bounding from wall to wall. "Nice cell. Shandor keeps you in style."

"You should have seen the first place he put me in."

"Well, this is comfortable, yes? And all this gold. Maybe it's worthless but by damn it *is* pretty. You need some jewels, though. A little color contrast, too much yellow here." He pulled a red leather pouch from under his cloak. Ghost-leather. "Give me a good jewel any day. Emeralds, rubies, sapphires. Not diamonds. Diamonds have good fire in them but I miss the color. I like my jewels to have color." Pouring the contents of the pouch into his huge hand as he spoke. A mountain of jewels. He thrust them in my face. "You could string them right across the room from wall to wall, hey? Light the place up a little."

"Ghost-jewels, Valerian. What good are they? I can't even touch them. All they are is colored air to me, you know?"

"Oh, shit, yes," he said morosely. "That's right."

"I think I'd rather have real gold than ghost-jewels. But thanks all the same."

"Damn," he said. He was crestfallen. "I completely forgot about that. They look pretty fucking real to me."

"You're a ghost, Valerian."

"Right. Right. Ah, too goddamned bad. You need some color in here. But look, I tell you, Yakoub: when you're king again I'll come to you real, okay? And bring you some real rubies, some real emeralds."

"When I'm king again? When will that be?"

He wasn't paying attention. "I have jewels galore, you know. Beaucoup jewels, that's what Julien would say, right? I took one hell of a cargo, last year. Out by Jerusalem Spill, somewhere between Caliban and Puerto Peligroso, big transport ship belonging to—well, who cares who it belonged to. Enough rubies on board to dam up a river with. A big river." Valerian laughed. "I could break the market, you know? Dump them all at once, make rubies as worthless as gold. Just like I did that time with the drugs, when they brought me up on charges before the kris. You remember? That time when you adjusted the verdict for me. Not that I see any sense in busting the ruby market. Not with the inventory I've got. But somebody's bound to do it sooner or later, some damned fool, you watch and see. It's inevitable. They've got a planet out that way somewhere that's as full of rubies as Galgala is of gold."

That was news to me.

"You sure of that?"

"You should see what was on that ship I took. Ten enormous overpockets loaded with them. A ton of rubies here, a ton there, sticking out into all kinds of storage dimensions, dimensions nobody ever heard of before. You know what I had to do to get them to unlock those pockets for me? No, you don't want to know. I don't even want to think about it. I'm really a very gentle man. You know that, don't you, Yakoub? But sometimes—sometimes—"

"Tell me about when I'll be king again."

"You want me to tell you that?"

"You just heard me say it."

"But that's the future!"

"So?"

"It is the future, isn't it? For you, I mean? Yes. Yes, sure it is. You want me to tell you the future?"

"Why not? You can tell me. Nobody will know but you and me."

"I can tell you, yes. Why shouldn't I tell you?"

"That's right."

"I can tell you if I feel like it. Whatever you want, I can tell you."

"Absolutely."

"There's nothing stopping me from telling you."

"Right," I said. "So tell me."

But he *wasn't* telling me. Just talking about telling me. And flying around the room like a berserk parakeet. The manic son of a bitch! I wanted to clobber him. Clobber a ghost, sure.

"It's the future," he said. "We aren't supposed to tell people their futures."

"Since when did you ever do what you were supposed to do?"

"Maybe it makes sense, the rule."

"Oh, come on, Valerian."

"But maybe it makes sense."

"At least tell me what's happening out there right now, then. There's no rule about that."

"You mean, in the Empire? The Kingdom?"

"Yes. Since Shandor arrested me. What's been happening."

"Plenty's been happening," he said. He floated across the room and came to rest in mid-air right in front of my nose, hanging sideways with his feet just grazing the golden wall. In a much quieter voice he said, "I never thought you were going to get away with this thing, this lunacy, handing yourself over to Shandor. I thought it was the most cockeyed thing you had ever done in your life. I owe you a big apology, I guess, Yakoub."

"So I got away with it, did I? It worked out all right?"

"Don't you know?"

Maddening. Still playing question and answer games with me.

He was worse than Polarca. Polarca didn't even *offer* to tell me anything when he came ghosting. Valerian has no scruples at all. Rules mean nothing to him. The only rule that has ever seriously mattered to him is the one that says, *Whatever you do, don't get caught at it.* Despite all the prohibitions Valerian would certainly be capable of revealing the future to me if he felt like it. And if he could manage to understand how important it was to me to know. But getting him to stay on the subject was more work than shoveling salizonga dung.

Exasperated, I said, "How would I know? It's still the future to me. I'm still here, remember? Still a prisoner. And nobody's been telling me a thing."

Valerian drifted down until he was standing practically upright and gave me a close look, and drifted back up at right angles to the floor again. "I forget," he said after a while. "That was dumb. Being a ghost all the time like this, I get mixed up. I lose track of what comes before which, you know. Of course if you're still here you probably don't know anything."

"Come on, Valerian."

"You want to know? All right. I'll tell you."

"You keep on saying that."

"I'm trying to tell you." He took a big breath, which lit him up in sixteen ghostly up-spectrum colors. The moment of revelation at last. He said, "Everything's going to be fine. It'll turn out just like you said it would."

Great. Polarca had said that too. But he had refused to give me any details. Just vaguenesses, same as Valerian. They were both in a conspiracy to drive me crazy.

I worked at keeping my temper, though. No sense yelling at ghosts: they just go away.

"How so? What's this *it* that turns out right?"

"I'm not supposed to tell you stuff like this. But you know me, Yakoub."

"Come on."

"Just between you and me, you have Shandor on the run."

"Tell me."

"You don't know *anything?*"

"Not much. Syluise was here and she said things are pretty bad. Breakdown of interstellar commerce. Starships going to the wrong destinations. Things like that. But I don't trust Syluise to give me straight news. Tell me."

"That's the straight news. It was a mess out there."

"*Was?*"

"Will be. Is. Whatever. You know, it isn't so simple for me, remembering what's future and what's past. It's all past to me, you know, Yakoub? Your future is my past. A lot of things have happened that haven't happened yet."

"Try to keep your mind on it. If you can. Do I get out of here soon?"

A long pause.

"Do I?"

"I think so."

"You think! You think! You never thought in your life, Valerian. All right. What's happening to the Empire?"

"Breaking down," he said, brightening. He was making a real effort now. "The old emperor's still alive. Hanging on like he means to stay forever. But nobody can understand what he says any more. Sunteil's trying to run things and Periandros and Naria are trying hard to get in his way. Doing a damned good job of it."

"More."

"More what?"

"More news. Keep talking."

"A ghost isn't supposed to—"

"Fuck what a ghost is supposed to. When the great kris found you guilty, was I supposed to let you go free? But I did it."

"You know I'll always be grateful for—"

"Fine. Tell me more."

He thought a moment. "Well, there's Shandor. Shandor's panicky."

I felt my pulse rate picking up. We were getting to the core of things now. Maybe.

"He is?"

"Scared completely shitless. He's just realizing who he's up against and it terrifies him. You've been fighting one hell of a war, you know. Without lifting a finger, without getting a word out of here to anyone."

"So you understand that, finally."

"It's amazing what you've accomplished just by handing yourself over to Shandor. Your boy Chorian escaped, you know, and he told everyone Shandor had you locked up here."

"I was wondering about him."

"And that's when things started to fall apart for Shandor. It made a lot of Rom very angry, hearing what he had done to you. Especially the pilots: they've begun doing all sorts of wild things to protest, flying to the wrong planets, messing up everybody's schedule. Some worlds are practically cut off altogether. Clard Msat: you just can't get there. Iriarte, I think."

I felt like crying for joy, hearing that.

But was it true? Past and present were such a jumble for Valerian. He might be reporting rumors, or fantasies, or events out of some other era entirely. I closed my eyes. So frustrating to have to depend for news on a couple of hyperkinetic ghosts and a gilded viper. I wanted desperately to feel the pulse of the worlds with my own hand. I had been here alone so long, isolated from the ebb and flow of the galaxy. My plan, my strategy, a shrewd one but a painful one. Attack by surrendering. Nobody had understood. They all thought I was crazy. All of them except Bibi Savina and Thivt. But my lunatic gamble seemed to be paying off. Valerian wouldn't lie to me. He might be confused but he wouldn't lie. Out there, the thousands of worlds, the millions of Rom, the billions of Gaje, all the human turmoil and bustle: was the whole thing tumbling into chaos? Useful chaos, on which I would be able to build?

I said, "I like what I'm hearing. Keep going."

"You know about the krisatora?"

"I told you. I don't know anything."

"Damiano has called them together. For a ruling on Shandor's conduct. They're going to denounce him."

"You know that for sure?"

"I'm trying to talk in your time, not mine. That's why I say they're *going* to denounce him."

"Denounce him?"

"That's what I said."

"Yes. Right. So they held a kris right here on Galgala under Shandor's nose and he didn't do anything to stop it? Or try to take control of it?"

"God, no. Who said anything about Galgala? The kris is being held on Marajo. Was held. Will be? Was."

"On *Marajo?*"

"Damiano picked his own krisatora. He said he didn't trust the kris that was in session on Galgala, because it was Shandor's."

I groaned. "So it isn't legitimate, the kris?"

"As legitimate as anything is."

"No," I said. "It's a kangaroo kris. Damiano's own private kris. What does he want, a civil war? Shandor will simply refuse to accept its jurisdiction."

"The time they brought me up on trial, that was Damiano's private kris too. That time they collared me for grabbing the Kalimaka ship. You remember? Suppose I had tried to refuse to accept its jurisdiction? Suppose I had said, This isn't a fair trial, this is a kangaroo kris, Damiano's got it in for me. What good would that have done me, hey? Where would that have gotten me?"

"But that *was* a legitimate kris. That was the great kris of Galgala, for Christ's sake. Its decrees are binding on all of us. This other kris of Damiano, this Marajo kris—what if Shandor says it isn't a true kris, that he's not going to accept its edict?"

"Don't worry. It's all over and done with—"

"Not for me it isn't."

"Over and done with," said Valerian dreamily. He was drifting again, hovering sideways in mid-air. Growing transparent now, becoming a blur of bottle-green light up near the ceiling. "That was really bad," he said. "That time they brought me up on trial." I saw that I was starting to lose him. He was beginning to wander further back into the past. The focus was shifting for him. I should never have allowed him to change the subject. Once he started reminiscing about that trial of his, there might be no bringing him back. "That was the worst time ever, for me. I was really suffering. You remember how bad it was, Yakoub?"

He was fingering the golden flecks in the wall in an absentminded way, as if trying to pry some of them loose. He seemed very far away.

"Valerian?" I said.

"You remember? I was really suffering."

"Of course I remember. But you deserved it."

He had suffered, all right. Scared out of his wits. Facing absolute ruin, and he knew it. The only time I've ever seen him in such pathetic shape. All the swagger and bluster squeezed out of him. But why bring it all up again now? I had to know about Shandor, about the Imperium, about what was happening behind the golden walls of my cell, and here he was giving me the angst and grief of that long-ago trial of his. The biggest trouble with egocentric people like Valerian is that they can't keep their minds focused on your problems for very long, no matter how urgent they might be.

He was still at it. "The way you all were looking at me—like I was an enemy, a traitor—a Gajo—"

"But you were pardoned," I said. "Look, come down from there, will you? I can't talk to you when you float around like that."

"Realizing you were all serious, that you actually were going to put me on trial. And punish me. I couldn't believe it was happening to me, Yakoub."

"Will you come down?"

"And then everybody testifying against me—my friends, my cousins—"

"Hey, it's all ancient history now, Valerian."

"Is it? Is it?" His voice was very faint. I wondered whether he might be ghosting within a ghosting right now, jumping back to the time of his trial, living through it all again in the moments between moments. I wondered how often he actually did relive it. His big trauma. His ordeal.

Valerian had grabbed one ship too many, that time. The wrong ship. And we had to make him suffer for it. And then I had taken pity on him despite everything. Saving him at the last minute from the worst punishment a Rom could receive.

"Yakoub?" he murmured. "Yakoub, I was afraid, do you know I was actually afraid?"

"I know."

It was hopeless, now, trying to get him to talk about the current affairs of the Kingdom. Or anything else that might matter. I had lost him. I was sure of that.

"Is that when you decided to pardon me? When you saw the fear?"

"I thought you had suffered enough," I told him.

"I was really suffering," he said again, very far away. "I was really afraid. Thinking you were all going to cast me out. That I would never hear anyone speak Romany again. Or laugh the way a Rom laughs. You know what I mean, Yakoub? You understand what I'm saying?"

"Of course I understand, Valerian."

He fell silent. He became fainter and fainter. He was almost invisible now, a thin shadow high overhead. I was sure that he was leaving me. I could have killed him. Try killing a ghost. The son of a bitch. Coming here and doing this crazy dance of past and present and future and then bugging out on me without providing me with any real satisfaction. I knew that in another moment he'd be gone, and me no better off than when he had come.

No. Wrong. Suddenly he grew solid again. He swooped down toward me, his feet practically touching the golden floor. Bright green sparks radiated from him. He was crackling with all his old vitality and energy again. We stood face to face, nose to nose. Valerian pressing in hard on me.

The abrupt shift amazed me.

"And you, Yakoub?" he challenged. "Is it your turn now? We were talking about fear, weren't we? My fear, when I was on trial? But now you're the one who's afraid."

He had me off balance, baffled, confused. There was a buzzing in my mind. Valerian was rough around the edges but he could be perceptive just when you least expected it.

"Afraid? Of what?"

"I don't know. Shandor?"

I shook my head. "No. He's never scared me. He doesn't scare me now."

"Good. Just hold on. Keep your courage."

I felt my annoyance with him vanishing in a flash.

"Yes. That is what I must do, Valerian."

He said, "And yet there is still fear in you, isn't there?"

Just when I was beginning to love him again, he has to start bothering me some more about my being afraid.

"No," I said, even more annoyed than before. "It isn't so."

"I think you do fear something. I see it in your eyes."

"Listen, Valerian—"

"I want to help you. Tell me what you fear."

"You aren't helping me. You're pestering me."

"I was afraid once. You can be afraid too. It's all right to be afraid, Yakoub. You just have to remember which is the fear and which is Yakoub. The fear can be in you but it mustn't become you."

I turned my back on him and started to count to ten. Ek, dui, trin, chtar, pansh—

But he kept after me. He was determined to pursue me forever on this thing.

"What do you say to that, Yakoub?"

"I don't know what you're talking about. Nothing has ever made me afraid and I'm not afraid of anything now."

"That sounds good."

"It's the truth."

"Is it?"

"No," I said, after a moment, in a different voice. Something had snapped in me, all of a sudden. A strange feeling but a liberating one. Why keep secrets from Valerian? Open up, let the truth out. "It's a lie," I said.

It was. Of course it was.

I had feared many things great and small, just like anyone else, although I had always been able to conquer my fear. That had been just so much noise, when I tried to tell Valerian that I had never been afraid.

And also I was beginning to bring myself to acknowledge—after the first moment of anger, after the first sting of pride—that Valerian was right, that he wasn't deceiving himself when he felt that he saw fear in me. For I did fear one thing above everything else, and I feared it terribly. Not death. Not Shandor. Not sitting here being a prisoner. Not even civil war among the Rom. It was something I feared so much I had never been able to speak of it to another person. Or even to confront it squarely myself. It was something I had kept locked for years in the deepest oubliette of my soul.

Valerian said, "Will you tell me what you're afraid of, Yakoub?"

I hesitated. This was very hard for me.

"I've never told this to anyone."

"Tell it to me. What is it that you fear?"

"Why should I tell you, Valerian?"

"So that perhaps I can help you stop fearing whatever it is that you fear."

"No one can do that."

"Perhaps I can. Tell me."

He hovered very close to me. The hum and crackle of his ghost-aura thundered in my ears.

Uncertainly I said, "I fear—I fear—"

"Go on, Yakoub."

I was soaked with sweat. There was a hand at my throat, choking back my voice.

Suddenly I felt the words escaping from me in a hoarse ragged blurt.

"What I fear, Valerian, is that Romany Star is a lie."

"What?"

"That the whole story is just a myth," I said. It amazed me to hear the dread words coming out. But somehow it calmed me to be saying these things. I was speaking more evenly and freely now. "That the red star we pray to doesn't have a damned thing to do with us. That we never came from any such place, that the swelling of the sun never happened, that if we ever do go there we'll find that it's just one more uninhabited planet."

Valerian was silent a while, thinking, frowning.

"That's the thing that you fear, is it?"

I nodded. I felt easier, having it out at last.

"Why?" he asked.

"Because I've aimed myself toward Romany Star for my entire life. Because all this lunatic scheming of mine has been devoted to one thing and only one thing, which is to bring us back to the Homeworld, to restore us to the place where we belong, the one place where we aren't intruders and outsiders and aliens. I've thrown myself headlong toward Romany Star, do you understand? I live only for the day when I set foot on that place, do you realize that, Valerian? And if it isn't there? And if some day I find out that it's all nonsense, that we really started from Earth just as the Gaje did, that all we really are is funny-looking Gaje who speak a funny old language, that Romany Star is nothing but somebody's poetic fantasy—"

"No. That isn't how it is," Valerian said. He sounded confident.

I paused, sweating, astounded. "No?"

"The whole story is true, everything that's in the Swatura. Believe me. The life we had there, the great cities, the omens, the swelling of the sun. The sixteen ships that went off into the Great Dark and brought us to Earth."

It was a different Valerian who was speaking now, no swaggerer, no blusterer. Quiet, serious, intense. I scarcely recognized the man.

"How can you possibly know that?"

"Because I've been there," he said. "I've seen the burned hills. I've seen the melted valleys. I've held the ashes of Romany Star in my hands, Yakoub."

I stared at him, not believing a word. He was only trying to tell me what he knew I desperately needed to hear.

"You couldn't have done that."

"Why not? It's a place, isn't it? I have a starship, don't I? What could stop me from going to take a look?"

"But it's forbidden!" I yelled. "It's absolute sacrilege for anyone to set foot on Romany Star until after the third swelling, until we get the call, until—"

"Yakoub," he said. "Don't be naive. It doesn't sound right, coming from you."

He said it gently, almost tenderly. He was smiling. There was something a little shamefaced about that smile, and also something a little patronizing.

I realized that I was trembling uncontrollably.

"You're serious? You actually and literally went there?"

Softly Valerian said, "When did I ever give a shit about the rules, Yakoub?"

7.

HE WAS GONE BEFORE I REALIZED WHAT WAS HAPPENING.
I thought he had just faded from visibility for a moment, but no, he was really gone. Leaving me alone with my astonishment.

Typhoons were roaring through my soul. Hurricanes, tidal waves, earthquakes. I was hanging on to my sanity by my fingertips.

I had told him the one thing I had struggled to keep from everyone, even myself, since the day the poisonous filthy idea first had crawled into my mind. The unthinkable thing, the truly unthinkable thing: today I had not only thought it but I had spoken it. But that wasn't all.

What he had told me—his own little secret, that he had given me by way of exchange—

I was stunned. A voyage to Romany Star? Landfall on the holy of holies, the forbidden planet, violating the sacred Motherworld? Before we had received the call to return? Amazing. Incredible. Only Valerian could have done something like that. How I despised him for it! And how I envied him! Such casual blasphemy, such lighthearted trespassing against the holiest of Rom beliefs? Against the Law itself. *"It's a place, isn't it? I have a starship, don't I?"* And then casually to tell me about it? The king? I could have him up before the kris for that. Even now, here in my prison, one word from me and he would be cut off forever from his own kind. They would crucify him. They would slaughter him.

Of course I wouldn't call down the kris on him. He knew that or he would never have said a word. No matter what his indiscretions, I had always protected him, somehow. He was like a part of me, shameless and wanton and uncontrollable but part of me all the same. You don't go mutilating your own arm simply because it reaches out and pinches the empress' ass while your attention is directed elsewhere.

But still—

Romany Star? *Romany Star!*

"I've seen the burned hills," he had said. "I've seen the melted valleys. I've held the ashes of Romany Star in my hands, Yakoub."

I was sick with envy and longing, with anger and joy. I was furious with him for not having asked me to go along, whenever it was that he made that blasphemous expedition. I would have refused to go, of course—in fact I would have threatened him with life imprisonment if he had tried to go through with the voyage, and by God and all His demons I would have made good my threat, too. But I wished he had asked me. I wished I had been there. To see with my own eyes that it was all real, to sift those ashes through my own fingers. I could taste it like bile in my throat, my yearning to have gone with him. No wonder I protect Valerian. I am as wanton as he is. Worse. I pretend that I will uphold the laws. And the Law. He does as he pleases and makes no pretenses. Which is the more moral man, the pirate or the hypocrite?

Romany Star.

I thought my breast would burst with the amazement and excitement within it. I thought my head would spin loose from my shoulders. I wanted to weep. To dance. To sing.

I've seen the burned hills. I've seen the melted valleys.

A soaring craziness enveloped me and I went spontaneously ghosting off, flinging myself into the darkness like a skittering meteor tumbling freely through the cosmos. I went here and there and there and here, back and forth and forth and back, Xamur, Megalo Kastro, Nabomba Zom, Vietoris, even the Capital. Nothing would come into clear focus. Nothing would hold still. I was floating free, unmoored from time and space, blowing in a gale that had come rushing up wildly out of my own soul.

One scene recurred again and again. At first it was only fragmentary but then I was able to make it hold, and I entered it to see what it was, where and when I was. Faces drifted past me. Damiano. Valerian. The phuri dai. A row of solemn-faced krisatora sitting in the judgment hall. So I was still on Galgala. But when? They were all much younger, Valerian, Damiano, all of them. Look, there I was myself, sitting in the king's chair, listening to the deliberations. I looked younger too. Not younger in the face, but younger in the eyes.

"I have never knowingly done harm to any Rom in my life," Valerian was saying. He looked pale, sweaty-faced, frightened. His mustache was drooping. "I ask the court to take it into consideration that my spirit has always been true to the Way. May God rip my tongue from my throat if I have spoken falsehood."

He was squirming like something skewered on a barbed hook.

Valerian at his trial, yes. That time long ago, brought up on charges before the great kris.

Everything wavered and for an instant I went wandering away, sliding like a stone on ice into some other epoch in some other quadrant of the galaxy. I think the place where I went may have been Earth, though it could just as easily have been Barma Darma or Duud Shabeel. I pulled myself back. I wanted to watch Valerian's trial.

We had had him but good that time, not for piracy but for unethical mercantile practices. It was all coming back to me as I hovered there, invisible. What he had done was intercept a cargo tanker loaded with belisoogra oil, the stuff used to make the blood-flushing drug essential to the remake process. In a moment of sudden magnanimity Valerian had decided to wipe out the belisoogra cartel by making the whole cargo available in one shot to some drug-brokers on Marajo, instead of dribbling it out over a number of years the way the cartel does. Break the market, he figured, make cheap remakes possible for all the poor folk who can't afford the treatment.

That's Valerian's Robin Hood facet. Comes over him like a fit, sometimes.

I saw Damiano rise, eyes bright with anger and outrage. "This man who says he is our brother, who says that he serves the interests of the Great People—he stands indicted for his greed, but I say we must punish him for his stupidity!" There was laughter. I joined in it myself: not my ghost-self that was watching but the other Yakoub who was slouched there in the royal chair. Poor Valerian. "A greedy Rom we can accept," Damiano went on. "Greed is not unusual nor is it entirely to be deplored. But a stupid Rom, my friends—ah, a stupid Rom endangers us all. Should we not chastise such a creature with whips and with scorpions, to teach him a little sense? I ask you!"

Poor Valerian.

He had made one big mistake. Valerian in all his grand magnanimity had unfortunately overlooked the fact that the belisoogra cartel happens to be a Rom operation from top to bottom—one of our greatest mercantile triumphs, in fact. We own the market and that gives us a death-grip on the whole remake industry, though the Gaje don't fully comprehend how important we really are to their continued good health and youthful vigor. In some subliminal way I think they know that we have them by the balls, but we don't go out of our way to call it to their attention. Apparently it had escaped Valerian's attention too.

By shattering the price structure of the belisoogra market that way he had skunked a few thousand of his cousins, bankrupting a surprising number of them who had rashly gone too far out on that particular limb, not expecting one of their own people to cut it off behind them. He had also cost us a lot of good political leverage vis-a-vis the Gaje. It would be years before all the cheap belisoogra he had dumped could be absorbed by demand. I have always been fond of Valerian but this time he had been really dumb, and, as Damiano so eloquently had told the kris, dumbness in a Rom has to be punished. The universe will punish dumbness in anyone, sooner or later, of course. But our position in the universe has always been pretty precarious and we can't afford the luxury of waiting for natural corrective processes to do our work for us.

"I call upon the victims of this man's foolish greed to stand forth and tell the kris of the injuries they have suffered through his unthinking action—"

We had gone through the whole formal traditional procedure. Bayura were brought in against him, the bills of complaint. Then we waited for Valerian to turn up on Galgala—he came for a feast in his honor, all unawares—and he was duly taken into custody and brought up on trial, actually for the first time in his life. The Gaje had never been able to hang anything on him in all his years as a pirate. But we did. Damiano himself was the krisatori o baro, the chief judge, and Damiano was out for blood. He could easily have been an injured member of the belisoogra cartel himself, he was so fierce and angry. Not that anyone seriously accused him of that. We are a civilized people, after all. Still, Damiano has a real dislike of losing money and he probably wouldn't have seen any particular conflict of interest in sitting as judge over the man who had done it to him.

I drifted through the judgement hall, keeping myself invisible. Once I saw myself look up at the place where I hovered, and I wondered if I was seeing me. I couldn't remember.

What I did remember was that the trial had started badly for Valerian and gone downhill all the way. He swore mighty oaths that his intent had been purely humanitarian, which in this instance may actually have been true. But he had a cost a lot of Rom a lot of money, all the same. He offered to pay it back. Well, that sounded good. But

Damiano kept hammering away. What about the weakening of our position among the Gaje by the breaking of our belisoogra monopoly? How did the defendant plan to reimburse for that? The krisatora nodded and murmured. Everyone loved Valerian but he had plenty of enemies too, and many of them were the same ones who loved him. In the course of piracies past he had done more than a little injury to various Rom merchants, all in the same casual and almost accidental way. The krisatora very clearly were out to get him. He knew it and so did everyone else.

Now came the solakh, the final interrogations and the sentencing. Valerian was somber and subdued. He knew what was coming. And what was coming was terrible. We were going to cast him from our midst. To proclaim him marhime, unclean. To call down the wrath of all Rom past and present, alive and dead, upon anyone who had any further dealings with him. Which would not only have deprived him of the comforts of his family, of the whole grand kumpania of the Rom, but would also have stripped him of his crew and his livelihood, and left him exposed to the vengeance of the Gaje, who had been trying to get their hands on him for a very long time indeed. And then for Valerian there would never be any voyages to Romany Star.

Like a wraith I floated over the heads of the krisatora as they moved toward their verdict. I paused above Yakoub the king. The king looked bored. The king *was* bored. Trials like this had always wearied me; it was a part of the job I would gladly have handed off to someone else. The endless medieval taking of oaths and crying out of curses upon would-be perjurers, the interminable trotting forth of evidence, the vast outpourings of woe and sweat and anguish and complaining—I saw the virtue and importance of it all. And I hated it. But nevertheless I did my duty. I have a great sense of duty. But that doesn't mean I have to enjoy it.

I made myself visible for only a moment, and only to my earlier self.

"Be merciful," I whispered. And winked. And went skittering off again in a ghost-ricochet to God knows where at the far end of time and the far end of the galaxy. When I knew where I was again I was back in my cell, sitting quietly on my couch hearing Valerian's voice in my mind for the eighty thousandth time, saying, *I've seen the burned hills. I've seen the melted valleys.*

The verdict on Valerian was guilty and the sentence was absolute expulsion from the Romany people. Cut off, cast out, excommunicated. Unlawful now for any Rom to speak a word to him, even his mother, even his brother, on pain of the same penalty. Whatever he touched would be deemed unclean and must be destroyed, whatever its value. In other words the complete cataclysm; the fullest punishment of our Law in all its ancient and apocalyptic severity. In due course the decree of the kris came to me for review, and, as I suspect everyone involved except perhaps Damiano was really hoping I would do, I found it far too severe, and voided it. Instead I ordered Valerian to make a huge restitution payment and a ceremonial act of penance, instructed him to keep his hands off Rom vessels for the rest of his natural or unnatural days, and sent him off, shaken and sobered and officially rehabilitated and eternally grateful to me, to continue his piratical ways in the spacelanes. Damiano gave me a hard time about my leniency. "That slippery bastard needed a good lesson," he said. And said it again and again in case I hadn't heard the first time.

"He's had one."

"Not good enough. He's going to go right on thinking it's safe to do whatever he damned pleases. He'll just try harder not to get caught again, that's all."

"Isn't that what everyone does?"

"You shock me, cousin."

"Do I? Do I really, cousin?"

Damiano had to yield, of course. I was king, as I reminded him two or three times, and he went away grumbling. Later on he and Valerian made peace with each other and Damiano even invested in some of Valerian's ventures, which is so perfectly in character for Damiano that I could have hugged him for it. Of course Damiano was right that Valerian would go on believing he could do whatever he felt like, so long as he took care not to get caught. And so he has.

I've held the ashes of Romany Star in my hands, Yakoub.

Did I dare believe him? Did I dare not to?

8.

THEN SHANDOR CAME STORMING IN, HIS FIRST VISIT TO me in a very long time, and distracted me. He was so lit up I would almost have thought it was Shandor's ghost coming in, all sparks and crackles and hums. But both his feet were on the floor and the sparks were metaphorical, not electrical.

He was enraged and practically incoherent. He paced up and down, back and forth, sputtering and twitching. Despite his recent remake he looked like an old man, this firstborn son of mine. I took real malicious pleasure in seeing how gray his skin was, how sharp his nose was getting, how rounded his shoulders. This babe that I had bounced on my knee only a hundred years ago, give or take ten or twenty.

He was burning up. He was consuming himself. He was the candle that was all flame from tip to tip.

That is a thing the Lowara Rom like to say: "A candle is all flame from tip to tip." In other words a candle is supposed to burn, and the thing to do is to let it burn, to let the tallow be translated into the flame that is the candle's true destiny. It is an argument against thrift. Polarca lives that way: he sets nothing by for the future, but burns and blazes all the time. He is lavish and generous to the point of craziness; but he does burn brightly.

Among us Kalderash the same saying has a different shade of meaning. Which is that when you merrily let your candle burn from end to end it gives you much warmth and light, but eventually it is consumed and then you are left in darkness. Therefore burn what you need, but nothing more. Especially when the candle that you burn is yourself. Shandor, it seemed, was wasting himself in the fervor of his rage.

It was quite a performance. I watched in amazement. I doubt that I could have done better. Finally he got himself enough under control to speak words that made sense, but even so they came out in a thick-tongued frantic way. "One last chance, God damn you!" he thundered.

"I can be merciful if that's what I have to be. I'll give you goddamned mercy, you cagy old bastard. But you have to cooperate. You have to cooperate! Or I'll finish you."

"Finish me how?"

"Finish you! Don't ask me. Just don't ask!"

"You don't look good, Shandor. Are you sleeping well these days?"

"I'm going to hold a coronation."

"Are you, now?"

"Stop talking to me in that patronizing tone of voice!"

"I'm trying to hold up my end of the conversation, that's all. I was inquiring about your health. There are things you could take. Water from nine places, you know that one? You'll need a drabarni to throw charcoal embers in it first. Maybe Bibi Savina would do it for you. And then there's bear's grease—you could send to Marajo for some, I think Damiano keeps bears there—eye of crayfish, powdered cantharis beetle—"

"I'll cut your tongue out if you don't shut up."

"The merciful Shandor, yes."

"There will be a coronation," he said, forcing the words out as though they were teeth bursting through his lips. "A nine-world ceremony, first here on Galgala, then Xamur, Iriarte, Nabomba Zom, Clard Msat—"

"You may have trouble with part of that. I understand that for some reason the starships aren't landing on Iriarte or Clard Msat these days."

"—and after the rite has been sanctified on all nine of the kingly planets, you and I will go to the Capital and present ourselves before the emperor to receive confirmation."

"Confirmation of what?"

"My title to the throne. The legality of my succession."

"You still want to be king, Shandor? Give it up. It's a dreadful job."

"On each of the nine kingly planets you will stand beside me as the phuri dai puts the seal of office over me—"

"I will?"

"The passing of the mantle. The transfer of authority. You will do it freely and joyfully."

"I would freely and joyfully spend ten years in the tunnels of Alta Hannalanna first."

"It wouldn't be a big problem for me to send you there."

"You'd do it, too."

"I could. Maybe you'd prefer Gran Chingada? Megalo Kastro, in the mines? Trinigalee Chase?"

"That's the best you can do? Trinigalee Chase?"

"I can send you anywhere. How about Mentiroso again? I can really make you suffer, Yakoub."

"And make yourself even more beloved throughout the Rom worlds than you are already."

"Damn you, Yakoub—"

"Threaten me some more, my son. This is the best exercise I've had in months."

"There's war out there, do you know that? Rom turning against Rom. Whole kumpanias splitting in two over the issue of the kingship. And you are responsible."

"*I* am?"

"By trying to reclaim the throne. By trying to displace a king legitimately chosen and anointed."

"Pot calls kettle black."

He was looking more apoplectic by the moment. I had a quick satisfying fantasy of goading him into a stroke right here in my cell. But no, Shandor would never be so obliging. He went ranting on about this coronation he was going to stage, in which I would stand by beaming benignly while he put my crown on his head. Pig's eye, I would. Preposterous notion. But give me full credit: I didn't for a moment get angry. Here stood my own firstborn son going straight for the Freudian jugular and I listened to him amiably, interjecting a bit of easy banter whenever he paused for breath. I even told him about Freud. He hadn't heard of him, obviously. Ancient Gaje philosopher, said I. I reached into my anthropological storehouse and pulled out Uranus and Cronos, Cronos and Zeus, David and Absalom, and one or two other famous father-and-son goodies. I threw in Lear and his daughters, too, though that story wasn't entirely appropriate to the situation. Close enough, though. "Is that what you want?" I asked. "To reduce me to a mere archetype? How sharper than a serpent's tooth it is to have a thankless child!"

"What are you talking about?" said Shandor. "You crazy old bastard!"

I smiled sweetly. In the end the stalemate still stood; I remained his prisoner, he remained in questionable possession of a shaky throne. He got red in the face and went back to muttering threats. Mentiroso, he said again. Alta Hannalanna. He waved Trinigalee Chase before my nose again too. He might have gotten me to give in, if he really had tried to ship me off to Trinigalee Chase. A good thing I had never told anyone how much I loathed that place, or why, a policy that I intend to continue to honor until the end of my days.

In the face of Shandor's threats I kept calm and cool. He was furious. I grew wary of pushing him any harder. There comes a point with any enemy where you can get him angry enough to act against his own self-interest, and then you're really in trouble. If Shandor did away with me in a fit of rage, it would really foul up his position among the Rom; but even so, I'd be dead. As I had pointed out on Xamur to Valerian, I could be useful even as a martyr. Still and all, that wasn't my first choice. It wasn't even high on my list.

He went away, eventually, muttering and cursing. Something was going to happen now, of that I was certain. Sticking me in that damp rat-infested oubliette hadn't accomplished anything for him and nothing better had come of letting me sit here in this gilded cage. I had done a lot of waiting in my life and Shandor was beginning to see that I was capable of doing a great deal more. He had expected me simply to come around after a time and put my blessing on his kingship, but it hadn't happened, and now, I suspected, he was reaching the limits of his patience. He might very well start in on me now with some more active form of persuasion. Torture? Brainburning? Little softening-up trips to some of the uglier worlds of the galaxy?

Be prepared for the worst, I told myself. Something is going to happen.

Something happened, all right. The very next day when the robots brought me my dinner I found a grilled fish on my plate, swimming in a delicate creamy sauce. After months of mush and gruel, a grilled fish in a fancy sauce? This is Shandor's idea of torture? With it came elegant little potato puffs, thin brown crusts enclosing globes of air, and some kind of long bluish beans in a pungent and subtle gravy. A beaker of wine on the side, nicely chilled, and a crisp little loaf of bread.

There had to be a catch. Maybe this stuff is poisoned, and he figures I'll fall upon it with such greed that I won't even notice the faint trace of cyanide that it's laced with, right? For perhaps five minutes I sat there staring miserably at that beautiful food, afraid to touch it. Then I realized that I was very hungry and that I could die of starvation just as easily as I could from cyanide poisoning. If I passed up this lovely meal I might be passing up the cyanide, if there was any cyanide, but

I'd also be passing up this lovely meal, and either way I'd be dead before too long. So I took a gingerly nibble. Ecstasy! If Shandor had had my meal poisoned, it was at least a delicious poison. I waited and nothing sinister happened. Another nibble. Another. What the hell, I thought, this food is too good to be lethal. And I went at it with gusto.

I had lived on Shandor's prison garbage so long that my stomach nearly rebelled at cuisine of such extraordinary caliber. It was all I could do to keep the first few mouthfuls down. But I gave it a good fight, and I won. The bread and the wine helped. And after a while it became a lot easier. When I went to sleep that night—still wondering vaguely whether I'd been poisoned—I spent my last few moments of wakefulness brooding over the significance of Shandor's strange gesture. It made no sense. I hate things that make no sense. If he wasn't trying to poison me in some crazy roundabout way, did he seriously think he could bribe me into cooperating by feeding me fancy dinners?

Of course not. I decided that it must have been somebody else's dinner, delivered to me by mistake. A malfunction of the serving robots. Off I went to sleep.

And woke, unpoisoned, to find that the robots had brought me breakfast. Two crisp crescent-shaped rolls of surpassingly fine texture, a flask of coffee that was close to ambrosia, and a little plate of mild white cheese and assorted local fruits glittering with tiny flecks of gold. I was baffled.

To my shame it was another day and a half before I stopped eating long enough to figure things out. *Help is on the way.* Polarca had told me, early in my imprisonment. *When it gets here, you'll know it. The clue will be right on the plate in front of you.*

What kind of food was it that these demented robots had suddenly begun to bring me? Why, it was French food. And who did I know whose great passion it was to cook in the classic French manner? Why, Julien de Gramont, pretender to the throne of France and special adjunct to his lordship Periandros of the imperial court. Yes. Of course.

Somehow Julien had infiltrated this place and he was preparing superb meals for me that were actually intended as messages. What all these cassoulets and ragouts and terrines and sautes were meant to tell me, these mousses and aspics and souffles, was that I had friends on the premises. And help would shortly be on the way.

SEVEN

The Sixteenth Emperor

We start out stupid. All we have at the beginning is the built-in wisdom of the body, which tells us which end to eat with and which end to shit with and not much more. But we are put here to do battle with entropy, and entropy equals stupidity. Therefore we are obliged to learn. Our job is to process information and gain control of it: that is to say, to grow wiser as we go along.

If I am just as stupid when I am twenty as I was when I was two, if I am just as stupid when I am a hundred as I was when I was fifty, then I am not doing my job. I am occupying space and time to no purpose, and I might just as well have been a lump of rock.

Of course, a time comes when even the wisest of men stops growing wise and starts getting stupid again. It may take two hundred years for that to happen to him, but it will happen. I am reconciled to the inevitability of that, I think. All that means is that entropy wins in the end, which we knew all along. No matter. The fact that we're fighting a losing battle does not excuse us from fighting it. The great human achievement is to postpone the moment of defeat as long as possible.

1.

WHAT I DIDN'T KNOW WAS THAT THE IMPERIUM HAD UN-
dergone some major changes. The old emperor had finally died—without naming his successor—and the three high lords were making their
moves. So there was chaos now among the Gaje as well as the Rom.

Tucked away in my cozy cell I didn't hear anything about any of this.
My only visitors now were the silent robots that continued to bring me
ever more elaborate meals. I didn't even get any ghosts. Instead of news
from the outside, what I got was supremes de volaille, noisettes d'ag-
neau, grenadins de boeuf. My waistline was spreading wildly. Meanwhile, beyond the walls of my prison, the whole precariously balanced
structure that had held the human race together during the thousand
years of expansion into the galaxy was falling apart in one great triumphant burst of greed and stupidity.

Imagine! Kings and emperors, here in the thirty-second century! As
though we were living in the middle ages. Pomp and circumstance,
fanfares and panoplies. Crowns and scepters. Wars of succession. It
sounds childish, doesn't it? But what system, I ask you, would have
worked better? Democracy? A parliament of worlds? Don't make me
laugh. That stuff works well enough on a small scale, maybe. Within
a single country, say. You'll notice that Earth in its time never managed
to get representative democracy going on so much as one entire continent at any one time, let alone the whole planet. So how could it be
achieved on a galactic scale? We buzz around pretty spectacularly in
our faster-than-light starships, but communication between solar systems still has built-in lags. The parliament would always be six weeks
behind the times in knowing what was going on. The galactic president
wouldn't have a clue. And there are hundreds of inhabited worlds,
right? Thousands. You'd need a parliament building half the size of a
city to house all the delegates. Imagine the babble and yatter. What you
need is a symbolic figure, a kind of animated flag to hold all the worlds
together. We knew what we were doing when we revived monarchy. Of
course this really isn't the middle ages, and the monarchy we set up isn't
really much like the ancient ones. What the emperor is, basically, is a

message that is sent simultaneously to all the worlds of the galaxy. His very existence says, *We are human, we are members of one family.* The emperor is like a poem, if you take my meaning. When he speaks, you may not understand the literal sense of what he might say, but you get the impact on some other level.

What's that you're saying? Why bother trying to hold the fabric of the worlds together at all? Why not simply let each planet live in blessed isolation, wrapped in its snug blanket of light-years? And do without the whole intricate and costly structure of the Imperium entirely?

Now *that's* a medieval concept if ever I heard one. And even in old medieval Earth it wasn't possible to make it work, though they certainly tried. There was no way for any nation to keep aloof from other nations for long. Weak ones that attempted it inevitably wound up being subjugated in one way or another. Strong ones might make isolationist policies stick for a time, but sooner or later they'd become inbred and decadent and start to slide into a dismal irreversible decline. Only when the Earth folk accepted some notion of their interdependence did they begin to attain something like civilization. As the ancient Gaje poet said, No man is an island, entire of itself. Every man is a piece of the continent, a part of the main; if a clod is washed away by the sea, Europe is the less. Exactly. Europe was one of their most famous continents, a small one but very important. The same poet went on to say, Any man's death diminishes me. And therefore never send to know for whom the bell tolls; it tolls for thee. Yes indeed. It is the same for nations. And it is the same for worlds.

Now we have gone sprawling and brawling out into the stars, filling the many worlds with ourselves and with the beasts of lost dead Earth that we brought with us for company, cows and horses and snakes and toads. We have spread like an unstoppable tide across a universe that probably regarded itself as perfectly satisfactory without us, and we have overwhelmed great sectors of it. And yet, and yet, for all our tremendous outward spill we are nothing but a thin dark thread lying across the Milky Way. If any of us were to try to stand alone, he would be lost. So we reach out—we who are just so many scattered beads bobbing on this great ocean of night, if you don't mind my changing metaphors on you, and if a king can't switch metaphors I'd like to know who can—and we try to maintain connection with one another. And that is why there is an Imperium; and that is why there is an emperor; and that is why when the emperor dies we all stand at the brink of chaos.

You may have noticed that in venting all this passion upon you I did not stop to draw distinctions between Gaje and Rom. Indeed. We have our differences, yes—how great those differences are, the Gaje don't begin to suspect!—but we have our great similarities too, and I never allow myself to forget that, either. They are human and we are human. This ocean in which we drift is very wide and we are very small; and all of us need whatever allies we can find. The Gajo is the enemy, yes: so we are taught from childhood. But the Gajo is also the only friend. It is a very perplexing business. Most important matters in life are like that. We Rom have kept ourselves apart, an island in the vast Gaje sea, for if we had not done that we would have been lost; and yet we have joined hands with them also, as much as is possible, for if we had not done that we would also have been lost. We are a Kingdom outside the Imperium, but we are of the Imperium as well. That is not easy to understand. It was not easy to achieve, either. But I tell you this, that the death of the Gaje emperor diminishes us all, even us Rom. No man is an island.

2.

I HEARD RUMBLES AND DISTURBANCES WITHIN THE building. Maybe they were moving furniture, maybe they were tearing down walls: I had no way of telling. The noise continued for a day and a half and it began to sound like something more serious than sliding couches around. But for me, in my isolation, it was just one more day and a half of gluttony: fantastic sauces and creamy desserts and glittering wines. A culminating orgy of fantastic food, as it turned out. On the evening of the second day I got no dinner at all. The robots failed to show up, and the noise outside grew much louder. Now I was certain that something serious had to be going on.

My first inkling of the truth came when I heard footsteps in the hallway, the sound of running feet. Then shouts and alarums, a siren or two, the unmistakable hissing of imploder fire, the dull boom of heavier artillery. I put my ear to the door. There was fighting going on out there, yes, but who was fighting whom? I couldn't tell a thing.

At first I thought that Polarca or Valerian had arrived with an army of Rom loyalists to overthrow Shandor and set me free. God save me from that. If I had wanted to push Shandor aside by force, I would have tried it long ago instead of going through this whole elaborate charade. Rom should not lift hands against Rom.

But if this was a Rom invasion, what was Julien de Gramont doing mixed up in it? Obviously it was Julien who had been preparing my meals these past weeks; no one else would have had the skill. Perhaps it was Julien who had opened the gates to let the invaders in. He and Polarca were well acquainted: old whorehouse buddies on many worlds, in fact. Had they concocted some sort of alliance? Why? They seemed like odd allies. Julien was sympathetic to all things Rom but essentially he was the creature of Lord Periandros. Polarca had no use for any of the lords of the Imperium.

I have never wished so profoundly that it could be possible to ghost *forward* in time as I did at that moment. Only five minutes, or maybe ten: just enough for me to find out what in the name of the Devil was going on in the house of power of the King of the Gypsies. But all I could do was stand with my ear to the door of my chamber and guess madly at ungodly alliances and conspiracies.

Then the door burst open and five armed troops in the pale green uniform of the Imperial Guard came rushing in.

They were native of Sidri Akrak. I saw that right away, in their blank emotionless Akraki eyes and their glum downturned Akraki mouths and the stiff-jointed tight-assed Akraki way that they moved. But in case those hints weren't enough, they were wearing splashy armbands emblazoned with the garish vertical stripes of the Akraki flag and a big scarlet monogrammed P. For Periandros, of course.

The officer in command—she had the epaulet of a phalangarius on her shoulder—strode up to me and said in that brusque flat way of theirs, "What is your name?"

"Yakoub." I smiled. "Rom baro. Rex Romaniorum."

"Yakoub what?"

"King of the Romany people."

The five Akrakikan exchanged solemn glances.

"You assert that you are the Rom king?"

"I do so assert, yea and verily."

"Is this so? Demonstrate your identity."

"I don't seem to have my papers with me. As a matter of fact, I happen to be a prisoner in this place. If you don't believe I am who I say I am, I suggest you call in any Rom you can find and ask him my name."

The phalangarius gestured to one of her subordinates. "Find a Rom," she said. "Bring him here. We will ask him this man's name."

I could still hear explosions in the distant reaches of the building.

"While we're waiting," I said, "would you mind telling me who you are and what's happening around here?"

She gave me a sour look, as close to an expression as an Akraki is capable of mustering. She scarcely looked human to me. She didn't look much like a woman, either, with that close-cropped hair of hers and her stiff Akraki movements. Only the barest hint of breasts beneath the uniform provided any clue to her sex. That she was human I would have to take on faith.

"I will interrogate you. You will not interrogate me."

"Am I right, at least, that you're imperial guards?"

"We serve the Sixteenth Emperor," she was kind enough to reveal.

"The *Sixteenth*?" I gasped. I wasn't prepared for that. "But when—how—who—?"

"You knew him formerly as Lord Periandros."

I blinked and caught my breath. So it was all over, then? The struggle for the throne that we had dreaded for so long had taken place while I lay stashed away in here, and somehow little tight-assed Periandros had emerged as emperor?

What a jolt it was. The whole grand apocalyptic galacto-political drama had been played out so quickly. And behind my back. Me not even on the scene to cheer the heroes and boo the villains. Or maybe cheer the villains and boo the heroes. I had missed all the excitement. I felt left out.

But of course I was jumping to conclusions—and not the right ones. The struggle for the throne wasn't over at all. It was just beginning, though I had no way of knowing that then.

I brimmed with questions. How had Periandros managed to shove Sunteil out of the way? What had happened to Naria? Why were there imperial troops in the Rom house of power? Where was Shandor? Where was the Duc de Gramont? But I would have done about as well asking questions of my own elbow as I did trying to get information from this blank-eyed Akraki. She stood there looking at me in complete indifference, as though I were some dusty moth-eaten relic that had been stored in this room for the last five hundred years, some old overcoat, some pile of discarded rags. Meanwhile her companions were searching through my few pitiful possessions in a sluggish but methodical way, hunting for God knows what cache of hidden weapons, or perhaps the manuscript of some scandalous memoir. It seemed like forever before the one who had gone in search of a Rom to identify me returned.

When he did return, though, he was accompanied not by a Rom but by the Duc de Gramont.

"Mon ami!" Julie cried. "Sacre bleu! Ah, j'en suis fort content! Comment ca va?"

With enormous passion and verve. With the kiss on both cheeks, with the joyous clapping of hands against my shoulders, with the whole great Gallic embrace. And then turning to the five Akrakikan, gesticulating vehemently at them with both his hands as if they were so much vermin.

"Out of here, you! Out! Vite! Vite! Salauds! Crapauds! Bon Dieu de merde, out, out, out!"

The phalangarius stared at him in disbelief.

"Our orders are to guard this man until—"

"Your orders are to get out. Vite! Vite! You miserable emmerdeuse, je l'emmerde on your orders! Out! Fast!"

I thought he would throw her out bodily. But that turned out not to be necessary. He simply drove her from the room with thunderous fusillades of obscene outrage in a wild mixture of Imperial and French and even a little Romany. "Va te faire chier!" he cried. "Fuck off, hideous lesbian bitch! Kurav tu ando mul!"

The Akraki fled, taking her astounded subordinates with her. I collapsed on my couch. I thought I would have my death of laughter, right then and there. It was a long time before I could speak.

"You know what that means?" I said. "Kurav tu ando mul?"

"Of course I know what it means," said Julien with immense hauteur. " 'I defile your mouth,' is what it means. The pity of it is that *she* does not know what it means." He shut the door of my cell, taking care not to lock us in, and crossed the room to sit beside me. "Ah, mon vieux, so much has happened, so very much! You know I have been on Galgala these many weeks now? Secretly employed in this very building?"

"The meals they were bringing me had your signature all over them."

"I hoped you would realize that. I would have sent you a note, but I thought the risks were too great. If Shandor somehow had discovered my true identity—ah, it was dangerous enough simply preparing such meals for you. But to the robots it was all the same, rat stew or jambon au Bourgogne en croute, so I could play my little game. Ah, Yakoub, Yakoub!"

"Is Periandros the emperor now?"

"You know that, then?"

"The phalangarius told me so. But that's all I know. I need to have all the rest of the news. What's been going on here? I've been hearing sounds of fighting for hours."

"It was the decision of Lord Periandros to rescue you from this captivity," said Julien. "This in the final days of the life of the Fifteenth. As the emperor lay dying, the Lord Periandros saw the turmoil that would surely ensue if an imperial succession took place at a time when the Rom kingship was in the hands of a person so volatile, so unpredictable, as your son Shandor. You will recall, mon ami, that I hinted at this when I visited you on that world of ice. But you were adamant in your wish to retire from the fray. Nothing I could say would move you to return to the Imperium at that time, although I see that you did later change your mind, for reasons that I do not know."

"Damiano came to me right after you and told me that Shandor had made himself king. It wasn't ever my intention to clear a path to the throne for Shandor, of all people. So I came back." I could hear a fresh round of gunfire, seemingly not far away. Julien seemed untroubled by it. "Where is Shandor now?" I asked.

"He has fled with his bodyguard to another part of the Aureus Highlands. We took him utterly by surprise when we struck. Very gradually did we move our troops into position surrounding the royal compound and he was not in any way prepared."

"Akrakikan troops only?"

"Yes," said Julien quietly. "We could take no chances."

"No thought was given to having Rom in the rescue party?"

"This was an imperial mission, cher ami. And I know that you have an aversion to the spilling of Rom blood by Rom hands. The invading troops were entirely Akrakikan, of Lord Periandros' personal force."

"And Rom blood was spilled, then?"

Julien studied me a moment. "Evidently there are Rom who are loyal to your son, Yakoub. God knows why that should be, but it was the case. In any event one usually does not invade a royal palace without encountering staunch defense. Please understand that we held the casualties to a minimum."

A minimum, yes. But that meant some. Bleak news. I sighed.

"Those who guarded your son were informed that the new emperor did not recognize him as king. They were offered a chance to lay down their weapons peacefully. Many of them did."

"Some did not."

"Some did not," Julien said.

"Well, so be it," I said after a time. "They were serving the wrong man. Who *does* Periandros recognize as king? Me?"

"He will. You will be taken to the Capital and there will be a ceremony of reconsecration. I think it will be necessary for you to have the decree of the great kris also, will it not? But that can be managed. I have spoken with Damiano and with Polarca. You will be king again, Yakoub. I ask only this, that this time you do not amuse yourself with another abdication."

"The abdication was a carefully considered gesture," I said. "It's not one I'll need to make a second time." I was still for a moment, considering the things Julien had told me. Something seemed off key, but in the rush and flow of our conversation I had not noticed it at first. Now it returned to trouble me. "Wait a moment," I said. "You told me that the rescue mission was an imperial enterprise, Julien. But you also said that Periandros had decided on it while the old emperor was still alive. And that he had sent his own soldiers to carry out the job. The whole thing sounds more like a private project of Periandros' than any sort of governmental action. Which was it? He wasn't emperor yet when you came here, was he?"

"No," said Julien.

"Why rescue me, then? So that in my gratitude I'd support his claim to the throne?"

"Oh, Yakoub, Yakoub—"

"That's it, isn't it? But what if I didn't *want* to be rescued? Did Polarca happen to tell you that I put myself into Shandor's hands voluntarily? That I had political objectives of my own to gain by letting him imprison me? And I told you when you came to Mulano that I wasn't going to take any public position favoring Periandros' claim to the throne."

"The Lord Periandros is emperor now, Yakoub."

"So the Fifteenth did manage to name a successor after all?"

Julien shook his head. "No."

"Then how did Periandros become emperor? What happened to Sunteil? To Naria?"

Julien looked uncomfortable. He was too much the diplomat to let himself be seen squirming, but he must have been squirming desperately within.

"At the time of the Fifteenth's death," Julien said in a strangely remote way, "the Lord Sunteil had gone to the Haj Qaldun system to investigate certain disturbances on Fenix and, I think, Shaitan. As for the Lord Naria, he also was occupied at that time by matters of pressing importance on his own native world, which as you know is Vietoris."

I felt very somber now. My dear old friend Julien, who had sold himself long ago to Periandros, was here to try to buy me too. Quid pro quo, Periandros sets me free and I give my allegiance to him and he recognizes me as undisputed king. One quid, two quos, and none of them any good.

"It was a coup d'etat, then?" I asked. "The other two were away, and Periandros simply grabbed the throne?"

"The peers of the Imperium have confirmed his election."

"The same way the great kris of Galgala confirmed the election of Shandor as king?"

"Yakoub, mon cher, mon ami, I beg you—"

"Go on," I said, as he fell silent. "You beg me what?"

"We spoke of these matters on—what is that world's name, the icy one?—on Mulano. When there is a vacuum in the body politic, disruptive forces are set loose. Your own absence from the Rom throne and the apparent usurpation of Shandor, followed by your sudden return from retirement and your imprisonment here, had already loosed one set of disruptions in the Imperium. The death of the Fifteenth threatened to make matters catastrophically worse. In the judgment of the Lord Periandros the stability of the Imperium would have been in jeopardy had he not acted swiftly and decisively."

"And Sunteil? Naria? They've both acquiesced in Periandros' swift and decisive act?"

For a moment, only for a moment, Julien's eyes were no longer meeting mine. That momentary flicker of weakness was the most damning revelation of all.

"Not precisely," he said.

"Not precisely?"

"In fact, not at all."

"Neither of them?"

"Neither one."

"They both claim the throne?"

Julien nodded. I thought he would burst into tears.

"So we have not only a Sixteenth, but a Seventeenth and an Eighteenth as well? All at the same time?"

"No, mon ami. There is only a Sixteenth."

"But we don't know which one of the three he is?"

"The emperor is the former Lord Periandros, Yakoub."

"So you say. Because you've been on retainer from Periandros since the year six. But is his claim any better than Naria's or Sunteil's?"

"He is in possession of the Capital."

"Nine tenths of the law, eh? Well, Shandor was in possession of *our* capital until you threw him out. What if Sunteil invades the Capital the same way?"

Julien was squirming now. A little muscle was flickering in his elegant Gallic cheek.

"Or both of them?" I suggested. "Striking a deal. Flipping a coin, heads I'm emperor, tails it's you, let's both throw Periandros out. What then?"

"These are terrible times, Yakoub."

"Indeed they are."

"The emperor wishes to help you because he knows that you can help him, yes. We are entering a season of chaos and flame. You and the emperor, standing together, could prevent the worst of it from happening."

"So we could, perhaps. But it would be the same if I allied myself with Sunteil or Naria."

"They did not rescue you, Yakoub. And they are not at the Capital now. Believe me, Yakoub: the Lord Periandros is emperor. However it was accomplished, it is the reality. Sunteil and Naria are insurgents. They mean to lead insurrections against the reigning emperor. If you throw in your lot with one or the other of them, Yakoub, you are not preventing chaos, you are in fact increasing it."

"And if I prefer Sunteil? Or Naria?"

"Why should you? You dislike them both. I know that."

"I have nothing good to say about Naria, true. Sunteil is a different matter."

"You can find something good to say about that Fenixi?"

"He's tricky and dangerous, yes. But he has charm. Periandros is absolutely devoid of charm, Julien. You must know that yourself."

"Charm is not the primary quality we seek in an emperor."

"But as king I'll have to deal with the emperor all the time. Do I want to deal with someone stiff and dull and humorless and heavy-handed when I could be crossing swords with the playful Sunteil?"

"You are being frivolous, Yakoub."

"I am a frivolous man."

"You are the least frivolous man in this galaxy!" he cried, with an angry force and a vigor I hadn't heard from him in a long while. "And this is foolishness. Periandros has made himself emperor. All right: he is emperor, like it or not. The other two are rebels. The emperor has given you your freedom and offers to support you in the schism within the Rom. You can accept or reject as you please. But if you choose to reach your hand toward one of the rebels you will destroy what little stability the Imperium has managed to attain in these difficult days. And you may find that the emperor, in his effort to rebuild that stability, will choose to reach *his* hand toward someone else."

"You mean Shandor? Is that a threat, Julien?"

"It is the statement of a realistic man, nothing more."

"It sounds like a threat."

"I am your friend, Yakoub. You know that. How long has it been for us, since the old days on Iriarte? When you were a discoverer of planets for your wife's kumpania and I was the company dispatcher? I was there when you married Esmeralda, was I not? When they gave you the bread and the salt, who stood beside you? And when Shandor was born, who was it you asked to be the godfather? And me not even a Rom; but you wanted me, and I would have done it if her father had allowed it. Have you forgotten all that?"

"I have forgotten nothing," I told him. "Nevertheless, you have a strange loyalty to Periandros."

"Not so strange. There's mutual respect there. You underestimate that man because you find the Akraki style not to your liking."

"He recognizes you as King of France, is that it?"

Color flared in Julien's cheeks and he seemed close to bursting into tears of rage.

"What does that have to do with anything?"

"France, I think sometimes, is more important to you than any place in the universe that still exists."

He calmed himself. It took some effort. "You will never understand what France is to me. It is like your Romany Star, Yakoub: the great lost place, the only true mother. Why is that so hard for you to comprehend?"

So he knew of Romany Star? That startled me. I had never heard that name on Gaje lips before. Obviously Julien had been paying closer attention to the private words of his Rom friends than any of us suspected. It troubled me, his knowing. But I didn't feel like dealing with that question now.

In annoyance I said, "Romany Star still exists. Someday we'll return there. But your France—"

"Ah, so that is the distinction, Yakoub? Your fantasy is real and mine is not, you mean?"

"Fantasy?"

"I beg you, mon ami, let us not cloud the discussion with these side issues—"

"You think Romany Star is a myth? A fable?"

He made a sweeping gesture with his hands. "N'importe, mon cher. That does not matter. Let us put this debate aside, for the moment. For the moment, Yakoub. You say that my loyalty to Periandros is strange, that it is somehow linked to his recognizing my claim to my own ancient throne. In fact he cares nothing at all about my claim. He cares only for the Imperium. I am loyal to him, to use your word, because I think he is the proper one to rule. As I also think that you, you are the proper one to rule, eh, Yakoub? Bien. Enough of this talk, mon cher. Come out of this prison room of yours, now. The palace is yours, this house of power. We restore it to you. Shandor is gone. Take your seat upon your throne, and I will prepare one more meal for you, in celebration. And then I wish you to think of all we have said. And then I hope you will come with me to the Capital, and present yourself before our new emperor. D'accord? Eh? Eh, mon ami? Think on these things. Only think, Yakoub."

3.

THIS TIME HE OUTDID HIMSELF WITH THE BANQUET. I could not begin to list all the delicacies and the worlds from which they came, or the rare wines, or the sensations that they aroused in me. Wherever Julien goes, he fills the surrounding dimensions with enough stored delights to dazzle a dozen gourmets, and this night he decanted them all for me. If I could have been persuaded by food alone, Periandros would have had my allegiance without a qualm.

But first I had to think, yes. And there was so much to think about.

The death of the old Fifteenth, for one. Any man's death diminishes me, et cetera. But this one hit me especially hard. My colleague. My contemporary, more or less. A huge chunk of the past carved away. I had worked long and well with the Fifteenth. A comforting familiar presence, my counterpart, my opposite royal self. And now gone.

In effect he'd been dead for years, of course, ever since he had begun his long slow decline into indifference and incoherence. Sunteil had been the real emperor for the last few of those years, I knew. (A lot of good that had done Sunteil, when the actual moment of succession was at hand. Obviously that wily man had made some fatal slip in his planning.) But being dead in effect is one thing and being literally dead is altogether another. Now that the loss was final I felt it suddenly and sharply.

A man of Ensalada Verde, he was. That gives you a measure of his quality right there: that he came from a nowhere world like that and still was able to climb right to the summit of the Imperium. All the other emperors have been men of the great metropolitan Gaje planets —Olympus, Copperfield, Malebolge, Ragnarok, teeming places with plenty of political clout—except for the Sixth and Ninth, who weren't men at all. But even those two, the two empresses regnant, came from major worlds. And then there was the Fifteenth, from his little unspoiled backwater planet that had maybe a billion people at most. He had actually been born a shepherd. But didn't stay a shepherd for long. Not him.

Flashes of the distant past ghost me. Myself arriving at the Capital, the hub of the galaxy, that world that has no real name and needs none. I am the newly elected king. He has been emperor six, seven, ten years. Enough time to get used to the grandeur and the silliness of it all. There are the crystalline steps, stretching up and up and up to the throne-platform. There sits the Fifteenth with his high lords beside him.

Fanfare of trumpets. The sound is sky-splitting: I expect suitcases and melons and odd pieces of furniture to come tumbling out of nearby storage dimensions. Up the steps, slowly, solemnly. Resisting the urge to take them two at a time. I have to be serious now. I am a man of mature years. (Ancient, in fact, by the standards of the olden days.) I am a king. An emperor waits for me to confirm me in my office with the touch of his wand. Another blast of trumpets. Drums, too, and maybe fifes.

"Yakoub Nirano Rom, Rom baro, Rex Romaniorum!" comes the cry from a million loudspeakers floating in a glittering cloud around the throne.

Up, up, up. The emperor sits waiting. He looks very calm. Wand of office resting lightly in his hand, like a fly-switch. About him, the three high lords preen and pose, looking terribly important. (These were the old high lords, left over from the reign of the Fourteenth, all of them now long dead. How they must have hated it when a shepherd from Ensalada Verde was jumped up over their heads onto the throne!)

Now the emperor rises to greet me. Not a tall man, not physically impressive in any way. He doesn't need to be. His mind is extraordinary: phenomenal breadth, phenomenal depth. Astonishing grasp of detail and pattern both. Some people are good at detail, some are good at pattern; only a few are masters of both. I have reason to think I am one. You know that. The Fifteenth was another. Nothing escaped his attention. When he spoke with you of starship routes he knew not only the reasons why the great routes were laid out as they were but also the name of every port of call along the way. And probably could quote population figures, too. A remarkable man.

Handing his wand of office to the lord on his left, now. Taking from the lord on his right the cup of sweet wine that by tradition the emperor always offers the king when the king comes visiting. Formally allowing me my sip. Then the touch of the wand to my shoulders, nice medieval moment.

"Yakoub Nirano Rom," he says. "Rom baro. Rex Romaniorum."

I have been king under Rom law since the moment the nine members of the great kris made the sign of kingship at me. But now the Gaje have accepted me also. Only a formality; but in these matters we live by formalities.

And the emperor, having formally confirmed me as king, looks at me and smiles and winks.

A wonderful moment. A wonderful gesture, that wink. Telling me a thousand things in one quick twitch of his eye. *We understand this throne business, you and I,* is what that wink has said. Yes. *We know what a joke it is.* Yes. *We also know how terribly serious it is.* Yes. Yes. *You are big and dark, I am small and fair. You are Rom and I am Gaje. And yet we are brothers, you and I. Brothers of the crown.* Yes. *We are closer to one another than I am to these peacock lords beside me. And*

than you are to anyone of your grand kumpania. Yes. Yes. Yes. From
then on we were locked together, the Fifteenth and I, in the joint
endeavor that is the governance of the worlds. It would be our shared
task to keep the sky from falling: a great burden and a great joy. All
that was contained in that one wink, and much more.

And so it was, for the Fifteenth and me, during the great years of our
reigns. Many was the time I called upon him at the Capital and took
the sweet wine from his hands, and we talked all the night through of
the movements of the stars in their courses and the myriad worlds, and
we made great decisions and reshaped great destinies. And at the times
when custom demanded he came to me at Galgala—and even once
when I was in residence at Xamur—and I threw wondrous patshivs for
him, feasts of such glory that they came close to rivaling that ill-starred
banquet given by Loiza la Vakako long ago on Nabomba Zom. But
there were no Pulika Boshengros to spoil our feasts. In the fifty years
of our collaboration we worked together serenely and effectively, the
Fifteenth and I. Until he began to slip into weariness and senility, and
I to put my preoccupation with Romany Star before all else. (For which
I make no apologies!) It was many years since I had seen him, now.
Since my departure for Mulano I had scarcely so much as thought of
him. And now he was gone, and I realized that insofar as it is possible
for a Rom to love a Gaje I had loved the Fifteenth Emperor. I set that
down here, now, for all to know.

And one thing more. In the twentieth year of my reign I discovered
a surprising thing when I was going through some documents of the
reign of my predecessor Cesaro o Nano. Which was that it was the
Fifteenth himself who had put into his mind the notion of naming me
to follow him as king. How very strange that was, that the Gaje emperor should make such a suggestion, and how very much stranger that
the Rom king should follow it. The Fifteenth had often told me how
he had held me in high regard long before I became king; and now I
had proof of it.

I have concealed this ever since I found it out. But why hide it any
longer? Is there shame in it? The Fifteenth was right that I would be
a good king. Cesaro o Nano was right to have followed his advice. What
of it, that the advice came from a Gaje? From the highest Gajo of them
all? Was Cesaro o Nano the less for listening to him? Was I the less for
having been recommended by an emperor? During the thousands of
years since our two peoples first were thrust together by fate we have
feared and mistrusted the Gaje, for good reasons, and they have feared

and mistrusted us, for reasons that seem to me not so good. But perhaps some of that fear and mistrust was needless, on both sides. And now it no longer seems important for me to conceal the Fifteenth's role in making me king. In truth, considering the great changes that many recent events have wrought, I think it is a good thing to let the story be told.

How odd, you may say, that the Fifteenth was so concerned about the Rom succession, and failed to provide for his own! But he chose me as king long ago when he was still in the vigor of his middle years. His own decline must have come upon him more suddenly than anyone knew, and the effect on him must have been far more calamitous than we suspected. For I knew the Fifteenth well, and I don't think he would willingly have left the imperial succession open as he did. His wits must have gone from him before he could make provision for the succession, for surely he wouldn't have wanted to depart as he did, leaving Sunteil and Naria and Periandros to battle for the throne.

Or perhaps—knowing him as well as I did—I shouldn't say that. Perhaps—considering the events that have followed his death—the Fifteenth knew exactly what he was doing, when he neglected to provide the usual decree of succession. He was a remarkable man. He saw things with extraordinary clarity. Perhaps he was looking beyond his death and the chaos that would follow it, into the deeper future, when all would be quite different. I would like to ask him what he really had in mind. Of course he is gone now. But perhaps one day I will have the chance to ask him all the same.

4.

I THOUGHT A GREAT DEAL ABOUT SHANDOR, TOO, AS I wandered like my own ghost through the halls of the royal house of power.

There were signs of struggle everywhere. Someone had made an attempt to clean up, but I saw gouges in the thick leather wallcoverings, burn-scars on the floors, even what may have been bloodstains. And yet Shandor had managed to escape. He had even, so it seemed, taken some ceremonial objects with him, ancient emblems and regalia. I saw the empty places. The invading force must have deliberately allowed him to get away, I thought. As a kindness to me. Because he was, after all, my son. Surrounded and taken by surprise as he had been, Shandor would never have been able to fight his way out. Especially when he was encumbered by the ceremonial objects. They must have winked and looked the other way, for my sake.

Oh, was I wrong about that!

I have to admit that I felt strangely tender toward Shandor, even loving, now that he was gone and I was free again. I know it sounds peculiar. Considering Shandor's unloving and unlovable nature. But after all he was my son. And his attempt to seize the kingship had failed: he was a fugitive, he was on the run. I had nothing more to fear from him, did I? So I could allow my buried love for him to surface. And my pity. If you can't make sense of this, don't try. You'll understand some day.

I found myself thinking I could reclaim Shandor somehow. Sit down with him in the traditional way, pour coffee for him, pour wine, discuss the differences that had arisen between us. Work them out, get rid of them, embrace him in a hot Romany hug of love and kinship. As though he were simply a boy of twenty who had gone a little astray, and not a reckless and evil old man who had chosen the path of wickedness all his long life. Yes, I would reclaim him! Win him back to be my true son! Take him into my government, even. So I thought. My fantasy, my folly. I was entitled. I am not required to be ruled by common sense one hundred six percent of the time. He was my son, after all. After all.

And then, Periandros—

What to do about Periandros?

Deny him? Tell Julien I could not possibly accept him as emperor, and send word to Sunteil, or maybe even Naria, that I was giving my support to him?

Why? Simply because I disliked him? Did I like Naria better? Sunteil, perhaps, I did like; but did I trust him? What were the ambitions of these quarrelsome Gaje princelings to me? Why thrust myself into their civil war? I was king again; and if I had Periandros to thank for that, so be it. I owed him nothing but thanks. Now I must restore my command of the kingdom; and then there would be time to see how the struggle among the high lords resolved itself. Meanwhile Periandros held the Capital. Therefore Periandros was emperor. If Sunteil or Naria disagreed, let him change things: that wasn't my affair. As king I needed an emperor with whom to deal. For the moment, Periandros was emperor. For the moment, then, I would take him to be the legitimate holder of the Gaje throne.

I sent for Julien.

"While I was Shandor's prisoner," I said, "he told me that he had been to the Capital and that he had received the wand of recognition. From the emperor, by the emperor's own hand. Do you know anything about that? Could he have been telling the truth?"

"Do you think he was, mon vieux?"

"He said Sunteil and Naria and Periandros were right there, but the emperor himself held the wand."

"The old emperor was lost in dreams all the time of Shandor's reign," said Julien.

"So I thought."

"It was Naria who held the wand."

"Naria?"

"There was a great dispute among the lords. Throughout it the Lord Periandros spoke out for you, Yakoub. He regarded Shandor always as an interloper with no rightful claim. Sunteil wavered, now supporting Shandor, then you, then saying it was none of the Imperium's business who the Rom chose to be their king. Naria argued for immediate recognition of Shandor. He has always mistrusted you, do you know that? Because you were born on the same world as he, and you a slave and he a noble. He thinks you hate him for that, that in some way you blame him for your slavery."

"I am not fond of Naria," I said indifferently. "Perhaps his theory has some basis to it."

"He told the others that Shandor would be the Rom king no matter what the Imperium said; and that therefore it was good politics to give him confirmation. The Lord Periandros and eventually Sunteil would not have it. Then one day when it was Naria's turn to hold the orb of regency he simply summoned Shandor to the Capital and laid the wand upon him. Fait accompli, you see."

"And did the other two accept what Naria had done?"

Julien waved his hand at the dark scar of an imploder burn on the wall. "There you can see how impressed the Lord Periandros was with

Naria's recognition of Shandor. As for Sunteil, he has kept his own counsel on the matter. As Sunteil usually does. Now that Shandor is overthrown he probably will claim he favored you all along."

"Yes," I said. "That sounds like Sunteil."

"And now, mon ami? What will you do, now that Shandor is overthrown?"

"Go to the Capital," I said. "Speak with Periandros."

"With the Sixteenth, as we must call him now."

I gave Julien a long, steady, cool look. This time he returned it, just as steady, just as cool. My ancient friend, my Gaje cousin. Who had been a part of my life longer than anyone now living, other than Polarca. Whom I had known for a hundred years. What was he trying to do now? Was it not enough that I had agreed to meet Periandros, to deal with him as though he were truly the emperor? Did Julien have to force him all the way down my throat?

Then I thought: It costs me nothing to allow Periandros his title, for as long as he is able to hold it. And it seems important to Julien to give him that little honor. Very well.

"Yes," I said. "To speak with the Sixteenth."

5.

AS WE WERE MAKING READY TO SET OUT FROM AUREUS Highlands to the Galgala starport I heard the distant sound of explosions and saw white smoke on the eastern horizon. Julien told me that fighting persisted in the back country, that Shandor had holed himself up in an obscure pocket of the Chrysoberyl Hills and was standing off attack by the imperial forces.

Once long ago on Mulano—it seemed a million years—Julien had warned me that my continued abdication might lead to wars between worlds. "War is an outmoded notion," I had told him with splendid assurance. "It's an obsolete concept." And now there was a war going on right here under my nose on Galgala itself, our Rom capital. With the troops of the emperor laying siege to a son of the Rom king practically within sight of the royal house of power.

So war was not at all an obsolete concept. Nor had Periandros' soldiers gallantly allowed Shandor to escape, as I had so naively imagined. By cunning or stealth or treachery or sheer force he had won his way free of the house of power, yes, and they were pursuing him, they were besieging him. My son.

For a day, a day and a half, I thought about nothing but that: that warfare was taking place on Galgala, that Akrakikan soldiers were seeking to capture my son. Or to kill him.

I had to do something.

He would have overthrown me; but still he was my son. The firstborn. Once my pride, my joy, my miniature image of myself. A difficult boy, perhaps an unloving one, and a stranger to me for most of his life; and lately my enemy. Yet still my son. Blood was calling to blood. I had other sons, many of them in fact, and in one way and another, over the great span of time, they had all been lost to me, through distance, through their own needs to be apart, through ambitions that had taken them to the edges of the universe, through quarrels, through death. We are a family people, we Rom, we Gypsies, and how sad and painful it was that the Rom baro, the biggest Gypsy of them all, should have come down into the winter of his years with no wife at hand, no sons. Here was Shandor my son practically within my reach. I would go to him. Perhaps there would be forgiveness at last. At least there would be no more killing.

Just when everything was in readiness and we were about to depart for the starport I sent suddenly for Julien and said, "First we must make a little detour, old friend."

"What do you mean?"

"To the Chrysoberyl Hills," I said. "To put an end to this fighting."

"No," he said. "We must go to the Capital."

"First this."

"No."

"No?"

"Listen to me this once, Yakoub. Forget Shandor."

"How can I?" I said. And I told him all that had been passing through my soul.

Julien listened without saying a word. And stared at me with infinite tenderness and sorrow.

"That was what I had feared," he said at last, when I had run dry of speech. "That you would find love in your heart for him, that you would want to make your peace with him. I had hoped to hurry you off Galgala before you learned the truth, mon ami. But now you give me no choice but to tell you."

"Tell me what?"

He paused only a moment. "Shandor is dead."

"Dead?" I said stupidly. "When? How?"

"Yesterday, or the day before yesterday. They used dream-light; they slipped into his camp under cover of illusion. Shandor was seized and brought before the imperial general." Julien stared toward the floor. "They will say that he was killed while attempting to resist, Yakoub. I am greatly sorry for your grief, mon vieux, mon cher."

"Dead?" The word refused to register.

"A strategic decision. I had nothing to do with it. You understand, do you not, I had nothing to do with it? He was thought to be too dangerous. An immense destabilizing force."

"He was a fool. He was incapable of destabilizing anything."

"That is not how it seemed to the emperor, Yakoub."

"So Periandros himself gave the order to kill him?"

"Not so," said Julien. I think he was sincere. "It was not the Sixteenth himself, but the general of the Sixteenth, seeking to win the emperor's favor. Seeking too hard, I think. Believe me. I beg you, believe me, Yakoub."

"What is this?" I asked. "The thirteenth century? Not even then did they kill captured princes. Are we sliding back into barbarism, is that it, Julien?" I turned away from him, appalled by the power of my own feelings, stunned by the weight of the grief I felt. Shandor! Shandor! How I had despised him, that sorry son of mine! How he had shamed me! How often I had longed for his death, a hundred times over the years! And how I mourned him now! I was as shaken as I had been that terrible day on Mulano when Damiano had brought me the news that Shandor, against all custom and decency, had proclaimed himself king. Then, if I could have killed him with a snap of the fingers, I would have snapped my fingers; but now he was dead at some stranger's hands and a monstrous void had opened within me where he had been.

I swung around and caught Julien roughly by the shoulder, so hard that he tried to shrink back from my touch, and could not.

"Was there anyone who thought that it would please me to have Shandor lose his life? Was it Periandros' favor they were trying to win with this murder, or mine?"

"I beg you, Yakoub—"

"Well? Was it?"

Julien shook his head desperately. His eyes were wild; his hair tumbled into his face; all his careful elegance was gone. "No," he said hoarsely, after a time. "Je t'en prie, Yakoub! I beg you, believe me! I had nothing to do with this. Nothing! Nothing!" And I saw that he was speaking the truth. Letting him go, I turned from him and went to the balcony, and stood by myself looking toward the Chrysoberyl Hills.

All was quiet there now. No puffs of smoke, no sounds of warfare. It was over, then. I wondered how many other Rom had died with Shandor. Asking that of Julien, I thought, would be asking too much.

"Send word to the Sixteenth," I said, after a time, "that I will be delayed a little while in my journey to the Capital. We must hold the funeral first. And that will take some days."

"But the emperor—"

"Bugger the emperor! My son is dead, Julien. A king of the Rom is dead! There is the shroud to make. The white caravan to construct. You know the rites as well as I do. The music, the pilgrimage, the burial. The wine, the food. Where is the body of my son?"

"The Akrakikan—"

"Get it from them. And send me the officers of the court. We will do this in the proper way. And then, only then, will you and I make our journey to the Capital and present ourselves before the Sixteenth. Go. Go." I gestured furiously, impatiently. "Get out of here, Julien! Leave me alone!"

6.

THE WORLD THAT IS KNOWN ONLY AS THE CAPITAL, THE world that is the hub of the galaxy, is to me a pallid and dreary place. Why the Gaje decided long ago to make it their New Earth, the seat of the government, I will never know, or care; you will have to ask of the Gaje if you would understand that choice. In a universe that holds a Galgala, a Nabomba Zom, a Xamur, why plant the center of your empire on a planet like that?

But of course Galgala and Xamur and Nabomba Zom were never theirs to choose. Those worlds are ours by right of discovery.

The Capital is not a terrible place. It is a smallish world, one of six that orbit a pale yellow-green sun, and it has a mild climate, rivers and streams, flowers and trees, air that you can breathe without adaptors, a general feel of comfort and placidity. But its oceans are shallow and its mountains are low and blunt and its birds are gray and brown. A drab world, a safe little world, a decent middle-of-the-road world. Perhaps that is why the Gaje like it so much. But they have not even managed to give it a real name.

Naturally they have built themselves an absurd fantastical imperial city out of marble and flame, a great gaudy enterprise, shining towers and broad boulevards and blazing lights, the usual crystal and emerald and alabaster everywhere. But what else would you expect from the Gaje: showiness, theatricality, preposterous overmagnificence. But in that case they should have built their capital on some planet other than the Capital. Just as the Idradin crater seems incongruous in its ugliness against the matchless beauties of Xamur, so too does the imperial city look wildly out of place on the Capital. It is like a colossal coruscating diamond that has been set in a diadem of cardboard.

Be that as it may. The Capital is the great Gaje place, and I am a mere shabby Gypsy, who knows nothing of true splendor. Maybe some day I will come to understand the Capital better than I do now. But that is not important to me, understanding the Capital.

For all its grandeur the imperial center had an uneasy, makeshift look about it when I arrived. It was like a city just recovering from a war—or preparing for one. The green and red sky-banners that paid homage to the Fifteenth had all been turned off. Only a handful of new ones in the colors of the Sixteenth had been put up thus far, and so the sky looked strangely empty. In the outer ring of the city, where scores of dazzling light-spikes normally glowed in honor of visiting lords from other worlds, everything was dark. I had never seen it like that before.

That darkness puzzled me. Weren't there any other visiting lords here? If there were, didn't they object to the absence of their spikes? Perhaps all the imperial vassals were keeping clear of the Capital until they were absolutely certain that Periandros was the emperor they were vassal to. Well, even so, I was an imperial vassal, and I was here. Where was *my* light-spike? I missed it. Maybe I was the only one here. Maybe

Periandros had told all the others to stay away. Could it be that the Sixteenth, still uncertain of his throne, felt it might seem unduly provocative to be claiming homage from the planetary lords just now? I know that I wouldn't have felt that way. I would be making every show of power and rightful authority that I could, if I were in Periandros' shoes. But—thanks be to Holy God and the Divine Mother and Saint Sara-la-Kali—Periandros was in Periandros' shoes and I was in my own.

"Why is there no spike up for me?" I asked Julien, not long after I was installed in the opulent guest palace at the Plaza of the Three Nebulas that the Imperium maintains for the use of the Rom king when he is visiting the Capital.

"There is a problem with the spikes," said Julien diplomatically.

"I imagine there is," I said.

"They consume a great deal of energy. These are difficult and expensive times, mon ami."

"Ah. I forgot. The thrifty Periandros."

"He has ordered a cutback on superfluous expenditures of energy. Temporarily, I'm afraid, there will be no light-spikes. It is only idle show, is it not, mon vieux? These Roman candles blazing away?"

"The emperor has his own sky-banners up, I see."

"Only a very few," Julien said, looking uncomfortable. "He must assert his imperial presence, after all. But you will note that where the Fifteenth had hundreds of banners in the sky, the Sixteenth has scarcely any. A symbolic minimum."

"I have a presence to assert also," I said. "I would like my light-spike, Julien."

"Cher ami—je t'implore—"

"Yes," I said, "my good old light-spike, bright purple, five hundred meters high, telling all the Capital that the Rom baro is in residence awaiting audience with the emperor—"

Julien was miserable and made no attempt to hide it. But he took my meaning. Not that I give a tortoise turd about light-spikes or banners or flags or medals or any such trivialities, ordinarily. But this was a time of testing for everyone. Periandros owed me the courtesy of a spike. Subtly or not so subtly—what did I care?—Julien would have to convey my wishes to his master. Then Periandros would be compelled to weigh his need for pinching obols and minims against the desire of the venerable Rom king for a little pomp and pageantry. And I would find out just where I really stood in the esteem of the new emperor and how much leverage I might have over him in the difficult times ahead.

The sky remained dark the next night. But the night after that, I saw the traditional royal Rom light-spike spear the heavens as soon as the sun went down.

In his hospitality, at least, the new emperor was unstinting—or perhaps Julien had simply arranged things as he felt they ought to be arranged. That was more likely. Periandros would have had a stroke if he had known what Julien was spending to keep me amused while I was awaiting the advisers I had summoned for my meetings with the emperor.

The immense and splendiferous Rom palace was in immaculate order and I had platoons of servants—robots, androids, human slaves, doppelgangers of slaves—a staff so huge it was ridiculous. The finest foods and wines were available at any hour of the day and night. Musicians, dancers, minstrels, likewise. And other services. It was embarrassing. Who needed these crowds, this hoopla? Especially in light of the sort of hospitality my own son had been providing for me. Not that I wanted the crawling things and meals of mush back, mind you; but this went too far in the opposite direction. I think you know that it is not the Rom way, all this luxury. It is the Gaje idea of the Rom way, perhaps: or perhaps the Gaje are so guilty about the way they have treated us over the millennia that they feel they must make amends in this overblown fashion when the Rom baro comes to town.

Day by day my people arrived at the Capital, bearing news of the horrendous chaos that had spread through the worlds during the time of my imprisonment, and—may all the gods and demons be praised!—the wonderful restoration of order that had been effected since the collapse of Shandor's insurgency. The Gaje lords might be squabbling but at least we Rom had the spacelanes open again and the ships running on time.

Polarca came first, then Biznaga, then Jacinto and Ammagante, and the phuri dai. Followed soon after by Damiano and Thivt. But not Valerian. I hadn't sent for him, and not for his ghost either. It would have been unwise, and in very poor taste besides, to invite a proscribed enemy of the Imperium like Valerian to come to the Capital. Testing Periandros was one thing, thumbing my nose in his face something else entirely.

I had to do without Chorian, also. I had grown very fond of the young Fenixi—let me not be too coy here; I had come to love him as I would a son—and it was my plan to move him into positions of ever greater responsibility in the government. We were all antiques; I needed someone born in this century to help keep me in touch with realities. But although Chorian was among those I called to my side at the Capital, he didn't show up. I asked Julien about him.

"He will not be coming," Julien said.

"What's the problem? I thought the starships were running on schedule again, now that Shandor is—"

"The starships are running on schedule, yes, mon ami."

Instantly alarmed, I said, "Where's Chorian, then? Has something happened to him?"

"He is safe and sound among the Haj Qaldun worlds, so far as I am aware," Julien told me. "He has not received your invitation, that is all."

"He *what?*"

"Yakoub," said Julien reproachfully. "What is this foolishness? How can I summon him here? He is Sunteil's man, your Chorian."

I felt anger flaring up. "He is Rom, Julien! One of my most loyal and devoted—"

"Perhaps so. He is also Sunteil's man. What you ask is impossible, mon vieux. Light-spikes I can get for you, yes. And other things: you have only to ask. But one who is actually in the employ of a rebel against the emperor? Yakoub, Yakoub, Yakoub!" He shook his head. "Be reasonable, mon ami!"

I was annoyed, but I saw his point. King or no king, I was going to have to yield on this. It had indeed been foolish of me to think I could have Chorian here at this time. I regretted that greatly. I wanted him here. It would be good for him to become familiar with the Capital, and useful and instructive for him to observe the daily ebb and flow of my negotiations with Periandros. But of course he couldn't be here now. Whatever he might be to me, he was Sunteil's man also. I shouldn't have needed Julien to point that out. Chorian would have to stay away from the Capital.

For now. But he would be on hand to play his part in the cataclysmic events that lay just ahead.

7.

THE CRYSTALLINE STEPS ONCE AGAIN. THE THRONE-PLAT-
form, far above me. How many times over the many decades of my life
had I stood on the great slab of onyx at the base of that lofty seat of
power, staring upward at the ruler of all the Gaje worlds?

I had never seen the Thirteenth, not in the flesh. I was too far from
the center of power then. The emperor of my childhood, he was, and
well on into my early manhood too, living on forever and forever. I had
seen his image on the screens of a dozen worlds, though: the little weary
waxen-faced man, perched high atop his onyx platform. Who could
have imagined he would have lived so long? The Fourteenth was a
different story, young and vigorous, coming to the throne with the
avowed purpose of clearing away the cobwebs that had gathered during
his predecessor's interminable reign. I made my first visits to court
during his time. A slight-bodied dark-skinned man, almost Rom in
color, with keen golden eyes and an easy smile, and the strength of a
true emperor behind that smile. He came from Copperfield, as five of
the emperors before him had done. It would be a lie to say that I had
known him well, but I had seen him, I had even spoken to him two or
three times. And then suddenly he was dead. There were rumors that
he had been done away with, for having instituted too many reforms
too quickly. And so came the Fifteenth, the shepherd of Ensalada
Verde, in later years my friend and working partner, wise and good.
Well, he too was gone now but I was still here, waiting by the crystal
steps for the one who called himself the Sixteenth, this mingy miserly
Periandros, the fourth emperor of my life. If indeed this was an emperor
I stood before now, and not merely a vain pretender.

I listened for the trumpets. Yes, there they were. But not the old
deafening glory. More of a pathetic blatting whoosh. Another of Periandros' petty economies? Or was it merely the flavor of the times, that
made everything seemed a pale and meek shadow of its former self?

And the voice from the million loudspeakers. "Yakoub Nirano Rom, Rom baro, Rex Romaniorum!" They had the name and the titles right, yes. But there was no conviction there, no force. I remember once when I had been ghosting back to the old imperial Roman days on Earth—and this Gaje empire enjoys some pretension of a link to that one, at least in certain of its borrowed ways and terminology—and it was the final days, just before the barbarians came hammering at the gates. Ordinarily one does not know that one lives in the final days of a great empire; one is aware only that things are not as good as they were reputed once to be. Knowledge of finality comes only after the fact, when the historians have come mincing in to provide some perspective. But those Romans in the final days knew that it was not just a bad time but the end of time, and you could see it in their eyes, in the gray look of their faces, in the slant of their shoulders. Everything about them cried out that the apocalypse was just around the corner. It was a little like that now. Decline and fall was in the air of the Capital. The old order was ending and God alone knew what was coming next; and even the trumpets and loudspeakers were faint and mildewed over with doubts.

"The Sixteenth Emperor of the Grand Imperium summons the Rex Romaniorum before the throne," called out the major domo. And up those stairs I went. Again. Slowly. Not so much bounce in my stride as before. The gloom and depression here was contagious. I resolved to get myself away from this place as fast as I could, once I had completed my business with Periandros.

Within his fine robes he looked drawn, shrunken, haggard. The Periandros I remembered was a plump man, soft-skinned, with the look of a pleasure-lover about him, ripe or even overripe. Completely misleading, because he was no more pleasure-loving than your basic lump of stone. Probably some rocks of the igneous persuasion were even his superior in that department. Within that soft pampered body was a mean pinched hard soul, like a crab lurking within a tender melon. God knows why they are all like that on Sidri Akrak: an entire planet of miserable ghastly dour people suffering from constipation of the heart. Now the ripeness was gone from Periandros and only the sour withered Akraki core of him was left. Beside him, in the seats where the emperor's high lords sit, were three more Akrakikan. I had to admire the totality of the takeover, and the total foolishness of it. Usually the emperor has sense enough to give the high lordships to citizens of assorted major planets, by way of building a little political support for himself. But not this one, who was in more need of support from other worlds than any emperor who had ever ruled. Oh, no, not this one: he had surrounded himself entirely with his own kind. Three of his own brothers, for all I knew. If they had brothers on Sidri Akrak. It seemed more appropriate for people like him to be born from tubes, like androids. It was a disheartening sight, seeing those four glum passionless faces staring back at me from the summit of the throne-platform.

"This is a joyous day, Yakoub Rom," Periandros said in a voice lacking the merest molecule of joy. Flat monotone, an inhuman drone. "You are welcome before us."

Us, no less. He had reinvented the royal *we!*

He had the wine ready for me. I took the cup. That stuff too had lost its savor: thin and acrid, a bad year. I felt like telling him that the wine of welcome is supposed to be sweet.

Instead I made the formal gesture that the Rom baro makes when he stands before the emperor. Maybe Periandros thought it was in his honor but all I was doing was reinforcing my own. Affirming my state of kingship, rather than affirming his emperorship. He didn't have to know that.

He did manage a quick pale flickering smile. Real emotion, Periandros style. The Periandros equivalent of a great roaring hug, I suppose.

"There has been much confusion, has there not?" he said. "How I detest confusion!" (Forgetting his *we* already?) "But the time of chaos is ending. The crown imperial has descended to us." (No, just not consistent in its use.) "—and we will do our utmost to restore order in the Imperium." A self-satisfied smirk. "Already we have done much. For example we have aided our Romany brothers in their time of difficulty."

Butting in, killing my son. Yes, wonderful aid.

I said, "You really think the confusion is over, Periandros?"

Hisses and gasps of shock among the high lords. A fierce look of black loathing from Periandros. I realized my mistake too late. Calling him by name, and not even *Lord* Periandros at that. But no one could call him anything but "Your Majesty" now, not even me. The former Lord Periandros had vanished within the royal greatness, what Julien would call the *gloire,* of the Sixteenth Emperor.

I hadn't meant any insult. It had just slipped out. I remembered, after all, the day Periandros first had taken his seat among the high lords. Not all that long ago. The apologetic look in the eyes of the Fifteenth, as if to say, *He's a peculiar little creature, I know, but I find him useful.*

Hard for me to take the peculiar little creature seriously. Sitting in my old friend's throne. But he was the Emperor now. At least I had decided to regard him as the Emperor. For expediency's sake. I covered my gaffe with a quick apology. Old habits die hard, et cetera, et cetera. Periandros looked mollified.

"We are not yet fully accustomed to our high position ourself," he confided.

I admired the grammatical elegance of that confession. I might have said *ourselves,* which would have been silly. But then I haven't given as much thought to the niceties of the royal *we* as Periandros undoubtedly had.

Piously I said, "It must be a great burden, Majesty."

"We have prepared for it all our life. There is a long tradition of imperial service, you know, on my world of Sidri Akrak." (Still not getting it straight, his *we.*) "The Seventh Emperor, and again the Eleventh—and now once more our world has been honored by the summons of the Imperium—" He leaned in close, staring hard as if trying to read my mind. God help me if he could: he'd see the contempt for his small soul bristling all over my cerebral contours and five minutes later I might find myself wishing I was back safe and snug in Shandor's oubliette. He moistened his lips. "This abdication business of yours— how am I supposed to interpret that?"

"A purely internal Rom matter, Majesty. A political ploy, perhaps not too wisely conceived."

"Ah."

"It's been withdrawn. Nullified. So far as I and my people are concerned, there's been no break in my reign."

"And the claims of your son Shandor?"

"An aberration, Your Majesty. A desperate insurgency that has now been brought under control. And with the death of Shandor the whole issue becomes moot. There are no other claimants for the Rom throne."

Periandros looked genuinely bewildered.

"Shandor is dead?"

"Killed during the invasion of Galgala by imperial troops," I said, perhaps too sharply.

He consulted with his high lords. There was much rapid muttering in the opaque Akraki dialect of Imperial. From what little I could follow I saw that Julien had been telling me the truth when he said that Shandor's death was none of Periandros' doing, that it had been a free-lance contribution by an overzealous general. Which at least would make it a little easier for me to do business with Periandros. When he turned back to me there was a look almost of compassion in his eyes. Or discomfort of the bowel, but I took it as compassion. Give him credit. Human emotion ran against his natural grain but he was trying. He expressed condolences, and I thanked him. Told him that Shandor had been a great trial to me but nevertheless he was blood of my blood, et cetera, et cetera. The Sixteenth nodded solemnly. Probably he was immensely fascinated by our quaint old Rom custom of giving a damn about the members of our own families.

After a time, to his obvious relief and in fact mine also, we got off the subject of Shandor and back to the subject of power, where we were both more comfortable.

In his ponderously purse-mouthed way he allowed as how we were both in highly precarious situations. I thought my situation was considerably less precarious than his, but I allowed as how I agreed with his assessment. I was wise enough to know that it didn't take a monster like Shandor to topple a king. Someone as loyal and dedicated as Damiano could do it, if he began to think I was getting too old and unpredictable to entrust with the job. Maybe even with Polarca's connivance. There was plenty of precedent in human history for kings being removed by their own most trusted kinsmen and associates for the general good and welfare. Yes, the more I thought about it, the more risky my whole position looked.

"We need each other, yes, you and I," I told Periandros.

Politics, the old Gaje philosopher said—Shakespeare, Socrates, one of those—does indeed make strange bedfellows. I never imagined I would find myself angling for the embrace of Periandros. But, then, I had never imagined to find Periandros sitting on the imperial throne, either.

Very quickly we came to an understanding. There would be a showy public ceremony, the complete works, a grand pyrotechnikon and all, by way of reconfirming me as King of the Rom. The laying on of the wand of recognition, the whole business. The entire nobility would be invited, both Gaje and Rom, from all the worlds. The biggest spectacle in centuries, in fact.

"With light-spikes for everyone?" I said.

"Of course, with light-spikes," Periandros said, irritated. "How can we do without light-spikes, if we are to have the nobility gathered here?"

"I was just wondering," I said.

But no, he was planning to pull out all the stops, and devil take the cost. I could see how serious he was about this, considering what he would have to spend. Though it did cross my mind that he might well ask us to contribute too. That would be all right. The reconsecration ceremony would be of enormous symbolic benefit to both of us. For me it would wipe out the little ambiguity that had been brought into being when Lord Naria, acting as regent, had laid the wand on Shandor's shoulders. For Periandros it would serve similarly to expunge what Naria had done, thereby retroactively expunging Naria's one brave display of imperial authority. All the worlds would know that Yakoub Nirano was now and forevermore Rom baro, Rex Romaniorum; and implicit in Periandros' recognizing me as king was my recognizing him as emperor.

There was one other little part of the package. But even Periandros the shameless was too abashed to ask for it outright. What he wanted was for me to spy for him: to have my Rom star-captains keep me provided with reports on the movements of the Lords Naria and Sunteil, and for me to turn those reports over to him. The way he managed to phrase it, though, Sunteil and Naria weren't explicitly mentioned, and it was possible for me to interpret what he was saying as simply a request for detailed statistical analyses of the flow of commerce between the worlds. That was how I chose to interpret it, anyway.

"Certainly," I said. "I see no problem with that at all."

"Then we understand one another?"

"Perfectly," I said.

He rose and poured the wine of farewell for me. I came forward to accept it, and took a close look at him as I did. I had been noticing something odd about him, the last few minutes, and I wanted to check it out at close range.

It had seemed to me that he was flickering about the edges, so to speak. Losing definition, a little. I wasn't sure of it; but as well as I was able to tell from the distance where I was required to sit, the Sixteenth was having some trouble keeping the boundaries of his corpus firm. That is of course a characteristic of doppelgangers: they are always plausible duplicates of the human beings from whom they are generated, but they are in a steady state of degeneration from the moment they are struck off the mold, and the keen eye can spot it sometimes, very subtle though the effect will be in the early stages.

Had I been talking to a doppelganger of the emperor all this time? Sitting there sipping his wine and staring into his eyes and playing little political fencing-matches with him, and the whole while I had been dealing with a mere simulacrum, while the authentic Sixteenth—scared out of his wits by the fear of assassination, even an unthinkable assassination at the hands of the Rom king himself—was hiding somewhere out of sight, monitoring the whole thing by cortex wire, maybe even running a relay that told the doppelganger what to say? Jesu Cretchuno Moischel and Abraham! What an absurdity! What an insult!

If it was true. I peered close, but I couldn't tell. Maybe I had imagined the whole thing. Maybe the flicker had been in my eyes and not in the emperor's edges. At any rate I didn't have any way of poking and prodding to find out; I had to take my little sip of wine and get myself down from the platform.

"Well?" Polarca asked. "How did it go?"

"About as I expected. The pompous little shit: he really thinks he's emperor. The funny thing is, so do I think he is. But there was one damned strange thing."

"What was that?"

I told him that I thought I might have been having an audience with a doppelganger-emperor the whole time. Polarca clapped his hands and laughed.

"If that isn't just like Periandros!" he cried. "Did he think you had a bomb in your mustache? He really wants to live forever, doesn't he?"

"I think he wants to live long enough to get Sunteil and Naria to agree that he's really the emperor," I said.

"I don't think anybody's going to live that long," Polarca said. He shook his head. "A doppelganger! Can you beat that!"

"I'm not totally sure, you understand."

"But it's just like him. It absolutely is. What do you think, will he send a doppelganger to this big grand reconsecration ceremony of yours too? If anyone's going to try to assassinate him, that would be a fine place to do it."

"And take out everybody within ten meters of him too," I said.

Polarca scowled. "Maybe you'd better send a doppelganger to the ceremony too, eh, Yakoub?"

8.

BUT THE GREAT RECONSECRATION CEREMONY NEVER DID take place. And Periandros learned that no matter how many doppelgangers he tried to hide behind, a really determined and creative assassin would somehow be able to find him. It happened just three days after my audience with him: a homing wasp, in his bath, a diabolical little artificial insect that flew straight for its goal and killed him so fast that he died with the soap still in his hand. You can use doppelgangers for lots of things, but not to take your baths for you.

A few hours later, before I had heard anything about the tragic event in the imperial bath-chamber, the starship *Jewel of the Imperium* landed at the Capital bearing a most distinguished passenger: no less than Lord Sunteil, who was returning with remarkably fine timing after having spent the past few months in exile, or, if you prefer, in hiding. (Yes, that same Supernova-class *Jewel of the Imperium* that had taken me from Xamur to Galgala when I went to have things out with Shandor. The pilot of which was Petsha le Stevo of Zimbalou and whose captain, by a remarkable coincidence, was the dapper Therione, a native of Sunteil's very own world of Fenix.)

The first thing that Lord Sunteil did upon his arrival at the Capital was to proclaim himself emperor, news having reached him with surprising swiftness that Periandros was no longer among the living. In measured words Sunteil expressed his grief over the passing of the late Lord Periandros, whom he did not refer to as the Sixteenth Emperor. He himself, he declared, was the Sixteenth Emperor. And he had held that title, he said, ever since the instant of the Fifteenth's death, although he had been unfortunately detained all this while on urgent imperial business in the Haj Qaldun system and had been unable until now to give his personal attention to the problems of the central government.

The second thing that Lord Sunteil did upon his arrival at the Capital was to run desperately for cover.

He had just finished proclaiming his imperial authority when a detachment of imperial troops arrived to arrest him. Sunteil managed to clear out of the starport barely ahead of them and vanished back into hiding somewhere south of the city. Somehow, though he had been able to ascertain with such surprising swiftness that Lord Periandros had perished that day in a lamentable accident in the privacy of his palace, Sunteil had failed to discover one other significant datum, which was that his rival Lord Naria had been secretly on hand at the Capital for quite some time and that Naria—or the Sixteenth Emperor, as Naria preferred us all to call him—had quietly succeeded in winning the support of a substantial portion of the imperial military forces. While Sunteil was still making self-congratulatory speeches at the starport, Naria had taken possession of the imperial palace and was accepting the homage of the peers of the Imperium, who were nothing if not obliging, though I imagine they were becoming a trifle confused.

A little later on that remarkable day, which I'm certain will provide stimulating challenges to historians for centuries to come, the late Lord Periandros made an unexpected reappearance on the imperial communications channel. The reports of his death had been greatly exaggerated, he informed us. He was even now as heretofore the Sixteenth Emperor and he called upon all loyal citizens to denounce the lies of the criminal Lord Sunteil and the vile intrusion upon the imperial palace of the criminal Lord Naria.

In short, the fat was in the fire, the shit had hit the fan, and there were altogether too many cooks in the kitchen, which was sure to spoil the broth. Periandros' simple little coup d'etat had given way to a three-cornered civil war.

Fragmentary reports on all this began to reach my palace at the Capital about midday. The first thing we heard was Sunteil's starport speech, telling us that Periandros was dead and he was in charge. Polarca, Damiano, Jacinto and I sat transfixed in front of the screen, trying to comprehend what was going on. Abruptly Sunteil's speech was interrupted and the camera cut to the imperial palace, to the great council-chamber of the emperor. We were treated to a close-up shot of the defunct Lord Periandros lying in state. He was wrapped from throat to toes in glittering brocaded robes, but the camera lingered a long while on his face, and it was unmistakably the face of Periandros. He appeared to be quite authentically dead.

Troublesome sounds of warfare now could be heard in the streets outside: sirens and whistles, booms and crashes.

"I don't like any of this," Polarca said. He kept blurring. I knew that he was ghosting compulsively, as he always did when he became tense. Hopping around wildly through the epochs and the light-years, but absent no more than a hundredth of a second at a time from the present. "We ought to get ourselves out of here, Yakoub," he said between hops. "These crazy Gaje are going to wipe each other out and we're right in the middle of it all."

"Wait," I said. "Sunteil's clever enough to get things under control fast. He's probably trying to round up all of Periandros' Akrakikan loyalists, and then—"

"Look," Damiano said in a strangled-sounding voice, pointing to the screen.

And there was the flamboyant face of Lord Naria, suddenly, purple skin and scarlet hair and cold, cold, cold blue eyes, telling us that *he* was the true Sixteenth, accept no substitutes, and all was well.

"Yakoub—" said Polarca, ghosting like a madman.

A robot came rolling into the room. "A man at the gate, claiming sanctuary," it announced. "Shall we admit him?"

Damiano laughed harshly. "Probably Sunteil, looking for a place to hide."

"He gives his name as Chorian of Fenix," said the robot blandly.

"Chorian?" I hit the control and brought up the gate scanner image. Yes, indeed, it was Chorian out there, looking flushed and sweaty and frightened. He seemed to be alone. He was trying to press himself as close to the impervious skin of the gate as he could. I sent the robots out to bring him in.

"Check him for concealed weapons," Polarca called.

"Don't you think that's going too far?" said Damiano.

"This is a crazy day. Anybody might do anything. What if he's here to assassinate Yakoub?"

Damiano turned to me in appeal. "For God's sake, Yakoub, if the boy had meant to kill you, wouldn't he have done it on Mulano?"

"Check him all the same," I said. "It can't do any harm. Polarca's right: this is a crazy day."

But the craziness was only beginning, then.

Chorian—duly frisked and otherwise processed—was admitted to my presence a few minutes later. He was a pitiful sight: wild-eyed, trembling, exhausted. I summoned one of my medics, who calmed him down.

"Thank God you're safe," he said, practically in tears. "You can't imagine what's going on out there."

"What are you doing at the Capital?" I asked.

"I came in with Sunteil on the *Jewel of the Imperium.* There was an attack—at the starport—imperial troops, a whole horde of them—a madhouse, people being killed all over the place—don't know how I was able to escape—"

"Slow down, boy. Was Sunteil killed?"

"I don't think so." Chorian took a deep breath. "He was with his bodyguard and I think they fought their way out the side exit. I went through the baggage loop and crawled into a storage pocket and out the far side. Ran all the way here. They're fighting everywhere—I don't know who, troops loyal to Periandros, troops loyal to Sunteil—"

"Don't forget Naria," Damiano said.

"Naria?" Chorian said, mystified.

"He doesn't know," I said. "Naria's at the palace. He's the one who sent the troops to arrest Sunteil. We just heard him proclaiming himself emperor. Right after they showed the body of Periandros on the screen."

"They showed Periandros, did they?"

"In his funeral clothes, yes. Looking very peaceful. He's lucky to be out of this mess."

Polarca turned to Chorian. "Was it Sunteil who arranged Periandros' death?"

"Of course. An artifical wasp in his bath-chamber. And then Sunteil would land and claim the throne. I tried to send word to Yakoub of what was going to happen, but there was no way to get through—the imperials were monitoring everything—"

"Monitoring the communications channels of the Rom king?" Polarca cried, outraged. "The little shit-ass! The sneak! Doesn't the man have the slightest shred of decency in him?"

"The man is dead," said Jacinto.

"Don't be so sure of that," Biznaga said. He was pointing at the screen again.

"Lolmischo Melalo Bitoso Poreskoro," muttered Damiano in horror and amazement, making the signs of protection against demons. A moment later I was doing the same. For there was Periandros staring straight out of the screen, glum and dour as ever, telling us that he was most certainly alive and very much in charge of the government, and calling on all good imperial citizens to deal mercilessly with the traitors.

"How can this be?" Chorian asked. "The wasp—"

"Killed one of his doppelgangers, maybe?" I suggested.

"Impossible. It was a homing wasp, programmed to be life-seeking. There was a metabolism tropism built into it: it wouldn't ever have attacked a doppelganger. I don't understand how Periandros could still be alive, if he—"

Polarca laughed. "He isn't. *This* is the doppelganger."

"Making a speech?" Damiano said. "A doppelganger, making a speech, claiming to be emperor?"

"Why not? Yakoub thinks it was a doppelganger of Periandros that held the audience with him. But even so he wasn't sure. Periandros may have been using some new improved kind of doppelgangers, yes? And at least one has survived the assassination, and is trying to hang on to the throne—"

"Why would a doppelganger want to be emperor?" Biznaga asked. "It can only live a couple of years."

"It may not know that," Polarca said. "It may not even know that it's a doppelganger. It's just doing what Periandros would have done."

"Jesu Cretchuno Sunto Mario," I muttered. "Three emperors at once! And one of them not even alive."

From the shining streets of the imperial center came the sounds of warfare, louder and louder, closer and closer.

9.

THINGS GREW QUIETER TOWARD EVENING. THE GOVERN-ment news channel kept its focus almost exclusively on Naria, who appeared every hour or two to urge people to be calm. Now and again the broadcasts were interrupted by the faction of Periandros, asserting that he was still alive and in command. Whenever the Periandros image was on screen I peered close, trying to determine whether or not it was a doppelganger, but there was no way of telling, not on screen. If the assassination had been carried out the way Chorian claimed it had, though, then most likely Periandros was really dead and what we were seeing was his doppelganger, all right. Either way, Naria seemed definitely to be on top at the moment. He was at the imperial palace. Periandros, or Periandros' doppelganger, wasn't saying anything about his own location. From Sunteil nothing at all had been heard since his original speech at the starport.

We kept ourselves snugly defended at the Rom palace and awaited further developments.

In the middle of the night came word that Julien de Gramont was on the screen and wished urgently to speak with me. At that hour I didn't wish urgently to speak with him, but these were unusual times. I rolled over and switched on my screen.

Julien looked woeful. His eyes were puffy, his beard was askew, his collar was drooping. He offered me none of his usual little jaunty French pleasantries, only a perfunctory sign of respect for my royal rank.

"The Sixteenth Emperor," he said, "requests a conference with the Rom baro at the Rom baro's earliest convenience."

"*Which* Sixteenth?" I replied, pointedly and undiplomatically.

"The former Lord Periandros, of course," said Julien in a tired, deflated way.

How very much like Julien to continue to regard his patron and hero as the one and only Sixteenth, at a time when two other lords were claiming the selfsame title and when Periandros himself was in fact dead. Julien had always been obstinate about lost causes, I reminded myself. Why shouldn't he go on calling Periandros the Sixteenth? What else could you expect from someone who in the privacy of his own soul still dreamed of strolling the mirrored halls of Versailles as true successor to the grandeur of Louis XIV?

"The report is that Lord Periandros was assassinated earlier today, Julien."

"I have spoken with him within the past hour, Yakoub."

"With him or with a doppelganger of him?"

"You are making this very difficult for me, mon vieux."

"I can't negotiate with a doppelganger, Julien."

"He appeared to be real and alive, to me."

"And the body that Naria displayed in the council-chamber of the palace?"

Julien shrugged. "A dummy, perhaps? A projection? Some sort of image? How would I know? Nom d'un nom, Yakoub, I tell you I have spoken with Lord Periandros within the past hour! He lives and he rules."

"But Naria holds the palace?"

"So it seems. Yet the Lord Periandros is emperor. There has been a great disturbance, but the Lord Periandros is emperor. I beg you, mon ami, do not put me through any more of this. This has been a terrible day for us all. Will you speak with him?"

I nodded and Julien put Periandros on the line. Or what purported to be Periandros.

A funny thing. Adversity seemed almost to agree with him. He looked a good deal less gaunt, less haggard, than the Periandros I had seen in the throne-chamber a few days before. Almost the ripe sleek Periandros of old, matter of fact. That had me suspicious at once, of course. Then too he seemed a lot calmer than I would have expected from a man who had been pushed out of his own imperial palace in a coup that very morning. I put my nose close to the screen, scanning for the telltale flickering which would tell me that I was dealing with a doppelganger. And quietly I keyed in Polarca's extension and Damiano's: I wanted them scanning too.

"We have regretted your silence this day," said Periandros right away. Plunging in without the little niceties. At least he hadn't forgotten his royal *we*. "We had hoped a statement would have been forthcoming from you concerning the anarchy that has erupted in the Capital."

He sounded good. He sounded convincing. That ponderous solemn Akraki style of his. Could this be the real Periandros after all? The one who had been skulking in the background while I went up the crystalline steps to pay my obeisance to a doppelganger?

I said, "I've had very little reliable news of what's been going on. Seemed to me the best thing was to wait and see what was real and what wasn't. In any case it's inappropriate, wouldn't you say, for the Rom baro to comment on imperial matters of state?"

Not a difficult question. But it drew a momentary pause, a sort of mental shifting of gears. Doppelgangers sometimes do that. They aren't really wonderful at the give and take of conversation. But neither are Akraki. I still didn't know what to think.

Then Periandros replied, "It might have been possible for you to have acted as a force for stability. It is still not too late for that."

Was that a flicker, just then? A loss of definition around the edges? A little difficulty keeping the underlying bony structure intact?

And why did he look so damned sleek?

I asked him what he seriously thought I could accomplish. Would a statement from me persuade Naria to relinquish the palace, or get Sunteil to go back to Fenix?

"It would contribute toward the restoration of order," Periandros said. "That you continue to recognize us as the rightful emperor. That you call upon your own subjects everywhere to deny cooperation to the rebels. That you urge the rebellious lords to surrender for the good of all humanity."

He seemed perfectly serious.

It sounded rehearsed. Programmed, even. I tried to make allowances for the normally plonking cadences of Akraki speech. They were all so earnest, all so mechanical, grinding relentlessly on and on in their cheerless way. Not a scrap of poetry to them, not a bit of human flair. It was just their style. Still, I doubted more and more that I was talking to a creature of flesh and blood, especially as Periandros went on speaking.

Because what he began to talk about now was how greatly he and I needed to cooperate with each other: how precarious our positions were, how useful we could be to each other in securing our own thrones and in restoring the health of the Imperium. I had heard all that before from him, of course. He went on to speak of the grand ceremony of reconfirmation that he would stage for me as soon as I aided him in clearing the rebels out of the palace: the wand of recognition, the nobility coming in from all the worlds to attend, a great unforgettable spectacle. He ran through the whole thing precisely as though we had not discussed this very project at the time of our earlier audience just a few days before. Now I was convinced that I had to be dealing with a doppelganger. A spook. Whoever or whatever it was that had given me that audience from the throne, it was clear that this one had not been properly briefed on the content of that other conversation.

I could see the unmistakable doppelganger manifestations, now. The loss of definition, the coarseness of identity-density. It was utterly clear to me now, even on the screen.

I didn't attempt to interrupt. I let the spiel flow on and on, while trying to calculate my strategic options. There was no sense allying myself with a doppelganger. I had already compromised myself enough, I figured, simply by recognizing Periandros in the first place. But that could be dealt with. He had been the only emperor in town, after all, when I arrived at the Capital: what was I supposed to do, refuse to accept him? But now—with Periandros almost certainly dead, and his claim being carried forth by one or more short-lived and basically absurd replicas of him, and a rival lord already esconced in the palace, receiving the homage of the peers—

Yes, I thought, I will have to stall this doppelganger somehow, and come to an understanding with Naria—

On screen, Periandros was still talking, laying out the terms of the grand alliance that he and I were going to forge. I was only barely listening.

Then the door of my bedroom opened and Chorian came bursting in. I signalled him furiously and he dropped down, out of scan range. Wriggling along the floor, he made his way toward me and scrawled a note that he pushed within my range of vision:

Ignore that creature. Periandros is definitely dead and that is nothing but a doppelganger. And Lord Sunteil is here and wants to speak with you at once.

10.

SUNTEIL? IN MY OWN PALACE?

I must have looked extraordinarily startled, because even the pontificating doppelganger Akraki on the screen picked up my reaction and said, "Are you all right?"

"A touch of indigestion—the lateness of the hour—I need to think your proposals over—to return your call later—"

"You will be unable to locate me."

"Call me, then. At the noon hour. All right?"

I switched the screen off and turned toward Chorian.

"This is true? Sunteil is here?"

"In disguise, yes. He came five minutes ago. Said he would speak only with you."

"Bring him in," I said. "Fast."

An old man entered. Someone had done quite a job of disguise on him. He looked about two hundred twenty-five years old, and a rickety, spavined, hideously ancient two hundred twenty-five at that—a withered, shriveled, bowed figure, palsied and tottering, with a few coarse strands of white hair clinging to the bare dome of his head.

It was the complete shipwreck, the total terrifying cataclysm of time: a man at the end of his tether, down there where remakes are no longer possible. And it was utterly convincing. But it had to be phony. I hadn't seen Sunteil in eight or ten years, but it wasn't possible for him to have aged that much so quickly. He had been in the first prime of manhood when I knew him—sixty years old, maybe seventy at most.

The one thing that hadn't altered was his eyes. I could see them glowing with dark mischief behind that wrinkled terrible mask: Sunteil's own authentic eyes. His gleaming, wicked, devilish, unmistakable eyes.

"Well, Yakoub," he quavered, in a high, piping phony-senile voice. "So I am your elder at last!" He tottered forward and fastened one claw-like hand about my wrist. "Sarishan, brother!" he said, and delivered himself of a wild rasping laugh. "Sarishan! These are strange times, eh, Yakoub?"

I didn't like his greeting me in Romany. Or his calling me brother. Sunteil was not my brother.

"You look lovely, Sunteil. You must have had a hard night."

"Isn't it magnificent? An instant reverse remake, a brilliant up-aging." He was speaking in his normal voice now, strong and deep. "They charge more for an up-aging than for the usual thing, do you know? Even though you'd think there wouldn't be much demand. But it was worth it. No one bothers an old man. Even in crazy times like these."

"I'll remember that," I said. "Perhaps everyone will stop bothering me, too, when I look as old as you do."

"You? You'll never look like this. Tell me, Yakoub: have you ever had a remake? They say this is still your real face and body, that you have some secret for never growing old. Is that true? Tell me. Tell me."

"Rom never grow old, Sunteil. We live forever."

"You must teach me the secret, then."

"Too late," I said. "You chose the wrong ancestors. There's no help for you. Born a Gaje, die a Gaje."

"You are a hard man."

"I am gentle and kind. It's the universe that's hard, Sunteil." I was finding all this banter wearying. Giving him a sharp look, I said, "This visit surprises me. I had heard you were in hiding somewhere outside the city. Why have you risked coming to see me tonight? What is it you want, Sunteil?"

"To negotiate," he said.

"You're a fugitive. I'm a king. Negotiation is best done between equals."

"If you're a king, I'm an emperor, Yakoub."

"I am a king, yes, and no question of it", I said crisply. "The only other claimant for my throne is dead and my people recognize me as their sovereign. But Naria is emperor just now, if anyone is."

"Is he? Naria sits in the palace, yes. The drunken soldiers in the streets proclaim him, yes. But sitting in a palace and ordering up riots in your name doesn't make you the emperor of the galaxy. Do the other worlds of the Imperium give a damn what the soldiers are doing in the streets of the Capital? All they know is that the throne is in dispute. And Naria holds power illegitimately."

"He holds it, though. While you skulk around in disguise in the small hours of the night, entering and leaving through side doors."

"For the moment," Sunteil said. "Only for the moment. Naria can be pushed as easily as Periandros was."

"Are you planning another assassination?"

"Oh?" Sunteil said, smiling a sly Sunteil smile out of that parched and ravaged face. "Was Periandros assassinated? I thought he was stung by a wasp."

"A metal wasp that someone sent flying through his window."

"Is that so? How very interesting, Yakoub." He let his glance rove for a moment toward Chorian, who shrank back as if wishing he could make himself invisible. "But if that was the case, I suspect that Naria will be on guard against any attempt to do something similar to him."

"Then how do you intend to get rid of him?"

"You'll help me," Sunteil said.

I let the astounding effrontery of that complacent statement go sliding by me. It wasn't easy.

"Help you?" I said, trying to sound innocently perplexed. "How can I possibly help you, Sunteil?"

"You say you are the king. I suspect that you are. The Rom everywhere obey you. No starship in the galaxy will go forth if the Rom baro gives the word. Flights everywhere will halt. Stop everything dead and Naria will fall."

"Perhaps."

"No perhaps about it. Do I need to tell you that the Rom hold the Imperium by the throat? Without interstellar commerce there is no Imperium. Without the Rom there is no interstellar commerce. You send out the word, Yakoub: There is to be no star travel until the legitimate emperor has taken the throne. In six weeks commerce will choke. You have the power."

His eyes were blazing. I had never seen Sunteil like this before. He was saying the unsayable, openly acknowledging the reality that everyone pretended did not exist. One didn't have to be as astute as Sunteil to see the stranglehold in which the Rom held the Imperium. But it was a power we had never chosen to invoke. We didn't dare. We could shut down the galaxy, yes. But we are very few and they are many. In time the Gaje could learn how to pilot their starships for themselves. If the Rom walked off the job there would be an ugly and chaotic period of transition in the Imperium, and then everything would be for the Gaje as it had been before. And then they would kill us all.

I was silent for a time.

Then I answered, "Possibly what you say is true, Sunteil. Possibly with my help you could force the Imperium to accept you as emperor. And possibly not. What if Naria survives the breakdown of commerce and keeps his throne? What will happen to me, then? What will happen to my people?"

"Naria will fall within weeks. Within days."

"And if he doesn't?"

"You know that these are idle questions, Yakoub."

"I'm not so sure. Tell me this, Sunteil: What do I have to gain by meddling in your civil war? If I back the wrong side, I destroy myself and perhaps the whole Rom kingdom. If I do nothing, you and Naria fight it out and the winner will have to recognize me as king anyway."

Out of Sunteil's grotesque skull of a face came the brilliant flashing Sunteil smile again.

"If I win without your help, Yakoub, what makes you think I'll necessarily recognize you as king?"

I heard Chorian smother a gasp of shock. I had wanted him beside me here to learn the craft of statesmanship; but this was a post-graduate course.

Carefully I said, "Surely you imply no threat, Lord Sunteil."

"Do you infer one?"

"I am the legitimate king of the Rom, chosen by the great kris and ratified by the Fifteenth Emperor. The Sixteenth, whoever he may be, has no way of undoing that ratification."

"It was my understanding that you abdicated, Yakoub, and that your son Shandor was chosen in your place by the great kris. And that no less a personage than Lord Naria, acting as deputy for the Fifteenth, laid the wand of recognition upon your son Shandor. All I would need to do is ratify Naria's action once I became emperor."

"Shandor is dead," I reminded him.

"Then the Rom throne would be vacant. I would nominate a successor."

"A blatant attempt to interfere in Rom sovereignty?"

"Don't try to be naive, Yakoub. It's never very convincing when you do. When Periandros pulled you out of Shandor's prison and set you up as king again, what was that if not interfering with Rom sovereignty? I concede that you Rom have a certain power over us, but we're not without power of our own. You know that the Rom king serves at the sufferance of the emperor."

"And apparently the emperor serves at the sufferance of the king, also."

"Exactly," Sunteil said. His smile returned, bizarrely benign this time. "Therefore why are we speaking of threats? I have no desire whatever to interfere in Rom sovereignty, to meddle with your right to the throne, or anything else of the sort. I simply want to be emperor. And I want you to help me."

"I told you. There are risks for me in it. And I see no reward, except to be allowed to keep what is already mine by absolute right."

"Oh, there would be a reward, Yakoub."

"I suggest you name it."

"Romany Star," Sunteil said. "What do you say? Give me your support and you can have Romany Star."

11.

I HAD TO LOOK AWAY, SO THAT SUNTEIL WOULD NOT SEE how stunned I was. Romany Star? How did he know that name? How was it that a lord of the Imperium was speaking of Romany Star?

I felt a moment of terrible vertigo. My face grew hot and my knees went weak and sudden bewildering terror stabbed my heart. For one flailing instant I thought I was going to fall. It was a bad moment, a dropping-through-the-hidden-trapdoor sort of moment. Then I managed to get the upper hand over my glands and transformed my fear into rage, which was no more useful but less debilitating. In God's name, who had told Sunteil about Romany Star? Who had revealed our most precious secret to this slippery Gajo? I would throttle the traitor with my own hands. Who could he be? I glared across the room. Chorian! Chorian! Of course. Sunteil's own little personal Rom, his Gypsy aide-de-camp—currying favor with the Gajo lord by letting him in on the deepest mysteries of our people—

I gave Chorian a look that I wished could blast his soul. He turned scarlet. And into his eyes came a piteous expression of—what? Anguish? Bewilderment? A yearning for the forgiveness that he knew could never come?

When I was a little more calm I turned back to Sunteil and said in a tight voice, "What do you know of Romany Star?"

"That isn't important. What is important is that I guarantee it will be yours, Yakoub, when I take the throne."

"You've already said that. But what do you think you're talking about? What do you mean when you say 'Romany Star'?"

Sunteil seemed very uneasy.

"A red star, it is. With a single planet circling it, that is also known as Romany Star."

"Go on."

"A place that for some reason is holy to the Rom people."

"For some reason, Sunteil? What reason?"

"I don't know."

"You don't?"

"How would I? It's some private Rom thing. All I know is that you want this Romany Star terribly, but you don't dare go there and claim it, either because it currently belongs to someone else or because you think we'll want it for ourselves if we find out that you're after it. I don't know and I don't care. I don't even know where it is. What I'm telling you, Yakoub, is that Romany Star will be yours if you help me become emperor. Isn't that enough for you? My solemn promise."

A Gajo's promise, I thought bitterly. A Fenixi's promise.

"You have no idea where it is or what it is, but you'll let me have it?"

With some exasperation he replied, "I'd take your word for it. You say, 'This place is Romany Star, Sunteil,' and I'll say, 'All right, it's yours.' Wherever it may be. No matter who claims it at the moment. All I know is that it means a great deal to you, the possession of this Romany Star. All right. It means a great deal to me, becoming emperor. You can give me that. And then I'll give you Romany Star. What do you say, Yakoub?"

I studied him. It began to seem to me as though he genuinely did not know anything more of Romany Star than what he had told me. Making allowances for the fact that he was Sunteil, that he was a man of Fenix, that he was famed for his deviousness and his deceitfulness. Nevertheless he had sounded uncharacteristically muddled and irritated as he responded to my questions about Romany Star. My instincts told me that this once, at least, he was being sincere when he said that that was really all he knew. Which was too much for any Gajo to know; but it was not in fact very much.

"I need time to think about this," I said.

"How much do you need?"

"I have advisors to consult. Options to weigh."

"Are you in touch with Naria?"

"I don't see why I need to tell you that. But in fact I haven't heard a word from Naria since all this began. Only Periandros. Who is still begging me to ally myself with him."

"Periandros is dead."

"Someone looking like Periandros and sounding like Periandros called me only a little while ago. A doppelganger, perhaps."

"A doppelganger, most certainly," Sunteil said. "Periandros is dead. I can give you the firmest assurance of that."

"I thought you could," I said.

"You'll be hearing from Naria sooner or later. Probably sooner. But I don't think he can offer you anything that can top my offer. How long will it be until I hear from you?"

"Not long," I said. "Only give me time to think. It has been an honor to speak with you, Lord Sunteil."

"The honor is mine, Yakoub."

Sunteil beckoned toward Chorian, as if expecting the boy to escort him out. I shook my head and indicated with the movement of a single finger that I wanted Chorian to stay; and Sunteil, nodding, went doddering from the room.

The moment he was gone I looked toward Chorian in terrible wrath. He was pale beneath his midnight-black skin.

"How is it that your master knows of Romany Star?" I asked him in a very quiet voice.

"He is not my master, Yakoub."

"You are in his pay. He knows of Romany Star. Not much, so it seems, but he knows. How is it that he knows, boy?"

"I beg you, Yakoub, believe me—" He faltered. "Believe me, Yakoub—"

"Say what you mean."

"If he knows anything—and it isn't much, what he knows, it is very little, of that I'm certain—if he knows anything, Yakoub, he did not learn it from me."

"No?"

"I swear it." He had shifted to speaking Romany now.

"You swear, do you?"

"By Martiya the angel of death, by o pouro Del the god of our fathers, by Damo and Yehwah, by all the spirits and demons—"

"Stop it, Chorian."

"I will swear by other things. By anything you name."

Coldly I said, "You've learned your ancient Gypsy folklore well, haven't you? Studied the Swatura like a good boy? And sold it all to Sunteil? All those quaint little scraps of myth and tradition, eh, boy? Did you get a good price from him, at least?"

Tears glistened in his eyes. "Yakoub! I have sworn!"

"Someone who will sell Romany Star to the Gaje would swear on the muli of his dead mother, and what would it mean?"

"I was not the one, Yakoub. When Sunteil began speaking to you of Romany Star I wanted to hide, to die, because I knew it was wrong for him to know anything of Romany Star, and I knew you would think right away that I must be the one who had told him. But I was not the one. What can I say to make you believe that?"

He came to my side and stood towering over me. He was trembling. His tears were flowing. Was he that good, to be able to feign tears? He was Fenixi, yes, and Fenixi can fool almost anyone; and he was Rom besides; but I didn't think he could counterfeit emotions like these. There is acting and there is true feeling, and if I am unable to tell the difference between the one and the other at my age then it has been pointless for me to bother to live so long.

In a voice that was scarcely loud enough for me to hear he murmured, "Yakoub, on Mulano you told me the story of Romany Star, and much else besides. And afterward, as I was waiting for the relay-sweep to come for me, I told you that I had discovered at last, while spending those few days with you, what it was like to have a real father. Do you remember that? The story of Romany Star was your gift to me. *You* were your gift to me. Do you think I would sell those gifts to Sunteil? Do you? Do you?"

And I had to say, though only to myself, No, Chorian, I do not think that you would.

To him I said, "I would prefer to think you are innocent, if I could."

"I *am* innocent, Yakoub." His tears were gone and he was no longer trembling. Perhaps the conviction of his own innocence was strengthening him now. "Believe me. I can say no more."

"I think you tell the truth," I said.

"For that I thank you, Yakoub."

"But how, then, did your master learn of Romany Star?"

"I tell you again, he is not my master. And I have no idea how he learned of it. But if you wish I will try to find that out."

"Yes," I said. "That would be—"

Just then the screen lit up and there was Julien, calling back to ask if I would speak with Periandros now, even though it was still early in the morning and I had promised to hold my next conversation with him at noon. Periandros did not want to wait until noon.

I took a long look at Julien.

I had the answer to the mystery of Sunteil's familiarity with Romany Star.

Julien! Of course! *He* knew of Romany Star. I remembered now what he had said on Galgala, when I had spoken of France as an unreal place, and he had said to me that France was to him what Romany Star was to us, the great lost place, the only true mother. That had amazed me. We do not speak of Romany Star with the Gaje. But Julien had learned of it, God only knew how. Perhaps it was not too difficult for him, in a long lifetime spent mainly around Rom. A few bottles of his fine red wines, a long evening of rich French foods, some Rom star-captain of his acquaintance lulled into an expansive mood, and it would all have come rolling out, the Tale of the Swelling Sun, the loss of our home and the dispersal into the Great Dark, and everything else. Yes. Yes. And Julien had filed it all away, our legend, our scripture; and he had saved it for the right moment and he had sold it to the right man.

Not to Periandros, whose cerces he had been taking all these years. But to Sunteil. Periandros was dead, and Julien knew it, no matter how many doppelgangers of the late lord were stored in the hiding-chambers. Periandros the doppelganger might yet prevail in this three-cornered struggle, but it was unlikely, and Julien was wisely placing his bets on Sunteil now. Cutting a little side deal for himself while there still was a chance. I had to admire him for that. But he should not have sold Romany Star to Sunteil, even so.

I had long ago fallen into the easy temptation of thinking of Julien as Rom, or almost Rom; but he was not Rom. Not at all. And this proved it.

"The emperor wishes to know," said Julien, "if the Rom baro has had sufficient time to consider their earlier conversation."

I wanted to reach into the screen and strangle him. My old friend, my rescuer. What I strangled instead was the impulse to do any such thing. If Julien had betrayed us, so be it. A Gajo is a Gajo, even Julien. You had to expect that from them. And in any case the damage was done. I had other problems to deal with. I didn't want to talk to Julien at all. Or his doppelganger master.

I told him that it had been a frantic night for me, that I hadn't had any chance to reach decisions about Periandros' offer. Hoping Julien would take that and go away before I had a chance to get really furious with him. He didn't.

"A thousand pardons, mon ami, but the emperor asks me to stress the fact that time is of the essence."

"I understand that, Julien."

"And if you are willing to negotiate on the points already discussed, then there is no time like the present for—"

"Julien?"

"Oui, mon vieux?"

"What's the point of this dumb game? We both know that Periandros is dead and that you're dealing on behalf of a doppelganger. So why are you bothering to bother me with all this shit now? What good is pretending that a doppelganger can actually function as emperor? Especially in view of the fact that you're getting ready to jump ship anyway and go over to Sunteil's side."

"To Sunteil's side? But I do not understand, Yakoub! What you are saying is incomprehensible to me!"

"Perhaps you might understand it better if I could say it in French. But I can't. Merde is the only word of French I know. What you're trying to tell me is so much merde, Julien. That's a French word, isn't it? If you don't understand it, maybe I should try speaking to you in Romany."

"You are so angry. My old friend, what have I done?"

I didn't want to start in on the whole subject. But he was irritating me at a time when I didn't need irritation.

"You don't know?" I asked.

A pause, minute but revealing.

"Whatever I may have done," he said after a moment, "it was for the sake of the Rom as well as for the sake of the Imperium, Yakoub. N'est-ce pas? It is the truth."

"Whatever you may have done," I told him, keeping tight control over my rage, God knows why, "was probably for the sake of Julien de Gramont, n'est-ce pas? With some slight thought, maybe, for the incidental damage it might cause, but that was purely secondary, I suspect." I amazed myself with my own ability to hold my fury in check. A trick one sometimes learns, with time. And sometimes forgets. "Just tell me this: whose pay are you in today? Periandros or Sunteil?"

Silence. Consternation.

"Both?" I suggested. "Yes. Yes, that would be more like you, wouldn't it? And right now you're calling to do Periandros' work, or what passes for Periandros these days. An hour from now you may be scheming with Sunteil. And—"

"Please, mon ami. I implore you, no more. Truly, I have done you no harm. I feel great love for you, Yakoub. Do you comprehend that? It is the truth. La verite veritable, Yakoub." He held his hands outstretched toward me. "I call you now on behalf of Periandros, yes. He wishes to speak with you. It is what I am asked to tell you."

"Then I ask you to tell him that I can't be bothered with doppelgangers at a time like this. Tell him he can go off somewhere and fart in his hand, for all I care. Tell him—" A stricken look appeared on Julien's face. "No. No. All right, tell him what I told you a minute ago. That I've simply been too busy to decide anything. Just stall him. Sidetrack him. In your slick diplomatic way."

"Until—?"

"Until never," I said. "This struggle is a two-sided triangle now, Julien, and there can't be any transaction between Periandros and me that would mean anything any more, whatever he may think. Doppelgangers fade. Maybe they don't know that about themselves, but I know it. I don't have time for him. The poor unreal bastard. All right? Do you understand what I'm telling you?"

"He may be dead, Yakoub, but he is not yet without power."

"He will be. He'll be nothing at all, very soon. I have to save my energies for dealing with the emperors who aren't dead. I'm working for the long run, Julien. Periandros is already decaying. Whether he knows it or not."

"But while he lives—"

"He *doesn't* live. He's a zombie. He's a walking mulo. And I ask you to keep him out of my hair. For the sake of the great love you claim to bear for me."

"Your voice is so harsh, Yakoub. There is such enmity in it."

"Perhaps you know why that is."

"D'accord," said Julien gloomily. "I will tell Periandros you need more time for your decision."

"About eighty million years," I said. And I broke the contact.

The next moment Polarca came striding into the room, looking distraught, waving a sheaf of reports.

"They're fighting in the Gunduloni district," he announced. "A bunch of Periandros loyalists against a detachment of Naria's militia. And troops wearing Sunteil's insignia have seized a whole block of streets just south of the imperial district, and they're going from house to house, forcing people to swear allegiance to him. And over on the other side of town there's a battle going on and nobody's been able to tell who's on what side."

"Is there anything else?" I asked.

"One thing more," said Polarca. "Naria has summoned you to the palace. He wants a parley right away."

12.

IT WAS INEVITABLE, OF COURSE: THE DROPPING OF THE third shoe. Periandros and Sunteil had been heard from, and finally the last of the high lords was putting in his bid for my support. Or so I assumed. I was requested—and Naria's adjutant had sounded pretty damned urgent about it, according to Damiano, who had taken the call —to come at once and to bring with me not only Polarca but the phuri dai. Shrewd Naria, angling for Bibi Savina's backing as well: maybe my seat on the Rom throne might be a little wobbly, but Rom everywhere revered the phuri dai, without exception.

We held a conference on the advisibility of my accepting Naria's invitation and I got a mixed response. Jacinto and Ammagante, cautious as ever, wondered if it might be some sort of trap, a ploy designed to give Naria control over the entire Rom high command in one swoop. Damiano and Thivt agreed that that was a possibility but they thought the notion was far-fetched. Polarca, plainly itching to get out of this palace in which we had hidden ourselves for what was starting to seem like weeks, didn't care: he was willing to take the risk, such as it was, rather than remaining holed up here any longer.

I looked toward Bibi Savina. "What does the phuri dai say, then?"

She looked at me and through me, into realms far, far away.

"Does the Rom baro refuse the summons of the emperor?" she asked.

"But is Naria the emperor?" Jacinto said.

"He holds the palace," said Bibi Savina. "One of the other two is dead and the third one is in hiding. If Naria is not emperor, no one is. Go to him, Yakoub. You must. And I will go to him with you."

I nodded. The phuri dai and I generally have seen things the same way over the years. To Damiano I said, "Tell him we'll be there in an hour or less."

"He's promised to send an imperial car for you."

"No," I said. "The last thing I want is to go driving around the

Capital today in a car that bears the imperial crest. We'll take one of our own cars. Three cars, in fact. Nobody's going to try to get in the way of the Rom baro if they see a whole cavalcade of Rom vehicles.''

Bold words. But in fact we were fired on five times during the thirty-minute ride to the imperial palace. There were no hits: our screens were good. Still, it wasn't a good sign. All this artillery action was twentieth-century stuff, and it felt out of place, a thousand years out of place and then some. I hadn't thought that a little thing like a struggle over the imperial succession could have sent the Gaje heading back down the evolutionary trail so fast. War is an obsolete concept, I had been telling Julien de Gramont only the other day—so to speak —during the tranquility of my retirement on icy Mulano. And in the short time since then I had found myself in the midst of a small war on Galgala and now in what had the look of a very large one here at the Capital. First our seat of government and then theirs.

At any rate, we got through the city in the same number of pieces with which we had set out. We never knew which side was doing the firing. Most likely all three factions were taking turns, and nobody having any idea of who it was that they were firing at, any more than we could tell who was shooting. An anonymous war: more twentieth-century stuff. If there has to be fighting, give me the medieval days, when at least you knew your enemy's name.

The city was a tremendous mess. I wouldn't have thought they could smash so much of it up so quickly. At least half a dozen of the loftiest towers had been sheared right off in mid-loftiness. Mounds of rubble strewn high as houses in the wide boulevards. A pall of black smoke staining the sky. Here and there an arm or a leg sticking out of the ruins: death, actual death, irreparable and irreversible. Whole lives cut in half as those towers had been, men and women robbed of a hundred years apiece or even more. And for what? Some petty dispute over whether the Gaje crown should go to a man of Fenix or a man of Vietoris, or perhaps to the animated image of a dead man from Sidri Akrak?

In that scene of devastation there were, nevertheless, incongruous signs of imperial splendor. Sky-banners, symbolic of the presence of the emperor at the Capital, were blazing away in the east, the south, and the north. But it was a display of banners such as never had been seen here before, for they glowed in three different sets of colors, one for Periandros, one for Naria, one for Sunteil. Wherever those warring lights met and clashed overhead, there was such turmoil in the sky that it befuddled and baffled the eye.

And farther to the north, in the city's outer ring—what were those plumes of brilliant purple light there? Why, they were the light-spikes of the Rom baro, of all things, returned at last to their proper place! Naria's doing? Sunteil's? Well, it was all useless flattery now. Did they think my allegiance could be bought with a show of light?

The palace was guarded by level upon level of fantastic defenses. A ring of deflector screens, first, casting a purple glow over the whole place. Within that, a row of gleaming tanks, all eyes and cannons. Then a phalanx of robots. An android militia. A vast host of human soldiers too—or, more likely, doppelganger-soldiers, hastily stamped out to meet the emergency. Scanners. Sky-eyes. Floating clouds of lethal anti-personnel pellets held in check by webs of magnetic force. And more, much more. State-of-the-art stuff, all of it, a wondrous and preposterous array of technological wizardry. Naria's incredible defensive deployment told me as much about Naria as it did about the current state of military preparedness in the Imperium.

It took more than an hour for us to be escorted through all the checkpoints. But at last we entered into the presence of the man who for the moment held the title of Sixteenth Emperor.

No throne-platform now, no crystalline steps. An immense cube of what looked like glass, but probably wasn't, had been set up in the enormous high-vaulted council-chamber of the palace. A warning line of blue fire rose from the stone floor on all four sides. High above, scanner beams searched constantly through the air. And deep within the cube, enthroned like a pharaoh of old in absolute inaccessibility, sat the self-proclaimed Emperor Naria, motionless as a statue, taut and slender as a whip, solemn as a god. Darkness surrounded him but he himself was illuminated by a confluence of spotlights that imparted a fierce blaze to his shoulder-length scarlet hair, his dark purple skin, his implacable yellow eyes. He wore a richly brocaded garment of some stiff green fabric that rose up behind his head like a cobra's hood, and the crown imperial floated above him in holographic projection.

All very impressive. All very ludicrous.

I saw Polarca struggling with a smirk. The phuri dai was smiling seraphically; but then she often does that, in all sorts of contexts.

"We are grateful for your coming here, Rom baro," Naria declared in slow, measured, absurdly pretentious tones. His voice emerged from behind the glassy walls of that cube out of a thousand speakers at once, and went rebounding dizzyingly around the vast room.

Such ridiculous theatricality! Who did he think he was talking to? And the royal *we* again. For century upon century the Empire had managed to survive and even thrive without any such idiotic affectations. But suddenly these uneasy lordlings were reviving it as they made their little snotnosed forays toward the throne. I felt sorry for them. That they should need to inflate themselves that way.

Still, I gave Naria the formal gesture of submission that a Rom baro traditionally makes to the emperor. Even though he had not offered me the traditional wine. It cost me nothing and might win me a point or two with him. And it rarely pays to be discourteous to megalomaniacs when you're standing in their living room.

Then I said, gesturing at the glass cube and everything that surrounded it, "How sad that all this should be necessary, Majesty."

"A temporary measure, Yakoub. It is our expectation that peace will be restored within a matter of days, or even hours. And that there will never again be such a breach of it, once we have completed the task of imposing our authority upon the Imperium."

"Let us all hope so, Majesty," said I most piously. "This war is an agony for us all."

The solemn bastard! Saw himself as savior. Well, meet hypocrisy with hypocrisy, if you have to.

He gave me his grave-and-thoughtful-ruler look. "There is much damage in the city, is there not?"

"Too much, I'm afraid."

"The Capital is sacred. That they should dare to harm it—! Well, we will make them pay for it, every minim, every obol." He studied me in frosty silence for a time. I returned his glare, unfazed. He wasn't a likable man, this scarlet-and-purple Naria. Reptilian. Dangerous. This was the man, after all, who had taken it upon himself to ratify Shandor's unlawful appropriation of my kingship, even while the old emperor still lived. What was it about our unhappy era that had loosed these Shandors and Narias in it?

Then he said, his tone changing entirely, shifting from stiff imperial pomp and bluster to sly and almost intimate insinuation, "Do you know where Sunteil is hiding?"

That was a really unexpected shot. I'm afraid I let myself show my surprise.

"Sunteil?" I said idiotically.

"The former high lord, yes. Who is now in rebellion, as you certainly must know, against the legally constituted government of the Imperium. He's here at the Capital. I wondered whether you happen to know where."

"Not a clue, Your Majesty."

"Not even an unfounded rumor or two?"

"I've heard that he's somewhere south of the city. More than that I couldn't say."

He looked at me like a bomb that was deciding whether it wanted to go off.

"Or rather, more than that you don't choose to say."

"If the emperor thinks I'm concealing things from him—"

"You've had no dealings whatever with Sunteil, then?"

The interrogation was starting to slide into new and perilous territory. Carefully I said, "I have no idea where Sunteil may be."

Which was true. But it wasn't the answer to the question that Naria was asking.

He let my little evasion pass without comment. Reverting now to his loftier imperial voice, he said, "When Sunteil comes to you again, Yakoub, you will seize him and deliver him to us. Is that understood?" Amazing. Rolling right over me like an avalanche. "This is war, and we can allow no niceties. You will have a second chance to capture him, and this time you will take it." *When he comes to you again?* How much did Naria know? I heard Polarca gasp in astonishment, and Bibi Savina lost her smile. *Seize and deliver him?* I had expected to hear Naria beg me for an alliance, not give me orders.

I stared. For a moment I was at a loss for words. Actually speechless. Me!

Naria went on serenely, "The hand of Sunteil has been raised against his emperor, which is to say that it has been raised against every citizen of the Imperium. He is the enemy of us all. He is as much the enemy of you Rom as he is the enemy of—of—what is it that you call us?"

"Gaje, Majesty."

"Gaje. Yes."

I said, "And why does Your Majesty think that I will be visited again by Lord Sunteil?"

"Because you will arrange it."

That simple. I will arrange it.

The response of Yakoub is the dropping of the jaw, the gaping of the mouth. Only metaphorically, of course. Calm on the surface, I am.

Taking all this very casually. Mustn't let him see how astounded I am. What a marvel you are, Naria.

"Ah. Because I will arrange it."

Saying it very lightly. Merely repeating what should have been obvious to any moron. You will lure my rival into your clutches, Yakoub, and then you will nail him for me. Of course, Your Majesty. Of course.

He said, "There will be a meeting, at some carefully devised neutral point. By your invitation. Another part of the planet, or perhaps some other world entirely. At which you and he will discuss the prospect of an alliance between the Rom Kingdom and an Empire led by Sunteil. You will charm him, as you do so well. You will lull him off his guard. And then you will capture him and turn him over to us."

I felt almost like applauding. Bravo, Naria!

He was speaking to me, to the King of the Rom, as though I were nothing more than some minor phalangarius of his staff. That took daring. Audacity. Stupidity.

"And Periandros?" Polarca said suddenly, a wicked gleam coming into his eye. "Are we to catch him for you too, Your Majesty?"

Within his cube of glass Naria remained as motionless as before, but his eyes turned toward Polarca and there was no look of amusement in them. It seemed to me that a chill wind had begun to blow through the council-chamber.

"Periandros?" said Naria. "There is no Periandros. Not many days ago the body of Periandros lay in state in this very room."

"But his doppelganger—"

Naria waved him to silence. "There are three doppelgangers of Periandros. They cause trouble, for the moment, but they are nothing. Time will steal their life from them and turn them to the clay from which they were made. Sunteil is the enemy. You must deal with Sunteil." He skewered Polarca with a baleful glance. Polarca had the good sense not to make any more little lighthearted sallies. After a time Naria looked toward Bibi Savina, who seemed lost in dreams, or perhaps off ghosting. "You, there, old woman! You stand there saying nothing, and your mind is far away. What are you doing? Peering into the future?"

The phuri dai laughed a wondrously girlish laugh. "Into the past, Your Majesty. I was thinking of a time when I was very young, and was in a swimming race with the boys, from one shore of the river to the other."

"But you can see the future, can't you?"

Bibi Savina smiled pleasantly.

"Of course you can. Tomorrow is as clear to you as yesterday, eh, old woman? Old witch. And the day after tomorrow, and the day after that. Do you deny it? How can you? Everyone knows the powers of the Rom fortune-tellers."

"I am only an old woman, Your Majesty."

"An old woman to whom the future is an open book. Is that not so?"

"Sometimes I see a little way, perhaps. When the light is shining for me."

"And is the light shining now?" Naria asked.

Again Bibi Savina smiled. A sweet smile, a childlike smile.

"Tell us this, at least," said Naria. "Will there be peace in the Empire?"

"Oh, there can be no doubt of that," said the phuri dai easily. "When war ends, peace returns."

"And the new emperor? Will his reign be a happy one?"

"The new emperor will reign in prosperity and grandeur beyond all measure, and the worlds will rejoice."

"Ah, you old Gypsy witch!" Naria said, almost affectionately. "You say things that are so full of cheer. But we are not deceived. The game's an old one, isn't it? Tell your listeners what they want to hear, and take their money and send them away happy. Your kind's been playing that game for thousands of years. Eh? Eh?"

"You are wrong, Your Majesty. The things I have told you are not necessarily the things you would want to hear."

"That there will be peace? That our reign will be a glorious one? What better prophecies could you have given me?"

The phuri dai smiled and made no reply, and once more her gaze wandered off into the distant galaxies. Naria, still staring at her, seemed for the moment to follow her there. There came the sound of more explosions outside the palace, some long and muffled like distant thunder and some, not at all far off, sharp and quick and percussive. Naria showed no sign of noticing them. After a time he turned his attention back to me.

"Well, Yakoub? Now we understand each other totally, is that not so?"

Periandros had asked me the same thing, I recalled, the day I had ascended the crystalline steps for my audience with him atop the throne-platform. Without hesitation I gave Naria the same answer I had given his predecessor.

"Perfectly, Your Majesty," I said. Though I doubted that very much. But at least I understood *him,* better than ever before.

"Then there is no need of further talk. You may go. When you have Sunteil, return to us."

This, said to a king!

Incredible. Utterly incredible.

"And then we will have much to discuss," he went on. "The new order of things, eh? The emperor and the Rom baro. It is our intention to make many changes, as the Imperium enters the time of prosperity and grandeur that the old phuri dai has foretold. And we will need your cooperation, eh, Yakoub? Emperor and Rom baro, working together for the good of mankind."

"As always, Your Majesty," said I obligingly.

"Good. Your first task is to bring us Sunteil. Nothing else matters until that is done. Go, then. Go now."

Grandly—yes, imperiously—he waved us from the room.

"Can you imagine it?" Polarca exclaimed. We were making our way warily through the shattered city. Sirens sounding, blurts of gunfire breaking out randomly here and there. "He tells you what to do, and then he tells you that you can go. A little wave of his imperial finger. Dismissing a king the way you would a stablehand."

There were implosion craters everywhere. Now and then a screening bomb went off, blanketing a whole zone of the city with dark clouds of communications-muffling murk. Or an explosion far overhead would send down showers of brilliant golden metallic threads, as though this were not a war but some sort of grand merry pyrotechnikon.

I said, "King, stablehand—it makes little difference to me, Polarca."

"*Less* than a stablehand! You wouldn't even talk to a stablehand that way!"

"No, I wouldn't," I said. "But I am not Naria."

The threads were clusters of picosensors: espionage devices, gobbling up data in mid-air as they floated. Sunteil's little spies? Naria's? Who could tell? Perhaps the doppelganger generals of the doppelganger emperor Periandros were the ones who had ordered them to be dropped.

And still the sky-banners of the three emperors rippled like auroras above us. And on the horizon, too, the brilliant purple light-spike that was the mark of the Rom baro, telling all the world that that great personage was in residence at the Capital in this very hour. Which I was beginning profoundly to wish was not the case.

Polarca was still furious. He couldn't let go of it.

"You aren't angry at being treated like that, Yakoub?"

"Angry? What good is being angry? Will it make him more courteous? Naria does as Naria must."

"The bastard. The pig."

"If I allow myself to become angry," I said, "I lose sight of what a formidable adversary he is."

"You think he is?"

"Can you doubt it?"

"Just an arrogant boy, puffed up with his own importance. How old is he? Fifty? Sixty? Not even. Sitting there in that glass box on display like the wonder of the galaxies. Calling himself 'we,' and handing out orders to kings. Going out of his way to let us know what a big deal he is. Playing games with you, leading you around by your nose. I'm surprised you put up with it like that, Yakoub."

"He is emperor," I said.

"That pimp? That fop? You call that an emperor?"

"He has the palace and the army," I reminded him. "And is very quickly going about the business of consolidating his power. Periandros is dead and Sunteil, who everyone thought would reach out and take the throne like a ripe fruit the moment the Fifteenth departed his body, runs and hides. And Naria knows how many doppelgangers there are of Periandros; he knows that Sunteil came visiting us in secret this morning. I think we need to deal with him as though he is truly the emperor, Polarca."

"What do you mean to do, then? Will you recognize him? What about Sunteil?"

"What about Sunteil?" I asked.

"He, at least, pretends to treat us as equals. Naria treats us like dogs."

"You prefer the pretense?"

"We live by pretense," said Polarca. "And what we pretend is that the Gaje respect us, when we know that they merely fear us, because they need us, because they depend on us. But the pretense of respect feels better than the reality of contempt. I like Sunteil's style better than I do Naria's."

"So do I," I said. "We may have no choice, though."

"Will you give Sunteil to Naria as he asks?"

I shrugged. "I don't know, Polarca. It's not a notion that pleases me a great deal."

Our cavalcade of cars came to a halt. We were at the palace of the Rom king, in the Plaza of the Three Nebulas. Suddenly I had a profound wish to be alone. For an instant I almost wished I was back on white glittering Mulano, squatting by the Gombo glacier and trawling for turquoise spice-fish with a vibration net. Far from all this, far from everyone, the wagging tongues, the clamorous ambitions, the murderous schemes, the noise, the blood, the idiocy.

Chorian came running out to greet me. He was agitated: an implosion bomb had gone off next door to the palace half an hour ago. He pointed to the palace walls: great ugly cracks ran from floor to ceiling. These lunatics would not be satisfied, I thought, until they had destroyed their entire absurd Capital. Well, so be it. So be it. The cities of mankind are temporary things. Let it all come down, I thought. Let the Gaje ruin all the worlds. And then we will lift ourselves from their midst and return to Romany Star to live in peace. As soon as we receive the call.

As soon as we receive the call.

Chorian tried to tell me that I should leave the Capital at once, while starships were still running; that I should take myself back to Galgala and await the resolution of the imperial civil war in relative safety.

"There is no safety anywhere," I told him. "I will stay here."

They all surrounded me, bubbling with conflicting advice. I sent them all away and went to my private suite, to my only refuge in this hubbub. I needed to rest, to think, to weigh alternatives.

But even there I could not be alone.

Hardly had I settled down but the familiar figure of Valerian's ghost came drifting through the walls. He was wearing magnificent robes of red fur trimmed with ermine, and he was buzzing and crackling with enough electrical intensity to light up half a planet. In the true Valerian manner he hovered erratically in mid-air, skittering this way and that.

I felt no joy in seeing him. "You? Here?" was the best I could manage by way of greeting.

"I had to come. Even if you didn't want me. You need to get out of here right away, Yakoub. This planet isn't safe."

"You're telling me that?"

"For God's sake, a war is about to break out here, Yakoub. Do you want to be killed? The crazy Gaje bastards are going to bomb each other into oblivion."

"You're out of phase, Valerian. The war has already begun. Look, can't you see the cracks in the wall, here? An implosion bomb across the street, half an hour ago."

"It'll get much worse. I'm trying to warn you."

"All right. What's going to happen?"

"Everyone's going to die, Yakoub. Get out while you can. Get everyone out with you. Listen, I'm only two weeks ahead of you in the time-line. That's all it is, two weeks, and in those two weeks all hell breaks loose at the Capital. I'm not even sure what happens. I came right away, as soon as I heard what was going on here. You've got to go. Now."

"You aren't the first to tell me that today."

"Well, I may be the last, if you don't get moving."

Wearily I said, *"You* get moving, Valerian. Go ghost Megalo Kastro, all right? Iriarte. Atlantis. I need to be by myself for a while. I need to think things through."

"Yakoub—"

"Go. Go. In the name of God, Valerian, let me be."

He gave me a long reproachful look, shaking his head sadly. And then he was gone. Leaving behind his buzz, leaving behind his crackle. Not in the room, just in my brain. I began to realize that I was starting to come close to the overload level.

A hot bath, I thought—a nap—a little flask or two of brandy—some quiet time to myself—

So much to decide. Leave the Capital as Chorian and Valerian urged, and let the Gaje lords do as they wished with each other? Or stay, and continue to try to shape the pattern of events? Snare Sunteil, and give him to Naria? Or send out word to the Rom star-pilots everywhere that ships must not go forth so long as Naria holds the throne, as Sunteil had urged? Ah, Mulano, Mulano! Peace! Quiet! Solitude!

There was a colossal blast just outside the palace. The entire building trembled and I thought it would collapse; but somehow it held firm.

"Yakoub? Oh, you Yakoub!"

What now? I closed my eyes, and suddenly I felt the presence of all the Gypsy kings once again burgeoning within me, the whole horde of them, pushing and shoving for my attention. Red-bearded Ilika, and little Chavula, and Cesaro o Nano, and all the rest of them, kings of lost Rom realms and kings of dominions still unborn, some whispering to me and some shouting. They were telling me tales of past and future, filling me with visions of glories gone and glories yet to come, but they were all speaking at once, and it was impossible for me to understand a thing. Their eyes were wild, their foreheads glistened with sweat. I begged them to give me peace. But no: they grew more impassioned, they circled round and round me, plucking at my sleeves like beggars, telling me this and that and this and that incomprehensible thing until I was ready to bellow and roar with mad anguish.

"Yakoub?" said a familiar voice, through all the hubbub. "Yakoub, listen to me!"

My voice. My own ghost, striding into the room.

I stared into my own face. It seemed strangely transformed, oddly different from the face I had looked upon all my life. Something about the eyes, the cheeks, even the mustache. An older Yakoub, an ancient Yakoub, Yakoub with all his years finally showing: still strong, still vigorous, not at all a walking cadaver such as Sunteil had made of himself, but nevertheless clearly a Yakoub who had come to me across a great distance in time. Which told me one thing that gave me comfort in that hour of madness, which was that my skein was still a long way from being fully spun.

He reached out toward me, that other Yakoub, and his ghostly hand rested on my wrist as if to hold me in place. His face was close to mine; his eyes searched me deeply.

"Has Valerian been here yet? To tell you to clear out of here?"

I nodded. "Five minutes ago. Ten, maybe."

"Good. Good. I was afraid I might be too early. Listen to me, Yakoub. Valerian doesn't understand a thing. He comes from just a couple of weeks down the line, did he tell you that? Too soon to know the full story. He's wrong to want you to leave the Capital. You have to stay. Do you hear me, Yakoub? Stay right here, no matter what happens. It is absolutely essential that you remain at the Capital. Do you understand me?"

My head was throbbing. I felt six thousand years old. A hot bath, a flask of brandy—sleep—sleep—

"Do you hear me, Yakoub?"

"Yes. Yes. Stay—at—the—Capital—"

"That's right. Say it again. Stay at the Capital, no matter what happens."

"Stay at the Capital. No matter what happens."

"Right. Good."

He disappeared. A tremendous explosion rocked the building. Another. Another. I ran to the window. The sky was aflame. And against the soaring tongues of fire the sky-banners of the three rival emperors rippled and blazed.

I felt myself caught in a whirlwind. Again and again came the terrifying sound of the war outside. The world was breaking apart, and so was I. I tried to hold myself together but it was impossible. I was whirling out of control. Some force beyond all resistance was pulling me free from myself. Sending me hurling like a handful of scattered atoms into the turbulent tempests of space and time—

Whirling—whirling—

It was like the first time I had ever ghosted. I felt my soul splitting in half.

EIGHT:

The Grand Kumpania

What we call the beginning is often the end
And to make an end is to make a beginning.
The end is where we start from.

We shall not cease from exploration
And the end of all our exploring
Will be to arrive where we started
And know the place for the first time.

—ELIOT, *LITTLE GIDDING*

1.

THIS PLACE WAS NABOMBA ZOM, THIS MAN WAS LOIZA LA
Vakako. Or so it seemed. I had little doubt that I was on Nabomba
Zom, for how many other planets do we know where the sea is red as
blood and the sand is pale lavender? But was this really Loiza la
Vakako? He seemed so young. The man whom I had known once could
have been any age at all except young. But this one, strolling by himself
along the shore of that boiling sea, seemed no older than I had been
myself in that far-off time when I had lived the life of a young prince
at the palace of Loiza la Vakako.

I appeared right in front of him, ghost-high above the moist sand. He
seemed not at all surprised, almost as if he had been expecting me.
Smiled the quick sly smile of Loiza la Vakako. Studied me with those
awesome eyes. Young, yes, no doubt of that, hardly more than a boy.
But already he was Loiza la Vakako, complete and total. That regal
presence. That austerity of spirit, that leanness of soul. That penetrating
shrewdness. That calmness that was not mere cow-like placidity, but
represented, rather, the absolute victory over self.

"First ghost of the day," he said. "Welcome, whoever you are."

"You don't know me?"

"Not yet," said Loiza la Vakako. "Come. Walk with me. This place
is Nabomba Zom."

"I know that," I said. "I'm going to live here for a few years, one
day when you are older and I am younger. And I will love your
daughter. And I will share in your downfall with you."

"Ah," he said. "My daughter. My downfall." He seemed uncon-
cerned. "You're the one, then. You are a king, are you not?"

"Can you see that?"

"Of course. Kings can see kings. Tell me your name, king, and I'll
wait for your return with great eagerness."

"I never knew anyone like you," I said. "You are the wisest man who
ever lived."

"Hardly. All I am is less foolish than some. Your name, O king."

"Yakoub Nirano. Rom baro."

"Ah. Ah. Rom baro! You will love my daughter, eh?"

"And lose her," I said.

"Yes. Of course, you will. And find her again, perhaps, afterward?"

"No. No, never again."

His elegant face grew solemn. "What will her name be, old man?"

I hesitated. This was all forbidden, what I was doing. But it seemed to me that I had lived on into a time beyond the end of the universe, when all the old rules were cancelled.

"Malilini," I said.

"A beautiful name. Yes. Yes. I will call her that, most certainly." Again the quick smile. "Malilini. And you will love her and lose her. How sad, Yakoub Nirano."

"And I will love you," I said. But already I felt myself growing transparent; I was being whirled away. "And I will lose you." And I was gone. Out of control. Whirling. Whirling.

2.

THAT BEAST THERE, STRANGE BEYOND WORDS, THE DOU-ble humps, the great jutting rubbery lips: I think it is the thing they called a camel. So this must be Earth. I am in a dry sandy place, jagged gray hills jutting at disturbing tilted angles in the distance, whirlwinds circling restlessly over the scrubby plain. A caravan of extravagantly costumed people with dark skins, coarse black hair, sparkling eyes, brilliant grins. Black felt tents. Hats with wide turned-up flaps. I have never seen this place or these people before, but I know them.

An open-air forge here, goatskin bellows, great heavy hammers, two smiths banging at red-hot metal. Here, three girls striding side by side, aloof and mysterious, like priestesses of some unknown order. A woman with ten thousand years of wrinkles, busy with beans and slivers of dried grass and the knucklebones of sheep, foretelling the future for a wide-eyed young Gajo. The sound of a flute nearby. The aroma of roasting meat, seasoned with sharp spices.

I allow myself to become visible. A boy dances up to me and stares, unafraid.

"Sarishan," I say. "San tu Rom?"

He has huge shining eyes, a cunning smile, a quick, agile way about him. He says nothing. He continues to stare.

I point to myself. "Yakoub," I say. I touch his scarf. "Diklo." My nose. "Nak." My teeth. "Dand." My hair. "Bal." He seems not to comprehend a thing. A few of the other Gypsies are looking toward us, now. The old woman fortune-teller smiles and winks. I keep myself invisible to the Gajo. A smaller boy jogs up to us and clutches the other's arm as he peers at me. "Tu prala?" I ask. "Your brother?" Still no reply. This must be one of the far lands of Earth, I decide, where the Rom speak a language other than Romany. From my tunic I take two glittering gold coins of the Imperium, bearing the features of the Fifteenth on one side and a scattering of stars on the other. I hold the coins up before the boys.

They are ghost-coins, without substance, without weight. They will vanish like snow in summer the moment I depart. But the boys stare at them with awe. They know gold, at any rate.

"From Galgala," I tell them. "From the stars, from the time to come." I lay the coins in the palms of their hands. They poke at them, frowning, trying to touch them. But to them the coins are nothing more than golden air. "I wish I could give you a more lasting gift. I am your cousin Yakoub."

"Yakoub," the smaller boy murmurs.

The whirlwinds are starting up again. I begin to fade. The boys look saddened. The coins are fading too.

"Yakoub!" the smaller boy cries. "Yakoub!"

"Ashen Devlesa," says the older boy suddenly in clear Romany as I disappear. "May you remain with God!"

3.

OUT OF CONTROL. ONWARD I GO. WHIRLING. WHIRLING. I might almost have been on a relay-sweep journey. I had that same sense of hanging suspended above the entire universe, flying swiftly from somewhere to somewhere through a vast soup of nowhere, with nothing to shelter me from the black inrushing strangeness of the cosmos except an imaginary wall of force not even as thick as a bubble. And I could no more govern the direction of my flight than I could the movements of the suns.

But this trip of mine now, it was free fall through time as well as space. I was going everywhere. I was going anywhere. Nothing at all held me in place; I was without moorings; I was a straw blown by the gods.

I needed to regain command. But how? How?

4.

MENTIROSO, NOW. UNQUESTIONABLY MENTIROSO. THAT sense of inexplicable and inescapable fear, bubbling through your veins, stirring in your gut. The closeness of unfriendly gods conjuring panic without reason. The hot scent of terror on the thick heavy breezes.

Look, there: the synapse pit of Nikos Hasgard. Those men sitting side by side in the stirrups, twitchy little Polarca, big sturdy Yakoub. They both look exhausted. Bowed, trembling, pale. I keep myself hidden from them as I float down. I stand behind them and let my right hand rest on Yakoub's shoulder and my left on Polarca's. I will try to send my strength into them both. Is that possible? A ghost aiding two living men? Well, I try. I try. I reach into myself and find the core of my vitality and tap it, and draw power forth from myself, and send it down my arms into my fingers and attempt to thrust it on into them.

Is it working? They seem to sit a little straighter. They regain some of their color. Yes. Yes. Here, Yakoub, here, Polarca, take, take, take!

They look at each other. Something is happening but they don't have any idea what it is.

"You feel it?" Polarca says.

"Yes. As if energy is coming up out of the equipment instead of going down into it."

"No. Not out of the equipment. Out of somewhere else. Out of the sky."

"Out of the sky?" Yakoub says.

Polarca nods. "Or out of the air. Out of the fog. Who knows? Who cares?"

I will stay with them as long as I can. A day, a week, a month—it is all the same to me. I live outside of space and time. And they need me.

But the fear—the fear—

Even ghosts feel it.

And I feel it reaching me, coming up through them in amplified strength. The fear that makes your teeth clack and your balls contract and your urine turn to ice. That fear is the glue that binds the cosmos together. The fundamental substance, the universal matrix. Conquer it at your risk; for if you do, you drive a wedge between atom and atom, and the universe begins to crumble. Nevertheless I struggle against it. I will not let the terror overwhelm me. I fight and I fight well, and I thrust it back; I beat it down; I trample it, I crush it, I destroy it. I am on Mentiroso and I am unafraid. And in that moment of no fear I see the little line of black that is the first crack in the fundament of the worlds. I have done it, I, me, Yakoub Nirano, I have driven the first wedge, and now it widens, now it yawns, now it is a broad dark chasm reaching outward, devouring everything it touches—

I am swept away in the gale of chaos.

5.

MEGALO KASTRO—DUUD SHABEEL—ALTA HANNALANNA—
Trinigalee Chase—
Vietoris, Mount Salvat, standing beside my huge father Romano
Nirano—
Megalo Kastro—
Alta Hannalanna—
Xamur—Galgala—Earth—Earth—Earth—
Mulano—
Alta Hannalanna—
Earth—Earth—Earth—
Whirling—whirling—helpless—out of control—

6.

THE WINTER IS ENDING. THE WARM WINDS ARE BLOWING
from the south. The Rom will take to the road again soon. Green
pastures, fields of oats and barley ahead. Cool clear mountain springs.
Horses hooves' thudding against the roads still damp from melting
snow, the wagon wheels rattling, the intoxicating joy of movement,
fresh air, the rebirth of life.

We come to the camp of our cousins down the road. We do not know
them, but they are our cousins. Sixty campfires burn that night. The
scent of roasting meat is everywhere. It is a glorious patshiv, a feast of

feasts, two kumpanias meeting on the great highway of the world. Our men are singing by the fire now, toasting our cousins, our hosts. Old songs, songs of our grandparents' grandparents, telling of travels long ago.

A girl comes forth, very dark, very young. Her eyes are shut; she might be in a trance. She sings and a boy hardly a year older than she comes up and stands before her: he has entered her trance. When she is done he begins to dance around her, feet slapping the ground almost angrily, but there is no anger in him, only delight and exuberance. His body leaps, but his arms and torso remain almost still. He sings to her. She laughs. His song ends and he stands staring at her, but he does not speak. They exchange shy smiles and nothing more. And then they retreat, she to her kumpania, he to his; but perhaps he will find her again before the night is over.

Roast beef, chicken, suckling pig. An old grandfather is dancing now, slapping his knees, clicking his booted heels together. Faster, faster, hands clapping, arms swinging. And now the boys; and now the men; and now everyone, first in a circle, then in a long oval loop, then in no pattern at all, for there are too many to hold in a pattern.

Ah, this is the life! The life of the road!

Dogs barking now. Sudden cries of alarm from the darkness on the rim of the encampment. Shouts, the sound of a shot, another shot. "Shangle!" someone cries. "Police! Police!" Riding on horses, coming to drive us away. What have we done? Only to camp here, and make a feast for our cousins, and sing, and dance. Maybe singing and dancing are unlawful in this place. "Shangle! Shangle!" Horses. Police dogs. Shots fired in the air. Men shouting in anger. Cursing, spitting. What have we done? What have we done? It must be the singing. It must be the dancing. They ride right through our midst and we dare not lift a hand against them. For they are the Gaje police; and we, we are only the dirty homeless Gypsies, who must move with care in their world. So we scatter, and the feasting is no more.

7.

I HAVE NO CHOICE. IF I LET MYSELF GO WHIRLING ON randomly through time, I am lost, all is lost. This is mere wandering. Randomness is meaninglessness. We have wandered long enough. Now it is time to find meaning. I need to impose control over my voyage. I need to impose meaning.

Who am I? *I am Yakoub Nirano, King of the Gypsies.*

Where was I born? *I was born on Vietoris, long ago.*

Where do I live? *Everywhere and nowhere.*

Where am I bound? *Nowhere and everywhere.*

What am I searching for? *For the true home of my wandering people.*

Where is that? *Everywhere and nowhere, nowhere and everywhere.*

Lost in time. Lost in space. But not beyond the possibility of finding.

I will look. I think I know where to look.

Back—back—

8.

I AM SWEPT AWAY AGAIN, BUT THIS TIME IT IS DIFFERENT. I am no longer floundering helplessly. This time I begin to feel some measure of command over my voyage.

9.

I KNOW THIS PLACE. EVEN IN THE THICK MIST THAT shrouds everything I can see the blueness of the sky, I can see the bright gold of the sun, I can see the whiteness of the thousand marble columns in the plaza. I have gone very far back now. I know this place, yes. I have been here before. This is Earth, the ancient Earth beyond history; and this place is lost Atlantis. This is the great Rom city, the most beautiful place on Earth that ever was.

How serene it is. Our island kingdom, white sands and sparkling sea. How well we have built here: what grace, what order. Alone and undisturbed I move through the long straight streets, among the dark slender people in white robes and sandals. Past the Concourse of the Sky, into the Street of Starwatchers, down the marble causeway to the waterfront. The city gleams through the mist. I envy those who live here in the city's own time, for they can see it plain; this dense mist is none of theirs, but is something I bring with me, out of the thousands of years across which I have come. It is unavoidable, so far back. But if Atlantis is this lovely, shrouded for me as it is, what must it be to those who see it shining brightly in the full sun!

I am at the water now. To my left stands the Temple of the Dolphins, pure and serene, a symphony in white stone. To my right is the Fountain of the Spheres; and straight in front of me lies the Grand Quay, with six fine ships riding at anchor, and one more farther out, coming in with its cargo of gold and silver and apes and peacocks, of precious stones, of pearls, of odors and ointments, of frankincense, wine and oil, all manner vessels of ivory, all manner vessels of most precious wood. This world of Earth is ours and all good things that are upon it; for we alone are civilized folk. The Gaje who live everywhere about us, beyond the waters of the sea that shelter us from them, are little more than beasts, and some not even that. So we go forth and take what we want and our ships bring it to us across the shimmering blue-green sea, and with it we make our city wondrous beautiful.

I will stay here forever, is what I tell myself now.

No matter the mists. No matter that I am only a ghost. I will become a citizen of this Atlantis and dwell here to the end of my days. I will drink the thick red wine in the taverns and I will dine on roasted meats and olives. No matter that I am a ghost and have no need of wine and meats and olives. I am here and here I will stay, deep in the depths of time, cloaked by mist, in a place where the Rom are lords and there is nothing to fear.

But what's this, now? Wavelets tremble at the edge of the shore. A fringe of gentle surf clear as glass laps against the marble piers and jetties, and pulls away, and surges back, not nearly so gentle this time.

The ships riding at anchor rise and fall, and slap the breast of the sea with their hulls.

The ship that is still out at sea vanishes for an instant beneath the horizon, and reappears, lurching, rolling.

The ground trembles. The sky shakes.

Ah, what is this, what is this? A roaring in my ears. The mist clears and I turn to see the mountain behind the city belching fire and black smoke. Great slabs of marble drop from the pediment of the Temple of the Dolphins. Farther up the slope in the Plaza of the Thousand Columns I can see the columns toppling like sticks. The roaring grows louder and louder.

There is no panic. The men and women in the white robes and the sandals move purposefully about, heading for their homes. A marble street splits and rises in the center, revealing steaming black earth below. Horses bolt and run whinnying through the marketplace. A chariot without a rider comes my way and passes through me and is gone.

Atlantis! Atlantis! Today I will see your ruining!

Where is the mist? I want the mist to come back. But no, now everything is clear, mercilessly clear. Every jagged crack, every furrow in the stone. There is still no panic, but I hear them crying out now, begging for the mercy of the gods. Have we not suffered enough? Must we be shattered here also, after we were driven forth from that other place of beauty in the stars?

Atlantis! Atlantis!

Alas, that great city—

Alas, alas that great city, that was clothed in fine linen, and purple, and scarlet, and decked with gold, and precious stones, and pearls! For in one hour so great riches is come to nought. And every shipmaster, and all the company in ships, and sailors, and as many as trade at sea, stood afar off, and cried when they saw the smoke of her burning, saying, What city is like unto this great city! And they cast dust on their heads, and cried, weeping and wailing, saying, Alas, alas that great city! For in one hour is she made desolate.

10.

*ATLANTIS IS NOT THE ANSWER. PERHAPS THERE IS NO AN-*swer. I am swept away. I am hurled far and far and far, deep and deep and deep. There is no answer. Or if there is one, I do not have the courage to seek it. I spin once more like a seed on the wind. I go on and on, not knowing where, not caring, giving myself over completely into the power of the gods that drive my fate. What does it matter, where I go? What does anything matter? All is lost, is that not so? The Imperium is fallen. Quarreling little lords pick and snarl over its yellowing bones. There is no center; there are no boundaries. And in that chaos how can we survive? The Rom will be blown once more on the winds. As I am now.

On. Far. Deep.

Whirling randomly once again, Yakoub?

But this is wrong. If there is an answer to the riddles of your life, you will never find it in this aimless fluttering. You had control; take it again. Go back again. Go back as far as you dare, and then go back even farther. Go to the source, Yakoub.

Go to the source.

Risk it all, or all is lost. Back. Back. To the source, Yakoub.

On. Far. Deep.

11.

INTO A LAND WHERE THE MISTS OF TIME ARE SO THICK and heavy that they shroud everything like a winding-sheet, binding tight and close. And mist within mist, clotted masses of white within white. What could have woven this cocoon about the world? Why, it is time itself that has done it. I have gone very far back, farther than I ever thought was possible. I am beyond Rome, beyond Egypt, beyond Atlantis, deep in antiquity. Nor is this Earth. I have no idea where I am, but it is not Earth: it does not have the smell of Earth, it does not have the feel of Earth. Perhaps I have gone back beyond Earth. Perhaps I have reached the source. Is that possible? The idea frightens me. I grope through dark realms of whiteness. Soft strands of mist entangle me. Smothering wisps of it cover my eyes and my nose and my mouth. I see mist; I breathe mist; I eat mist. There is nothing here but mist.

Have I come to the beginning of time?

In the dimness, by the lightless light of a shrouded sun, I imagine now that I can see shadows, or at least the shadows of shadows. Perhaps there is something here after all, some substance, some tangibility. A city? That shadowy arch there: is it a bridge? And that, a tower? That, a boulevard? Do I see trees? Figures moving about? Yes. I think my eyes are growing accustomed now. It takes some getting used to, this mist. Or perhaps what it takes is a colossal effort of will, in order to see here. Not-seeing is easy: your eyes will do that for you. Simply open them and they will show you the mist. That is all your eyes will show you: the mist. But seeing something more takes work. You have to throw all your soul into it. It is like a game where the odds are stacked so heavily against you that a small wager is useless; gamble everything on the next toss of the dice, or else move along to a different table. Do you want to see what is here, Yakoub? Then meet the stake. Put up all you have. And then even more. Yes.

I think the mists are beginning to clear.

Yes. Yes. Beyond question, the mists are beginning to clear.

There is a chrysalis within this cocoon. Everything is being revealed to me. Here is a city indeed. I see bridges, towers, boulevards. I see trees. I see figures. I see a sun in the sky.

This place is no place I have ever seen before. And yet it seems to me I know it like the fingers of my own hand. The mist is completely gone now and I see everything clearly, with an odd dreamlike intensity, as though through a glass that magnifies. How strange this place is! I have seen so many worlds that I can no longer count them all, worlds of such strangeness that the mind can scarcely encompass it; and yet I feel something here that I have never felt anywhere else.

I move slowly and warily through these strange streets. Timid ghost, glancing this way and that. The city is vast. It sweeps over hills and valleys as far as I can see, dense and populous, though broken frequently by plazas, parks, watercourses, promenades. The people have dark solemn eyes that sparkle with unfamiliar knowledge. Their black hair is braided in elaborate knots. Their clothes are shimmering strings of beads falling in free cascades. They pay no attention to me; perhaps they are unable to see me, or perhaps they have no interest in me. Where am I? What world is this? I know this place, though I have never seen it before. These buildings, these streets. The streets are straight but they cross at angles that bewilder the eye. The buildings have an eerie alien beauty that is nevertheless familiar. This is not my first visit to this place where I have never been before. What does that mean? What am I trying to say? Words I never thought to speak. Streets I never thought I should revisit, when I left my body on a distant shore.

The sun is red. It fills a fourth of the sky.

But though that great sun blazes above me, I am able to see the stars also, thousands of them, millions, a field of light in the heavens. There are no constellations here; there is only light.

And the moons! Jesu Cretchuno Sunto Mario, the moons!

They are like a jeweled belt across the whole vast arc of the sky. From horizon to horizon they hang in a sublime row, glittering, burning, seven, eight, ten dazzling moons—no, eleven, eleven moons, bright as little suns. If this is how they look by day, what must the night be like here?

Eleven moons. Red sun. The stars shining by day.

Eleven moons.

Red sun.

The stars shining by day.

I know where I am now, and the astounding truth sweeps through me like the wave from the sea that carries the mountains away. I have traveled a long way, and I have arrived where I meant to go all along. Despite the fears and the hesitations that have held me back, the long quest has ended in success.

Tears flood my eyes. I want to drop to my knees in awe. This is the place, yes. Here in our first world is where I am. The forbidden place, the holy place. At the still point of the turning world, where past and future are gathered. We may go ghosting anywhere in time and space, but not here; it is not lawful to go here, it is not even possible to go here. It is beyond reach. Or so I have thought. So have we all thought. And yet I have achieved it. I am here. I have come home.

This is Romany Star.

How can I doubt it? There is Mulesko Chiriklo, the bird of the dead, swooping, soaring: silent wings, bright staring eyes. I have passed through that unknown, remembered gate, into the one place that is all places for us. The gales of time have blown me to the far end of time. Those were the mists of dawn that I had had to push aside. And now I see with terrible clarity, in this place which has always been forbidden to us, and which we have believed to lie beyond the range of all ghosting. I am here. I alone have made the impossible journey. Time past and time future point to one end, which is always present. For me now there can be neither past nor future. My destiny has come round upon itself. In my end is my beginning.

The sky over Romany Star is exactly as it is said to be in the legends. Red sun, eleven moons, stars shining by day. The tale-tellers were faithful to that much, at least, in the thousands and thousands of years of the telling of the tale.

But nothing else is as I expect it to be. Shining marble palaces, says the Swatura. Splendid towers, vast concourses, broad highways, gleaming temples of many columns. No. That is Atlantis, not Romany Star. We built differently in our second home, and forgot that we did. Here is beauty also, but of another sort, less formal, less monumental. Nothing seems permanent. They use no stone here. They have woven this city of some delicate reed; everything is pliant, everything is yielding. Towers, yes, and bridges and boulevards, but they ripple in the gentle breezes, and change form at a touch. There will be nothing left of this place when the time of the swelling of the sun arrives. A dry wind, a gust of heat, a puff of flame: and then nothing but ashes within hours. No charred monuments for future archaeologists to puzzle over; no stumps of fallen obelisks; no foundations, no walls, no mosaics. Nothing. Ashes. Instantly. It is all very beautiful now; it all will perish in a very beautiful way, in a moment, in the twinkling of an eye, leaving no doleful relicts behind.

Hundreds of people stream past me into a building larger than the others just across the way from me. I join the flow and enter with them, unnoticed, unhindered. A green light shines inside, but its source eludes me. I pass through corridors strewn with woven mats into rooms that yield to other rooms, and at last I come to one room of great size, plainly a meeting-hall, where the citizens of Romany Star have assembled by the thousands.

At the far end of the room a sort of hammock which is also a sort of a throne has been strung high above the floor. It is occupied by a man who by his look could well have been my brother. There is kingliness about him: I see it at once, and I would have seen it even if I had simply met him in the street and not come upon him enthroned in a great hall. His hair is braided in the ancient way and he wears the beaded clothing. But his face is mine, his eyes are mine. He is my brother. No, we are closer than that. He is me.

He is speaking to his people. Not a word that he says can I understand; and yet I feel reassurance emanating from him, I feel his strength, his calmness. He speaks gravely and they listen to him gravely. It is a long speech, and everyone remains perfectly still to the end of it. Then, in silence, one by one, they go to him and they touch their hands to his. The ceremony continues for hours, an endless procession of the people to their monarch. I find it tremendously moving and I am unable to leave; the line edges forward and I edge with it, until I see that I am near the front, that in another moment I will be at its head. There is no way that I can turn away. I am visible to them all. It would be a dire insult to spurn this man's blessing now, whatever it may mean. So I go forward and I stretch out my hands and he touches his hands to them. Even though I am here as a ghost, he touches my hands, just as he has touched those of his own people.

For all the others, the touch was only a moment. But me he holds, me he detains. I feel the tremendous vitality of him flowing into me. I see the great sadness and wisdom of his spirit shining in his eyes. Yes, he is a true king. There are only a few kings born in any epoch, and they know from birth who they are. I am one, even if I have not always lived up to my kingliness. This man is another. We are of one soul, he and I. I love him for his strength; I love him for his sadness; I love him for his wisdom. I love him as one loves a king. I love him as one loves a father. I love him as one loves one's own self.

He holds me a long while. It seems like hours.

He says nothing, but I feel that we are conversing at length. Much is passing from him to me, and from me to him. Behind me no one moves; we could be alone in the hall. In the spark that travels from his hands to mine and from mine to his are all the Rom who ever lived; we bridge the race from end to end, this king and I. Within him is a sense of all our destiny to come, and within me is a sense of all that has befallen us; and we pass these things back and forth between each other. Time past, time future, pointing to one end. Which is always present.

He offers me courage. Mere death is not the end of anything, he says. It is only an interruption. Men die, women die, planets die: but certain things continue. What matters is to continue; and there are many ways of continuing. We have sent our sixteen ships out into the Great Dark. That is our way of continuing.

And in return I give him hope. You have achieved what you meant to achieve, I say. You have allowed us to continue; and we have done the job. Look, I am here to show you that we still exist at the far end of time. We are all part of the grand kumpania, all we Rom, your people and mine. One blood, one people. One grand kumpania. We have continued you. We have wandered very far, as was the gods' decree for us, but we have not lost our sense of who we are. And—look—I am here to pledge to you that soon we wanderers will be coming home, to this place that has always been ours.

I am you, I tell him. And you are me.

I am you, he tells me. And you are me.

He releases me. When I walk away, I carry within me the fullness of this great Rom civilization of Romany Star: its grandeur, its tragedy, its wisdom, its poetry. Its grandeur is its tragedy; its wisdom is its poetry. These are people who are waiting to die. I know now when I have arrived. The omens have come, the lottery has been held, the sixteen ships have been built and have gone off into the Great Dark. These are the ones who were left behind. They will die. Everyone dies, and for each it is the end of the world; but for these millions here the death of one will be the death of all. They have made their peace with death. They have made their peace with the end of the world.

And in their end is their beginning. For I am the emissary from worlds to come, testifying to their continuation down through the passageways of time. I have come to tell them that the circle will be made whole, that the exile will soon be ending, that I am the one who will bring our people home.

I find myself outside this great building of woven reeds again, this palace of the last king of Romany Star.

I stare at the red sun that nearly fills the sky, until my eyes begin to throb and ache.

Ah there, you red sun, you are Romany Star, and I am staring right at you! I tremble. O Tchalai, the Star of Wonder. O Netchaphoro, the Luminous Crown, the Carrier of Light, the Halo of God. There you are hanging in the heavens before me! Star of wonder, star of night. And star of day as well. Star of Gypsies, toward whom we have yearned throughout all our days. There you are.

I tremble and the red star trembles with me.

It seems to me that its color has deepened and that eddies and whirlpools are moving on the face of it. This is the last day. The air grows warm. Yes, yes, the red star is warmer now. Swelling. Churning. O Tchalai! O Netchaphoro! This is the moment, yes, the time of the swelling of the sun, the moment of Romany Star! The Rom have come forth from their houses by the thousands, by the millions, and they stand beside me in the streets, joining their arms together, watching. Waiting. Someone begins to sing. Someone else picks up the song. And then another, and another. The language in which they sing is unknown to me, though it must be some grandfather of the Romany that I speak. Nor do I know the words of the song, nor the melody. They are all singing now, and now I join them. I throw my head back, I open my mouth, and my heart gives me the song; and I sing, loud and clear. I can hear my own voice above all the others for a moment, and then it blends with them in a perfect harmony as the red sun grows larger and larger and yet larger in the sky.

12.

THEN A WRENCHING, A TWISTING, A PAINFUL SENSE OF being torn loose—

Of movement across time, across space—

The smell of burning was in my nostrils when I opened my eyes. As though I was breathing ash; as though the air itself was singed. I felt lost. Where was the red glow of Romany Star? Gone. Gone. The sound of the singing on that last day still echoed in my ears; but where were the singers? Where was I? Why had I not been allowed to remain with them for their last moment?

Perhaps I had, and I had died with them, and I had gone to hell. Had I? Was this hell that I was in now? I had traveled so far, to so many places; why not hell too?

I was lying down, perhaps in a bed; there were people around me; their faces were indistinct, indistinguishable. Their voices were vague murmurs. My eyes were betraying me. My hearing. Everything was a blur. Romany Star was gone. That was the one certain reality. Romany Star was gone. And that smell of burning—that hideous taste of ashes that came to me with every breath I drew—

"Yakoub?"

A gentle voice, far away. I knew that voice. Polarca, my little Lowara horse-trader.

"Yakoub, are you awake?"

Not hell, then. Unless Polarca was in hell with me.

I managed a scowl and a laugh. "Of course I'm awake, idiot! Can't you see that my eyes are open?"

He was bending close over me, nose to my nose. Seeing him helped me bring into focus the others, those blurred shapes behind him. Damiano my cousin. Thivt. Chorian. And others, farther back, not so easy for me to make out. Bibi Savina? Yes. Was that Syluise? Yes! Biznaga, Jacinto, Ammagante. Was *everyone* here? Yes, so it seemed.

Even Julien. The treacherous one, even him, at my bedside. All right, I would forgive him. He was my friend; let him be here. And who was that? Valerian? Not Valerian's ghost, but the actual Valerian? How could that be? No one ever saw the actual Valerian any more. Was I dreaming that he was here?

I have been to the morning of time. I have seen Romany Star. And now I have come back.

"What is this?" I growled. "Why are you all hovering around me? What's going on?"

"You've been asleep for weeks," said Damiano.

"Weeks?" I sat up, or tried to, and found myself infuriatingly weak. My arms and elbows refused to obey me. Like strands of spaghetti, they were. Damn them! I pushed myself up anyway. "What world is this?"

"The Capital," Polarca said.

I shook my head, letting things sink in. "Asleep for weeks, and this is the Capital. Ah. Ah. How could it be weeks? I was off ghosting— just for a minute or two, ghosting never takes very long—"

I looked around. Medical equipment everywhere.

"Have I been sick?"

"A long sleep," Polarca said. "Like a coma. We knew you were in there. We could see your eyes moving. Sometimes you shouted things in strange languages. Once you sang, but nobody could make out the words."

"I was ghosting. A great many places."

Syluise came forward and took my hand. She looked as beautiful as ever, but older, more somber, the flash and glitter gone from her beauty. "Yakoub, Yakoub! We were so worried! Where did you go?"

I shrugged. "Atlantis. Mentiroso. Xamur. All sorts of places. That doesn't matter." *I have seen Romany Star.* "Why does it smell like this in here? Am I imagining it? Everything smells burned."

"Everything is burned," Chorian said.

"Everything?"

"There's been a great deal of damage," said Polarca. "The lunatic Gaje have smashed their Capital to shards in their lunatic war. But it's done with now. Everything's quiet. You should see what it looks like out there, Yakoub."

"Let me see."

"In a little while. When you're strong enough to get up."

"I'm strong enough to get up now."

"Yakoub—"

"Now," I said.

They were exchanging troubled glances. Trying to figure out some way to prevent me. Not strong enough, was I? To hell with them. I swung my legs out of the bed and put some weight on them. The first pressure against the floor was agony; I thought my feet were on fire, that my ankles were exploding. I didn't let it show. I kept pushing forward, forward, levering myself up. Tottered a little, shifted my weight. Now it was the knees that were screaming. The hips, the pelvis. I hadn't been standing for weeks. Lying here in a coma, dreaming I was in Atlantis, dreaming I was on Romany Star.

No. Not dreaming. Ghosting. Truly and literally there.

I have seen Romany Star.

I walked to the window and switched it to view capacity.

"My God," I said in awe. "My God!"

There was a vast rubble-field outside, stretching as far as I could see: broken statuary, sundered pavements, toppled buildings, charred walls. It was an unreal sight, a stage-set of devastation. Here and there a building rose intact out of the ghastliness. Incongruously, unaccountably. It seemed wrong that anything should still be in one piece on this world. The undamaged buildings were out of place in this architecture of destruction. I had not seen anything so frightful in my life.

I turned away from the sight of it, numbed, shaken.

"What have they done here?" I asked.

"It was the war of everybody against everybody," said Polarca. "Three different armies at first, Periandros, Sunteil, Naria. And then a second doppelganger of Periandros broke away from the first and made war on him. And after that it was Naria's forces dividing against themselves; and then there was a new army that didn't seem to belong to anyone. After that, no one could make sense out of anything. The fighting was everywhere and everything was destroyed. We survived because they didn't dare aim at the palace of the Rom baro, and we had your banners out, and your light-spike. But even so we took a few bad hits. One whole wing of the building was gutted. We thought we were going to die. But there was no way to leave the Capital. The starport is closed. No ships are moving anywhere."

"Gaje," I muttered. "What can you expect?"

"Somehow you slept through it all. We thought you were never going to wake."

"The fighting is over now?"

"All over," Polarca said. "There's no one left to fight."

"And who ended up as emperor, when all the fighting was over?"

There was silence in the room. They looked stunned and dazed, all of them. Polarca, Damiano, Chorian, Valerian and the rest, silent, dazed.

"Well?" I said. "Is that such a difficult question? Who's emperor now? Tell me. Naria, is it, still?"

"No one," said Damiano.

"No one?"

"There is no emperor."

It made no sense. No emperor? No emperor?

I said, "How can that be, no emperor? There were three!"

Damiano said, "Periandros' doppelgangers were destroyed by Periandros' own troops. There was a confrontation, at the headquarters of Periandros, two of the doppelgangers face to face. Everyone could see now that there was no Periandros, that there were only doppelgangers. So they destroyed them both, and then they hunted down the third one and finished it too."

I nodded slowly. "And Naria? What happened to him? Behind that ring of defenses. His deflector screens, his tanks, his robots. His glass cube."

"Dead," Polarca said. "A plasma bomb, a direct hit on the imperial palace. Thirty seconds of thousand-degree heat. The palace was hardly damaged but everyone inside died instantly. Naria was cooked in his own glass cube."

"That leaves Sunteil."

"He went to take possession of the palace after Naria's death," Chorian said. "Naria had booby-trapped the throne-platform. Three lasers sliced Sunteil into pieces the moment he took the imperial seat. A hidden scanner, coded for Sunteil and only Sunteil, that would respond to no one else's somatic specifications." He looked away. "I was there when it happened," he said quietly.

"Dead?" I said, not believing it. "The high lords? All three dead? No emperor at all?"

"No emperor at all," Polarca said.

"What will they do? There has to be an emperor!"

"Go back to bed, Yakoub."

"No emperor—"

"That's not our problem. Go back to bed. Lie down. Rest," Polarca said.

I glared. "Who do you think you're ordering around?"

Syluise took my hand. "Please, Yakoub. You've been seriously ill. It's just a little while since you regained consciousness. You mustn't put a strain on yourself now. Please. Just rest a little more."

"I was ghosting," I said. "Not ill at all."

"Please, Yakoub."

"Do you know where I was? Do you know what I saw?"

"For me," she murmured. "Lie down again. So I won't worry. We can't afford to lose you too, now. No emperor, no king—"

I looked around the room. I felt like shouting, raging, blustering. Was I so fragile? Was I so decrepit? Look at them all! Staring, gaping! They were all like pale phantoms to me. Unreal. This whole place seemed unreal. Romany Star still glowed in my mind. That palace of reeds, that long line of quiet citizens, that king in his vast and solemn dignity—that great red sun, swelling, swelling, growing larger and larger and larger—

"Mon ami, I implore you." Julien. "You will be fine tomorrow. But you must not tax yourself overly, you must not place demands on yourself that you are unable to meet. I implore."

"You," I said.

His face colored. "Whoever I may have served in the past, Yakoub, it makes no difference now. Now I serve only you. And I beg you, Yakoub. Rest yourself. The pitiful pretender begs the true king. You need your strength for tomorrow."

"Tomorrow? What, tomorrow?"

He glanced toward the others. I saw Damiano nod, and Polarca.

Julien said, "The audience, tomorrow. The peers of the Imperium, the new ones, those who survived the holocaust here. For days they have hovered about the palace, pleading to speak with you the moment you regained consciousness. A matter of the greatest urgency, they say. You are the king and there is no emperor: they need to see you. They need your help. They're totally bewildered."

I stared. "Peers of the Imperium? Greatest urgency? Totally bewildered?"

"Tomorrow may be too soon," Damiano said. Always cautious. "We don't want to overtax you. They've waited this long, let them wait another couple of—"

"No," I said. "Tomorrow may be too late. They need my help. How can I ignore that? Get them here right away, man!"

"Mon vieux, mon ami!" Julien cried. "Not today! Not so soon! You have but hardly awakened. Let it wait."

"Send for them."

Polarca threw up his hands in despair. Damiano, tight-faced, furious, clenched his fists. Syluise clung close, appealing. I saw the stricken face of Chorian, and even some boy standing beside Chorian, one who I had not even noticed before and that I did not know at all, was shaking his head as though to say, No, no, Yakoub, not so soon, not until you're stronger.

I was determined. There had been enough anarchy; if I was a king, and I *was* a king, then I must take up my task. At once. At once.

"Send for them!" I thundered.

But it was the last thundering I did that day. Even as the words escaped my throat, the force of my own outcry undid me. I swayed and grew dizzy and sagged down toward the side of the bed. I think for a moment my soul tried to bolt free of my body. I forced it back. Wondering if this was the final moment of Yakoub, stupidly, prematurely, just when so much remained to complete. No! No! By the holy turds of all the saints and demons, not yet, not yet, not yet!

A bad moment. A foolish moment.

"Easy, there," Valerian whispered, lowering me to the pillow. "You're all right. Easy, you Yakoub! Give him a drink, fast! No, not the water, you idiot! Here. Here. Sip this, Yakoub. There. Another. Julien's finest cognac. Here."

I felt life returning, as the rich fiery brandy hit my gullet. But even so it took me an embarrassingly long while to recover a little poise: thirty seconds, perhaps a minute. Then I smiled. I winked. I belched. I made the good Rom sign that says, *Not dead yet, cousins, not yet!* But I knew that the peers of the Imperium, whoever they might be and whatever they might need to hear from me, would have to wait. I would have to curb my roaring impatience. I was a little frail today. I needed a little more rest. It had been a busy time for me, and I am not young, I suppose. That is the truth: I am in fact not young.

13.

NOT THE NEXT DAY, NOT THE DAY AFTER THAT. PERHAPS it had taken me close to two hundred years, but I had learned a little patience after all. I waited until I had some strength again.

Then I sent for them. And then they came.

I was in the audience-room of the palace that the Gaje had so kindly provided, all those hundreds of years ago, for the use of the Rom baro when he is in residence at the Capital. But I think they had never expected to see that audience-room put to such a use as it was put this day. No, not in a million years would they have anticipated a day such as this.

It was a very formal occasion. I dressed in my finest finery and mounted my throne and sat among the ceremonial objects of my power: my silken scroll of office; my silver scepter that bore the five holy symbols of axe, sun, moon, star, cross; my statuette of the Black Virgin Sara; my wonderwheel; my shadowstick. A grand and primitive display. Here sits the Gypsy king in all his majesty, yes. All hail!

"Send them in," I said.

A demon-figure at the door, bizarrely masked. Red straw beard, bulging green eyes, white horns. Cloak of brilliant stripes, a dozen colors. He pauses, makes a gesture of respect, bows stiffly from the hips. Takes up a position to my left, near the window.

Another. A woman, supple, sinuous. Golden mask, slits for eyes. Firm chin visible below, painted with interwoven blue lines. A gown that glistens like cold fire. The same gesture. Stands beside the first.

What is this masquerade? Who are these demons and witches?

A third. Savage spikes at his collar; giant black antlers rising high above a domed head. Bows. Moves to his place. The room is very silent. Polarca's eyes are bright as beacons. Damiano stares, lips clamped tight. Valerian ghosts nervously in and out of the scene; I see the energies flickering around him.

The fourth peer of the Imperium. Crocodile-head, stubby furry beast-legs. Pitchfork in his hand.

The fifth. Bat-wings, fangs, a torch smouldering in his black long-clawed hand.

Monsters and demons. These are the peers of the Imperium?

A fish-woman, scales and breasts. A goat-man, snorting and preening. One with a great bird-beak, and brilliant plumage that glows with a light of its own.

Lion-head. Frog-head.

Nine nightmare monsters arrayed in a semicircle before me. How still they are! What now? Will they leap upon me, will they devour me alive as I sit on my throne?

A signal. Antler-head comes forward. Kneels. Touches my foot. "Majesty," he says. What? *What?* The voice, rumbling from the depths of the heavy mask, is deep, hoarse, rough.

"Majesty," says lion-head, coming forward.

"Majesty," says fish-woman.

One by one. It is a dream. It is some fantastical moment out of space and time. The universe has ended; spirits float freely about.

"Majesty." "Majesty." "Majesty."

Now they are reaching into their costumes and pulling forth small objects which they place before me: a sphere, a rod, a string of interlocking golden balls. Not a masquerade, then, but a game? What am I supposed to do, solve the puzzle of these toys? Should I be wearing a mask of my own?

Why are they calling me *Majesty*? That is no title of mine. The Rom baro is beyond such pomp. My people call me Yakoub. These lords could well do the same.

Crocodile-head draws from the depths of his garb something that looks like a short sword in its scabbard. Polarca tenses and prepares to leap forward. I wave him back with the smallest motion of a finger. Crocodile-head places the scabbard before me: fine purple velvet, rich, lustrous. Places a furry hand on the head of the weapon within and begins slowly to pull it forth.

It is no weapon.

I know what it is. I have seen it before, many times, in my visits to the Capital. It is the wand of office that the emperor holds when he occupies the throne-platform atop the crystalline stairs.

What is this? What is this?

"Will you pick it up, Majesty?" asks crocodile-head.

"That wand is nothing of mine."

"It will be yours the moment it touches your hand," he says.

I had thought that after seeing Romany Star I would be beyond all awe; but now I am awed to my roots. What are these crazy Gaje doing, all bedecked in these nightmare costumes and crawling about down by my feet? What strange rite is this, that no Rom has ever seen or even heard about before, this procession of phantasms, this presentation of the wand?

Are they making me emperor? *Me?*

"You have all gone mad," I say.

"Majesty—" says crocodile-head.

"Majesty—" from antler-head.

"We beg you, Majesty—" It is frog-head, groveling.

"Up, all of you!" I stare in amazement. "On your feet! Take off those hideous masks!"

"Majesty—"

"Off with them! Unmask! Unmask at once!" I snatch up their Gaje wand of office and wave it around. "No nightmares in here! Get rid of those masks!"

They turn to one another, making bewildered little gestures with their claws and paws and flippers. Consternation. Uncertainty. Then lion-head lifts his mask, and the face of a man of Vietoris, unknown to me, looks out. Frog-head reveals a Copperfield face, ruddy, wind-burned. Antler-head has the fair skin and golden hair of a man of Ragnarok. Nine worlds of the Imperium have yielded these nine peers. Without their masks they look absurd in their costumes, caught in mid-mummery, childish, foolish, embarrassed.

"What is this?" I ask, brandishing the wand. "Why have you come here in these outfits? What are you trying to do?"

"The tradition," one whispers. "It is only a little pageantry, Majesty. To lend a heightening touch to the old secret rite—"

"What rite?"

"The naming of the emperor, Majesty."

Yes, I was right. Madness.

"Have you all lost your minds? I am Rom! What are you doing, coming to a Rom like this?"

"The throne is empty. The three high lords are dead. The ships remain in the starports. The worlds are helpless," says the Ragnarok man.

"The time has come for the uniting of the peoples," says Copperfield.

"You are the one. There is no one else. This was the will of the Fifteenth, sealed in the moment of his death, revealed to us now in the time of the destruction of the Capital. He chose you. This terrible war has been the consequence of ignoring that choice. Spare us further grief. Surely you will not refuse the will of the Fifteenth?"

The will of the Fifteenth—

"Majesty!" they cry again. I look across the room. Polarca is laughing or crying, I am not sure which. Damiano is down on his knees, shivering and praying. Chorian looks as though he has been struck from behind by a falling star. Only Julien de Gramont is totally calm: he looks transfigured, ecstatic, as though France itself is being reborn before his eyes.

"Majesty! Majesty!"

I look at the wand in my hand. The will of the Fifteenth? Jesu Cretchuno Sunto Mario! Emperor Yakoub? The same man, king and emperor? What do they think I am, Gaje as well as Rom?

By damn, why not?

The first Rom emperor. And the last. Take the throne, proclaim the harmony of the peoples, rebuild the web that links the worlds. Send forth the starships again. And then, then, the rebirth of Romany Star under my auspices. The return, the resettlement. For this must be the call that we have all awaited: when the Gaje turn to a Rom and say, Bring us together. So will we come together at last. And then we will go home.

"Will you accept?" the Gaje lordlings ask, astounded themselves by what is happening. "Do you yield to the will of the Fifteenth? The throne of the Imperium is waiting for you, Majesty. Say the word, and we will proclaim it: the Sixteenth has been chosen at last!"

"No," I say, and there is a terrible stunned silence.

"No?" they mutter. "No?"

A smile. "No, not the Sixteenth. That's an unlucky number, I think. Let *them* have been the Sixteenth, all three of them. The Sixteenth and the Seventeenth and the Eighteenth. We accept your homage, and we proclaim ourselves to rule from this moment forward as the Nineteenth of our line, and so be it."

"Long live the Nineteenth Emperor!" cry the peers of the Imperium.

"Long live the Nineteenth!" From Chorian, resonantly, joyously.

"Long live the Nineteenth!" From Julien, from Polarca, from Valerian. And then from all of them.

"We are greatly pleased," I say, benevolently waving the wand of office from one side of the room to another.

The royal *we*. How wonderfully silly that sounds.

I love it.

14.

BY THE TIME I HAD BEEN ROBED AND ANOINTED AND driven across the smouldering rubble-fields of the Capital to the imperial palace, which still stood intact despite all the carnage that had taken place in and around it, night was falling. On the horizon the sky-banner of a new emperor was aglow in every direction.

Once more I climbed the crystalline steps, huffing, I must confess, and puffing, all the way. No emperor waited at the top to hand me my cup of sweet wine. No loudspeakers boomed out my name as I ascended.

The peers of the Imperium clustered below me as the Nineteenth Emperor held the first procedural session of his reign.

I appointed Polarca and Julien de Gramont as my first two high lords. Polarca, of course. And Julien because a majority of the high lords would have to be Gaje, and he was *my* Gajo. The other one I would choose from that gaggle of masked monstrosities, as soon as I had had time to learn something about them.

When I was done with that, I issued some decrees having to do with the reconstruction of the Capital—we would do it in a somewhat less gaudy and grandiose way, but there was no need to say anything explicit about that just yet—and the reorganization of the imperial guard in the wake of the civil war. Then, in my capacity as Rom baro, I told Polarca to send word to the Rom star-pilots in every corner of the galaxy that the starships must start going forth again at once. How else would the joyful peoples of the Imperium be able to send their delegates to the Capital to celebrate the coronation of the glorious Nineteenth?

"All right," I said finally. "Enough of this. Help me down these goddamned stairs, you two."

Polarca blinked. "Did I hear you ask for help?"

"Crystalline steps are very goddamned slippery, Polarca. Do you want the Nineteenth to fall and break his ass right in front of the worshipful peers? Here. Take my arm. And you, Julien, you walk in front of me. If the Nineteenth *does* slip, at least his fall will be broken by the King of France."

Of course I wasn't all that worried about slipping. But I thought it would reassure them, knowing that I was at least beginning to take a few sensible precautions in deference to my age. You have to humor people, sometimes, or they'll drive you crazy with oversolicitousness.

"Who'd have imagined it?" Polarca murmured, for something like the ten thousandth time that day. "The Nineteenth Emperor descends the throne-platform, and who is he? Who is he? Do you believe you are emperor, Yakoub? Would you have thought such a thing was possible, that the Gaje would come to the Rom baro, that they would lie down in front of him in their masks and robes, that they would hold out the wand to him, that they would say—"

"I knew it all along," I told him grandly. "I saw it in the lines of my palm."

"And me a high lord of the Imperium!" Polarca cried.

"And you knew *that* all along, too, didn't you? Didn't you, you Polarca?"

Chorian was waiting below. He had that boy with him, the one who had been in my bedroom when I awakened. I wondered who he was. Some young brother of Chorian's, perhaps? No, there wasn't any resemblance. This boy had nothing like Chorian's long legs and slim, rangy build. He was short, deep-chested, fair-skinned; he didn't quite look Rom at all.

"Majesty?" Chorian called.

"To you I am Yakoub," I said.

"But—but—"

"Yakoub."

He nodded. "I have someone here I'd like you to meet."

I looked at the boy. "A friend of yours? A relative?"

"His name is also Yakoub."

"Not an uncommon name."

"He is the son of your son Shandor," Chorian said.

"*What?*"

"Majesty!" the boy said, and I thought he would cry. I thought I would, also. He dropped down before me and began kissing the hem of my garment in a disgusting way. I had to pluck at his hair to pull him up and away.

"Don't," I said. "Let me look at you, boy."

Not much Rom in him, no. Except in the eyes. Shandor's eyes, bright and fierce. My eyes. I felt a little shiver go running down my back.

I drew him close to me and held him, and kissed him in the Rom way.

Chorian said, "He was found on Galgala, in Shandor's camp. They shipped him here just before the starships stopped running, but there was no time to bring him before you until now."

"Yakoub," I said, trying out the name. It is not all that common, that name. It has an ancient heritage, yes. But there are very few of us today. He was smiling and crying at once. Named for me. What, I wondered, did that tell me about Shandor? A handsome boy in his way. Fifteen years old, maybe? Maybe younger. Shandor's son by that Gaje woman of his. A poshrat, a half-breed. Well, no matter. I was starting to feel half Gajo myself, now that I was their emperor. It was time to put aside some of the old prejudices. This boy united both the races in himself. Good. With my own name stuck to him. Good. I wondered how much Shandor there was in him. Shandor's energy and cunning, maybe, but none of Shandor's vileness, eh? One could hope. I smiled. "Come with me, Yakoub. And you, you Polarca. Julien. Chorian. I need some fresh air."

Out under the stars. That burning smell was starting to fade, now: it was days since the fighting had ended, and most of the fires were out. The sky was ablaze with light.

I looked up, searching for Romany Star.

"Can you see it?" I asked. "It should be there, somewhere off to the north, eh?" I narrowed my eyes, squinting, peering. Frowning. As I looked I said very quietly, "I went there, you know. While I was off ghosting. I went all the way back, and shook hands with the king. The last king of Romany Star, and what a great man he was!" They were all staring at me. "You don't believe me? Well, no matter. No matter. I was there. I said I wouldn't let myself die until I had been to Romany Star, and I have kept my vow." Odd that I couldn't find it up there, though, after having seen it almost every night of my life. That great red blazing thing. Where was it? More trouble with my eyes, maybe? "Do you see it?" I said. "Polarca? Chorian?"

They didn't seem to see it either. We stood there in the darkness, peering, frowning, squinting. I could hear the song of Mulesko Chirilko, rich and strange in the night.

"I was there on the last day," I told them. "As the swelling of the sun began. And I said to the king that we would be back, that I would lead the return. That much I promised him. As I have promised myself all my life. As I promised you."

Polarca said, "Could we be looking in the wrong place, Yakoub?"

"It's usually—right—there," I said. "Ah, holy saints and demons!"

"What do you see?" Chorian asked.

"There," I said. "I see it now. Not red any more. There it is, that bright star there. The blue one, do you see? That's Romany Star. Changing. Swelling. The third swelling of the sun has started, do you see?"

"I don't see the one you mean," said Chorian.

"There. There." I pointed, and he stared, and Polarca stared. And my grandson stared. They didn't seem to see. I tried to guide them, describing the pattern of the constellations all around. It was unmistakable now. The great blue star shining where the red one had been. The third swelling was under way at last; and after that it would be safe for us to go back. Then I would send my people in ships, hundreds of ships, thousands of ships. How long would that be, before it was safe? Ten years? A hundred? Well, I would find out. I would ask the imperial astronomers tomorrow.

What if they said five hundred years? Well, no matter. No matter. Someone else would lead the return, I suppose. Chorian? I would like that, if it were Chorian. Or this young Yakoub, maybe. Or maybe *his* grandson. That would be all right. I had kept my vow. I had lived long enough to see Romany Star with my own eyes. And to set us upon the path that would take us home.

And now? There is work to do, for the king, for the emperor. Great tasks await, and I will do them, for I am the man for the tasks. I knew that all along. And now you know that too, for I have told you my story, which now is finished, though my work is not. What is still to come, we will see. This is my story, and I have told it. Chapite! A Romany word, which storytellers use, when they have come to the end of their tale. Chapite! It is true! It is all true!

P. 8-25-86